Igniting the Flame

Rise of the Giants Series: Book 6

Theo Mann

The Invisible Publishing Company

Rise of the Giants Series

Contents

Chapter 1

Kuvik yelled out in pain as a rough length of rope dug into his side. Bone-breaking force threw him in the air and knocked him down hard to yank him against the rope again and again.

He struggled to get out of the stranglehold tangled around his body, but nothing could break the tough cordage. The rope held even when his whole weight slammed down against it.

He roared out again and again until, by some unknown miracle, the rope loosened and he slammed down even harder on the ground.

The giant Ashtaw to which he'd gotten accidentally tied kept charging away across the countryside. The creature didn't notice him, either while he'd been tied to its body or after he fell off.

He landed between the Ashtaw's feet and it accidentally kicked him as it thundered past and kept running into the distance. At least the enormous creature didn't step on him. He would have been dead for certain if it did.

He groaned in agony and lay flat on his face in the dirt for a minute. He didn't want to move. Everything hurt, especially his sides and back where the rope had cut into him.

He wore only a thin, threadbare pair of pants torn off above the knees. The rope had slashed, burned, and cut into his flesh all over his back and torso, but at least he didn't feel any broken bones.

He finally pried his aching corpse out of the soil. He allowed himself to whine and moan about it while he sat up and pushed himself back on his knees. He was all alone.

He looked around him as the truth sank in. He didn't recognize where he was. The Ashtaw stampede must have run a lot farther away than he realized.

He thought fast. He'd gotten tangled in that rope while trying to ride the Ashtaw with the Godless men of Hangman's band. Hangman's band couldn't be too far away from the Ashtaw Valley right now.

The Ashtaws had churned up the soil in a wide swath of broken ground leading back in the direction from which they'd come. Kuvik only had to follow the Ashtaw's path to the valley. Then he could head east and meet up with Hangman's band.

Kuvik tried once to stand up, but pain and exhaustion knocked him back down on the ground. Getting tied to the Ashtaw had injured him more than he realized. He only glanced down at his chest once before he looked away.

He needed leaf paste first. Then he needed Gooji juice so these wounds wouldn't get infected. He was also unarmed. He'd dropped his metal kukris somewhere along the way.

He wouldn't get any of those things sitting here feeling sorry for himself. He had to go somewhere—anywhere but here.

The Ashtaws usually stuck to open country. They didn't like traveling through the jungle. He'd fallen off on a grassy hilltop between two different valley systems. Impenetrable jungle blocked him from seeing anything in either valley.

He didn't give himself the option to use his arms to help him get to his feet. He pushed himself up and staggered back along the Ashtaws' trail.

Kuvik followed the broken sod down the back of the hill, into a different patch of jungle, and slumped at the base of a tree. Some of the wounds in his torn skin were starting to bleed. He had to seal them before the blood attracted dangerous creatures to attack him.

He really would have liked to crawl into the treetops, find a nice secluded hiding place, and curl up and go to sleep there until he healed.

He couldn't do that—not with all this blood all over him. He would probably lose consciousness and go into a delirium when the wounds got infected.

He really missed Yoa right now. She would have taken care of everything if she'd been here with him. She would have made the leaf paste and put it on his back in all the parts he couldn't reach.

She would have gone through the whole laborious process of making Gooji juice for him. Then she would have guarded him while he slept. He would have given anything to have her here right now.

He kicked himself for holding her at arm's length for so long. She was the best woman he'd ever known—and he loved her. He loved her as much as she loved him. He should have married her a long time ago.

Yoa wasn't here to do anything for him. He had to keep staggering through the trees while he gathered the leaves to make paste. Every movement racked him in agony.

He felt himself starting to break down in tears. He couldn't do that. He planned to initiate into the Godless Clan. Godless men bore their pain and kept going.

He'd been telling himself for years that he wasn't good enough to be Godless. Now he'd finally made the decision to initiate so he could marry Yoa and become one of Hangman's men.

He already was one. Everyone said so. No one knew it better than Kuvik. He had been Godless for a long time. He just had to make it official by going through his initiation.

He would take care of that the very instant he made it back to the band. He wouldn't make it back to the band if he died of an infection out here on his very first night.

Hangman would have been able to handle this situation. Hangman would have been able to push through this pain, make his leaf paste, boil his Gooji juice, and find his way back to his band. He'd done it countless times before.

Kuvik pulled another handful of leaves off the branches and sent a blast of pain through his body. He screamed out and his cry turned into a bellow of pure mindless rage.

He channeled that rage into pushing through the jungle no matter what. He roared every time he tore the leaves off. He made sure to do it extra hard and inflict the most damage possible on the trees around him.

He stopped now and then whenever he came to a stream and rinsed the blood off himself until he gathered enough leaves. He lacked the strength to climb into the treetops, so he squatted by the stream and ground the leaves on a rock.

He spread the paste on every wound he could see and as many on his back as he could get to easily. He spent some time stretching his arms behind him to make sure he found them all.

He would have liked to collapse right then and there, but he wasn't finished yet. Just a little longer.....

He had to climb the trees to find the Gooji sap. Then he had to climb down to build a fire on the ground.

He gathered sticks, made a tinder bundle, and blew it into a flame. He found a smooth rock, put it in the embers, and started to hollow out a chunk of wood to fashion into a basin to boil the water.

He didn't even have a knife he could use for any of that. He had to use his fingernails to scrape the sap off the trees. Then he used another stick and a flat rock to gouge out the basin.

He was in the middle of that when he heard a clicking noise in the treetops above him. He froze in place and glanced up. He didn't need to see the Krakelow moving through the branches toward him.

His wounds weren't bleeding anymore. The leaf paste sealed them, but that sound brought the truth home more than anything else could.

Kuvik needed weapons. Getting stuck out here alone was bad enough. Getting stuck out here unarmed would be disastrous.

He thought fast while he finished gouging out the basin. He had time before the Gooji juice cooled enough to drink. He didn't trust himself enough to sleep before then.

The sound didn't stop. That sound on its own kept him awake. He kept a much closer watch on the treetops and surrounding jungle for any creature coming close enough to attack him.

He kept looking up from his work of making the basin and cast his mind around for something he could use as a weapon.

He finished the basin, used two sticks to lower the glowing stone into the water to boil the juice, and left it to cool while he searched the streambed for the right kind of rock.

Hangman had chipped his own kukris out of stone. Kuvik didn't find any of that kind of stone here, so he would have to improvise. He could always use bone once he made his first kill. He would need food soon anyway.

He selected a random stone, picked up another much larger stone, and smashed the smaller stone against another to fracture it. It pulverized into powder, so that was a complete waste of time.

The leaf paste eased the pain and stiffness in his arms and chest, but not completely. He could move around better now, so he did the same thing to a dozen rocks before he found one that shattered into a pointy fragment he could use.

He took it back to his fire and used a vine to lash the stone shard to a long pole to use as a spear. It wasn't the greatest weapon, but it was better than nothing.

He squatted down by the fire and stuck his finger in the Gooji juice to see if it was cool enough to drink. He normally wouldn't have drunk it yet, but he wanted to get it over with so he could climb into the branches and go to sleep.

Something like a soft hiss made him look up. His skin prickled again when he spotted a group of Demonex padding through the jungle. They headed back in the direction from which Kuvik had just come.

They wouldn't have seen him if not for his fire. They glanced over, paused, and turned in his direction. He got to his feet and brandished his spear at them.

Then he had another idea and dropped another, longer piece of wood into the flames so its end would catch fire. He could use that as a weapon against the Demonex, too.

He didn't dare to take his eyes off them. Three of them were enormous males with spiky manes and ridges running down their spines. The other six were females. They flared their nostrils when they smelled his injuries.

Nine massive creatures stalked out of the jungle and surrounded his fire to box him in. They left only one way out—straight up.

He told himself to jump into the treetops right now, but he would have had to drop his spear if he did that. The Demonex might jump up there after him and then he would be completely unarmed.

The Demonex didn't give him a chance to make that decision before two females rushed him around both sides of the fire. He couldn't fight them both. He wasn't sure he could even fight one of them.

All of the others dove in at the same time. He had to pull some trick out of thin air.

He spun to the right, stabbed his spear into the female on that side, and rolled sideways onto the ground. The other female coming in behind him took a flying leap to pounce on him and landed on the other female.

The female that Kuvik stabbed tumbled sideways with him. The second female's weight drove the first female all the way down onto the spear. She let out a spine-chilling shriek mixed with a roar that vibrated through her into Kuvik's ribcage.

The spear impaled through her body and pierced the second female, too. She bellowed in agony and tried to spring clear, but all the other Demonex jumped in and blocked her. She couldn't get away.

The two females pinned Kuvik down, but the first dead body protected him from the worst. He slithered his arm out, grabbed the burning stick, and thrust it into the face of the biggest male trying to bite Kuvik's head off.

The burning end of the stick hit the male in the eyes. He bellowed, reared away, and took off into the jungle. Kuvik swiped the stick at another male, but he dodged in time.

The two males and four females got jumbled together with each other. None of them could decide whether to attack Kuvik or jump clear. They wound up conflicting with each other and interfering with each other's efforts to do both.

Kuvik couldn't pull out his spear to stab any other Demonex, so he fell back on the only weapon within reach. He thrust the burning stick at another female and the embers seared into her side. She withdrew, too.

Kuvik tried to hit one of the males and missed, but the Demonex still retreated out of Kuvik's range. Kuvik swiped the branch back and forth trying to drive the Demonex off, but the embers were already starting to die down.

Kuvik needed some other weapon. He glanced sideways, snatched a big rock from the ground right next to him, and he smashed it into another female's head.

The blow stunned her for a second and he struck out at another female. She roared and tried to lunge at him. First she tried to bite him in the face. Then she tried to bite the hand holding the rock.

His fury erupted again and he struck even harder. She tried again and again to get her fangs close enough to his face. He took advantage of her efforts by pulverizing her in the skull every time she moved her head within arm's reach.

He eventually stunned her, too, but he didn't stop. He kept smashing her in the skull with all his strength until he imploded it and reduced it to a squishy, shattered mass.

She slumped on top of the other two dead females lying on top of Kuvik. Their weight crushed his ribs and stopped him from breathing. He heard himself yelling at the Demonex—and they finally heard him.

The two males and three remaining females pulled away and circled the fire a few times while he lay there helpless—but he wasn't helpless. They found that out the hard way. He had his rock.

He took that moment to stick his branch back in the flames so he would be able to use it again if the Demonex tried anything. They didn't. They watched his every move like they understood exactly what he was doing.

He bared his teeth in a feral snarl of pure bloodthirsty survival rage. He would kill them and a whole lot more before he let them kill him first.

He heard himself yelling out with every tortured breath. He didn't try to be quiet even though he heard other creatures moving in. Demonex blood covered him from his neck down to his knees.

The remaining Demonex must have realized the same thing. They didn't reengage. They glanced around at the darkening jungle and then paced off into the trees to continue on the journey they'd been going on before they came over here.

They left three of their females lying dead on top of Kuvik. The surviving Demonex met up with their other male friend. One of his eyes had completely burned over. A massive black scorch mark covered half of his face. He didn't come near Kuvik again.

Chapter 2

Kuvik yelled a few more times in a frenzied mixture of rage, pain, and fear for his life. He glanced around everywhere.

He had to get out from under these Demonex and somehow, some way or other, clean the blood off himself before something else decided to attack him.

Getting one fully grown Demonex female off him would have been difficult enough. The two closest to his body made it impossible for him to move.

He had to put down his rock and let go of his spear shaft. The spear wasn't doing him any good right now anyway, but he didn't like to let go of any weapon.

He'd never spent this much time alone before. He felt how exposed, injured, and vulnerable he was. This was the worst situation for him to get caught in.

He couldn't get hold of any of the Demonex from this position, so he finally had to grab the squishy, smashed head of the female he killed with the rock. He yelled again from the effort of twisting her neck enough to roll her body off the pile.

She tumbled away and he tried to do the same thing with the second body. He couldn't budge it. The spear went through both of the other two bodies.

He fought in every possible way to free himself. In the end, he had to twist onto his side, pull his legs up underneath the lower Demonex, and then turn over so he could kick them off.

All three bodies thumped into a pile right there on the ground. He staggered to his feet still yelling out in exhausted strain every time he took a breath. He used all his strength to pull his spear out of the two Demonex and practically toppled down the bank into the stream.

He collapsed on the bottom, sat up to his chest in the water, and then lay all the way down to wash himself off.

He struggled to think straight with all this adrenaline coursing through his veins. He couldn't waste this Demonex meat. He had no reason to go hunting for anything else and he didn't want to.

Other creatures would come for the bodies. He had to act fast. Three adult Demonex would be a lot of meat.

He would need to process the meat and dry it for long-term storage. He wouldn't have to hunt for a long time after that. He would be able to recover while he ate it all.

He could only dry the meat on the ground. He didn't like his chances of defending his camp alone while he did it, but he would just have to try it. He didn't go to all the trouble of killing these Demonex just to leave them for the ants and Abnormits.

He floundered up the bank and approached the bodies. That was the moment when he noticed the overturned basin lying across the fire. The Demonex had upset and spilled his hard-earned Gooji juice. Now he had to start all over.

He sighed heavily and turned back to the matter at hand. He didn't have a knife or any other tools to butcher these Demonex, so he dragged the bodies into the trees, left them there, and went to gather some more sap while he thought it over.

He came back, straightened out the basin, filled it with water, and put the flat rock back in the embers to heat. Then he bent over the dead Demonex.

He picked up the head of the female he'd stabbed first with his spear. Her two front fangs formed downward-curving swoops with two razor-sharp edges, one on the convex side and one on the concave side. They would make perfect butchering tools.

He got a different rock from the streambed, sat down with the creature's head wedged between his knees, and used the rock to smash the fangs out of the creature's upper jaw.

He took a few minutes to examine the rest of the creature's teeth while he was at it. He'd never seen a Demonex's teeth this close up before. He'd never wanted to.

Some of them would make excellent weapons of different kinds—and he had six whole jaws full of these weapons right here in front of him.

His fury and intensity to save his own life kept him awake all night long. He worked for hours to butcher the three Demonex, cut the meat into strips, hang it on tripods built over the fire, and roast some of the meat to eat right now.

He drank two doses of Gooji juice during the night. His own efforts to survive fired him up too much to notice if the juice helped him at all.

He finally sat down and gorged himself on the roasted meat. The food calmed him down considerably, but not enough for him to stop.

He returned to the dismembered carcasses. He'd stripped off their hide and all their flesh. He dumped the organs away from his camp. The Abnormits had already discovered them.

He beheaded the three Demonex and boned out all six enormous femurs from the creatures' legs. The ball-and-socket joints on these weapons would make perfect clubs.

He took a dozen other bones, saved the hides, and then dragged the remains away for the Abnormits to eat. He took his time studying all the bones and skulls to decide how to use them the best way.

The two fangs would make outstanding knives. He just needed to attach the teeth to handles. The cutting teeth along the Demonex's lower jaw also intrigued him. The jaw stretched as long as his forearm and ended with six shorter curved fangs, three on each side.

He took one of the skulls and carved off the lower jaw. He held it over the fire to burn off the skin down to the bare bone. Then he used another large rock to split the jaw right down the center at the point where the creature's chin would be.

He ended up with two curved weapons lined with razor cutting teeth along the inner surface and three larger pointy fangs at the end. The two halves of the jawbone mimicked the shape of kukris.

The back part of the jaw where it connected to the skull even gave him a perfect place to hold the weapon.

He could wrap strips of Demonex hide around the handles to make them more comfortable to hold, but these weapons were perfectly good the way they were. He could definitely defend himself with these.

He worked for another several hours to remove the upper curved fangs and lower jaws from the other two skulls. He wound up with six kukris and six knife blades. This was more than he could reasonably use at one time, but it would be better to have too many.

He took occasional breaks to turn the meat on the tripod to make sure it dried evenly. He felt himself getting too exhausted to go on. He needed to rest, but he didn't want to do it on the ground.

He needed a way to carry all his weapons and supplies, so he spent the next few hours sewing together six shoulder bags for himself, three for each side of his body. He cut strips of hide, tied thongs around his jawbone kukris, and stashed the six blade fangs in his bags. He would work on those later.

He wrapped the dried meat in hide bundles as he took the food off the tripod, but he kept one full Demonex hide intact. He didn't know when or where he would need it, but he didn't want to waste it in case he did need it.

He finally passed out under his tree with his kukris in his hands. He couldn't keep his eyes open a second longer, but he could finally rest at ease. He was armed and as ready for this as he ever would be.

Chapter 3

Kuvik woke up at dawn when it started raining. The first patters of raindrops struck his face and startled him awake. The fire had started to die while he'd been asleep. He must have been a lot more exhausted than he realized.

He scrambled to his feet and checked the remaining meat on the tripods. Most of it was dry enough to store, but he had to get it out of the rain before it got too wet.

He wrapped it up in another hide bundle, but he made sure to keep it separate from the rest. He would have to eat that meat first before it spoiled.

He also wrapped up the last hunk of freshly roasted meat and cast a glance around at his camp. He had no more reason to stay here, so he climbed up into the branches and found a sheltered spot to wait out the rainstorm. Now he could relax as much as he wanted to.

He would have liked to continue his journey immediately, but he decided to take another day to recover, let his wounds heal, and regain his strength. He would need to be much stronger if he faced and fought any creatures alone—not to mention human enemies.

He went back to sleep, ate the rest of his fresh meat, fell asleep again, and then spent hours working to perfect his weapons. He fashioned handles for all six teeth knives, added thongs and handgrips to his kukris, and hung two of them from his waistband.

He didn't need the others, so he tied them together to make a bundle he could carry on his back. Now he was as ready.

He went back to sleep and woke up on the third morning. The rain had stopped, so he climbed all the way into the highest canopy to observe the country. He still didn't recognize any of it. How far did the Ashtaws really take him?

He traveled through the branches until he got to the open country and the torn-up Ashtaw track.

He had to go out into the open to follow it, so he took a little more time to grind a supply of leaf paste and collect a small packet of Gooji sap before he left the shelter of the jungle.

He didn't want to delay any longer, so he walked right out into the open and followed the trail. It led away from the jungle and crossed miles of open country. The trail led up hills and down into valleys.

He didn't think at the time that the Ashtaws had run that far, but he must have been wrong. Then again, they could run a lot faster on their long legs.

He diverted into the jungle to make camp for the night and then did it twice more before the trail descended into another jungle valley.

He didn't remember the Ashtaws running through any jungle, but they must have. Their footprints tore up the sod and snapped off huge branches even here.

He still didn't recognize any of this country. Was he even heading in the right direction anymore? Would this trail lead him back to the Ashtaw Valley at all?

He would have abandoned the trail if it hadn't still headed south. How far would he have to go before he found any country he recognized?

He left the trail on the fourth day, climbed into the branches, and put his head down on his arms for the night. Maybe he should just give up on following this trail and try to find his way back to where Hangman's band had traveled south in the first place.

Kuvik still hadn't made up his mind what to do before he fell asleep. He woke up when it started to get light the next morning. He ate some of his food, climbed down to the ground, and turned around to return to the trail. He might not follow it anymore.

He decided to go out there, look at the trail, and then survey the countryside for any high mountains he could climb. One of them was bound to give him a view of some mountain range or other feature he could use to orient himself.

He didn't see how the Ashtaws could have run this far and carried him so far away from where he started. He had to be within sight of something he recognized.

Mountains surrounded the Ashtaw Valley on all sides. Hangman's band had been traveling through that country for months. Kuvik would recognize something. He had to.

He set off through the jungle toward the trail, but he stopped when he heard laughter not far away. The voice sounded high and melodic—like a woman or a child. The sound sent a shiver over Kuvik's scalp.

He stopped in his tracks, rested his hand on one of his kukris, and strained his ears to listen. He didn't hear anything for a minute. Then he heard a soft murmuring voice like a woman or young girl talking to someone in a confidential undertone.

He set off sideways to track the sound. No woman or young girl should be out here alone. Every woman and young girl Kuvik knew spent their lives learning to keep quiet in the jungle. They wouldn't needlessly give themselves away like this.

The voice kept rising and falling, giggling, laughing occasionally, and talking to someone. No other voices answered. Whoever this was really was alone.

He slowed when he got closer enough. He inched through the undergrowth to sneak up and see the person.

He stared through the branches into a clearing hardly believing the evidence of his senses. It really was a young girl. She must have been fifteen or sixteen in the flush of young, unsullied beauty.

She wore a long white dress made of flimsy, fragile, gossamer fabric. It draped to the ground and surrounded her body in a billowing cloud. Her black hair hung free and swayed in liquid darkness when she moved.

She sat on a fallen tree trunk holding out her arm. A large Blitzword perched on the bare skin of her forearm—right where it could bite her and kill her with its poison.

Kuvik watched in slack-jawed horror while she stroked its wings and tickled its back. She laughed when she made it buzz its wings in annoyance.

She held a flat piece of tree bark in her other hand. The Blitzword tried again and again to bite her arm, but she kept sticking the bark between its mandibles and her own skin to block it.

She laughed at the creature's frustrated efforts. The Blitzword buzzed each time it bumped its mouth against the bark and had to pull its head back to try again.

She spent the time in between attempts tapping her bark on different parts of the creature's body. She tapped it on top of its head, used her bark to swat the Blitzword's tail sideways, and even used the bark to make the creature raise and lower some of its legs.

Her constant interference distracted it from biting her. Then it would try again and she blocked it by sticking her bark in front of its face.

She talked to it in a cheery undertone while she did all this. "Be careful. Don't fall over," she told it and then tapped her back on its head again. "Does that hurt? What's that sound? Huh? What's that sound? Ooo! Be careful. You almost lost your balance on that one." She stuck her bark in front of its mouth again. "Ooo! That was a close one.

You almost had that, but you missed. Sorry. Try again. Oh, be careful! Something might come along and make you fall off."

Kuvik couldn't watch this. He stormed out of his hiding place, barged up to the girl, swatted the Blitzword onto the ground, and stomped his foot on it to crush it.

"What are you doing—playing games with it?!" he demanded as soon as he killed the thing. "Don't you know how dangerous those things are?"

She blinked up at him, down at the dead Blitzword, and then her expression cleared when she looked back up at him. "I was just having fun."

"You don't have fun with those things! It could have killed you!" Kuvik looked around. "Where's your Clan and band? Where are your people?"

She shrugged that away. "I don't have any." She burst into a glowing smile. "You can be my Clan and band. You can be my people."

"I'm just one person." He took hold of her elbow and pulled her to her feet. "You can't stay out here alone."

"*You're* alone. Do you have a band?"

He decided not to answer and pulled her back into the trees. "What are you doing out here alone?"

"I live out here. Don't you see? I live out here alone. I don't have a band. I'm on my own."

He turned around to stare at her. "That's impossible! I don't believe you."

She shrugged. "It's true. I don't need anyone else."

"How do you survive all the creatures? How do you hunt for food?" He glanced down at her dress and looked away. He couldn't see her body through it, but it didn't hide her shape.

She laughed at his questions. "Come with me. Come this way." She walked off into the jungle on the other side of the clearing.

Kuvik hesitated. Should he go with her? Any creature could come along and kill her in a matter of seconds. She didn't have a single weapon on her. He doubted she would have known what to do with one if she did have one.

She wouldn't have the strength to use a weapon either way. He was used to seeing muscular, toned women among the Godless. They knew how to take care of themselves or at least put up a fight.

This girl's thin arms barely looked strong enough to carry a bundle of firewood.

Chapter 4

T he girl strolled off into the trees and even started humming to herself under her breath. Kuvik couldn't take it anymore. He pulled his kukris from his waistband, glanced around on both sides, and followed her.

Her attitude made him a hundred times more watchful than normal. He held his breath waiting for something to attack her. It never occurred to him that someone might attack him instead.

She couldn't be living out here alone. He would never believe that if he lived a thousand years. She couldn't have survived—so what was she doing out here alone?

She didn't look crazy or deranged or even lost or distressed. She looked a sight less distressed than he felt right now.

He followed at a distance at first, but he had to catch up with her if he planned to protect her—from anything.

"Where are we going?" he asked. "What is it that you want to show me?"

"You'll see," she replied over her shoulder.

"Which Clan do you belong to?"

"I belong to the Ages Clan."

"I've never heard of that," Kuvik replied. "What country are we in? I don't recognize it. Are we anywhere near the Jagged Points?"

She laughed again. "I don't know what that is. How can you not even know what country you're in?"

"I got tangled up.....with a rope.....one of the Ashtaws carried me here. It's a long story. I got separated from my band. I'm trying to get back to them."

She turned around and gave him another beaming smile. "That's nice. Which Clan do you belong to?"

He opened his mouth and stopped himself. "I guess I don't really belong to a Clan. I've been living with the Godless for four years. Before that, I was with the Hungry Ghosts for almost fifteen years, and before that....."

He trailed off. He hadn't said that name to anyone. He hadn't even told Hangman or Yoa the name of his original Clan. He didn't want to name them. He didn't want to make them real.

The girl stared at him and waited for him to answer. He changed his mind. "What's your name?" he asked.

"Dana." She started walking again. "What's yours?"

"Kuvik," he replied.

"You don't look Godless. You don't dress like them and you don't have long hair."

"I'm not Godless—not yet."

"What does that mean? Why do you say, 'not yet'?"

"I was going to initiate into their Clan before I got lost. They're the closest thing to a Clan I've ever had. I suppose I'll have to start dressing like them and growing my hair out if I do initiate, but I don't suppose anyone will care if I keep doing what I'm doing now."

"Look at this!" Dana rushed forward and squatted down next to a different fallen log. Brightly colored fungi grew all over it in many-tiered shelves of orange, white, and shades of brown and yellow.

She raised her hand to touch them. Kuvik stopped her. "Don't touch them! They're poisonous. The poison can seep through your skin and kill you. Don't you know that?"

She smirked at him. "I was just going to have some fun. Watch."

She picked up a stick off the ground and poked it into one of the fungi. It writhed, undulated, and let out little puff-clouds of spores. She laughed again.

Kuvik grabbed her and pulled her away. "Stop it! Those spores can cause blindness and madness! You really shouldn't be out here."

He steered her to her feet and got her moving again. Now what was he going to do with this girl?

He followed her for another twenty minutes before he decided to call it quits. "I think you better come with me," he told her. "You won't be able to protect yourself out here by yourself."

"Nothing bothers me." She smiled at him again. "I'm fine."

He couldn't see anything wrong with her, but his every instinct told him not to let her keep going. "Come this way. You can show me whatever it is later."

"No, I have to show you now."

Kuvik bristled. "Tell me what it is first. Otherwise I'm going to take you back to where I found you and you can come south with me. I can't leave you out here. That wouldn't be right."

She opened her mouth to say something. A deep thump resounded through the ground right then and interrupted her. Kuvik spun around and stared at the treetops. Rhythmic thumping sounds traveled through the ground coming from somewhere.

He didn't wait around to find out where it was coming from. He grabbed her hand and pulled her back in the direction from which they'd come. She giggled again—maybe because he was holding her hand.

He paid no attention. He wasn't trying to imply anything. She was too out of it to know what was good for her.

Maybe there really was something wrong with her brain. Maybe she had gotten separated from her people and got lost without realizing the danger she was in.

He didn't recognize her clothes from any other Clan he could remember. He didn't think it was possible that the Ashtaws could have carried him all the way into another part of the country with completely different Clans.

They couldn't have because they'd been running for less than a day before he fell off. He might have gotten confused about how long they actually did run, but they definitely didn't run past sunset.

The thumping sounds became more distinct as they got louder and faster. They came from the right. Kuvik glanced in that direction and saw two Crushers coming closer, but they didn't come directly toward Kuvik and Dana. The Crushers didn't see them—not yet.

Kuvik reacted without thinking, stuck his kukris back in his waistband, grabbed Dana with his arm wrapped around her waist, and launched with her into the treetops. He climbed one-handed and carried her up into the canopy where the undergrowth would hide them.

He settled on a branch and lowered her onto it next to him. "Don't make a sound," he whispered. "They'll pass us by without seeing us."

He tried to unwrap his arm from around her waist, but she'd somehow put her arms around his neck when he picked her up. She didn't take her arms down when he let go of her.

She smiled at him from extra close. Her beauty and radiant smile made him uncomfortable. He took hold of her arms and pried them off as gently as he could. He had to make sure he didn't knock her off the branch.

She couldn't balance as well as a Godless girl. She held onto other branches to steady herself, but she never stopped smiling in the same cheery way. "Thank you," she breathed. "You're really sweet."

He looked away in another direction. "You can't take care of yourself."

"So you'll take care of me?"

"How long have you been out here alone?"

"Always!" she chirped.

She said it too loud and one of the Crushers roared right then to remind her to be quiet. They drew level with Kuvik's hiding place. The Crushers still didn't turn in his direction.

"What's the last thing you remember before you found yourself out in the jungle alone?" he asked after a minute.

She only beamed at him. "You don't believe me."

"How do you find food?"

She shrugged. "I don't know."

He looked away again. Now he knew there was something wrong with her—something a lot more wrong than getting stranded alone in the jungle. He had gotten stranded alone in the jungle. Not even he was as lost and brainless as this.

He decided to give her some of his dried Demonex meat. Maybe that's why she was so thin—because she hardly ever got any food.

She looked healthy enough, though. Her cheeks glowed with vitality and a noticeable layer of healthy flesh padded her jawline. She ate well, whoever she was.

She didn't have sunken cheekbones or the hollow, shadowed eyes he would have expected if she had been going without food.

He handed her three sticks of dried meat. She beamed at him, thanked him, and started chewing on them.

She didn't ask what kind of food it was. She didn't complain about eating dried meat. She didn't act at all surprised by this kind of food—which meant she must have eaten it before. She must have eaten it a lot.

The Crushers passed, but a handful of Gorlocks came through the area a little while later. Kuvik stayed where he was. No way would Dana know how to travel through the branches. He would have to take her down to the ground.

That would make traveling with her much more dangerous—as if she wasn't in enough danger already.

He considered carrying her on his back and staying in the branches anyway—but he would have to go out into the open country pretty soon anyway to go back to the Ashtaw trail.

Hadn't he just been thinking about leaving the trail? Why did he keep following it at all?

Time passed. Other dangerous creatures passed his hiding place and then an army of ants came through. Dana tore off a piece of her dried meat off her last strip and dropped it into the middle of the ants. Four of them stopped to devour it.

"Hey!" Kuvik exclaimed.

She laughed at the ants' behavior and then at his reaction. "I just wanted to see what they would do."

He blinked at her as a dozen different thoughts passed through his head. He'd never met anyone anywhere ever who would deliberately waste food like that.

His mind went into a tailspin. Should he tell her what this meat cost him? Should he tell her that he would have to risk his life to get more of it—for her?

She just went back to watching the ants. She did all these dangerous, reckless things just to entertain herself. What if.....What if she was the one who was dangerous? How could she be? She had no weapons and she didn't have the strength to fight anything.

Kuvik could overpower her easily. He could have overpowered a woman her size if she'd been born Godless and knew how to fight.

Something strange was going on here. He just didn't know what it was. What if she decided to throw *him* to the ants just to see what they would do? How did he really know she wouldn't?

He realized one thing in that moment. She would never lift a finger to help him if he did get into trouble.

He might put himself in danger defending her. He would defend her against a Gorlock or a Crusher or a Krakelow or a Stalkion or a Demonex or any of a thousand other creatures.

She wouldn't help him. She wouldn't even pick up a stick or a rock to make it easier for him. She would stand off to one side and let him take all the risk.

He couldn't even console himself that she would stand off to one side because she was weak, helpless, and in fear for her life. That wouldn't be the reason she stood off to one side—not at all.

She would stand off to one side so she could see what happened to him. She would do it so she could watch for pure entertainment value.

She would never go to the effort of making leaf paste for him or put on his wounds. Forget about building a fire, gathering Gooji sap, boiling it for him, and helping him drink it in the middle of the night.

He stared off into the distance and drifted back to that night he spent alone with Yoa in the jungle. He thought at the time that it was the worst night of his life, but he found out he had been wrong.

He would give anything to trade Dana for Yoa. She took up weapons to help him against the Bounty Hunters. That was the night when he fully let himself feel how much he cared for her and wanted her for himself. He never let himself do that before.

He didn't leave the branches before night fell. He needed to make up his mind what to do about Dana. He really didn't look forward to traveling all the way south with her. That would be a nightmare.

He couldn't leave her, though. She might have been telling the truth that she really was alone. Then he would have no choice but to take her with him.

He'd been learning that lesson from Hangman all these years. A man of the Godless band always protected anyone weaker than himself. Dana definitely qualified.

He squatted on the branch, folded his arms, and put his head down while he let himself drift off. He would make it back to the Godless sooner or later. Then he would initiate.

He wanted to be able to say when it happened that he had conducted himself as a true Godless man while he'd been gone. He wouldn't be able to live with himself without doing everything possible to protect Dana, even from herself.

Chapter 5

K uvik climbed down to the ground, set Dana's feet down next to him, and turned south. "Let's go," he told her. "We have a long way to go."

"We're going this way." She waved behind her.

"No, we're going south toward Godless country. You have to come with me. You won't last a day on your own."

"I can't go south. I have to go this way. I told you. I have to show you."

"Show me what?" Kuvik started to lose his patience. "It can't be more important than your life."

She grabbed his hand and pressed it between both of hers. "Just come with me for a little way. Just let me show you and then we can go south. I promise."

"Tell me what it is first."

She burst into another grin. He was really starting to not like that grin. "I can't tell you what it is. It's a surprise."

"Forget it." He turned south again. "Come on. You can show me another time."

"I can't. It has to be now." She squeezed his hand tighter. "Come on, Kuvik. Just this once. Please? It will only take a minute."

He considered refusing her, but that would mean walking away. "Fine, but make it quick."

She practically jumped up and down in delight. She didn't let go of his hand until he deliberately pulled it out of her grasp. He didn't want her touching him like that or any other way for that matter.

She headed off into the trees in the same general direction she'd been going to begin with. She headed northwester—away from where he wanted to go. At least she did that much consistently.

He cast wary glances all around him. He didn't like this at all. He seriously considered walking away right now.

If whatever she wanted to show him was anything malicious or if she showed any further sign of messing with him in a mean-spirited way, he would abandon her in a heartbeat.

He also decided that he wouldn't continue with her heading northwest past sunset today. He wouldn't let her continue to lead him anywhere but south—not after today.

If she didn't come to whatever she wanted to show him—if she just kept saying over and over again that she wanted to show him something—forever—he would call it a day and go south alone.

She walked for half an hour before his temper started rising. "So where is it?" he demanded.

"Just a little further. You can see it from here." She moved to one side so he could see in front of her.

He stepped forward and drew level with her so he could see what she was looking at. He didn't see anything until he noticed a gap in the undergrowth ahead. The trees started to thin.

He pushed his way through to a break in the tree line. He came out of the jungle in another open channel between the jungle and a hill climbing on the other side.

He spread the branches with both arms and glanced right and left. There was nothing here. "What am I supposed to see here?" he snapped over his shoulder.

"This is it," she told him. "Isn't it wonderful?"

He compressed his lips in annoyance. This was the last straw. He'd wasted enough time with her already. She was either insane or so mentally unstable that she might as well be.

He almost turned around to walk away before he heard a high-pitched cry in the distance. It floated over the hill in front of him.

He froze and his blood ran cold when a whole army of Bounty Hunters charged over the hill heading straight for him. His first instinct was to turn around, push Dana into the trees, and run for it. He might even have carried her if she couldn't run fast enough.

Right at that moment, at the worst possible time, he felt her hands grab hold of his kukris from behind. She yanked them out of his waistband from behind and pulled the string to untie the bundle binding the other four jawbone kukris to his back.

The sensation wiped everything else out of his mind. He might have believed right up until that moment that she was just too oblivious to realize what she was doing.

He spun around to confront her. She grinned at him and held up his kukris in one hand to dangle them in front of his face. "Looking for these?"

Another war cry echoed across the landscape behind him. The Bounty Hunters were getting closer. She took his kukris. She left him unarmed.

"How could you do this?" he croaked.

She laughed at him. "You're gonna love it. I promise."

He heard the Bounty Hunters coming closer. He heard their feet pounding on the sod out there.

He made one last desperate dive to grab his kukris out of her hand, but she yanked them away and laughed at him again. "Ooop! Not fast enough! Did you want these?" She bounced them up and down in front of him and then moved her arm to hold them out of reach.

He couldn't believe it—and yet he should have known. He had gotten a bad feeling about her. He should have listened to his instincts.

He didn't try to fight back. He already knew what was coming.

He stood where he was and stared into her eyes right up until the moment when the Bounty Hunters tackled him from behind, slammed him down on the ground, bound his wrists together, and pulled a sack over his head so he couldn't see anything.

Chapter 6

A kick landed on Kuvik's ribs and then dozens more pummeled him all over his body. He didn't even try to fight back. He knew better from his previous encounters with the Bounty Hunters.

A few of them kicked him in the head just because they always did. He heard Dana laughing in the background. The Bounty Hunters had already taken his bags away and she had his kukris.

He regretted losing those weapons. He was really starting to like them. He'd always admired Hangman's weapons. Kuvik had only been satisfied to give up the idea of having some like that when he found those metal kukris he had taken from the Bounty Hunters.

Now Kuvik had found something he liked even better. Maybe the way he had gotten those weapons made him particularly attached to them. He wanted more of them. All he had to do was kill Demonex. He already knew he could do that.

Hangman was the killer of Crushers. Kuvik would be the killer of Demonex. They would become his new specialty.

He used those thoughts to carry him farther and farther away from the beating. The Bounty Hunters kicked him black and blue all over his body. They kicked him six or seven times in the head and stunned him.

That made it a lot easier to slip away from all of this. His previous captivity with them made it much easier. The process happened quicker this time, thank goodness. He didn't have to think. He just had to get through it—and then what?

He already knew the fate that awaited him on the other end. This beating was just the first of many. This was the warmup that would soften him to whatever happened after this.

The Bounty Hunters would keep him brutalized and beaten down. They wouldn't give him one minute of peace. They would keep at him until they made him a mindless slave like all the others—or he would die from the ordeal.

A secret flame of defiance flared in his heart. No! He would escape. He had done it before. He could do it again.

He had slaughtered all the Bounty Hunters who captured him and threatened Yoa. He could do the same thing to these people....but he couldn't do it now. He had to measure his chances and take the right opening.

He let himself drift a little farther away. He didn't need to be here for this. He numbed himself to the pain and let himself think about his kukris.

The Bounty Hunters made a habit of collecting all kinds of weapons from the people they captured. The Bounty Hunters especially collected unusual weapons they never saw anywhere else.

They might keep his kukris. He might get them back—and his teeth knives.

It didn't matter if he did get them back because he could always make more of them. The jungle never ran short on Demonex. They all had the same kind of teeth and jaws. It comforted him to know the jungle would provide his favorite kind of weapon for him.

He had to stop thinking about his kukris. They made the flame of defiance flare higher. He would have liked to use those weapons on the Bounty Hunters right now. He would have known exactly what to do with them.

The good news was that the Bounty Hunters brought him weapons without even trying. They all carried weapons of one kind or another. Most used metal-pointed spears. Kuvik already knew how to use those.

They would take the bag off his head eventually. Then he would be able to see where he was. Then he could really start to plan how to escape from them.

One of them kicked him in the head again and he passed out. He woke up feeling sick and swollen all over. He lay huddled on the ground—but he didn't have the bag over his face anymore.

He lay in front of some of the makeshift huts the Bounty Hunters used when they traveled. He winced when he picked his pounding head up off the ground and tried to pry his swollen eyelids open to see anything around him.

A lot of the huts crowded the jungle everywhere he looked. He didn't see the end of them. The Bounty Hunters had brought a lot of men to capture him—or the Bounty Hunters had brought a lot of men wherever it is Dana arranged for them to capture him.

Where was she right now? She was the first woman he'd ever seen cooperating with the Bounty Hunters. He'd only ever seen beaten, subservient, heartless slaves before.

She looked too beautiful and healthy to be a slave. Was it possible she was one of the Bounty Hunters themselves? He didn't think they had wives and children in that sense.

Then he remembered the other village—the second village away from where the Bounty Hunters kept all their slaves.

Everyone there had been healthy, well fed, and living in luxury compared with the Bounty Hunters—the male warriors Kuvik had thought were the real Bounty Hunters.

He didn't really know anything about their society. They could have had two castes—or whatever they were. The upper class could live in one place wearing fancy clothes with all the food they could eat.

Then the warriors might live separately. Maybe the Bounty Hunters took these slave-captives to do all the manual labor and act as servants to the warriors. That made more sense, but Kuvik could only guess.

That might explain Dana's dress. She might have come from the second village—although he'd never seen anyone dressing like that there—not that he'd seen much of the place while he was there.

Sunlight streaked through the trees from one side. The beams came through the foliage at an almost horizontal angle. It must be dawn now. The jungle smelled like it.

Right at that moment, a woman started screaming in one of the huts behind him. It wasn't a pained or tortured or terrified scream. She shrieked in rhythmic outbursts of ecstasy in time to deep thumps of wood against wood.

A man started grunting in the same rhythm and then he bellowed out as she screamed in one high long, trembling cry. She immediately started to cycle down and whimper in shattered bliss. Was that Dana? Did she belong to one of the warriors—or all of them?

He tried not to think about that and the noise died in a minute anyway. Her screams woke up the other warriors. They came out of their huts and started moving around their camp.

They kicked him occasionally when they passed him, but none of them tried too hard to be systematic about it. They left him there and ignored him.

This must have been a big camp—which made sense considering how many Bounty Hunters had come over that hilltop to attack him.

They couldn't have all come out here just to attack him. They couldn't have known the Ashtaw would drop him here of all places. The Bounty Hunters must have been here on some other campaign.

Dana must have already been with them. He still couldn't imagine why she had been out there in the jungle by herself playing games with dangerous creatures.

He should have known she wasn't out there alone. That was the thing. He already did know she wasn't alone. He had never thought she was alone. That was impossible. He just never thought this would be her real situation.

He tried to figure out where he might have made a mistake that led to his capture, but he would have done everything the same if he had it to do over again.

He couldn't and wouldn't leave a helpless girl out in the jungle. He had no way to know she wasn't helpless or that she would betray him so badly.

Now he was stuck here, but even this wasn't as bad as it might have been. He knew enough about the Bounty Hunters to escape eventually. They wouldn't kill him outright before he saw an opening and took it.

The Bounty Hunters spent hours organizing themselves to leave their camp. They used a lot of slaves to do the hard work. Everyone ignored Kuvik—right up until the very last moment before they moved out.

The slaves loaded huge bundles of stuff on their backs. The Bounty Hunters themselves carried almost nothing except their own weapons.

The Bounty Hunters and laden slaves formed a big line and started heading off into the jungle. The column took a long time to leave the area. Those in the back had to wait for those in the front to leave first.

Seven Bounty Hunters came over to Kuvik and started kicking and beating him with clubs again. They beat him much more severely this time and kicked him in the head a lot more.

He slipped back into his trance. He could expect a lot more of this. He was ready for that. He knew how to deal with it. He might even have lost consciousness a few times. He could practically lose consciousness at will when it suited him.

He came back to awareness when a different kind of agony stabbed him through the body. It came from all his limbs and even his head.

He jolted back to consciousness and realized the Bounty Hunters weren't beating him anymore. He didn't even see them.

A bunch of male slaves came over to him, picked him up, and put him on some kind of sled made of two branches tied together at one end. The other ends rested apart on the ground with a piece of hide stretched between them.

The slaves put Kuvik on the hide. One of the men picked up the tied branches, positioned the cross in front of his chest, and towed the sled by leaning his weight into the tie.

Kuvik's body held the rear ends apart. They scraped along the ground to carry him where the Bounty Hunters wanted to take him. He didn't have to walk anywhere. He couldn't have walked if he wanted to.

He slumped on his little hide bed and rested his aching head and body. He wouldn't be much good for anything if they kept beating him like this. They would have to let him recover sometime if they wanted to use him for slave labor.

All the slaves showed signs of bruising all over their bodies. The Bounty Hunters kept all their slaves beaten down and cowed into submission. The Bounty Hunters wanted to do the same thing to him. They did it to all their captives.

They set off through the trees. Kuvik floated in a hazy half-zone between consciousness and unconsciousness.

He drifted back to his senses when the slave pulling him put him down and another man took his place. The slaves surrounding Kuvik kept changing shifts when one man got too tired.

Kuvik pried his swollen eyes open and looked around. He stayed awake this time when the slave pulled Kuvik's sled forward.

The Bounty Hunters were in the process of crossing another hilltop right at that moment before they descended the other side into another valley full of jungle.

That moment gave Kuvik just enough time to see which direction the Bounty Hunters were going. They were heading straight north.

He put his head back down and shut his eyes. He didn't need to keep them open anymore. The Bounty Hunters could take him as far north as they wanted to. He would still escape. Then he would just travel back south until he found Hangman's band again.

He would go home. His band would welcome him as one of them. He already knew where he belonged and who he belonged with. The Bounty Hunters couldn't stop that. No one would ever be able to stop it. It was written in his blood now.

Chapter 7

K uvik yelled out in pain when the slaves dumped him off the sled in another patch of jungle somewhere. None of the slaves paid any attention to him. They left him there, bound, beaten, and lying in the dirt.

Any movement sent lightning bolts of pain shooting through him, so he lay still and concentrated on trying to heal from all these beatings.

The slaves ignored him and went back to work helping their comrades set up the Bounty Hunter camp. The slaves built all new huts, lit fires, and unpacked the Bounty Hunters' belongings.

Some of the slaves went hunting and brought back their kills to butcher and prepare for the Bounty Hunters to eat.

The Bounty Hunters went through the crowd striking the slaves with sticks, whips, and clubs whenever it suited the Bounty Hunters to do so. They occasionally chastised one of the slaves for doing something wrong, but not often.

More often the Bounty Hunters struck for no reason at all. They seemed to do it just to teach the slaves to get used to being beaten any time and all the time just because they were slaves.

Kuvik tried not to pay attention to any of this. It was nothing he didn't already know.

He wound up watching anyway. He saw plenty of Bounty Hunters taking the female slaves into their huts with them.

Some of these females screamed a lot. Some made no noise at all. Some came out and went back to work. Some didn't come out at all. The male slaves pretended not to notice. The other Bounty Hunters laughed about it.

Kuvik didn't see Dana anywhere. He hadn't seen her all day. In fact, he hadn't seen her at all since she betrayed him and took his weapons away from him.

Part of him became convinced in an irrational way that she wasn't here at all—that she must have gone somewhere else. He couldn't picture her as part of any of this.

Some part of him wanted to believe she was too clean to associate with something as crude and degrading as all of this.

He already knew that wasn't true. He wasn't even surprised when he saw her moving around the camp. She wore the same long white dress for some reason. She looked so out of place among all these dirty, beaten slaves and hulking Bounty Hunters.

Her presence didn't cause a stir with anyone. None of the slaves or Bounty Hunters treated her presence as anything out of the ordinary. She moved through the camp like she belonged here.

She barely glanced at the slaves. She must have been so used to seeing them that she hardly saw them at all. Only Kuvik seemed to see anything noteworthy about her behavior or theirs.

She walked straight through the camp until one of the Bounty Hunters called out something to her from the side. She turned off and crossed the camp to join that man where he stood with another cluster of warriors. They milled around talking in front of one of the huts.

She stepped into their cluster and that one man reacted by sweeping his arm around her waist from behind. He pulled her toward him, crushed her against his body, and got in her face murmuring something in a low, fast undertone.

She pretended to squirm in his grasp and turned her head to answer in the same undertone, but she wouldn't stop smiling and blushing at what he did and said.

Her eyes darted to the other men watching like she didn't want them to see—or she pretended that she didn't want them to see.

They all saw when he lifted her tighter against him, grabbed her leg high up the back of her thigh where it met the crease of her buttocks, and tried to pull her leg around his. He stuck his knee between her legs, but her dress got in the way and he couldn't go very far.

She colored even more and her hair swept over her face in a wave of pure sexual heat. She grabbed his shoulders, but she didn't try very hard to push him away. Her lips parted and her eyes softened.

The man dove in and kissed the side of her neck where it arched away from him when she turned her head. He kissed her once very quickly and let her go enough for her feet to sink to the ground.

They both straightened up and her dress fell back into place, but he let his hands linger on her a little too long.

His hand slid up to her hip in a possessive way and he kept his arm behind her back even when she straightened up and turned away from him to face the group.

None of the other Bounty Hunters reacted to the scene. They either watched it without reacting or they kept talking through the whole thing. The other warriors acted like Dana and this man did this kind of thing all the time.

Kuvik didn't know what it meant or if it meant anything at all. It made him think a lot of things—not that he should be thinking about her at all.

Whatever she was, whoever she belonged to—whatever she was in the habit of doing with these men—none of it concerned Kuvik now or ever.

He tried to put her out of his mind, but she didn't make it easy. She stayed in his part of the camp for the rest of the evening. He tried not to pay attention to whatever she did with one man or another, but he didn't see her doing anything with anyone, not even that one man.

The camp started to wind down for the night. More Bounty Hunters went into their huts, either alone or with their female slaves. The male slaves kept working as long as any Bounty Hunters remained awake.

Kuvik turned his head away, shut his eyes, and put his pounding head down on the bare dirt to go to sleep, too. At least the Bounty Hunters didn't come back to beat him again. They didn't need to. He was already as beaten as he could possibly be.

They couldn't beat him again—not without injuring him beyond the point where he would be useful to them. He had to remember that. They would keep him brutalized and beaten down just like all these slaves.

Then the Bounty Hunters would put him to work the same way they put all these other slaves to work. That's where this was going.

He was just about to check his brain out of reality again so he could stop thinking about all of this. He had enough to think about just feeling sorry for himself.

Dana startled him by squatting down in front of him right at that moment. Her stark white dress made her impossible to ignore.

He hurt himself again by jolting away from her too fast, but he couldn't move anywhere with his wrists and ankles tied, much less moving anywhere fast in his condition.

He reared away to put as much distance as he could between him and her, but he couldn't get away. She gave him a look and started spreading leaf paste on his injuries.

He roared in pain when she touched his chest. "Leave me alone, you filthy witch!" he snarled. "Get your hands off me! Don't you dare touch me!"

"Lie down and be quiet, Kuvik," she snapped. "You'll die of an infection if I don't treat your injuries."

"Do you think I care?!" he fired back. "Do you think you could ever convince me that you give a crap about me?! Leave me alone! I'm here because of you."

"Then you're mine to do with as I please." She kept spreading the paste on and blasting him apart with pain. He hated to admit that the paste really did make him feel better.

He couldn't stop himself from jerking his head away when she spread the paste on his eyebrows. "You rotten tramp!" he snarled. "You betrayed me! I tried to help you! I tried to protect you—and this is how you repay me!"

She only shrugged it away. "It's the Bounty Hunter way. You're a captive. I'm a Bounty Hunter. What did you expect me to do?"

He turned his head away again. He wanted to be anywhere but on the same continent with her.

She used the opportunity to move behind him. He gritted his teeth and tried not to groan in torment when she spread the paste on his back, but he wound up doing it anyway. Maybe now she would leave him alone.

She didn't. She pivoted around him and positioned herself right in front of him again where he had no choice but to glare at her. At least he didn't have to pretend to like her.

She was his enemy. She was a Bounty Hunter as much as the warriors. She was just as dangerous, but in her own, more feminine way.

She pulled forward a long cylindrical piece of wood that she held straight upright. The interior had been hollowed out to make a long drinking vessel.

"Now you need to sit up and drink some Gooji juice," she told him.

"Leave me alone," he snapped. "I never want to see you again!"

"You'll die without the juice. You don't want that, do you? Just drink it, Kuvik. You know you need it. You aren't ready to die yet, are you? You still want to get home to your band, don't you?"

She didn't wait for him to ask permission. She took hold of his pulverized body. He gasped and whined in pain while she wrestled him off the ground into a sitting position.

She had to hold him up with one arm. She steadied the vessel with the other, guided it to his mouth, and held it in place while he gulped down the juice.

She went through the whole procedure like she really did care to heal him with this treatment. She didn't. That was the worst part. She told him straight to his face that he was a captive—which meant he was a slave.

She was doing this to save him for the work he would do for her Clan later. She didn't care about anything else.

No wonder she'd been so delighted about watching other creatures suffer. He should have known then, but he couldn't have.

Chapter 8

Dana lowered Kuvik back down onto the ground, put the empty drinking vessel aside, and picked up a wooden bowl with a wooden spoon sticking out of it.

"Now eat something." She brought a spoonful of whatever it was close to his mouth. It wasn't meat. "You plan to escape, don't you? You'll need your strength for that."

Her words made him open his mouth. He already knew she was manipulating him. She must have seen it a thousand times with a thousand other captives. They probably all wanted to escape at first.

The Bounty Hunters knew exactly what to say to break down their captives' defenses. The Bounty Hunters would do the same thing to him.

They didn't feed him at all during his first captivity. He didn't know why except that the warriors were the ones who took responsibility for him then. They didn't have one of their women around to do it for them.

He would have expected them to send one of the slaves to feed him and give him Gooji juice. Maybe they didn't want him to talk to any other slaves until the Bounty Hunters broke down his spirit a little further. Maybe they didn't want him to influence them.

That gave him an idea. These slaves might still want to escape. He might be able to influence them, but he would have to talk to them first. He would have to find times to do that when the Bounty Hunters weren't around.

He refused to look at Dana when he opened his mouth. She put the food in his mouth and he ate it. He kept his eyes trained on the details of the dirt in front of his nose. She didn't say anything else, thank the stars.

The food was some kind of small white grains flavored with some other different-colored specks he didn't recognize. The food tasted good, but it had a strange texture. He wasn't used to it.

She spooned all the food into his mouth and left him alone in merciful peace. The rest of the camp wound down getting quieter and quieter. More Bounty Hunters went inside. More slaves curled up on the ground and went to sleep.

Anyone still awake worked quietly. The slaves hardly ever talked to each other.

Only one thing Dana said meant squat to Kuvik. *You aren't ready to die yet, are you?*

He wasn't ready to die. The urge to die—the driving insanity that told him to stop eating and drinking—to find a weapon to kill himself to end his suffering—that urge came from the Hungry Ghosts.

He'd spent decades of his childhood struggling against this feeling when everything and everyone around him told him it was the right thing to do—that ending himself was the nicest, most noble thing he could do for this wretched world.

Some hidden spark in his soul always knew it was wrong. Some part of him always wanted to live no matter what anyone else said. He might be selfish for that. He might be inflicting a terrible wrong on the world by staying alive.

He'd spent years telling himself to just go ahead and do it. His life before the Godless had been a lot worse than anything the Bounty Hunters could dish out. He had survived all of that and the Godless still wanted him. Hangman still wanted him.

Kuvik wasn't ready to die—not yet—not ever. He would never let the Hungry Ghosts pull him down—especially not now when he had something worthwhile to live for.

Hangman and his men had been absolutely horrified by seeing someone kill themselves. Seeing the Hungry Ghosts kill themselves was the worst thing the Godless could possibly imagine.

Hangman was the first person who had ever told Kuvik straight out that his life had any value—and that Hangman wanted Kuvik to live.

Kuvik would never be able to throw that gift away—not if he lived a thousand years. He might spend the rest of his life as the Bounty Hunters' tortured, brutalized slave.

He would just have to live it through, but he would live. His life would always have value thanks to Hangman and the others.

They had welcomed Kuvik. They had shared their food with him. They had all cared for him. Even the women had cared for him even though he was a total stranger to them. The men had respected him and fought alongside him as a brother.

They would gladly have made him Godless to call him brother for the rest of his life.

Thinking about them almost made him want to cry, but he pushed that feeling away. He would get back to them. They were still there waiting for him to come back.

Hangman would always welcome him. Mora, Viking, Red, Wildling—they would all welcome him—and Yoa would always welcome him. One or more of them dying didn't matter because the others would still remember him.

He fell asleep and woke up exactly the same way. He woke up when he heard women screaming in the huts. Some of them really did scream this time. Then the Bounty Hunters pushed them out of the huts bleeding and cradling broken bones in certain places.

The camp roused and everyone went through exactly the same routine. The slaves broke down the camp and packed up everything. The slaves put Kuvik back on the sled and the column moved off heading north.

He recognized the five slaves responsible for loading and dragging him on the sled. The same five came each time. He stayed conscious enough to watch them during the day. The same five pulled him all day long.

They were all men in their late twenties. They all suffered a range of injuries, both old and recent. They made slightly more eye contact with him today, but they didn't talk to him.

The throb in his head started to ease today, but not the pain and swelling in his face and body. The thick, swollen bruising in his cheeks, jaw, and eyes got hot and pulsed with painful swelling. He couldn't do anything but put his head down and rest until it went away.

The column kept slogging north—always north. Kuvik didn't see what the Bounty Hunters wanted there. They usually went into other Clans' territory, but they didn't overtake any other Clan.

The warriors didn't send out raiding parties. He saw enough of the column when the group crossed tall hillsides. None of the Bounty Hunters left the column.

He also so one tiny speck of white in the group from this distance. Dana walked along with the warriors. She was the only female Bounty Hunter in the column. He didn't understand why—not that it mattered much to him.

The five slaves tipped him out of the sled and onto the ground when the column made camp again on the second night. Everything went the same way. The slaves built the huts. The slaves lit the fires. The slaves did the hunting, butchering, and cooking.

Kuvik lay where he was. He would be one of those worker slaves pretty soon. He better relax and rest while he had the chance.

Some of the slaves walked around with bruising as bad as his or sometimes worse. Some of them worked with broken bones, cracked skulls, blood dripping from their noses or mouths, or flayed, slashed, weeping skin.

Some of the women walked around with blood running down the insides of their legs and whip marks all over them. Kuvik didn't envy them one bit.

He tried not to look at these people, but he found it impossible not to. His heart went out to them, especially after saving those people from the first Bounty Hunter village that had captured him.

Maybe he could do something like that with these people. Maybe he could set the Bounty Hunter village on fire, free the slaves, and take them back to the Godless with him. That would be the best thing to do with them.

He started to relax for the night when dozens of screams broke out on the other end of the camp. He jolted upright and tried to spin around to see what the problem was.

He expected creatures to attack. The Bounty Hunters never took precautions against creatures. The Bounty Hunters seemed to think they didn't need to—that they were strong enough and had enough people to protect themselves.

Kuvik cringed when a solid line of twenty Bounty Hunters marched through the camp shoulder to shoulder. The line stretched from one side of the camp to the other. They advanced herding everyone before them.

The Bounty Hunters swung whips made out of braided vines and slashed the slaves right and left whenever anyone came within range.

The slaves tried to flee, but they only wound up clustering more closely together and making bigger targets for the Bounty Hunters to attack.

The line stopped whenever one part of it encountered these clusters. Then multiple Bounty Hunters fell on all the slaves and whipped them to the ground. Only then did the line advance farther across the camp.

The remaining slaves retreated, but their own numbers worked against them. They crowded against the houses, got stuck there, and fell under the Bounty Hunters' whips.

Dana stood in the middle of the line between two men. The man on her left was the same guy who had grabbed her yesterday. Kuvik didn't know the others, but he definitely recognized that one.

She whipped the slaves just as hard. She flailed her whip with a sick leer of pure malicious fun plastered across her pretty face. That smile made her look so hideously cruel.

She whipped the slaves with special enthusiasm. Hurting these people gave her more thrilling energy than anything else Kuvik had ever seen.

The only other time he'd seen her look so happy was when she stole his kukris so he would get caught. She loved doing stuff like that.

The line crossed the whole camp. The Bounty Hunters eventually came to Kuvik. He couldn't get away, but fortunately, Dana was nowhere near him.

He tucked himself tighter into a ball, turned his face away, and curled his chin close to his chest to protect himself. The other Bounty Hunters whipped him across the back five times. Then they stepped over him and kept going.

Shrieks, screams, and broken sobs filled the camp long after the Bounty Hunters got to the other end and the line broke up. The Bounty Hunters came back, split up to their huts and fires, and went back to whatever they were doing before.

Some of them struck out with their whips at random slaves—even slaves who'd already received vicious whippings just a few minutes before. Some of the slaves didn't get up after the Bounty Hunters' attack.

Kuvik stayed where he was and didn't draw any attention to himself. The whip cuts on his back hurt, but he was one of the few who got off easy in that attack. Some of the slaves carried their motionless comrades into the jungle and didn't bring them back.

Everyone else kept working and pretended the attack never happened. No one had to explain why. The Bounty Hunters could do anything like this anytime and they did.

The camp went on with its business on both sides. Both the slaves and the Bounty Hunters played their parts. They went through the same combination of routines until the Bounty Hunters started to take their female slaves into their huts for the night.

It was already starting to get dark by the time one of the male slaves in Kuvik's party came over to him. The guy put another vessel of Gooji juice aside along with another bowl of food while the guy applied fresh leaf paste to the whip cuts on Kuvik's back.

The slaves had to be careful to take time away from their work to apply the paste to themselves and each other. They had to be subtle about placing rocks in the embers to boil Gooji juice for their injured comrades.

The hunters were the only slaves allowed to leave the camp. They were the ones who gathered Gooji sap for everyone.

The Bounty Hunters saw the slaves doing all of this, but the Bounty Hunters didn't intervene as long as the slaves made sure not to let the process interrupt their work. The slaves had to maneuver each action into the rest of their duties and tasks.

The man finished with Kuvik's back, squatted in front of him, and got busy applying a fresh coat of paste to all of Kuvik's other injuries.

Kuvik studied the guy. He was young—or he ought to have been if he wasn't so torn down by mistreatment and neglect.

He probably would have been about twenty-five. His black hair had been cut too short and unevenly as if someone had to saw it off with a blunt knife. He and all the male slaves kept their faces clean-shaven for some reason.

The guy didn't raise his dark eyes to look at Kuvik except when the guy applied leaf paste to Kuvik's face.

"Thank you," Kuvik murmured.

The guy didn't answer. He put the leaf paste aside and picked up the vessel of juice. Kuvik didn't protest when the guy picked him up and dumped the juice down his throat.

Kuvik waited while the guy put the vessel aside and picked up the bowl of food. "What's your name?" Kuvik asked. "Mine is Kuvik."

The man didn't answer. He raised a spoonful of the food, put it in Kuvik's mouth, and waited for Kuvik to chew it before feeding him another one.

A woman's laugh startled Kuvik into glancing across the camp. Dana stood over there talking and joking around with the warriors again. The same man stood at her side, but he didn't try to touch her again.

"Do you know that man standing next to Dana?" Kuvik asked. "Is he her husband or something?"

The slave guy didn't answer that, either. He put the next spoonful of food in Kuvik's mouth.

"She was the one who tricked me into walking into a Bounty Hunter ambush," Kuvik went on more to himself than anyone else. "I've never heard of the Bounty Hunters taking one of their women on a raiding party. Maybe they brought her because she enjoys it so much to see other people suffer and bleed. Maybe they brought her along just to give her the special pleasure of disarming me while my back was turned so the Bounty Hunters could make me a captive."

"Zehir," the slave guy muttered under his breath.

Kuvik spun around fast. "What?"

"Zehir," the guy murmured again. "His name.....it's Zehir."

"Who is he? Are they married?"

The slave shrugged and spooned another mouthful into Kuvik's mouth. "I don't know what they are or why they bring her. She's as bad as they are."

Kuvik swallowed his food with difficulty. "Who are you?" Kuvik asked. "Tell me your name. Please."

The guy looked down into the bowl and pushed the food back and forth for a minute. Kuvik couldn't see what the guy would be looking at in there.

Kuvik didn't expect the guy to say anything, but he eventually mumbled, "Dorei."

Kuvik's heart leapt. "Which Clan are you from originally?"

Dorei shrugged. "I don't remember. They took me, my parents, and my whole band when I was too little to remember. I've been moving around from one Bounty Hunter band to another as long as I can remember."

Kuvik opened his mouth to tell Dorei that they could work together to escape from the Bounty Hunters, but Dorei cut him off. Dorei used the moment to feed Kuvik the last spoonful of food and turned away to pick up all his stuff.

"They won't let you lie down for much longer," Dorei murmured. "You better sleep while you can."

He walked off and returned to his work, but Kuvik couldn't have been happier about the way that conversation went. Dorei had told Kuvik his name. Dorei had told him about Zehir even if Dorei couldn't tell him much of anything else.

Kuvik settled down much more peacefully that night. He'd made one connection with the slaves. He would build a core of allies he could get to help him escape. They could do it together.

Chapter 9

The Bounty Hunters didn't make Kuvik walk the next day. Dorei and the other four slaves came back, loaded Kuvik onto the sled, and went through the whole agonizing ordeal again the next day.

Kuvik looked forward to the time when the column would make camp that night. He would get another chance to talk to Dorei or one of the other men assigned to transport him.

Kuvik would just keep building these connections the longer he stayed here. He didn't need any more encouragement than that.

He did start to get extremely hungry and especially thirsty during the day. The Bounty Hunters didn't give him any water except for the Gooji juice and one bowl of food each day. It wasn't enough.

None of the slaves got enough to eat. They all staggered around like living skeletons. Their condition made them especially vulnerable to the Bounty Hunters' attacks. The slightest strike could break bone.

Kuvik found himself studying his five handlers much more closely. He could pay more attention as his injuries healed.

He paid special attention to Dorei. The guy was skin and bone with hollow, sunken, distant eyes and a pained, soulful expression Kuvik understood only too well. He knew exactly what Dorei had been going through all these years. No one knew better than Kuvik.

Dorei worked hard. He sweated, panted, and strained his thin, wasted muscles to pull Kuvik across the countryside. Dorei threw all his weight into the job and never stopped working even after the column made camp. He never shirked.

Kuvik didn't see why Dorei gave so much extra effort to the Bounty Hunters. Kuvik understood the slaves better when they did the bare minimum to escape punishment. Why should they break their backs for these violent tyrants?

The slaves made a special point to avoid Dana. Kuvik noticed that more and more as time went on. They couldn't avoid the warriors, but she stuck out for all the world to see.

The slaves saw her coming and maneuvered themselves into positions and places to protect themselves even from her noticing them.

Not all the Bounty Hunters lashed out at the slaves out of vindictive spite or even sadistic pleasure. She was one of the few who did. Most of the others did it systematically—almost grudgingly because they thought they had to.

Not many others actually enjoyed it. Dana and Zehir definitely did. They shared that quality. It bonded them and they exercised their pastime together whenever it suited them.

Kuvik saw them together a lot. He never saw Zehir do anything overtly sexual toward her again.

In fact, Kuvik never saw Zehir touch her again at all. Were they even in a relationship? Kuvik wouldn't have thought they were in a relationship at all except for that one incident.

He couldn't think of any other explanation for why Zehir would act that way toward her. Kuvik couldn't imagine any man acting that way toward any woman other than his wife—and even then, never in public.

The other Bounty Hunters didn't seem to think anything of it. Kuvik shouldn't have thought about it or anything else related to Dana, but he found it impossible not to.

Now Kuvik understood who and what she really was. He understood her place in Bounty Hunter society—or almost.

Was Zehir the one who let her come on this journey? Was he the one who decided she might be useful to have around to help lure captives into Bounty Hunter custody?

Kuvik lost sight of her in the crowd. He barely paid attention to anything else going on in the camp. He spent the time counting down the minutes until Dorei came back and they could talk again.

Kuvik's first question would be to ask the names of the other men in Dorei's group. Kuvik wanted to know them, connect with them, and start building trust with them. He needed friends and he already felt closely bonded to these men for some reason.

Dana startled him out of his thoughts by coming out of nowhere and sitting down in front of him. He jerked back too hard and hurt his shoulders. They had started to ache from lying on his side all the time with his wrists tied behind his back.

She smiled at him. "I brought your dinner. Open wide."

Kuvik glared at her. "Why do you keep coming back to gloat over me? Don't you have anything better to do?"

She smirked even more dangerously. "I come back to gloat over you. Don't you know that by now?" She bent in low and dropped her voice to a sultry murmur. "Did you think we would get closer if we stayed out in the jungle together?"

She stroked her hand down his chest to his stomach and then to the waistband of his pants.

He tried to struggle away from her, but she grabbed his waistband and tugged him closer.

"You felt so good when you carried me into the branches, Kuvik," she purred. "I would have straddled you that night if you let me. What's the matter? Do you have a wife back home with the Godless? Is that why you're so virtuous?"

She lowered her hand, grabbed him between the legs, and squeezed. She must have done this a lot, too, because she knew exactly how to touch him to make him hard.

"You would have loved it, wouldn't you?" she husked. "You would have loved making me scream like that in the dirt on the jungle floor. You would have made me your beast and planted your seed in me. Don't worry. You'll think about me that way tonight. I promise."

She let go, straightened up, and left him lying there seething with fury and confused tension.

He had never thought about her that way before, but he sure thought about it now. She made sure of it. He couldn't get those pictures out of his head no matter how hard he tried.

She picked up the bowl, scooped out a spoonful of the food, and held it in front of his face for him to eat.

He had to find a way to turn the tables on her. He had to find a way to block her from stabbing him in the guts like this. She had found his greatest weakness. She would keep exploiting it until she broke him.

He understood these methods. He recognized someone using them on him. He had to find a way to reverse it.

He looked up and opened his mouth for her to put the food into it. She started to smile.

"Is Zehir your husband, Dana?" Kuvik asked. "He handles you like his wife, but you can't be legally married. You're underage, aren't you? You aren't over the age of gathering."

The smile evaporated off her face. She stared at him in stupefied horror for a second. How many of these Bounty Hunter warriors put two and two together?

"He treats you the same as one of his slaves," Kuvik went on. "Does he take you into his hut and make you his beast? Does he make you scream like that in the dirt on the jungle floor? Does he ever plan to marry you? It's too late if he's already done it with you. He doesn't have to marry you. He can keep treating you like one of his slaves and you'll keep going along with it, won't you? Is that you I keep hearing screaming first thing in the morning? Do you think anything will change when you come of age? Why should it? What's the stop him from passing you around to his friends when he gets bored with you?"

Her face transformed into a mask of brutal rage and she shot to her feet. She hurled the bowl onto the ground hard enough to splatter the food into the dirt in front of Kuvik's face.

He didn't regret that he wouldn't get anything to eat tonight. His ploy worked. He wouldn't think of Dana tonight—at least he wouldn't think about doing anything to her himself.

He thanked his lucky stars he had never touched her before his capture. Now he wouldn't think of anything except that she was one of Zehir's women—maybe even one of many.

She couldn't be more than sixteen or seventeen. He could have any and as many slave women as he wanted. He didn't need Dana—for anything.

Kuvik didn't know or care if Zehir had been doing anything with Dana. Kuvik planted the seed of doubt in her mind. That's all he needed to do.

She wouldn't open her mouth to twist his heartstrings again. She would avoid him—which meant he would be free to talk to his slave handlers instead. He could wait for that. It would definitely be worth missing one night's food.

Dana stormed off to the other side of the camp. He didn't expect to see her again at all, but she came barging back a few minutes later. She carried one of the Bounty Hunters' clubs about two inches thick.

Her face twisted in fury told Kuvik all he needed to know. He braced himself for the worst, but even then he knew it was worth it.

He had found her vulnerability and exploited it. She had given him the only weapon he needed while they were out there alone together in the jungle.

She raised the club while she was still walking toward him, wound back, and swung. She plastered him hard across the face, made his head snap back, and went to town on the rest of his body and limbs in between kicking him in the head.

He dropped down into his distant quiet place. He passed out completely long before she finished. She kept going on and on and on. She might not stop until she killed him.

Chapter 10

Kuvik woke up to the sharp, excruciating pain of the slaves moving him onto the sled again. He didn't open his eyes all day. He didn't care about anything. He really did want to die, but he had no way to make it happen.

He still couldn't bring himself to regret baiting Dana into beating him like this. The Bounty Hunters would just come around and do it again soon anyway.

He'd been getting better these last few days. Dorei had said the Bounty Hunters would make Kuvik get up and work soon, so of course they would let him recover again.

Every pebble in the landscape exploded his head and body apart with pain. He whimpered in agony every time a bump or clump of grass made the sled bounce.

The rough terrain made this ordeal so much harder to endure. The constant pain in every part of his body wore down his resolve. He found it harder to keep the spirit of escape alive, but he had to.

His one consolation in this was that Dana wouldn't come back to toy with him again. She did more than not come back. She stayed completely out of his sight that evening when the column made camp.

He kept looking around for her. He actually would have liked to see her. He wanted to see how she reacted to his counterattack. Did she change her behavior? Was Zehir feeling the effects of Kuvik's maneuver? Kuvik certainly hoped so.

Maybe Zehir would get angry when Dana stopped responding to him. He might throw away all pretense and really start treating her as a slave.

Then Kuvik had a crazy idea. Maybe she already was one. Maybe she had started out as a captive. Maybe Zehir or the other warriors had given her special treatment to turn her against her fellow captives. Maybe that's how she had gotten like this—to save herself.

Kuvik didn't care about any of that. He didn't care if his jabs made her life a living hell. He really hoped they did after what she did to him. He would do a lot worse if he ever saw her again.

He hoped his words shattered the illusion of her carefully constructed fantasy world that these men would ever treat her differently.

He hoped she had to live with that realization from now on. He hoped she would never be able to retreat back into her pleasant little fairy tale where she was one of the oppressors instead of one of the cattle.

Kuvik looked forward to Dorei coming back to feed him. One of the slaves would have to give Kuvik Gooji juice again after Dana's beating. She sure did a number on him. Dorei had been right about her. She beat Kuvik far worse than any of the men.

They did it systematically. They knew just how far they could go without doing any permanent damage. She would have done permanent damage if she had been as strong as they were. Maybe one of them stopped her from outright killing him.

He had won. That's what the beating meant. She couldn't counter anything that he said because she knew it was all true. That's why she beat him while he was tied up. She had no other way to attack him.

Not even touching him again would work because he knew her secret. Was he the only one? Should he circulate it among the other slaves so they could use it against her, too?

These slaves didn't seem too interested in outsmarting their captors. Maybe none of them had thought of it before.

He got another surprise when a female slave came over to feed him tonight. She also brought leaf paste and Gooji juice, but he barely noticed that.

She was older than the men who dragged Kuvik's sled around. She might have been in her thirties or maybe as old as forty. She looked absolutely terrible with a lot of different colored bruises all over her face and bloody cracks in her lips.

She kept sniffing and running her right wrist across her nose. She looked wretched, miserable, and utterly defeated. Her dark eyes overflowed with so much pain, loss, and hopeless despair.

"Who are you?" he gasped.

She barely looked at him. "Sit up and drink this." Her voice cracked like she might be on the verge of tears.

She helped him sit up and held the vessel for him to drink the juice. Then she laid him on the ground and started applying the paste to all his injuries.

"Maybe you should use this on yourself. You look like you need it more than I do." He hesitated. "My name is Kuvik. What's yours?"

She sniffed again and rubbed her nose. Her lips trembled. "Just eat your food and don't make me have to go back and tell anyone that you didn't."

"I wouldn't do that. Hey! Look at me."

She refused to look at him. He should just leave her alone, but every fiber of his being told him to help her. He had to do something for this poor woman.

He couldn't just come right out and offer to help her—not when he was tied up like this. He would have to get untied before he did anything. She might think he was going to ask her to untie him. That could get her killed.

She picked up the bowl and started feeding him. "Do you know Dorei and the others?" he asked. "Is that why you're here?"

She still didn't look up. "Dorei is my son," she mumbled.

Kuvik had to blink at her for a second before he could believe that. She didn't look old enough to have a son Dorei's age—and then he remembered what he said about the Bounty Hunters capturing him and his whole family.

He didn't say which Clan he'd come from. Maybe he and his family had come from a Clan that didn't believe in the gatherings.

Kuvik knew of a few that didn't. The men could take any female they wanted no matter how old she was. His original family Clan had been one of those.

Kuvik scrambled to come up with another question to ask her in between spoonfuls of the food. "What's your name?" he asked.

She didn't get a chance to answer before one of the Bounty Hunters stomped over and kicked the bowl out of her hands. The bowl overturned on the ground again.

"Get back over there where I told you to go!" the guy blared. "Don't let me catch you disobeying me again."

He grabbed her by the arm, yanked her to her feet hard enough to make her cry out, and practically hurled her away. She took off running toward the other side of the camp and vanished behind the huts.

Silence fell. Kuvik didn't expect anyone to come back and feed him again, but Dorei showed up a minute later. He picked up the fallen bowl and spoon, used it to scrape up the dirty food, took it away, and came back with a fresh bowl a second later.

"I'm sorry if I did anything to get your mother into trouble," Kuvik told Dorei while Dorei fed him. "I was trying to talk to her."

"It wasn't you," Dorei mumbled under his breath. "It was Osid."

"Who's that?"

Dorei inclined his head to one side. "That man that came back for her. He's.....you could say he takes a special interest in her."

Kuvik looked away and didn't ask what that meant. He already knew. "Is she your only relative here?" Kuvik asked. "Is the rest of your family here?"

"A few of them are here. I don't know where the rest are."

"Tell me the names of the other men who pull me around on that sled. Do you know them?"

Dorei nodded down at the bowl. "Garvis is the young one who walks with the limp. Phiri is the tall one. He's stronger than we are."

"Why? He looks like he gets more to eat?"

"The Bounty Hunters use him for heavy labor back in the village. He gets more food—more meat. All the heavy laborers do. They have to or they wouldn't be strong enough to do the work. Akli is the one who always looks angry. Don't make him mad. Don't say I didn't warn you."

"Thank you," Kuvik replied. "I'll be careful."

"Nelv is the other young one. He keeps to himself. He doesn't get close to anyone, but he's a good hard worker."

Kuvik opened his mouth to ask why Dorei worked so hard and why he valued hard work in someone else considering their circumstances.

Kuvik stopped himself from asking that. He didn't want to offend Dorei by making it sound like Kuvik was finding fault in anything Dorei did.

Dorei waited for Kuvik to say something else. Dorei fed Kuvik a few more mouthfuls.

Kuvik couldn't think of anything else to ask—not anything that wouldn't have been too provocative this early in the game. He had to pace himself and give these people time to get used to him.

Dorei startled Kuvik out of his thoughts. "What did you say to Dana that made her so mad?"

Kuvik couldn't make eye contact with the guy. "I was traveling south to find my family band. I got separated and lost in the country. I found a young, unarmed, helpless girl all alone in the jungle. She couldn't defend herself, so I couldn't leave her on her own. It seemed like there was something wrong with her mind—like she might have been born defective or something. She didn't recognize the danger. She kept trying to show me something. I told her I would see what it was and then I would take her south to my band for her own protection. She led me into a trap, disarmed me from behind, and got me captured."

Dorei stared straight into Kuvik's eyes and didn't look away through the whole story.

Kuvik made eye contact with him once. Kuvik couldn't handle more than that. "She acted so young and innocent then—and then a few days ago, I saw her walking across the camp....over there....near that hut right there. She met up with Zehir and he put his arms around her and pulled her against him in a sexual way like she belonged to him—but he did it in front of all the other men—like he wanted to take her right then and there where they could all see her. She smiled and blushed through the whole thing like she enjoyed it."

"He does that kind of thing with her all the time," Dorei remarked. "It's one of their games."

"I asked her if they were married. I said it couldn't be legal because she's underage. I said he has no reason to marry her if he can have her whenever he wants the same as any of his slave women. I asked if he takes her any way he wants in between all the slave women he can help himself to when he feels like it. I asked why he would marry her when he doesn't have to."

Dorei clucked his tongue and shook his head, but his lips quivered like he had to stop himself from smiling. "No wonder she beat you so badly. You took a big risk saying all of that. She could have killed you."

"Is she a slave herself? Is that it? Is she the Bounty Hunters' plaything and they get some kind of sick thrill out of training her to brutalize the captives for them?"

"I've thought that before." Dorei put the last spoonful of food in Kuvik's mouth. "I've wondered about that—and I can tell you for a fact that he does do it with her. He takes her into his hut with him at night and keeps her there. I've heard her screaming."

Kuvik looked away again. He told himself he didn't care, but he actually did. He couldn't help it.

What did the Bounty Hunters do to her? Did they brutalize her first to get her addicted to good treatment? Is that how they corrupted her against the other captives? Or was she born among the Bounty Hunter elite and handed over to Zehir for some political reason?

Kuvik still had to consider the possibility that she went along with all of this willingly. It was possible that none of the Bounty Hunters did anything to her and she did all of this because she enjoyed it.

Dorei got to his feet. "I better go. The Bounty Hunters will get angry if they see us talking too much."

He picked up all the stuff his mother had left behind. Kuvik realized too late that he'd forgotten to ask her name.

Dorei left him alone with plenty on his mind. Finding out that Dana was intimately involved with Zehir didn't change anything. It didn't answer any of Kuvik's questions and it didn't get him out of here.

Chapter 11

K uvik roused from a deep sleep when someone touched him and moved his body around. He jumped out of his skin when someone cut the thick vines binding his feet together.

He floundered out of a sound sleep and looked up at the five men who usually handled him. He tried to figure out what they were doing to him and why.

He'd been a Bounty Hunter captive for a week with no change in his circumstances. The Bounty Hunters hadn't given him any more beatings after Dana attacked him.

The Bounty Hunters had let him heal, but that only brought him closer to the moment when they actually did beat him up again. It was only a matter of time.

The five men pulled him to his feet. He stumbled and had to struggle to keep his balance. This was the first time the Bounty Hunters had let him stand up since his capture.

The five men stood him up straight, cut his wrists from behind his back, and took hold of his arms with two men on either side. They raised his arms above his head.

He barely noticed what they were doing until another slave guy laid a heavy log across Kuvik's shoulders. The four men on either side of him tied his wrists to the log. They immobilized him as well here as he had been a few minutes ago.

He glanced around and tried to make eye contact with the men. He'd developed an unspoken bond with all five of them. Dorei was the only one who had come to feed him at night, so Dorei was the only one of the five Kuvik had gotten a chance to talk to.

Maybe they would let him walk on his own now. He could only hope.

They dashed all his hopes when a dozen Bounty Hunters came over and beat him as badly as before. He couldn't fall to the ground or protect himself with his wrists tied to the log across his shoulder.

They made this beating much worse than before. They covered his whole body in bruises. They stopped short of breaking any bones, but they made sure to kick him in the head a lot. They seemed to do it more this time than the others.

He gave up all resistance and just let it happen. They kept pulling him to his feet and clubbing him across the back and in the knees to make him fall down. The Bounty Hunters made sure not to leave a single inch of him unbeaten.

He became aware of the whole column standing around watching. Everyone waited for the Bounty Hunters to finish before the column moved out for the day.

They left him on his feet to walk on his own. He wished now that they hadn't. His legs ached from all the strikes and kicks.

The five slave guys came back and tied a thick rope around his ankles, but they left it loose enough for him to stumble in short, faltering steps. He wouldn't have been able to run anywhere.

One of the Bounty Hunters tied a rope around Kuvik's waist and the guy tied the other end around his own waist so he could walk hands free. Then the guy kicked Kuvik to make him walk with the rest of the column.

His head swam. He had to struggle not to fall over. He could barely see where he was going, but he didn't need to. Dorei and the others pushed him whenever Kuvik stumbled off course.

The Bounty Hunter who had leashed Kuvik to his waist laughed at Kuvik's struggles. The other Bounty Hunters joined in the joke, but they all forgot to appreciate it after a while. Kuvik's ordeal became just another feature of the journey.

At least the five slaves didn't have to pull him anymore. He could be grateful for that for their sakes. He would rather walk even if every step caused him excruciating pain.

Having his arms tied up to this log made his shoulders ache even more than having them bound behind his back for a week. He couldn't decide which was worse.

The log turned out to be a lot heavier than he realized. Carrying that extra weight became the worst part of the ordeal.

His knees gave out more than once before sundown. Dorei and the other four slaves dragged Kuvik to his feet and got him moving again. They didn't speak to encourage him, but their presence made him feel better.

They understood. Some of them must have gone through something like this at one point or another.

The Bounty Hunters camped in the jungle again that night. The five slaves led Kuvik to a tree at the edge of the camp. He buckled there and collapsed half-sprawled against the trunk. He couldn't have run or walked anywhere even if he tried.

The Bounty Hunter untied the leash, dropped it on the ground, walked away, and left Kuvik there unguarded. No one needed to guard him. He was too beaten, exhausted, and disheartened to try anything tonight.

They left his legs free, but no one untied his wrists from the log. He longed for the days of having his hands bound behind his back. This was the most uncomfortable position he'd ever been in.

Everyone ignored him until darkness fell and Dorei came back to feed Kuvik. Dorei had been giving Kuvik plain water for the last few days. He hadn't needed Gooji juice before, but he definitely needed it now.

Dorei helped him sit up to drink the juice, laid Kuvik back in the same position, and started feeding him as usual.

"Did you ever think about escaping, Dorei?" Kuvik asked at last.

"Sure," Dorei mumbled while he scraped the bowl for the last spoonfuls. "I used to think about it all the time when I was young."

"Why didn't you do it?" Kuvik asked. "Why are you still here?"

"I saw what happened to the others who tried. Nothing is worth that. I wouldn't do it unless I could be certain I would get away without getting recaptured. I wouldn't risk something like that and escape is impossible anyway. No one ever succeeds."

"I did it once," Kuvik told him.

"I don't believe you," Dorei countered. "You don't know what being a Bounty Hunter prisoner is really like. You think you can escape whenever you want to. You're wrong."

"I know what being a Bounty Hunter prisoner is like because I was one before. I got captured and taken to a village in the south. They made me fight a juvenile Crusher while the warriors stood around and laughed and cheered. Now do you believe me?"

Dorei's eyes blazed. He didn't look away.

"I escaped," Kuvik went on. "I went back in and deliberately got myself recaptured because I saw the Bounty Hunters bring in a young girl from my family band. I went back to get her out and I escaped a second time with her. We made it all the way back to our band for over a year before this happened. I did it before. I can do it again."

Dorei went back to scraping the bowl. "You should talk to Akli. He's the one who always wants to try to escape. He's tried it before, but they always bring him back."

"Do they punish him?"

Dorei nodded down at the bowl. "He's the reason I never tried and I never will. I wouldn't want to go through that. Anything would be better than that."

"What did they do to him? He looks healthy enough—as healthy as any of you can possibly look."

Dorei looked up and glared at Kuvik. "I'm going to tell you, but only if you promise never to tell him that I told you. Don't let on that you know—and don't ever let him find out that I'm the one who told you. Give me your word, Kuvik."

"I swear it. I won't tell anyone that I know—not even him."

"They emasculated him. That's why he's so angry all the time. He's tried to escape countless times. They tried everything to break him. They beat him. They raped him. They killed his relatives in front of him. They did everything. They hurt him worse than anyone I've ever seen, but he still kept trying. They finally couldn't think of anything else bad enough to do to him, so they did that. That was the last time he tried it, but I'm pretty sure he still thinks about it. He just keeps getting more furious and enraged with every passing year. It's a miracle he hasn't killed all the Bounty Hunters by now."

Kuvik didn't answer. He couldn't think of anything to say to that, so he didn't say anything. He could only think one thing about Dorei's revelation. Kuvik thought he'd finally found the ally he should have been looking for all this time.

Someone like Dorei couldn't help Kuvik except by giving him critical information. Kuvik needed someone like Akli—someone determined to escape—someone who wouldn't hesitate to fight back and kill Bounty Hunters if it came to that.

Dorei gave Kuvik the last mouthful of food and left him alone in the silence. The five slaves happened to settle down and sleep near enough for Kuvik to watch them tonight. The five slaves didn't always do that.

Kuvik found himself studying Akli more closely. He walked around with a permanent enraged scowl etched into his face. Now Kuvik knew why—like Akli needed more of a reason than all the rest of these people.

He didn't act meek and beaten down. He walked around simmering away like a volcano ready to explode. Kuvik really needed someone like that, but Akli never came near Kuvik. They'd never shared a word in the whole time Kuvik had been here.

Chapter 12

Dorei and the other four slaves pulled Kuvik to his feet for another long hard slog heading north. The journey took forever. He couldn't even keep track of how long he'd been traveling with these people.

They left his arms tied to the log all the time. They never freed him. The same Bounty Hunter came back to pick up the leash tied around Kuvik's waist, but the guy didn't tie it around his own waist.

He handed it off to Dana. This was the first time Kuvik had seen her since that night. She smirked at him while she tied the leash around her waist.

He didn't understand why until she stepped behind him and slashed him hard with a whip across the back. It left a deep cut and made him writhe in pain, but she only kicked him from behind and told him to start walking.

The column moved out with him stumbling along with the others. The five slaves guided him when he veered off track. Dana stayed behind him all the way whipping his back to bloody shreds.

She didn't stop all day. She changed arms when she got tired. She drove him before her and grinned and sometimes laughed when he yelled out in pain at her strikes.

He lost his mind in a sea of pain long before the column stopped for the night. He passed out under another tree, woke up just long enough for Dorei to pour a dose of Gooji juice down his throat, and passed out again.

The next week blurred in a dull grey fog of pain, stumbling marches, choking down one meager bowl of food each evening, and getting shaken awake and pulled to his feet to do it all again the next day.

The Bounty Hunters didn't whip him again. Dana didn't show herself to him again. None of the other Bounty Hunters paid any attention to him at all except when that one man leashed Kuvik around his waist every morning.

They left him to sleep the rest of the time. He didn't try to talk to Dorei again. Kuvik probably wouldn't have talked to Dorei again—not about anything important. Kuvik might have talked just to be polite.

Dorei didn't matter anymore. He was one of the lost—one of those who had decided it was better to cooperate. That must be why he worked so hard. He didn't want to risk anything—and so he wound up risking everything.

Dana's whipping gave Kuvik the excuse he needed not to talk to Dorei at all. Kuvik kept his eyes closed through two more doses of Gooji juice.

Kuvik kept his eyes closed during meals for the first couple of nights. He didn't want to talk to anyone and Dorei didn't try.

Kuvik recovered enough to open his eyes, but he didn't try to talk. He let Dorei think that maybe Kuvik was becoming withdrawn or angry or hostile because of his ordeal. Kuvik never let on the real reason why he stopped talking to Dorei.

Kuvik directed all his mental energy toward figuring out a way to talk to Akli. Kuvik's whole life seemed to hinge on accomplishing that one task.

Akli never came near Kuvik for the whole journey, and the next day, the party started winding its way down into a valley with a large Bounty Hunter village in it.

This one resembled the second village where Kuvik had stayed during his first captivity. Everyone in this place looked like either a warrior or a slave. He didn't see any of the people in fancy clothes. Would Dana stay here, too?

None of the Bounty Hunters or slaves showed any particular excitement or happiness about coming back here. Kuvik wouldn't have expected the slaves to get happy or excited about it, but he would have expected some positive reaction from the warriors.

They hardly acted like they were entering a village at all. They spread out to the different houses. The slaves returned to work and everyone went on exactly the same way they had been the whole time they'd been traveling here.

The five men who usually handled Kuvik went off in different directions, too. They all seemed to forget that he existed.

He stopped in the middle of the village and looked around. No one untied his wrists from the log. No one untied the rope from his ankles. He might have been able to stumble away into the jungle, but he wouldn't have gotten far.

He turned all the way around in a circle waiting for someone somewhere to do something with him or two him, but no one did. Everyone went off to different houses, went inside, and ignored him.

That was the moment when he saw one of the slaves enter a different house. This man had been walking behind Kuvik all this time. That was the reason Kuvik never noticed the guy before.

He carried an enormous bundle of jumbled weapons of all kinds from dozens of different Clans. Kuvik understood those weapons instantly. He'd seen them before the night he and Hammer had killed those Bounty Hunters and took their weapons—the night Kuvik had gotten his first kukris.

The man vanished inside the house and then another slave entered behind him carrying a second bundle of mixed weapons. Kuvik thought fast. He didn't see his jawbone kukris in the pile, but that hardly mattered.

The second man went inside and both men emerged without their bundles. They must store the weapons in there. Kuvik's heart stopped. He was standing just a stone's throw away from one of the biggest weapons caches he'd ever seen in his life.

He had to find a way to get into that building—sometime when he had his hands free and could fight.

Now he knew where to go and what to do. Should he make his move now? He would be able to use a blade from the pile to free his hands. He could throw off this log and fight his way out of here.

Right then, a woman stormed up to him, grabbed him by the back of the neck, and yanked him sideways. "You!" she snapped. "You come with me!"

She dragged him through the village. He yelled in pain every time she almost pulled him off his feet. He stumbled more than once and went down on one knee before she grabbed some part of him and pulled him upright.

"Quit your whining!" she barked. "I can make it a lot worse for you if you really want me to. Shut up! You have nothing to complain about. Now get over here and don't make me have to get rough with you."

She dragged him to a large house at the edge of the village. It was almost as big as one of the big meeting houses where the warriors met to drink and make their slaves fight each other.

She didn't enter through the front. She towed Kuvik around to the back of the building, opened a different door, and propelled him inside. She did it hard enough to really knock him over this time.

He sprawled across a flat stone floor like the ones in the meeting houses. This place had the same kind of construction except that the room was much smaller.

A fire blazed in a circular hole in the middle of the floor. Four pillars of flat stone mortared together rose from the corners around the fireplace, met in the middle, and continued together in a unified chimney to a hole in the ceiling.

The rest of the room had no furniture in it. Various implements, bundles of dried flowers, and cured haunches of meat hung from the walls and roof beams.

The woman stormed past Kuvik to the other side of the room, pulled a metal knife from some hidden place, and came stalking back with a murderous scowl on her face.

This was the first time he'd gotten a look at her. She was a thickly built woman about forty-five years old with heavy jowls and a small, pinched mouth to match the venomous expression on her face.

She wore a full-length dress very similar to Dana's except that this one was grey. It didn't billow around her because she didn't have a shapely body. The dress only made her look worse.

She passed the fireplace on her way toward him with the knife clasped in her hand. He thought fast for a way to get out of this and tried to get to his feet.

He made it as far as his knees before she slashed the knife at him and cut the cord holding his wrist to the log. His arm fell down and dangled from his aching shoulder.

Her sudden move upset the log. It toppled off Kuvik's shoulders and the other end hit the floor hard enough to almost twist his other shoulder out of its socket.

He yelled out in pain, but she didn't listen. She cut the other cord, freed his other wrist, and the log fell the rest of the way off him. It still managed to hurt him by scraping the torn skin across his back on the way down.

He jumped out of the way so it wouldn't crush his feet, and just as fast, the woman snatched a switch from the fireplace and started whipping him with it.

She struck fast and hard. His ordeal over the last three weeks made him spring away from her and throw up his arms to protect himself.

He only wound up backing into a corner of the room where he couldn't get away from her. She laid into him much harder than Dana ever did.

This woman cut him deep enough to make every wound bleed—and she didn't stop. She slashed him all over the arms, shoulders, chest, stomach, sides, and legs. He buckled onto the floor and covered his head just praying for the end.

She used that opening to whip his back just as hard until she tore open every inch of his skin. He lacked the strength to resist. She injured him as badly as he ever had been before if not worse.

He toppled all the way onto the floor as soon as she finished. His blood soaked the stones underneath him. They felt warm and slick instead of flat, cold, and smooth.

She threw the bloody switch down by the fireplace and kicked him in the stomach. "Now get up and clean up that mess. You don't think I'm going to do it for you, do you, you worthless piece of trash? That's what you're here for. Be grateful I don't kill you with my bare hands."

Just then, a man's voice echoed from somewhere else in the building. "Noya!" the man called. "Where are you?"

The woman froze. That man must be calling her.

She spun around and yelled back. "I'm coming, Aigo! I'll be right there!"

She hustled to one side of the room, came back with a rope, and cinched a noose around Kuvik's neck. She almost strangled him dragging him to the edge of the fireplace.

She tied the rope around one of the pillars, used the other end to bind his wrists together, and left him bleeding on the floor while she hurried away to answer Aigo's call.

Chapter 13

K uvik woke up when someone kicked him again—in the back this time. "I told you to clean up this mess!" a woman's voice snapped. "Do you think you can sleep all day?"

Kuvik floundered to wake up and figure out where he was. He had to pry himself out of a film of dried blood on the stone floor. He was still in the room behind what looked like a Bounty Hunter meeting house.

He took a second before he remembered the heavy-set woman who had whipped him so badly. He must have passed out because the first faint glimmer of dawn light was just streaming through the open door behind him. He must have slept all night.

He took even longer before he remembered her name and everything that had happened after the Bounty Hunter column brought him to this village. Her name was Noya. She was the one who whipped him into this bloody condition.

He tried to sit up, but the rope around his neck and wrists wouldn't let him. She stormed up to him, cut the rope around his wrists to free his arms, and cut the rope around the fireplace pillar. She led a length of rope in a tight noose around his neck.

He staggered to his feet. Dried blood caked every inch of his skin. Moving anything disturbed the painful whip cuts all over his body. She only spared his face, neck, and scalp.

He barely got a chance to stand up before she threw a wooden bucket at him. She hit him hard enough in the stomach to make him wince.

"Go get the water," she snapped. "There's a stream behind the meeting house over there. Don't let me find out you looked sideways at anything on the way there or on the way back. I'll be watching. Hurry up. I don't have all day. You're lucky I put up with you at all."

Kuvik struggled to think straight. Should he try to escape now? He wouldn't be able to get to the weapons store fast enough—and he wouldn't be able to travel fast enough to get away from this village even if he did find a way to arm himself.

He wouldn't be going anywhere in this condition. He turned toward the door, but right before he walked out into the dawn fog, Noya called out behind him again. "If you get this cleaned up and obey me, I might give you some Gooji juice later."

He didn't respond. So that would be the new incentive. Obey, cooperate, and submit—in exchange for Gooji juice. The Bounty Hunters probably attached all kinds of rewards for their slaves' cooperation.

The most obvious reward would be escaping this kind of pain. Kuvik hobbled out of the building, paused there until he spotted the stream, and then limped off in that direction.

Noya came to the door and watched his every move. She never let him out of her sight for an instant. She would have been the first to see him go to the weapons store.

He winced every time he took a step. She really messed him up this time. This might be the worst yet. It would take him a long time to recover from this—and she didn't look very likely to let him do it.

He couldn't bring himself to bend his legs enough to squat by the edge of the stream. He buckled onto his seat, put the bucket aside, and eased himself into the water. He didn't care if Noya saw him.

The cold enveloped him and washed the extra blood off. He didn't rub himself hard enough to open any of his wounds. He just cleaned himself and his pants enough to make himself a tiny shade cleaner. That would have to be enough for now.

He felt only slightly better when he got out. He didn't have any way to dry off, so he filled the bucket and limped back to Noya's house—or Aigo's house—whoever's house it was.

She paced around on the other side of the room when Kuvik slouched in. She didn't turn around. She waved at the bloodstained floor. "Get to work. It won't clean itself up."

He glanced down at the bloodstain. He'd never done anything like this before. He didn't even know how to start.

He decided to start by pouring water on the stain. She threw a hard brush at him. It had an oval wooden back with hard bristles sticking out of one side. He'd never seen one before, but it seemed perfect for this job.

He couldn't kneel or squat, so he sat down and started scrubbing. Noya threw a bunch of pieces of old, frayed, tattered cloth down on the floor next to him. He didn't know what he was supposed to do with them.

He tried using them on the wet, bloody floor and found that they soaked up the bloody water. He wrung it out in the bucket and cleaned up the rest of the floor. He got it as clean as it possibly could be.

He barely finished throwing the water into the trees outside before Noya yelled at him from inside the same room.

"Come butcher this Gorlock for me!" she snapped. "I don't have all day. Hurry up, you piece of trash. You're lucky I put up with you at all. Look at you. You're useless. You can't do anything right, can you? Why do I even waste my time?"

He took the bucket back into the same room. He didn't see any Gorlock until she opened another door on the inside of the room.

It opened into another much larger room—also with no furniture. This one had multiple fire holes in a similar stone floor, but none of them had pillars or chimneys.

A dead Gorlock occupied almost the entire room. Noya threw one knife on the floor.

"Now get to work and don't make me have to give you another whipping. Be grateful I don't keep you tied up around the clock in a pool of your own filth. That's what you really deserve. Cure all the meat before sunset today. Don't let me find out you slacked off or it will go worse for you."

She left him there alone and slammed the door behind him. The silence pulsed in his ears, but at least he didn't have to worry about her coming after him again—not for a while.

He could definitely butcher a Gorlock. Doing it alone would be a lot harder than doing it with a team of powerful Godless men helping him, but anything was better than dealing with her.

He would almost have rather fought a living Gorlock than deal with her again.

He got to work, cut up the meat, and then went into the nearby jungle to cut sticks to make a tripod. He also made several trips to the stream to get water.

He used each of these outings to scope out the weapons store. A lot of people walked around the village and worked in different spots during the day. He wouldn't be able to get near the building in daylight. He would have to escape at night.

He had to pass through the first room with the chimney and fireplace pillars to get into and out of the Gorlock room. Noya wasn't in the outer room, so he used some embers from the fireplace to start fires in the Gorlock room.

He erected tripods over each fire and sliced up the meat to dry it. He worked all day without stopping even to wash the blood off his arms.

So he was back in one of these villages. The men didn't come to make him fight any dangerous creatures, but Noya was turning out to be much more intimidating.

He finished butchering all the meat. She didn't say anything about curing the hide, so he skinned the Gorlock and hung the hide up to dry, too.

He found himself studying the skull and jawbones. The teeth weren't exactly the same as Demonex teeth, but the teeth would still be useful.

They curved in smooth cylindrical points that came to one sharp end. They would only be good for stabbing, but that was better than nothing.

The Gorlock's claws interested him more. They would make perfect weapons—almost as perfect as Demonex fangs. He also studied the Gorlock's razor feathers.

He had to pluck the feathers from different parts of the hide. He separated six large features half the length of his forearm and two others longer than his forearm. He just had to find a place to hide the weapons so no one would see them or find them.

He selected a hollow on top of one of the ceiling beams in the fireplace room. Noya would probably keep him in that room more often.

He sectioned up the rest of the carcass and took it out into the jungle to feed to the Abnormits. He cut four claws away from the Gorlock's feet, stashed the claws in his pants pocket, and used a large rock to smash out three of the sharp fangs.

He returned to the Gorlock room which was now the meat-processing room. He had nothing to do but wait and continue to turn the meat over on the tripods while it dried.

He sat down next to one of the fires and used the coals to char away the extra flesh, skin, and sinew from the fangs and claws. He wound up with four long curved stabbing spikes and four sharp curved slashing weapons. These would do nicely.

He decided to attach one of each to the end of the same handle. Then he could use the weapon one way or the other depending on whether he wanted to stab or slash.

He had to scramble to his feet when he heard Noya coming. He crammed all his weapons into his pockets and pretended to be checking the meat when she looked into the room to see what he was doing.

He pretended not to see her until she left again. Then he hid all his weapons on top of the same ceiling beam with the Gorlock feathers.

He spent the rest of the day curing the meat and planning his escape. The first step was to get his health back. Noya didn't say anything about feeding him. That would weaken him, but he at least had to be able to move around. He couldn't do that now.

He took all the dried meat off the tripods at sunset just as Noya returned. He stacked everything in the center of the room. He'd even cleaned the floor to remove all the bloodstains.

She only humphed at the meat, dragged him back to the fireplace room, and shoved him down on the floor. He expected her to tie him up again, but she didn't.

She dropped a small leather packet of something on the floor in front of his eyes along with five strips of the meat he'd just worked so hard to cure. Then she walked out heading deeper inside the meeting house and shut the door with him in the room.

He hardly dared to move. His eyes riveted to the little packet in front of him. Was this what he thought it was? His heart pounded in anticipation. He didn't know how he would handle the disappointment if it wasn't.

He pushed himself up, sat on the floor in front of the fire, and unfolded the packet with shaking fingers. A medium-sized pile of Gooji sap nestled inside. He had to put the packet down so he wouldn't drop it.

He sat still and chewed his meat while he stared at the sap for a long time. He had to make a batch of juice and take it tonight. He'd already waited too long.

He didn't feel any infection from Noya's whipping, but he couldn't take any chances. He wouldn't be going anywhere tonight—not that he planned to anyway.

He had to heal up—which meant he had to keep her happy enough to stop her from whipping him a second time. That would be terrible.

He finished his second strip of meat before he summoned the courage to go outside and fill his water bucket. He didn't know any other way to boil the juice, so he collected a rock from the stream while he was there.

His mind went into a tailspin on the way back. She had given him a lot more sap than he expected. It was almost more than he needed. He decided to use half of it tonight and save the other half—either in case he got reinjured or to take on his journey with him.

He put the rock in the fireplace embers as soon as he got back. Noya had also left behind the knife she gave him to butcher the Gorlock, so he stashed that with the rest of his weapons.

Then he built up the fire, brought in another armload of wood, and ate his next strip of meat while he waited for the rock to heat.

He genuinely enjoyed that evening by himself. Spending time alone had become one of the most exquisite pleasures he could remember ever since Dana's betrayal. No one bothered him. He had the whole evening to himself.

He savored the taste of the meat. He was the one who had prepared it. He didn't know or care who killed it. It still tasted good. He could relax here by the fire while he waited for his Gooji juice to cool.

Chapter 14

Kuvik finished his food and stretched out on his back to sleep. Noya probably wouldn't give him another night like this one. He wanted to enjoy it while it lasted. He left the back door open to the outside world. It didn't tempt him to run away into the night.

Actually it did, but he knew better than to try it in his condition. He at least needed to be able to fight any Bounty Hunters he happened to stumble upon in the dark, shadowy jungle.

He wouldn't make any escape attempt until he fashioned his weapons. That was the first job—that and regaining the mobility to use them.

He tested the juice, but it was still too hot, so he lay down again. He must have fallen asleep because he woke up in the middle of the night when a scream ripped through the house. He bolted straight upright and strained every nerve to listen.

Voices echoed through the house coming from somewhere out of sight. He couldn't see anything in the darkness. All the light had faded from the night sky outside.

Those voices rang out as clear as day. "I said get over here!" a man's deep voice boomed. "Shut up and quit your whining. Do you think you can mess with me? You're lucky I put up with you at all. Shut up, you piece of trash! You have nothing to complain about. I can make it a lot worse for you if you really want me to."

A crying woman answered him in a jumbled stream of what sounded like begging. Goosebumps erupted all over Kuvik's arms when he recognized Noya's voice. She sounded so different now.

"Get the hell over here and do your job!" the man snapped. It was Aigo. "You don't think I'm going to do it for you, do you? I could kill you with my bare hands. That's what you really deserve."

Noya started to answer and then screamed again when something made a low thump. More thumps and occasional whipping sounds came from deeper inside the house.

Her screams escalated as the attack got worse. Kuvik listened for a minute and then picked up his bucket of Gooji juice. He wasn't getting any sleep, so he might as well drink it.

This explained Noya's hateful attitude. She passed on what she got from Aigo to any helpless captive who happened to fall into her hands. How far would she go?

She didn't seem as sadistically evil as Dana. Noya struck Kuvik as more just mean and vengeful. She couldn't take out her resentment on the person who really deserved it, so she took it out on anyone weaker than herself.

Her crying, yelling, and screaming went on for a long time. It slackened off at times while Aigo told her to stop complaining, called her a worthless piece of trash, and told her all the ways he could make it worse for her if she didn't do as he said.

Kuvik finished his Gooji juice and stretched out on the floor. He didn't think he would be able to sleep, but he must have. He must have been too exhausted or else Noya and Aigo must have stopped after a while.

Kuvik was still lying there on the floor sound asleep when something hit him in the ribs—hard. He shot off the floor fast enough to hurt his injuries a second time.

He barely got his eyes open before he realized what was happening. Noya stood over him beating him with a one-inch rod cut from some tree branch. She pounded him hard enough to bruise him all over again. At least she didn't use the whip.

Kuvik thrashed on the floor. Part of him told himself to grab the stick away from her and maybe even turn it against her. He could overpower her. He had to—and then what?

He could run away into the jungle—only to get hunted down by more Bounty Hunters. Dorei's story about Akli came back into Kuvik's mind. He had never found out the punishment for escape attempts because he didn't get caught—not that first time.

He didn't want to attack Noya, especially not when he saw the expression on her face. Her dress hid enough of her body so that he couldn't see her injuries, but they must have been there. Aigo must have hurt her real bad.

Her sour, hateful expression from yesterday had changed to something very different this morning. Her features spasmed and she kept trying to fight her mouth under control. She didn't cry, but she looked like she wanted to.

Her expression alone stopped Kuvik from fighting back. She had to take out her grief and pain on someone. He was the only one here to whom she could express her heartache. Did she know he'd heard her last night?

Whatever room she and Aigo had been in last night might be close enough to this fireplace room. She might already realize that Kuvik would hear. Maybe she wanted to punish him for that—for knowing her weakness.

He let her do it. He didn't fight back. He didn't try to stop her. He curled into a ball and took it. He had nothing to lose at this point. He would escape eventually. Her mistreatment wouldn't stop him.

She eventually beat him until the stick broke. It shattered across his hip and the splinters scattered over the floor. "Now clean up this mess and get to work," she snapped, but he heard her voice shaking. "Be grateful I don't kill you with my bare hands."

He didn't answer. He sat up, collected all the broken pieces of wood, and threw them into the fireplace. The embers from last night still smoldered in the hole.

She put him straight to work doing all kinds of hard labor. She made him haul rocks from the stream to build a wall behind the meeting house. Then she told him to use an axe to hew some huge fallen logs into square beams for a new meeting house.

He barely made it through the day and almost collapsed from exhaustion. She came out to where he was working and told him to come back to the house. He expected her to leave him alone with his day's food, but she led him to the building's front entrance this time.

He realized a second too late what he was walking into when he discovered a whole bunch of people already in there. They all wore nice clothes—the kind of clothes he'd seen in the second village.

Dana was there dressed like all the other women. Why did she wear that white dress out into the jungle? He would never understand her.

He froze on the threshold—just long enough for one of the nicely dressed men to grab Kuvik by the back of the neck. Kuvik didn't have to guess who the guy was. Noya must have learned that maneuver from Aigo.

The men of this other faction of Bounty Hunters wore their hair trimmed short. This style somehow complimented their bizarre outfits. The men held themselves stiff in their tight jackets and decorated sleeves and collars.

Aigo overpowered Kuvik and shoved him into the middle of the room. "Come on in and have some fun, my boy," Aigo told him and hurled Kuvik hard enough to send him sprawling across the floor.

All his recent injuries exploded in pain. He struggled to hold it together and try to see everything at the same time.

Would this be another Crusher fight to the death or just another torture session like the one when the Bounty Hunters stood on him and crushed his testicles for the fun of it?

Everyone else laughed, especially Noya. She walked out of the crowd, raised another wooden bucket, and dumped a stinking wave of slopping excrement all over him.

The crowd howled with horrified glee, shrank back from the mess, and a few people threw things at Kuvik. This went on for a few minutes.

He waited for someone to come forward and try to hurt him worse, but they apparently didn't want to get their nice clothes dirty. They just enjoyed laughing at him and then left.

Aigo strolled up to the edge of the filth puddle. "Now clean up this mess—and clean yourself up. Don't come back until you do or I'll make you sleep in this. Don't let me find out you slacked off or it will go worse for you."

He walked out and left Kuvik lying there. He took a minute to catch his breath, but the smell eventually became too much for him.

He got up, went to the stream, and washed off his clothes and body. He spent longer than he needed to just lying in the cool water and letting it wash over him. It felt good compared to all the rest of this.

He didn't want to go back. He didn't want to stay here any longer. Noya didn't care about working him as a labor slave as long as she could vent her torment on him.

She didn't care about letting him heal between attacks. She didn't care if she beat and whipped him enough to kill him. He couldn't stay here.

It was still too early in the daytime for him to try to leave now, so he decided to clean up the mess, retrieve his weapons, and stay up tonight attaching them to handles.

Going back and forth to the stream for water would give him plenty of time to cut the wood to make his blade handles.

He got the bucket and rags from the other room and started work. He took his time. No one came around to watch, supervise, or check on his progress. No one wanted to come near the smell.

He gave himself another bath before he returned to the fireplace room. It was deserted. Noya didn't leave him any food this time. Would she come back at all?

He didn't want to wait around or fall asleep for her to wake him up with her screaming—or anything else.

He got the knife off the roof beam, sat down on the floor in front of the fire, and started whittling the handles for his weapons. He made the handles smooth along the shaft and bored holes in the ends to fit the teeth inside.

He had to split the end that would hold the Gorlock claw. He used vines from the jungle to lash the claw into place and then fitted the fang into the socket. He had no way to secure it, so he split that, too.

He lashed the two sides of the tube around the fang so the wood gripped it in a tight cylinder. He finished all the weapons, put them back on top of the roof beam, and waited for darkness to settle over the landscape.

He would have liked to figure out a way to turn the Gorlock feathers into weapons he could use, too. He could have embedded them into the edges of a staff and made them into some kind of combination blade and axe.

He would have to work on that later. He didn't have time to do it tonight. He would still be able to use the feathers for hand-to-hand combat if he needed to.

Chapter 15

Kuvik sat on the doorstep and watched the slaves and Bounty Hunters finishing their work for the day. They went into their houses one after another.

He still didn't understand where all the slaves lived. Did each of them have a small room behind wherever the Bounty Hunters lived? He would probably never find out.

He was just starting to settle into another relaxing evening by himself when Aigo came back. He entered the fireplace room through the inner house door—coming from the Gorlock meat-processing room.

Kuvik turned around expecting it to be Noya. Kuvik started to stand up when he saw that it was Aigo coming toward him instead.

Kuvik didn't have a chance to get off the floor before Aigo grabbed him by the back of the neck again and marched him outside.

Kuvik only had a split second to realize something was seriously wrong before Aigo hurled Kuvik at a bunch of other Bounty Hunters standing around. They caught him and started tying him up with another log across his shoulders.

He saw his one chance at escape slipping away from him and struggled, but one of the Bounty Hunters punched him in the stomach, grabbed him by the head, and slammed his knee upward into Kuvik's face to stun him.

That one moment gave the Bounty Hunters enough time to secure his wrists to the log, tie his ankles closely enough that he wouldn't be able to run, and then they tied more lengths of rope to the wrists of other slaves arriving in front of and behind Kuvik.

He blinked the stars out of his head to see more slaves assembling from all over the village. He didn't see if other Bounty Hunters brought these slaves—either the well-dressed Bounty Hunters or the warriors.

The warriors grabbed each slave as they arrived. More warriors assembled all the time to help out.

They doubled up on the slaves, tied them to logs, secured their ankles with short ropes to stop them from running, and then leashed all the slaves together in a long line with ropes connecting their wrist restraints.

Kuvik fought his mind back into some kind of working order. He'd never seen this before. He didn't know why the Bounty Hunters would tie all their slaves like this when so many of them acted so submissive and cooperative.

Darkness settled over the village as the process went on and on. The line in front of Kuvik kept getting longer as the Bounty Hunters added more and more slaves. He couldn't turn around to check, but he assumed the line kept stretching behind him, too.

Who else was in this line? Dana wasn't a captive and neither was Noya—not that their lots in life were any so much better than if they had been.

The process went on late into the night. The Bounty Hunters emptied the village of every slave and tied them all in line—but the Bounty Hunters didn't put everyone in the same line.

The Bounty Hunters kept out thirty men and bound them in a separate line. Each of these men carried an enormous bundle on his back—including all the weapons from the store building Kuvik.

The Bounty Hunters tied these men's hands next to their heads near their ears. The Bounty Hunters bound each man's wrists to the bundle itself—in the position where the man might hold the load to steady it.

The Bounty Hunters selected the strongest, healthiest men for this task. Each of them bowed under an enormous weight each man struggled to support. Kuvik didn't see what the other men were carrying. They must have been carrying supplies for the journey.

The Bounty Hunters carried nothing but their weapons. They called for the slaves to move out. The line with all the logs left first. Everyone had to start walking at the same time. No one could stumble or the whole line would come to a halt.

The Bounty Hunters flanked the column on both sides yelling instructions and insults at the assembled slaves. The Bounty Hunters kept yelling for everyone to keep going if anyone fell.

The column always wound up dragging the person along the ground. The Bounty Hunters would rush the person from both sides and yank at him or her to make the person get up if they didn't do it themselves.

If the person still didn't get up, the Bounty Hunters beat the person to the ground. This usually brought the column to a stop while the Bounty Hunters cut the person loose, dragged them clear, and retied both people in front of and behind the person's position.

Then the Bounty Hunters yelled for everyone to keep going while the Bounty Hunters finished beating the person to death. None of those people ever rejoined the line.

The column moved faster after that. Only those strong enough to keep walking remained. No one fell anymore.

Kuvik hardened his resolve and retreated into a quiet place in his mind. *You aren't ready to die yet, are you?* He wasn't ready to die and he wasn't going to die—not before he escaped and returned to the Godless.

The Bounty Hunters kept everyone walking into the night and through dawn the next day. Kuvik stayed on his feet without falling once all the next day.

The Bounty Hunters crossed hills, climbed through passes, descended into valleys, and reentered the jungle. They didn't stop until dusk on the second day. They made camp somewhere, but they didn't release the slaves to do the work for them.

The Bounty Hunters stopped the first slaves where the Bounty Hunters planned to camp and directed all the remaining slaves to walk around them in an ever-widening circle.

The cluster of slave-prisoners kept getting bigger and bigger. The Bounty Hunters made everyone sit extra close together—so close that the logs bumped into each other and even injured a few people.

The Bounty Hunters paid no attention to that. They pushed the slaves down on the ground in this tight circle, barked a few threats, and left them there.

The Bounty Hunters took the slaves with the loads to another side of the camp, unloaded them, and got those thirty to do all the tasks of making camp.

The Bounty Hunters didn't bring any females for themselves this time. They left all the women tied up to their logs with the first group. The Bounty Hunters slept alone that night.

Kuvik looked around him at the other slaves while he waited for night to fall. His heart soared when he saw Akli sitting near him.

Kuvik waited for all the Bounty Hunters to go into their huts for the night. The load-carrying slaves curled up on the ground and went to sleep. A few of the women started crying, but they made sure to do it silently.

"Dorei tells me you want to escape," Kuvik whispered.

Akli's head shot up. His eyes smoldered with even more fury than usual. "What do you know about it?" Akli snarled.

"Only that I want to escape and you want to escape. We should help each other. I escaped from the Bounty Hunters before. I know it can be done."

"Be quiet!" another man hissed nearby. "You'll get us all punished and maybe even killed!"

"You could come with us," Kuvik replied. "We'll have the best chance of success if more people make the attempt."

"How will you do that?" another asked. It was Nelv, the other young man who had been responsible for taking care of Kuvik on the march north. "We can't get free and we can't get away from the Bounty Hunters anyway."

"I just told you I've done it before," Kuvik told him. "I was bound to a post in a house in the middle of one of their villages and I escaped and took a girl from my family band with me. All of you can get free if you really want to. We have all the weapons we need right over there in those bundles. We could get free right now if we only had a way to cut these ropes."

"We don't have a way to cut these ropes," Dorei interjected.

"Does that mean you're in?" Kuvik fired back. "Don't join the discussion if you aren't all in and ready to do anything necessary to get free—including killing Bounty Hunters. You have to be ready to kill any of them that come after you. You have to be ready to die rather than let them bring you back."

"I'm in," Akli replied immediately. "Just tell me what I have to do."

"I'm in, too," Nelv added. "I would rather die than stay here."

"Don't do anything until we're all ready to strike together," Kuvik whispered. "No one do anything on your own. That's bound to fail."

"You did it on your own," Dorei pointed out. "Why can't we?"

"You would have done it on your own a long time ago if you could," Kuvik countered. "You told me you would never try to escape under any circumstances. Something drastic better have changed for you since that conversation. Otherwise, you better stay behind and keep working hard the way you always have. You'll be safer that way."

Dorei shut his mouth. He didn't reply.

Kuvik heard volumes in that silence and turned back to Akli and Nelv. "Do either of you know how to use weapons?"

"Not very well," Nelv replied.

Akli lowered his eyes and shrugged. "That's what got me caught before. I could have fought my way out, but I didn't know how to fight."

"Never mind. The important thing is that you tried," Kuvik told him. "It tells me you have heart and spirit. You have more heart and spirit than all the rest of these cowards put together."

"Watch it," an older man snapped nearby. "You are not sitting here calling us cowards."

"Have you ever tried to escape—even once?" Kuvik fired back. "Don't talk to me about heart and spirit unless you're at least willing to try. That's the least anyone should be willing to do. You aren't ready to die yet, are you?" He turned back to Akli and Nelv. "What about climbing trees? Do you know how to climb trees?"

"I know how, but I'm not very good." Akli frowned. "Why do you ask about that?"

"I'll tell you later. The first project is to get out of the camp and to do it under cover of darkness. Just remember what I said and don't try anything until we're all ready to move at the same time."

"What if we see an opening first?" Nelv asked. "Should we take it?"

"Not unless you know how to fight and climb trees. Just wait for my signal—and when it happens, stay with me so I can guide you. I'll help you in ways you won't be able to on your own. Trust me. I know how to get away from the Bounty Hunters as soon as we leave the camp. All we have to do is break out, arm ourselves, and get out into the jungle in the dark."

"Aren't there dangerous creatures out there?" a woman asked.

"Do you think they're more dangerous than the Bounty Hunters?" Kuvik asked. "I would rather take my chances with any creature in the jungle than to stay a Bounty Hunter captive for even one more day."

Silence answered him until another man said, "I'm in, too. I'm going with you. The Bounty Hunters took everything from me. I'm not going to let them take my life or even one more day if I can help it."

Kuvik smiled at the guy. He kept his head shaved like Kuvik's. "What's your name?"

"Beinu," the man replied. "What's yours?"

"I'm Kuvik. I lived for years with the Godless Clan and learned their ways. That's how I escaped last time and that's what we'll do this time." He glanced around. "Anyone else?"

"I'm going, too." A woman spoke up this time. "I'm going home to my family."

A bunch of other people chimed in and said they were going, too. None of them wanted to stay. Some of these people even had children with them. The Bounty Hunters had tied them up with logs, too.

Kuvik foresaw any number of problems trying to escape with this many people, especially if they didn't know how to climb trees.

They would have to learn to fight back. It would all come down to just how badly they wanted their freedom and what they were willing to do to get it.

All four of the other men who had dealt with Kuvik in the last march said they wanted to join him. Only Dorei kept quiet, but at least he had the sense to do that much.

"Everyone quiet down now," Kuvik told them. "We just need to sit tight until I find a way to cut these ropes. Don't give the Bounty Hunters any reason to think we're planning anything. That would destroy all our advantage."

Everyone responded to his instructions. They stopped talking and people started falling asleep after a little while.

They couldn't lie down with these logs on their shoulders. Most people just drooped where they were and slept until the Bounty Hunters woke them up in the morning.

Chapter 16

The Bounty Hunters kicked and beat the captive slave-prisoners awake the next morning. The Bounty Hunters made everyone stagger to their feet and unwind their cluster to form a column again.

Then everyone had to stand around while the thirty load-bearing slaves dismantled the camp, packed everything, loaded on their bundles, and the Bounty Hunters tied the men's wrists in place the way they did yesterday.

The two columns moved out again. No one stumbled or fell even though none of these people had eaten anything or drunk any water for two whole days. This couldn't last.

It didn't last. The party entered another stand of steep mountains and passed through a few different canyons leading to another valley. The column started to cross a rocky plateau covered in sharp flakes of chipped rock. They carpeted the whole ground.

Kuvik's hide shoes protected his feet, but some of the prisoners walked barefoot and cut their feet on the sharp stones. He realized in that moment that he was looking at an entire landscape paved in weapons.

He reacted instantly, stumbled over his own feet, and slammed down hard on his knees. He didn't have to pretend to let the log pull his weight to one side.

He would have fallen on his face, but he managed to twist enough to jam the log end on his right side into the ground. He adjusted just enough to get his hand down on the ground. His fingers closed on one of the shards.

The Bounty Hunters rushed him and started hitting him with their sticks. "Get up!" the Bounty Hunters yelled. "Get up, you piece of filth!"

Kuvik staggered to his feet. He had to use all his strength to haul the log back onto his shoulders—but at least he had the shard in his hand. He had to be careful not to hold it too tightly. It really was sharp—sharp enough to cut skin.

The shards had cut his knees. Blood ran down his shins, but he paid no attention. The cuts dried and so did the drips. They didn't attract any attention from creatures once the column reentered the jungle.

Kuvik kept quiet for the rest of the day. He didn't try to use the shard—not here out in the open where the Bounty Hunters might see him. He couldn't even be sure if any of the other prisoners had seen him pick up the shard.

The Bounty Hunters didn't stop to make camp until they returned to the jungle that evening. They circled the prisoners again in exactly the same way. Kuvik found Akli sitting near him again. Akli gave him a hard look and glanced at Kuvik's hand.

Kuvik didn't move or acknowledge. He waited for the Bounty Hunters to go to sleep again. Akli never stopped staring at Kuvik all evening. The guy's intensity really started to rack Kuvik's nerves.

Kuvik waited a long time after the thirty load-bearing prisoners went to sleep. He finally rotated the shard in his hand. He had to be careful to position it in the right place without cutting himself.

He finally clasped it between his fingers, bent sideways, and started using the sharp edge to cut the rope on Akli's right wrist. Akli had to brace his body to hold the log still. He pulled his arm down to stretch the rope tight so each pass of the shard cut more effectively.

Kuvik worked for a long time. He had to wrench his body and strain his already aching shoulders to position the shard at the right angle. Every pass cost him a massive effort. He grimaced and bared his teeth until the fibers parted and his wrist came free.

He pounced on the shard, grabbed it out of Kuvik's fingers, and Akli lowered the log to the ground so he could start cutting the strands on his left wrist. Kuvik was too exhausted to care.

Akli had to put his log on a few other people's laps. He wound up putting it on Nelv's and Phiri's laps. They were both on board with the escape plan and didn't protest.

"Stay low, Akli!" Phiri whispered. "One of the Bounty Hunters could see you!"

"Quit stepping on me!" one of the women whispered.

"You can stay here if you want to!" Akli snarled over his shoulder. He finished cutting his wrist free and started cutting the rope on Phiri's left wrist. He was closer to Akli now than Kuvik was.

"When do we go for the weapons?" Phiri whispered.

"Wait until we free everyone who wants to go with us," Kuvik replied. "Everyone who wants to stay behind can stay tied up. Then the Bounty Hunters will see that they didn't try to escape."

"Cowards!" Akli muttered. "The Bounty Hunters said they would kill me if I ever tried again. They won't bring me back as a slave—not again."

"Be quiet!" another man hissed from somewhere. "You'll wake them up with all this talk."

Akli freed both of Phiri's wrists. He started to untie his own ankles and then started untying the wrists of the person sitting next to him while Akli cut the ropes on Nelv's wrists.

Their efforts took them away from Kuvik, but he didn't care that they left him until later. Akli freed Nelv. Nelv freed Beinu and Phiri freed Garvis.

The five of them started working their way through the group freeing more and more people. The wave of free people spread outward.

A few of the captive prisoners reared away from the escapees and stopped them from untying them. The escapees left these people to their fate.

Akli finally made it over to Kuvik. A bunch of the others started to stand up. "Stay down!" Kuvik whispered. "Don't do anything until we can act at the same time."

Nelv, Beinu, Phiri, and Garvis all did as Kuvik said and sat down in their former places. A few others did the same, but too many stayed standing and even started walking toward the bundles of weapons.

"Hey!" Kuvik whispered. "Come back!"

They didn't listen. Phiri started to stand up to go after them. Nelv pulled him back down and it was just as well that he did. Fifteen people crossed the camp to the weapons stash and started rummaging in it. They made way too much noise.

Akli didn't notice. He kept working to cut Kuvik's wrists free. "Stop, Akli," Kuvik whispered.

Akli looked up. "Huh? What do you mean?"

"All of you get your logs back on your shoulders!" Kuvik hissed. "Hurry! Pick your logs up and hold onto the ropes. NOW!!"

He grabbed the rope that Akli had just worked so hard to cut. A few people took longer to figure out what Kuvik meant, but it became obvious when the escaped prisoners started pulling weapons out of the bundle.

They made a lot of noise. No one in their right mind could mistake the sound of weapons being drawn.

The rest of Kuvik's party scrambled to sit down, heft their logs back onto their shoulders, and to help their friends wind the cut ropes around their wrists in a desperate effort to make it look convincing.

Kuvik and his friends were still working on the project when the Bounty Hunters inevitably realized what was happening and rushed out of their huts. They took a matter of minutes to cut the escaped prisoners down until none remained alive.

The short fight gave Kuvik and his friends enough time to tie themselves up well enough. The Bounty Hunters didn't notice anything when they came over to check the rest of the slaves.

The Bounty Hunters went into a frenzy checking every single rope. They assumed that the escaped prisoners must have loosened the bonds on everyone else's wrists. The Bounty Hunters stayed awake for hours retying everyone as tightly as before.

Then the Bounty Hunters posted guards to keep track of everyone. Kuvik didn't see his shard anywhere. It had fallen among the other prisoners. He wouldn't have been able to use it anyway—not with the Bounty Hunters keeping an eagle eye on everyone.

None of the other prisoners talked or even made eye contact for the rest of the night. Kuvik stayed quiet and eventually fell asleep. Trying to free that many people had been a bad idea.

Those people should have waited like he told them to. He tried to warn them, but they didn't listen.

He wasn't sure he would have gone for the weapons first or just run for it into the jungle. He didn't take a weapon with him before he had escaped with Yoa. He just hid both of them and went after the weapons later.

He wouldn't have drawn weapons from inside the bundle within a few inches of one of the Bounty Hunters' huts. That was just foolish, especially when the escaping prisoners could hear the noise ahead of time.

They should have stopped when they first started rummaging in the weapons and realized their actions would wake up the Bounty Hunters. He had told them to stay with him and follow his instructions. They didn't.

He didn't like to see any of them die, especially not in such a needless way. He would have to be more selective about who he talked to and who he shared his plans with.

He still believed in Akli and the other three men. They obeyed him to the letter even if it meant becoming captives again. Not even Akli argued. Kuvik would have liked to praise them and Akli especially, but Kuvik kept silent.

The rest of the march kept going on. More people stumbled in the line the next day, so the Bounty Hunters decided it would be a good idea to feed everyone and give them water that evening.

The Bounty Hunters assigned the load-carrying slaves to do this job. The men had to do everything in the Bounty Hunters' camp and then go through all the other prisoners, give them water, and put the food into their mouths.

The men rolled a strip of dried meat into a ball and stuck it into each person's mouth. Then the person had to chew it up without letting any of it escape. That was the only food anyone got.

The meat was Gorlock meat. It might even have been the meat that Kuvik had processed. He wouldn't have been surprised if Aigo had gotten Noya to make her new slave do the job for this journey.

Kuvik let himself believe that while he chewed the meat. It gave him special strength and energy because he was the one who had cured it. All the effort he had put into that job came back to him now. Thinking that way made him feel better.

The party marched farther north for two more weeks. None of the prisoners talked about escape and no one tried it. No one even looked at each other.

None of the men in Kuvik's party gave any sign that they were watching him and waiting for him to bring it up again. He wouldn't bring it up in front of the others.

The party finally made it to another, even larger village. Kuvik completely blocked it out of his mind that he was traveling farther north by the day. None of that mattered. First he had to escape. Then he would travel south.

How far south he had to travel meant exactly nothing. He would travel a lot farther south than this. Hangman's band had journeyed for years from the northern mountains through treacherous country to get back to Godless country. He could do the same thing.

He had every reason to and absolutely no reason not to. He had nowhere else in the world to go and nothing else in the world to do that was anywhere near as important. It was worth spending the rest of his life on that one mission if he just could get back to his band.

Chapter 17

The prisoners slogged into the village at sundown. Hardly any of them stayed on their feet long enough for the Bounty Hunters to untie them.

This village didn't follow the same pattern as the other two Bounty Hunter villages that Kuvik had already seen. The nicely dressed Bounty Hunters didn't live separately from the slaves and warriors. Everyone lived together in one place.

All the nicely dressed Bounty Hunters—or whatever they were—and all the additional warriors gathered around to watch the slave marching in.

Then the warriors who escorted the column assigned each slave to a household of the nicely dressed Bounty Hunters.

Kuvik got assigned to one of the warriors. The guy grabbed Kuvik by the arm, marched him away to a house at the end of the village, pushed him through the door, and jerked Kuvik down on the floor.

The man tied a rope around Kuvik's neck, lashed the other end tightly to a post in the wall, and left him there. Kuvik could have untied the rope with his own hands, but he decided not to do that right in front of the guy.

The man started moving around the room doing something or other. Kuvik took that moment to adjust his whole world concept to his environment. He'd never seen a house like this, not even among the Bounty Hunters he'd seen.

Furniture packed the room. A giant table sat in front of a massive stone fireplace with a fire blazing inside it. It made the room sweltering hot. Not even leaving the door and the one shuttered window open made any difference.

All kinds of chairs, couches, and other stuff crammed the room to bursting. A set of stairs rose from one side of the room to another level on top. Kuvik had never seen that before.

The man who had brought him here was one of the warriors who wore his hair in spikes with a white loincloth tied around his waist. He looked utterly out of place in such a house.

"I hear you had an escape on the way here—or an attempted escape," the man muttered under his breath. "I better not find out you ever tried something like that. I don't deal kindly with that from any slave."

A woman's voice stopped Kuvik from answering—not that he had planned to answer anyway.

"Kogno!" she called from somewhere upstairs. "Are you back already?"

"Come down here, Zori!" Kogno called up the stairs. "You need to see this!"

"See what?" she asked.

"Come down and you'll see." Kogno crossed the room and pointed in Kuvik's face. "One wrong move around my wife and you're done. Understand?"

Kuvik didn't get a chance to answer before Zori came downstairs. She wore the same white billowing dress that Dana wore, so maybe that's what all the warriors' wives wore.

Zori was also very pretty, fresh, and Kuvik saw right away that she was underage, too. What in the world was wrong with these people?

She stopped on the stairs and stared at Kuvik across the room. "What is it?" she asked.

"You know what it is," Kogno replied over his shoulder. "It's a slave. He just came in with the others."

She came the rest of the way downstairs and scrutinized Kuvik extra closely. "He looks strange."

"That's because he cuts his hair. See? It will grow back unless he cuts it again."

She frowned at Kuvik. "Why is he so beat up? Look. Someone has been whipping him."

"He just got captured, so the others have to be extra hard on him to teach him his place. You know how it works."

"He looks terrible for someone who just got captured. They shouldn't have been so hard on him." She took a few steps closer and stopped in front of Kuvik. "What Clan are you from?" she asked.

"Don't ask him that!" Kogno interjected. "You don't want to get personal with a slave."

"I want to find out about him. He's interesting."

"He won't live long and then you'll be too disappointed when he dies."

"He might not die. Some of the slaves live a long time."

"I'm Godless Clan," Kuvik interrupted.

She spun around, gasped, and her eyes flew open. "Really?! That's so interesting!"

"It isn't interesting," Kogno growled. "It means he'll be extra defiant and extra hard to tame. It means he'll never obey and he'll never stop trying to escape."

Zori ignored him. "Aren't the Godless fearless warriors who are extra dangerous in battle?" She frowned at Kuvik and cocked her head to one side. "Why don't you have long hair? All the other Godless we've seen wear their hair long."

Kuvik opened his mouth to answer. He had no idea what to say to her, but at least she cared enough to ask.

Kogno didn't give him a chance to. Kogno stormed across the room, took hold of Zori's elbow, and pulled her away. "That's enough of that," Kogno snapped. "Don't talk to him. Don't pay any attention to him. He isn't here to be your plaything."

"But isn't he here to do work around the house? Isn't that what the slaves are for?"

"Not this one. He's going out to work. He'll only be here in the evening after he finishes his work for the day. Then he can do work around the house."

"I'll need to talk to him then," she pointed out.

"Then you can talk to him then—only enough to tell him what you want him to do—nothing else. Don't get close to him. I'll have to get rid of him if you don't listen to me."

She furrowed her brow, but he walked away from her to end the conversation. His behavior left no room for argument.

She finally turned away and started getting some kind of food from some kind of container set on a shelf in the fireplace.

She set out some kind of flat bowls on the table, but they weren't bowls. They didn't have upwardly rounded sides to hold the food in. These were made of some kind of hardened stone and they were just flat discs with a very small lip around the edge.

Kuvik had never seen these before. He didn't see how they would stop the food from spilling over the side.

She placed the container of food in the middle of the table and used a much bigger spoon to scoop the food onto these flat discs. The food was more of the tiny grains Kuvik's handlers fed him on the way here.

This food didn't spill off the side of the disc. The food just sat there in a mound in the center waiting for someone to eat it.

Zori didn't hand out spoons for people to eat with. She placed two different utensils next to hers and Kogno's discs. These looked like spoons except that the ends had been flattened into four sharp spikes like some kind of weapon.

Kogno sat down in a chair on one side of the table and Zori sat in another chair opposite him. They both started eating with these weapons and used them to scoop the food into their mouths.

They talked about a lot of things Kuvik didn't understand. He got so confused by their way of life that he didn't pay much attention to their conversation. They eventually finished and Zori stacked up all the utensils to take them off the table.

"Don't forget to feed the slave," Kogno told her.

"Oh, of course!" she exclaimed. "I did forget."

"He won't be able to work if you don't feed him. If you're so interested in him, you can start by taking care of him and making sure he gets enough to eat—and enough water to drink."

This project cheered her up more than anything. She scooped another massive portion of the grains onto a different disc, stuck one of the weapons into the pile, and brought the disc over to Kuvik.

She burst into a huge smile when she held it out to him. "Are you hungry?"

He didn't answer. He just took the disc from her. He had to balance it so he didn't spill the food all over the floor.

"What's your name?" she asked.

"Kuvik," he mumbled.

"I'm Zori, Kuvik," she informed him.

"He already knows that," Kogno interrupted. "He heard me calling you earlier."

She laughed. "Right. I forgot."

"You would forget your nose if it wasn't attached to your face."

She laughed again. Her eyes twinkled when she smiled at Kuvik. "Aren't you hungry? Don't you want to eat it?"

He nodded. He knew better than to trust sweet, innocent, beautiful, charming young girls like her—especially when they belonged to the Bounty Hunter Clan.

Zori was a warrior's wife—exactly the same as Dana. Kuvik would never trust Zori—not in a million years. He didn't even trust that she hadn't poisoned his food right now. He only dared to eat it because he saw her and Kogno eating from the same container just now.

He picked up the weapon. It functioned the same as a spoon except that it didn't have a bowl or curved sides. He had to hold the weapon steady and balance the food on top of it while he brought it to his mouth.

He made sure to hold the disc under his chin in case he dropped any of the food, but he didn't drop it. He could eat with it okay as long as he paid attention.

Zori grinned at him. "Haven't you ever eaten with a fork before?"

Kuvik looked back and forth between her and the weapon. That's what the Bounty Hunters must call these things—forks.

He shook his head.

"Do you like the food?" she asked. "Is it good?"

He only nodded and kept eating. Kogno was right. Kuvik wasn't here to get acquainted with these people. At least Kogno wouldn't try to make friends with Kuvik.

Zori left and started working around the room while Kogno did something else. Kuvik was too busy concentrating on his meal to care what Kogno did.

Zori boiled water on the fire and used the hot water to clean all the discs and forks. She was still doing it by the time Kuvik finished eating. She smiled again when she took the disc and fork away from him and gave him a gourd full of water.

This was the most water Kuvik had seen in one place since his capture. He gulped down half of it. He wanted to save the rest for later, but he ended up caving and drinking it all anyway.

Zori smiled when she came and got the empty gourd. "Where's he going to sleep?" she asked Kogno.

"He can sleep where he is," Kogno replied. "I see no reason to change it around."

"Aren't you worried he'll escape if you leave him down here alone?"

"You heard what Halmeron said. He's posting guards to patrol the village all night long. Some of these new slaves might have been involved in the escape attempt on the way here. The guards will have orders to kill any slave they catch outside between sundown and sunset. None of these new slaves is going anywhere."

Zori turned to Kuvik. "You wouldn't try to escape, would you? You feel comfortable staying here, don't you?"

"Will you stop it?!" Kogno snapped. "He's a slave. No one cares if he wants to stay here or if he feels comfortable. Now go upstairs and leave him alone. Don't let me catch you down here talking to him again."

She did as he said and went to the stairs. Kogno came toward Kuvik. Kuvik stiffened, but Kogno only tied Kuvik's wrists together and lashed them to the same post.

Zori watched the operation from the stairs. "Don't hurt him, Kogno," she called over.

"I'll hurt him if I want to," Kogno muttered and walked away.

He started climbing the stairs, so Zori had no choice but to do the same thing. They both vanished to the upper level and left Kuvik alone.

The journey here had exhausted him too much—and the food made him sleepy. He wasn't ready to escape anyway—not with armed guards patrolling the village. That was going to complicate his plans.

He rested his head against the post. He couldn't move it anywhere else. His exhaustion overcame him and he fell asleep.

Chapter 18

Kuvik didn't wake up until the next morning when Zori came downstairs. Her footsteps on the stairs startled him awake. He took a second to remember where he was and how he'd gotten here.

She smiled when she saw him with his eyes open. "Good morning, Kuvik!" she chirped.

He didn't answer. Kogno's words from last night came back to haunt Kuvik. Kogno didn't want Zori fraternizing with Kuvik—for obvious reasons. Kuvik really needed to take that lesson and own it. Kogno knew which end was up and so did Kuvik.

She got to work making a different kind of food in the fireplace. The fire had died down overnight.

The open door and window had let the room cool enough for Kuvik to get a decent night's sleep. He wouldn't have been able to if it had stayed that hot.

Now she built up the fire back into a blazing inferno. She built the fire up much higher than it needed to be. The Godless never built fires this big. They didn't need to.

Kuvik couldn't remember any other Clan building fires this big, either. In fact, he couldn't even remember any other Bounty Hunters building fires this big, not even Noya.

Zori hummed to herself while she worked. Kogno came downstairs a little while later and scowled at Kuvik once as if Kuvik was doing something wrong by sitting here bound by the wrists and neck. At least Kogno didn't hear Zori trying to talk to Kuvik again.

She finally took the container out of the fireplace. "You'll have to untie his hands so he can eat," she told Kogno.

Kogno came over and untied Kuvik's wrists and neck. Kuvik stayed sitting on the floor where he was even when Zori brought him a helping of food.

This was a different kind of grain cooked to a stick, gelatinous mass and flavored with some kind of sweet black dried fruits. Kuvik had never seen anything like this, but he was too hungry to inspect the food very carefully.

He started eating and didn't stop until he scraped the disc clean. Kogno and Zori sat on opposite ends of the table again. They were too busy talking to each other to notice when Kuvik finished. Zori didn't smile at him. She only paid attention to Kogno.

Kuvik stayed where he was until they finished. Then Zori started cleaning everything up. Kogno waved Kuvik forward. "You come with me."

Kuvik stood up and followed Kogno outside. Kogno led the way to the other side of the village. Kuvik hadn't been over here before.

Kogno pointed to another line of slaves. These men weren't tied or guarded. They walked in a long line down the back of a slope behind the village.

"You follow them," Kogno told him. "You work with them today and come back to the house in the evening after you're done. Understand?"

Kuvik nodded and walked away to join the line. He actually appreciated Kogno's straightforward, no-nonsense way of talking about everything. He wasn't sadistic or even cruel. He just went through the motions.

He didn't make a big deal about beating Kuvik down or trying to break him. Kogno didn't care about anything as long as Kuvik did his job.

Kuvik thanked his stars that he'd gotten assigned to someone like Kogno. At least he would be fair instead of impulsively violent or vicious like some Kuvik could have gotten assigned to.

Kuvik got in line with the other men. He didn't see anyone he knew, so he didn't try to talk to them or find out where they were going. Kogno said Kuvik had to work, so that's what this must be.

At least he could do it with a full stomach. Life could have been a lot worse. Kogno and Zori didn't beat him or whip him like Noya did.

Kuvik might be willing to say he felt comfortable in their house if things kept going this way. It would be the best Bounty Hunter house he'd ever set foot in.

The line meandered down the hill into a steep gully and eventually ended at a rocky quarry full of big stone blocks scattered on the floor around a crooked streambed.

The slaves in the line each picked up a block. Each man hoisted the block onto his shoulder and continued in the same line. The line passed up the quarry to another narrow path climbing out of the gulley to the village.

Kuvik could understand this. He didn't have to think. He just had to keep walking no matter what. Carrying the block for hours on end didn't hurt nearly as much as carrying that log with his arms tied up. He could at least adjust his position whenever he wanted to.

The other men in the line did the same thing. They switched the block from shoulder to shoulder every now and then.

They returned to the village, laid the blocks in a stack behind one of the meeting houses, and then every man in the line got to walk unburdened all the way back downhill to the gully.

The downhill trip turned out to be outright enjoyable compared to everything else Kuvik had been going through all this time. He didn't mind working all day long.

None of the Bounty Hunters interfered with the group at all. He didn't see any Bounty Hunters near the line, in the quarry at the pile behind the meeting house, or anywhere else in the area.

Kuvik returned to Kogno's house that evening. He didn't get there until sunset. He barely made it back to the house before the guards went on duty for the night.

The house door stood open, but he heard an argument going on inside long before he got there.

"He's supposed to be here to do work for me!" Zori blared. "How can he do work for me when he's never here!"

"I told you he has to work all day!" Kogno fired back. "That's a little more important than you sitting around doing nothing while he does the work you're supposed to be doing in the first place."

"You said he would be able to do work once he got home from the quarry, but now it's dark which means he can't even go outside and bring in water and firewood! Why are we supporting him if he can't work for us?!"

"You're perfectly capable of getting your own wood and water," Kogno returned. "You should have brought that in before now."

"I didn't think I had to!" she pointed out. "You were the one who told me he would be able to do it for me. Why did you even bring him home if all we're going to do is feed him?"

The patrols passed the house just then, so Kuvik had no choice but to go inside. Kogno and Zori both stopped arguing the minute he showed up. Kogno pointed to the same post. "Sit down."

Kuvik sat down and Kogno tied him by the neck again. Zori made no attempt to talk to Kuvik or to smile at him. She went back to her work and started putting the meal on the table as before.

She didn't forget to serve Kuvik this time. She laid out three discs and gave him one before she and Kogno sat down to eat their meal.

She didn't make eye contact with Kuvik when she handed him the disc. She brought a water gourd at the same time, set it on the floor where he could reach it, and turned her back on him for the rest of the evening.

She and Kogno sat down and ate in a tense silence. Kuvik kept his head down, ate his food, and drank his water as quietly as possible. He really needed to take his escape much more seriously.

He would need to take advantage of the quarry as an option as long as the Bounty Hunters left the slaves unguarded. Part of the downhill pathway led through the jungle. He could easily get into the treetops there.

Then he could just run for it through the canopy. The Bounty Hunters wouldn't be able to catch him there. They wouldn't be able to track him or even see him. He wouldn't even need weapons.

He decided to go ahead and do that. He wouldn't tell a living soul what he planned to do. He spent the rest of the meal retracing the route in his mind. The branches hung low enough in a couple of different spots for him to grab hold and swing himself up.

He might not be as strong as he used to be. He would need to account for that in his plans and make sure he could still make it without relying solely on his arm strength.

Those spots had especially dense canopy, too. They would be perfect for traveling and hiding out of sight from the ground.

He jolted back to high alert when Zori came over to pick up his utensils. He should have thanked her, but it would be better if he just didn't talk to her at all.

Kogno left the table. Did he and Zori say a word to each other through the whole meal? Kuvik couldn't remember.

Kogno didn't say anything while he bound Kuvik's wrists to the post. Then Kogno and Zori went upstairs. They started arguing as soon as they got up there. They started going back and forth again about Kuvik doing work around the house.

Zori got progressively more upset when she realized she couldn't budge Kogno on the subject of Kuvik doing hard labor. Kogno never lost his temper. He kept repeating the same remarks again and again until she gave up.

She eventually broke down crying. Then all talk died between them and silence descended over the house.

Chapter 19

K uvik stayed silent from the time he woke up the next morning until he walked out the door to go to work. He ate his food exactly the same way.

He didn't think twice about finding a weapon. He wouldn't need one once he got into the canopy.

He *would* need one if he encountered any dangerous creatures—when he encountered dangerous creatures. He would have to get weapons somewhere else. Trying to get them here would be too dangerous, would take too long, and potentially give him away.

He got into line with the other prisoner-slaves on their way down the hill to the quarry. He had five seconds to think about his escape plan before he saw something wrong. Bounty Hunters stood guard over the line.

He kept his eyes down and pretended not to be too surprised by this. He shouldn't have been. It didn't make sense to guard the prisoners at night but not during the day. Someone somewhere had been bound to figure that out eventually.

The Bounty Hunters had posted armed warriors everywhere along the route all the way down to the quarry and back up to the village. He made several rounds and checked out every place he'd been planning to jump into the branches.

He could still have gotten up there, but not without the Bounty Hunters seeing him. He would have had no lead time to get away from them before they came after him.

Too many things could have gone wrong, so he didn't do it. The Bounty Hunters set up more and more barriers as the day went on. They closed up every opening and became increasingly watchful for any slave trying to escape.

He couldn't break away now—or not as easily. He put his head down and let himself slip back into his trance of not thinking about anything. He played the role of the mindless slave so defeated that he'd completely given up on ever getting free again.

He didn't have to pretend. He knew this feeling only too well. It started to sneak back into his mind and take over. It would block out the drive to escape if he let it.

He let go of the idea of escape—for now—at least until he found a better way. He would go out into the jungle again one of these times. Then he would escape into the branches and never look back.

He dropped off his latest block of stone and headed down the hill to the quarry. He didn't even look up into the branches. Too many Bounty Hunters stood guard. He didn't want them even to suspect that he was thinking about climbing up there.

He entered the quarry and bent over to pick up another block. He could handle them more easily, thanks to eating more food more times of the day at Kogno's and Zori's house.

They didn't know it, but they really were helping him in ways they probably didn't realize. Just giving him the basics of human life, letting him sleep in peace every night, and not beating or whipping him all the time was a vast improvement on his previous experience.

He grabbed the block, but before he could lift it, one of the other captive-slaves bent over right next to him to pick up another nearby block.

The guy murmured in Kuvik's ear, "Are you still planning it?"

Kuvik looked up. The person standing next to him was Akli. They shared one brief moment of eye contact before they both picked up their blocks and got back into line heading up the quarry and back to the village.

Their movements positioned Akli in front of Kuvik. Kuvik had to wait until they both got far enough away from one Bounty Hunter guard and not close enough for the next guard to overhear what the two men said to each other.

"Yes, I am still planning it," Kuvik murmured. "But we can't move with these guards around."

"They patrol the village at night," Akli muttered over his shoulder.

"I know." Kuvik had to fall silent when the two men drew level with another guard.

"What do you think?" Akli asked the next time they found an opening.

"Keep watch," Kuvik replied. "Watch for another opening. That's all we can do."

They ended their conversation, but Akli's presence brought Kuvik back from the brink. He wasn't finished yet. He would get out of here. Nothing ever stayed the same around here. Something was bound to change and give the men another opportunity.

He didn't find it that day. The men changed their position in the line every now and then depending on when, where, and how long it took them to pick up their blocks in the quarry.

Kuvik saw Nelv, Phiri, and Garvis in the line, too. Kuvik found opportunities to hold similar conversations with all three of them. They all still wanted to escape, but they'd all come to the same conclusion. They had to wait for conditions to become more favorable.

Dorei didn't work in the quarry. He worked in the village, but Kuvik saw him around multiple times, too. The two men shared eye contact each time they saw each other, but they never talked.

Kuvik didn't try. He concentrated on the four men he knew he could count on—no one else. He didn't broach the subject with anyone else—not even people who had expressed willingness to try on the march here.

He returned to Kogno's house that night and found the couple in a much lighter mood. They didn't argue. Kogno tied Kuvik in the same place. Zori smiled at Kuvik when she served him his food, but she didn't try to engage him in conversation.

She and Kogno talked while they ate. They talked about all the Bounty Hunters standing guard and keeping watch over the slaves day and night. Zori remarked how unusual it was to think the Bounty Hunters had to do it that way.

She made it sound like she'd never seen it before that a village had to keep constant watch to stop the slaves from escaping. She made it sound like the slaves had always been docile, obedient, and cooperative before now.

Kogno shrugged her concerns away. First he said it was just a necessary precaution after the escape attempt on the way here. Then he said it wasn't his decision and attributed it to Halmeron, whoever that was.

Kuvik didn't see anyone around here acting as any kind of leader, but then again, Kuvik hadn't seen much of this village since he got here.

He supposed Halmeron must be this village's equivalent to Uthor from the first Bounty Hunter village that had captured Kuvik.

Halmeron meant nothing to Kuvik now. He finished his meal and waited in silence for Kogno to tie his wrists to the post so Kuvik could go to sleep. He just had to go through the motions and wait for something to change.

It happened much quicker than he expected. He roused sometime in the night when he heard yelling, crashing, and then screaming in the distance.

Kuvik raised his head. The sound drifted into the house through the open door from outside. The first hint of light was just starting to creep over the landscape. He could see everything outside, but full daylight hadn't spread over the countryside yet.

The noise woke up the whole village. Kogno came pounding downstairs, glared at Kuvik sitting there still tied up, and stormed outside. Kogno met up with a bunch of other Bounty Hunters who had been on guard last night.

Kogno left with them. The same combination of yells, screams, crashes, and thumps kept echoing through the village from out of sight.

All the other voices in the village erupted at the same time. Men yelled inside their houses and so did the women. More men flooded outside.

The houses with children living in them started up with their usual early morning noise of women trying to calm and quiet their children. Kuvik stayed where he was. He didn't want to get involved in whatever this disturbance was about.

Zori came downstairs in a few minutes, glanced at Kuvik, and started her work without trying to talk to him. She built up the fire, made the morning container of food, and served it to him, but he couldn't eat it with his hands tied.

He really hoped she didn't get the brilliant idea to untie him. Now would be the worst time for Kogno to come home and find Kuvik free—or even partially free.

Zori didn't free his hands. She left his food and water sitting on the floor in front of him and went back to her work without a word of explanation to him. She spent the rest of the morning pretending he wasn't there.

Kogno came back a few hours later. He started by throwing his spear on the table and then hurling himself down on the bench in front of his food. He started eating it and Zori sat down opposite him, but she didn't eat.

"What's happening out there?" she asked. "What's all the commotion about?"

"The patrols caught one of the slaves trying to escape early this morning. They brought him back. Halmeron had to decide what to do with the guy."

"What is there to decide? They executed him, didn't they?"

"Not yet, but they will. Halmeron wants to make a public example of him for the other slaves. All the slaves have to go watch later to make sure they all understand."

Kuvik waited for either of them to say something else. Kogno's words cast Zori into a thoughtful silence. She didn't draw attention to the fact that Kuvik hadn't eaten that morning because his hands were still tied.

Kogno glanced in Kuvik's direction, saw his hands still tied, and saw the food and water sitting there untouched. Kogno went right on eating. He didn't get up or interrupt his meal to free Kuvik.

Kuvik didn't ask him to. Kuvik barely looked at his food. He'd been living on borrowed time ever since he came to this house. No one knew that better than he did. Nothing this good could last. It was bound to end.

Kogno ate for a while before he broke the silence. "The slaves won't go out to work today. You can get him to do work around the house if you want to. I'll stick around and keep an eye on him—and enough of the men are patrolling the village during the day. He won't try anything."

That ended the conversation. Kogno and Zori finished eating and she started cleaning up. Kogno finally got up from the table, untied Kuvik, and Kuvik at his food and drank his water as quickly as he could.

Kogno stood guard over him until he finished. Zori came over, took the dishes away, and Kogno untied Kuvik's neck. "Come with me," Kogno ordered.

Kuvik followed Kongo out of the house, between a few other buildings, to the other end of the village. Which of the slaves had tried to escape last night and gotten caught?

Kuvik really hoped it wasn't Akli. Akli couldn't be so stupid as to try an escape now, so who was it? Kuvik couldn't guess.

Chapter 20

More and more slaves headed in the same direction to gather from all over the village. Plenty of Bounty Hunters came with them. Some of the warriors guarded their slaves the way Kogno did. No one dared to come near Kuvik as long as Kogno was here.

Everyone amassed in front of one of the meeting houses. A group of ten warriors had tied Dorei to the wall with his legs spread and his arms outstretched on either side. The warriors had already stripped him naked and beaten him severely.

Dried blood, mud, and what looked like excrement smudged his face and body all over. They'd tied a strip of hide thong around the base of his genitals.

The Bounty Hunters had slung a heavy rock from the line to cinch the noose tighten enough to make the flesh turn black. Dorei's eyes darted around the crowd.

He must have already known he was going to die. He bared his teeth grimacing in terror, pain, and misery watching everyone gather around to watch. His ribcage heaved and he kept letting out little whining gasps every time he took a breath.

Kuvik found himself glancing around the crowd. He saw a lot of warriors and a lot of the nicely dressed Bounty Hunter men gathering around, but he still didn't see anyone acting as a leader.

None of these men dressed themselves up or made themselves a spectacle the way Uthor did. None of them made a show of telling the warriors what to do—or telling anyone else what to do. Kuvik couldn't tell if Halmeron was here or not.

The warriors started at some unseen signal between themselves. One of them starting whipping Dorei. He didn't even try to act brave or tough. He cried out, sobbed, and even screamed for all the crowd to hear.

"Did anyone else try to escape with you?!" the Bounty Hunter whipping him demanded.

"NO!!" Dorei screeched. "I WENT ALONE!! I TOLD YOU THAT!!"

"Is anyone else planning escape?!" the same guy asked when he brought the whip down.

"NO!!" Dorei broke down sobbing for real. "I'M THE ONLY ONE!!"

The warriors kept interrogating him the whole time to find out if he had taken part in the escape attempt on the march north. Dorei said he didn't—which was the truth.

The warriors asked again and again if anyone else in the village was planning to escape. He denied it every time and insisted he had planned this attempt and carried it out alone. He claimed he didn't know of anyone in the village who was planning to escape.

Kuvik had to admire the guy's fortitude. He died protecting Kuvik and everyone else. Dorei already knew for an absolute fact that Kuvik, Akli, and the others were planning to escape.

Dorei might have thought he could buy himself a little more time by selling out the others, but he kept his mouth shut through it all. That took courage.

The Bounty Hunters whipped him bloody all over his body. He didn't even try to quiet his screams or make himself less wretched and pathetic. Kuvik could only feel sorry for the man.

Kuvik didn't know what Dorei had tried to do to escape. He must have been desperate to try it now at the worst possible time. He had taken a massive and unnecessary risk when he didn't have the skills and knowledge to pull it off.

The Bounty Hunters finished whipping him. The same man who did the whipping turned to the crowd and bellowed out for everyone to hear, "This is what will happen and a hundred times worse to anyone who tries to escape. You all belong to us now. Get used to it."

He spun around, slashed with a knife, and cut Dorei's genitals right below the noose. The rock pulled the flesh away, but the noose had already cut off the blood supply for so long that the wound hardly bled at all. Is this what the Bounty Hunters did to Akli?

Dorei burst into a fresh outburst of screaming and outright sobbing. He didn't stop this time, but the Bounty Hunters were only getting started.

One of them walked around the meeting house from behind it just then. The guy carried a large basket, stopped next to Dorei, put the basket on the ground, and took the lid off.

He stood up and another man stepped forward holding two sticks. They'd been tied together at one end with a round piece of rod jammed between them. They squeezed together to make tongs.

The guy bent over and used the tongs to lift a single Abnormit grub out of the basket. Dorei was already screaming and crying too much to stop now. He tried to struggle to get away, but he couldn't break the ropes tying him.

The man placed the grub on Dorei's stomach and the grub gnawed its way through his skin. The grub vanished inside his abdomen and started devouring him from the inside.

Dorei burst into full-throated screams as loud as he could shriek. He writhed, fought, thrashed, and convulsed in agony, terror, and hopeless panic. His abdominal wall rippled a few times and then the bulge traveled upward toward the cleft of his chest.

Dorei was too out of his mind in a frenzy to make eye contact with anyone, but Kuvik refused to look away. He watched the whole sickening ordeal until the grub crawled up inside Dorei's chest.

He collapsed there and slumped against his bound wrists. It was over. He was dead. Stunned silence fell over the crowd. Everyone stared at his body. No one looked away.

Kuvik expected the Bounty Hunters to warn all the slaves again that any escape attempt would be punished the same way, but none of the warriors said anything. Some of them left.

Kogno finally told Kuvik to go with him and they returned to the house. The rest of the crowd dispersed at the same time. Everyone went off in different directions. No one talked.

Kogno led Kuvik back inside the main room. Zori worked near the fireplace. She looked up when the men returned.

"You won't go back to the quarry," Kogno told Kuvik. "I don't know what Halmeron plans to do about that, but no one will leave the village today. You can work in the house. Zori will give you things to do. Enough of the men will be standing guard outside."

He didn't outright say that no one else would be able to escape, but he might as well have. He walked away to the other side of the room to go about his own business. Kuvik didn't know what to do first.

Zori handed him a wooden bucket. "You can start by bringing water and filling up that barrel there."

She pointed to a barrel sitting under the corner of the eaves outside. It sat farther down the wall where rain would spill off the roof and fill the barrel. It must not have rained very much recently because the barrel was getting empty.

"You can get water from the cistern at the other end of the village." She pointed back in the direction of the meeting house where the warriors had executed Dorei. "Go straight there and come straight back. Don't go anywhere else."

She didn't say it, either, but she might as well have. The thickest groups of warriors would all be down there at that end of the village.

Kuvik walked out of the house and headed in that direction. The slaves and the rest of the Bounty Hunter population started going about their business as usual. Everyone pretended that Dorei's execution had never happened.

Hangman had no choice but to think it had happened when he got to the end of the village and saw Dorei's body still hanging there on the meeting house wall. None of the warriors had removed the body yet.

The Abnormit grub was starting to eat its way up his neck and out through the space between his upper ribcage and collarbone. Kuvik looked away and spotted Nelv and Phiri across the village.

Neither of them would make eye contact with him. So that was the end of that. Dorei's execution would put the fear of God into everyone. No one would be willing to try to escape again.

That didn't matter. Kuvik would just go alone. He would stand a better chance alone anyway. Taking anyone with him had always been a losing proposition.

He didn't know what the word, *cistern* meant, but he found out after he passed the meeting house. Another hill rose on that side of the village and joined up with some higher mountains on the west side.

Someone had built a stone wall against the hillside using the same granite blocks from the quarry. A carved stone face in the shape of the sun covered half the wall with a spout coming out of the mouth.

Water poured from the spout into a carved stone pool underneath. A few different slaves stood around the pool filling their buckets before they left to return to their work.

Kuvik went over there and did the same thing. He didn't look at the other slaves. They didn't mean anything to him.

He would have liked to take Akli with him when he escaped. Akli deserved freedom more than anyone, but Kuvik couldn't risk delaying any longer—not with the Bounty Hunters cracking down on everyone.

The other slaves left the cistern first. He filled his bucket and pulled it up. He rested it on the edge of the pool for just a second to let the extra drips fall. A young woman came up to the pool on his right just then. He didn't look at her, either.

She startled him out of his thoughts. "You're Kuvik, aren't you?"

His head shot up. She was another slave covered in bruises, whip cuts, and wearing tattered rags. He immediately looked away and lifted his bucket off the rim of the pool.

"Almost all the slaves want to escape," she blurted out. "Please. You have to help us. We just don't know what to do or how to do it. Please help us. Don't leave us like this. We'll do anything. I heard what you said in the jungle. We'll fight. We'll do whatever we have to do. Everyone is just too scared to say anything."

He refused to look at her again. "I have no reason to help anyone. The people I try to help do exactly the opposite of what I say. They get killed and everyone else gets into trouble. I'm better off going alone."

"Please don't leave." Her voice broke and tears sprang to her eyes. She tried to shake them away, but they kept coming until they streaked down her cheeks. "Please...you don't know what it's like......Kannor.....he's so cruel....I don't know how much longer I have left....." She shook that away, too. "Some of us have been trying to escape for years. Akli isn't the only one. He's just the one most people know about. Those people who disobeyed you are just a few. The rest of us will follow you. We need someone who knows what to do and can tell us. Please. You're our last hope."

He started to say that he wasn't—that they could have escaped a long time ago if they really wanted to.

He couldn't leave these people behind—not if they really wanted to leave. He'd gone through the same thing with the first village he'd liberated.

He knew the story of Hangman and his men freeing all those captives from the Renegade Clan. No one knew those stories better than Kuvik. He'd spent years living side by side with people Hangman had freed.

Kuvik had watched Hammer and his men grow up into the strongest Godless warriors anywhere. Hangman had given them that.

Kuvik couldn't turn his back on these people—not when they asked him point blank to free them. He had walked away from Dorei—but that was before Dorei tried to escape on his own.

The woman placed her hand on Kuvik's arm. "You don't have to do anything right now. You don't have to put yourself in danger. I'll go around and talk to everyone. I'll find out who wants to help out. Then I'll find a way to let you know."

"We need weapons," Kuvik blurted out. "We need to find out where the Bounty Hunters are keeping their weapons horde."

"I already know that," she replied.

His head shot up and he stared at her again. "You do?! Where are they?"

"They're in that house over there." She pointed across the village to a small house next to one of the meeting houses. "They put the stash in there after the men carried it here from the south. Everything they brought is in there—and a whole lot more the Bounty Hunters have been collecting for a long time. Should I go get them now?"

"NO!!" Kuvik struggled to lower his voice. "Don't do anything. Just find out who is willing and who we can rely on. Then we'll take it to the next step. Make sure no one puts themselves in danger."

He picked up his bucket and walked off without looking back. He probably should have asked her name, but he didn't think of it in time. Kuvik took the water back to the house, dumped it into the barrel, and made a dozen more trips to do the same thing.

Zori sent him to another part of the village to collect firewood, but she didn't send him into the jungle. He didn't get a chance to get up into the branches, so he might as well stick around and see where this went.

That woman must have been willing to do a lot if she took all the risk of talking to everyone, especially now when the Bounty Hunters would be watching everyone so closely.

They walked everywhere all over the village and kept a sharp eye on all the slaves no matter what anyone did. None of the slaves could twitch an eyelash. The Bounty Hunters got suspicious if any of the slaves talked to each other.

Chapter 21

Kuvik came out of Kogno's and Zori's house for the morning and passed through the village. A week had passed since Dorei's execution. None of the slaves had been allowed to leave the village.

Halmeron had been keeping plenty of Bounty Hunters on watch day and night, but the Bounty Hunters who did stand guard did it more casually. No one expected the slaves to attempt escape—not now.

Kuvik returned to the place where he and the other men had started making the pile of granite blocks. Halmeron wanted them to build a wall around that part of the village. Kuvik didn't ask why.

All the men who used to be part of the line going down to the quarry now worked to build the wall. They had to mix mortar, which meant digging up sand and clay from the streambed on the other side of the village.

Certain men got assigned to the digging. Others got assigned to mixing. Another group carried the mortar back to the wall. Others lifted the blocks into place. Then other slaves positioned the stones and tapped them into place to make the wall straight.

Kuvik got randomly assigned to the job of mixing the mortar. This turned out to be the most strategically advantageous spot for him. More people had to come and go from this spot than any other part of the operation.

The Bounty Hunters stood guard over the slaves even here, but the guards kept their distance where they could survey a wider area. They didn't hover close enough to overhear anyone's conversation.

Kuvik got to talk to more people here. Akli, Phiri, Nelv, and Gravis all belonged to the mortar-carrying crew. All four of them had to come back and get fresh loads of mortar from Kuvik all day long.

The four of them exchanged snatches of conversation with him in those few moments when they got close enough. They usually had to break off as soon as anyone came near them, but at least the men could talk.

Others from the first escape attempt also worked in the same project. Beinu worked in the clay-digging group. He ended up coming to the mortar-mixing area pretty often, too.

He and dozens of others had been talking to the woman Kuvik met at the cistern. He only found out later that her name was Kesha. Kannor, the warrior whose slave she was, had a notorious reputation for being one of the cruelest Bounty Hunters anywhere.

He had already gone through dozens of young female slaves exactly like her. He used them mercilessly, beat and tortured them to stimulate himself, and eventually brutalized them so badly that they didn't survive their injuries.

He treated his wife just as badly. He only made sure to let her recover between sessions so she didn't actually die on him.

He didn't have to worry about that with his slaves. He and the other warriors brought in a constant supply of new captives. He could be as hard on them as he wanted to be.

Most of the men Kuvik talked to had already given Kesha up for dead. They all agreed that she really didn't have anything to lose by trying to escape. Her situation couldn't get any worse if she got caught.

She threw herself into the process with everything she had. She really was ready to do absolutely anything to get out with her life.

Kuvik didn't see her again. He only heard from everyone else that she was going from person to person getting everyone's agreement to join a mass escape attempt.

People joined more willingly when they heard that Kuvik was involved. Everyone wanted him to take charge of the mission—or whatever this was turning into.

Everyone got much more hopeful when they heard that he planned to raid the Bounty Hunters' weapons stash. Every slave in the whole village wanted to get their hands on those weapons, but no one dared to do it alone.

Kuvik didn't dare to do it alone, either. He still didn't know how or when he would get these people to make their move. He needed some definite opening.

The Bounty Hunters didn't give him one. They didn't come close to giving him one. They stood guard all the time. They hardly ever gave the slaves more than a few minutes to do anything.

He got to know his core people better through these snatches of stolen conversation. It wasn't easy, but he started to put together a more complete picture of who and what everyone was.

Akli had belonged to the Chosen Clan. He'd never learned to fight or hunt, which explained why he had failed to escape so many times.

Most of his family band had gotten wiped out when the Bounty Hunters first attacked. They carried off the rest. The Bounty Hunters had severely brutalized him, his mother, his sisters, his two brothers, and four of their surviving relatives in the early days of their capture.

Akli had suffered the tortures of the damned while watching his mother, sisters, and all their remaining relatives die off one after the other. The stories of how his mother and sisters had died made for the stuff of nightmares.

Eventually, only Akli and his two brothers remained. The ordeal had fired a resolve in all three to escape and return to their own Clan at all costs. Akli's two brothers had been the relatives the Bounty Hunters had killed to punish him for his repeated escape attempts.

Nelv had a similar story, but it took a long, long time before he opened up enough to tell Kuvik about it. Nelv had never told anyone. The horror of watching his family killed before his eyes had made him silent and reclusive.

He was the only survivor of the Bounty Hunter attack on his family band. He came from the Emerald Clan. They had all fought back and died down to the last man—except for Nelv.

He had been only three years old at the time. His mother had hidden him in the jungle to protect him from the Bounty Hunters. They had found him after they wiped out his band and they took him into captivity anyway.

He spent the first years of his captivity as the labor slave of a vicious couple from the nicely dressed side of Bounty Hunter society.

Both the husband and the wife liked to torment Nelv by reminding him daily that the Bounty Hunters had killed his entire family band, that he was the last of them still alive, and that he no longer had a family he could return to.

He had developed the habit then of simply not answering. He didn't answer anyone unless he absolutely had to. He showed no emotion. He didn't permit himself even to feel any emotion. Their comments and everything else everyone did and said rolled right off his back.

Phiri had belonged to the Followers' Clan, but he'd gotten captured as a boy. He knew how to read, but that was about all. He didn't have Mora's vast knowledge of so many subjects.

He'd made a strong effort to continue the Follower way of life by cooperating with the Bounty Hunters as much as possible.

He'd enjoyed some good and not-so-bad experiences in his time, but he'd become increasingly more accepting of the idea of fighting back. He'd come to realize as he grew up that the Follower way might not be the best.

Garvis had his own tale to tell. He'd been too young to remember the details of his capture or which Clan he'd belonged to beforehand. He'd been the Bounty Hunters' prisoner-slave for so long that he didn't even know if he had any relatives in any other village or in Bounty Hunter custody.

He had injured his leg when the Bounty Hunters took him on a campaign against a different territory of Godless.

Garvis didn't know enough about the country to tell Kuvik where these Godless lived. He had never gotten close enough to them to find out who they were or the names of their Krals.

The Bounty Hunters had invaded the territory the way they usually did. They had planned to raid all the bands, take whatever they wanted, and kill everyone else.

The Bounty Hunters didn't know that this particular territory was home to nine different bands all related to each other by blood. Their Krals consisted of four brothers, all the sons of one father, and their five cousins.

Their father and uncles had ruled one much larger band with the grandfather as the central Kral. He and his brothers had gotten killed fighting in another battle. That left the nine brothers and cousins.

They could have chosen the oldest as Kral, but all nine of these men had recognized that their band was getting too big anyway. Their camps had started to attract too many creature attacks. The creatures always knew they could find women and children there.

So the nine brothers and cousins decided to split up the band. They separated, but they remained closely bonded and helped each other when necessary. The Bounty Hunters carried out two attacks on the territory and scattered two of these bands.

The Bounty Hunters moved in on the third. They got a nasty surprise when they came face to face with all the other seven bands plus all the surviving warriors from the previous two attacks. The entire Clan joined together into one army to confront the Bounty Hunters.

The Bounty Hunters' reputation wouldn't let them back down even though they saw that they were outnumbered and outclassed by men much stronger, better trained, and better armed than themselves.

The battle joined and the Godless overran the Bounty Hunters. Garvis had gotten trampled and fallen on top of some dead Bounty Hunters' weapons when the Godless stampeded the area. That's how he'd gotten injured.

The Godless slaughtered most of the Bounty Hunters. The rest turned tail and ran for it. The Godless spared the slaves and sent them away to return to their own Clans.

These Godless had apparently never heard of taking in freed captives from another Clan. None of these Godless offered to take in the slaves left behind.

The Godless had put leaf past on Garvis's injured leg, dosed him with Gooji juice, and sent him and the other slaves on their way.

Two of these slaves belonged to the Chosen Clan. They offered to take Garvis home with them and the three men started traveling together. The Bounty Hunters had recaptured the three men a few days later.

These were the same Bounty Hunters who had fled from the Godless. Their own cowardice made them even more cruel toward the slaves who had witnessed the Bounty Hunters' humiliation.

The Bounty Hunters had refused to give Garvis any additional leaf paste or Gooji juice for his leg. It became infected and never healed completely, which led him to walk with a limp.

Seeing the Godless' bravery and ferocity had given Garvis an aching hunger to break free from his captivity. He knew nothing of fighting or survival in the jungle. He realized pretty soon how insurmountable the task would be.

He'd started to try to learn the skills he would need. He still didn't feel he was ready until he met Kuvik.

Kuvik loved that story—all except for the part about the Godless sending the slaves away. They shouldn't have done that. Hangman never would have done that.

Kuvik had plenty of time to tell these men his own story as well as the story of Hangman's band taking in the freed women and children from Renegade territory as well as all the freed slaves from the first Bounty Hunter village that Kuvik had destroyed.

He insisted that anyone who escaped with him would be more than welcome to return to Godless territory with him, join Hangman's band, and initiate into the Clan if they wanted to.

Phiri had also gone on multiple campaigns with the Bounty Hunters, either to carry their burdens or just as a laborer to make camp, hunt, and do any other jobs they wanted slaves to do so the warriors didn't have to.

He had seen the Bounty Hunters' cruelty firsthand. He had also seen bands and Clans fighting back against the Bounty Hunters and sometimes succeeding.

The notion had been growing in him for a long time that fighting back really was the best way—much better than just lying down and accepting whatever the Bounty Hunters dished out.

Phiri had seen the Bounty Hunters bring in plenty of other Follower captives. Some died within minutes because they couldn't or wouldn't defend themselves. He'd seen others tormented to death over days or weeks.

Some of these people died thinking they were being noble and righteous by not taking the most basic steps to protect themselves. Phiri had started to see a pattern here and realized that there was nothing noble about letting cruel people kill him for no reason.

Chapter 22

Kuvik woke up in the middle of the night when he heard Kogno and Zori talking upstairs. They always left him tied up downstairs. This was the first time he'd ever heard them talking in the middle of the night.

Kogno always tied Kuvik to the same post, but he'd cooperated so well that Kogno made the ropes long enough for Kuvik to lie down on the floor. Kogno had also given Kuvik some blankets and a small pad stuffed with dried grass as a cushion to lie on.

Kuvik raised his head to listen. Kogno and Zori weren't arguing this time. Kuvik had never heard them argue again after that first time.

"Why do we have to go?" Zori tried to keep her voice down, but it echoed extra loudly in the silence. "What's wrong with this village?"

"I told you it's Halmeron's decision," Kogno replied. "He didn't give the reason."

"He's had the slaves building that wall for two weeks. Why is he leaving now?"

"I don't claim to understand anything he does or decides to do. I only know we have to leave tomorrow."

"What about Kuvik?" Zori asked. "Are we taking him with us?"

"He didn't mention what will happen to the slaves. I assume he plans to take them, too. He'll need at least some of them to carry our supplies and all the spoils we've taken from all the raids. I guess that's what this is about. We have to take the spoils farther north. We have too much in one village. Halmeron doesn't want to risk anyone coming along and taking them before we take them north."

She sighed. "I wish we didn't have to go. We're settled here. Why can't some of the slaves take the spoils north while the rest of us stay?"

"I don't know if that's the reason. I'm just guessing. You would have to ask Halmeron and I couldn't let you do that."

"Fine," she groaned. "What do you want me to do?"

"Don't do anything until tomorrow when he makes the announcement to everyone. No one is supposed to know ahead of time. He'll tell us tomorrow how much of our possessions to take and how we'll travel. I'm sure he'll have some specific instructions to give us. Don't do anything until you hear what they are."

Kuvik didn't listen to anything else. Escaping would be a lot harder once the column moved out of this village.

The Bounty Hunters had become less vigilant with every passing day. The slave population had been so meek and compliant ever since Dorei's execution. The Bounty Hunters didn't see any reason to keep a constant watch on everyone else.

Kuvik sat all the way up from the floor thinking fast. He still hadn't set the time and day for the prisoners to escape, but the conspirators had put all the other preparations into place. They just needed to make their move.

Kuvik knew every detail of this village. He knew where the Bounty Hunters stored all their weapons. Kuvik could find that house with his eyes closed.

He couldn't risk the Bounty Hunters taking everyone farther north. The Bounty Hunters would be more watchful on the journey. They would probably bind everyone to those logs again. That would make escape nearly impossible.

He had to get out tonight—which meant waking up all the other slaves.

He pivoted onto his knees and moved his hands to his front pants pocket. He'd gotten assigned to help butcher a Demonex for the village two days ago. He'd used the opportunity to steal one of the curved teeth and stashed it in his pocket.

He hadn't been able to take any other part of the Demonex. This tooth was the only weapon he could conceal in his pocket. He had no other clothes. He went shirtless the rest of the time.

He jammed his bound hand into his pocket and took hold of the tooth to cut the ropes restraining him. Then he would have to sneak into the rest of these houses, find his comrades, wake them up, and wake up everyone else.

Some of his fellow escape conspirators had children they wanted to take with them. Waking them up in the middle of the night would be potentially disastrous—but he just had to do it tonight or never.

He started to pull the tooth out of his pocket when a woman yelled across the village outside. "Beinu's gone! He was here a little while ago! Now he's gone!"

All the guards on patrol came running. More men came out of their houses. Their voices flew back and forth carrying the message.

Kogno's footsteps pounded across the upper floor getting closer to the stairs. Kuvik let go of the tooth and curled up on his pad where he usually slept. He shut his eyes and waited for Kogno to run downstairs and across the room.

He burst out into the open village and exchanged a few words with the other warriors standing guard. They rushed back and forth talking loud and fast, searching everywhere for any sign of Beinu, and meeting back up to do it all over again.

Kuvik lay still in the dark not daring to move. Why would Beinu make his move now of all times? Did he overhear someone talking about going farther north? Did he think he had to act tonight?

Kuvik couldn't act tonight—not now—not with every warrior in the village on high alert and running around between the houses.

He forced himself to lie still and wait. Beinu might have ruined the chance for everyone else. What was wrong with these people? Why were they all so irretrievably incapable of following simple instructions?

Kuvik had to remember Kesha's words. Not everyone was like that. Beinu might have panicked. He might have been trying to contact someone to find out if they *should* act tonight. Beinu might have been trying to contact Kuvik to ask him the same question.

Kuvik still lay there straining his ears for any sound when Kogno barged back into the house. He stormed over to Kuvik, untied him, and took hold of his arm. "Get up," Kogno snapped. "Get up now. I know you're awake."

Zori came downstairs just then and saw Kogno marching Kuvik out of the house. "What's going on?! Where are you taking him?!" she cried out.

Kogno pointed at her and narrowed his eyes. "Go back upstairs, Zori! Don't you dare come out here."

Kogno towed Kuvik outside. It was still dark, but dawn would be coming soon. Kogno pulled Kuvik to the center of the village—the very same spot where the warriors had divided the captive slaves and assigned them to different houses.

Kogno yanked Kuvik down onto the ground. "Sit down here," Kogno growled. "Don't move. It's for your own safety. Just sit still and don't move."

Kuvik didn't understand, but he kept still just the same and didn't ask any questions. He didn't care where he went or what he did as long as the Bounty Hunters weren't out there looking for him.

He got all his questions answered when more warriors and even housewives showed up a minute later. They all came leading their slaves. Some did it politely. Others dragged their slaves by the hair or by ropes around their necks.

Kannor dragged Kesha through the dirt by her hair and one nicely dressed man kicked his slave all the way through the village making the poor slave guy fall countless times.

The Bounty Hunters herded all the slaves to the center of the village and pushed them down on the ground in another cluster around Kuvik. He didn't think he was anything special for getting here first. Kogno must have heard the word first to bring his slave here.

Everyone all over the village rounded up their slaves, confined there in a tightly packed group on the ground, and kept them under guard while the sun rose. The Bounty Hunters spent hours searching for Beinu. They eventually ransacked the whole village.

"What's happening?" Garvis whispered from Kuvik's right.

"Beinu tried to escape," Kuvik murmured back. "They're looking for him."

"Why did he try to escape?" Akli asked. "Aren't we supposed to go together?"

"The Bounty Hunters planned to leave today," Kuvik replied. "They were going to take us on another march farther north. Beinu may have found out and panicked."

Kesha sat up, sniffed, rubbed her eyes, and looked around. "Now what do we do?"

"Don't do anything," Kuvik replied. "We can't do anything while the Bounty Hunters are guarding us and searching for Beinu."

"We can't let them take us north," Akli pointed out. "That would make it a hundred times harder."

"Wait a little," Kuvik replied. "They won't leave today anyway. They might not leave for a while if they don't find Beinu. We might get another chance."

They had to break off their conversation when another group of Bounty Hunters reentered the village dragging Beinu between them. He was already unconscious and didn't see the other slaves sitting there under guard.

The Bounty Hunters dumped him there face down on the ground fifteen feet away where all the other prisoners could see him. He had failed to escape just like Dorei. When would these people learn?

The Bounty Hunters went off and did something else for a while. Maybe they had to consult Halmeron about what to do with Beinu. The wait gave Kuvik plenty of time to see all the people who had agreed to go with him.

One of them was Dorei's mother. Others were people Kuvik had been working with or had other dealings with since his capture.

The sun kept climbing. The Bounty Hunters kept not doing anything about Beinu or the other slaves. Hour passed upon hour. Kuvik's prediction came true. The Bounty Hunters didn't move out to head north that day. It was too late.

They came back hours later, dragged Beinu off the ground, and staked him to the wall of a different house where all the slaves could see him.

He didn't regain consciousness. He hung there by his wrists. Maybe the Bounty Hunters were waiting for him to come around so they could torture and execute him in front of the other slaves the way they executed Dorei.

Beinu didn't come around. The sun climbed to its zenith before the Bounty Hunters called it quits. Everyone returned to the cluster, pulled their slaves out of the group, and took them back home.

Kesha screamed when Kannor grabbed her by the hair. He punched her in the face, knocked her out, and dragged her through the dirt the rest of the way. Kuvik got to his feet when he saw Kogno coming. Kogno didn't march Kuvik back to the house.

Kuvik sat down in his place and Kogno tied him right up against the post this time. Kuvik expected nothing less.

A hush hung over the village for the rest of the day. The open house door gave Kuvik a clear view of Beinu still hanging on the side of the building. He didn't move. Kuvik couldn't see from here if Beinu was even still breathing.

The Bounty Hunters had plenty to occupy them for the rest of the day. They kept going back and forth all over the village even though they didn't have to guard or patrol for slaves. All the slaves stayed indoors for the rest of the day.

Kuvik stopped paying attention, leaned his head against the post, and shut his eyes. That was two of his potential allies gone. He hadn't gotten as close to Beinu as the others, but Kuvik still hated to lose people, especially like this.

All the slaves had a story like his. That was the thing about living with Hangman's band. The Godless had all been so much more functional than he was. They had all grown up with loving families and plenty of support. Even Mora had grown up with that.

None of them grew up suffering the kind of mistreatment he had suffered first with his own Clan and then with the Hungry Ghosts. The Godless had cared for him, welcomed him, took him in, and healed him more than he ever thought possible.

They didn't understand him. They couldn't. Not a single living one of them shared his experience or knew even half of what he'd endured.

Everyone here understood his past. He could tell anyone where he'd come from and what he'd been through. None of them thought it was anything unusual or out of the ordinary. It didn't make him different from them. It made him the same as them.

None of the Godless thought it made him different from them, but he thought it. He knew it. He *was* different from them and always would be. Was that the real reason he hadn't let himself initiate before? Maybe some part of him believed he would never be Godless.

Chapter 23

Kogno woke Kuvik up a few different times by coming into the house and going back out to join the other warriors. Kuvik didn't think too hard about what they were doing out there. Maybe they were getting ready to leave tomorrow.

Kogno finally came back and sat down at the table to sharpen some weapon. Zori came downstairs not long after that and started making the evening meal.

She asked him a few questions about the situation outside, but he shut her down, told her to mind her own business and keep her place, and refused to answer in any other way.

Neither of them spoke after that except when she asked him if the village was still moving out tomorrow.

He said yes and that the same rule applied. Halmeron would decide in the morning how everyone should do it, what they should take, and how to transport the slaves.

Kuvik couldn't think of very many ways to carry out a mass exodus less efficiently than this. This Halmeron wasn't much of a strategist if he left these details to the last minute without informing his people.

Darkness fell and Zori served the two men their food. Kogno untied Kuvik's hands right away so he could eat. Kogno retied them after he and Zori had finished eating.

Kogno left Kuvik's neck bound tightly to the post both during the meal and afterward. Kuvik had to sleep sitting up tonight.

He really didn't care about the luxury of sleeping on a pad. He didn't even really care about sitting up. He shut his eyes as soon as Kogno finished tying him.

Kogno and Zori stayed downstairs a little while longer before they went upstairs. Kogno left the front door open as usual. It didn't have any way to lock as far as Kuvik knew. They had to leave the door open to let the room cool off.

Kuvik didn't have to question if the Bounty Hunters were still on patrol outside. He heard them walking back and forth and occasionally talking in low tones. They walked more loudly and talked more than any other night he could remember.

He waited a few more hours before he opened his eyes and looked around. The fire was starting to die down. It didn't blaze as high. Just a few low flames illuminated the room.

He waited for the next patrol to pass the house. Then he maneuvered himself onto his knees and twisted sideways to face the post. He couldn't count the number of times he'd rehearsed this moment in his mind.

Kogno always tied Kuvik's wrists below the rope around his neck. Maybe Kogno was trying to be nice by not positioning Kuvik's arms too high above his head.

Kuvik wedged his neck tighter against the noose. He could get his fingers to touch the knot at his throat and he started to wiggle it loose. He had to stop when another patrol went by the door. He sat down in his old place before silence fell and he started up again.

He loosened the knot at his throat and freed his neck. Then he used his teeth to untie the knot around his wrists.

He sank down on the pad beneath him and took that moment to catch his breath. His blood pounded in his ears. Everything he did from now on would be a death sentence for him and everyone else who went with him.

He pulled the Demonex tooth out of his pocket and gripped it in his right hand to be ready to strike when he needed it. He would show no mercy. He was getting out of this village at any cost.

He waited where he was for another patrol to pass. Their noise told him exactly where they were.

Maybe they were trying to intimidate the slaves by making so much noise. Maybe the guards wanted to broadcast it far and wide that they were there so the slaves would know they couldn't escape.

He snuck around the table and found the place where Zori kept her three cooking knives. Kuvik took them all.

He flattened himself against the wall by the door and strained his ears until he heard the patrols move off. One of them headed down the village toward the west. The other went east.

Four more patrols circled the village perimeter. The six patrols constantly changed their rotation to move through the village and all around it.

He waited until silence returned outside. Then he ducked through the door, rushed around the house, and hid in the shadows. Darkness would be his best friend tonight—darkness and silence.

He skimmed along the wall, ducked behind another house, and came to the second one in the same row. This was Akli's house. He lived with two of the nicely dressed Bounty Hunters and their two young children.

The couple kept their slaves tied up in a cellar under the house. The cellar had separate stalls with strong wooden walls separating all the slaves.

Two female slaves lived upstairs with the two children. The parents didn't take care of their own children. Kuvik had already heard from Kesha that the two nurse slaves weren't interested in escaping. They thought they led a privileged existence.

Kuvik snuck around the back of the house and crept in through the back door. It opened into an empty fireplace room like Noya's. A set of stairs descended from here into the cellar.

Kuvik kept going through three other rooms until he found the stairs going up. He'd never been in the upper floors of one of these houses. He didn't know what to expect.

He was free and on the rampage in a Bounty Hunter village. All the pain, rage, despair, and horror of his captivity came to the surface.

He had no plans to take it easy on the Bounty Hunters by simply running away and vanishing into the jungle. That would be too easy—for him and for them.

He tiptoed down a narrow hall and glanced into every bedroom. The slave nurses slept on raised beds with the two children next to them—one child per nurse. Kuvik left them asleep.

He went into the last bedroom where the mother and father slept. He stood over them watching them sleep for a long time before he slashed his tooth across each of their throats.

He left both of them choking on their own blood, darted out of the room, and shut the door behind him to muffle the sound. He didn't want to wake up the children or the nurses.

He hustled back downstairs to the cellar. He already knew which stall Akli lived in. Akli was asleep, too.

Kuvik squatted in front of Akli and clamped his hand over Akli's mouth to silence him. Akli's eyes flew open and he tried to yell out. He couldn't see in the dark.

"Be quiet, Akli!" Kuvik hissed. "Don't make a sound! We're getting out of here! Just be quiet!"

Akli froze at those words. Kuvik cut the ropes binding Akli, freed him, and pulled him to his feet. "Go through the cellar and free everyone who is with us," Kuvik whispered and shoved one of Zori's knives into Akli's hand. "Make sure everyone knows to be quiet. Kill anyone who makes any noise. You can tell them I said so. Anyone who makes a sound could get us all caught and executed. If they aren't ready to be quiet, either kill them or leave them behind. Understand?"

Akli nodded.

"Bring everyone to the weapons store as soon as you get our people free," Kuvik went on. "I'll arm everyone and we'll leave from there. Hide from any patrols or kill them, but only if you can do it silently." Kuvik pushed Akli away and raced out of the house.

Kuvik had to dive behind the house when another patrol came through the area. He must have made some small noise to alert them.

They stopped on the other side of the house, held a whispered conversation to ask each other if they had both heard it, and separated to search around the house. Kuvik didn't wait for them to find him hiding there.

He scooted along the wall to one corner, grabbed the first Bounty Hunter when he came around it, hooked his arm around the man's neck, cut the man's throat, and dragged him further around the corner to hide the body from his comrade.

The second Bounty Hunter circled the house completely to search for the source of the noise and to find his missing comrade. Kuvik ambushed the second guy the same way and dragged both bodies into the fireplace room so no one else would see them.

He dove straight back out into the dark, sprinted from house to house, and didn't stop until he got all the way to a different house on the opposite end of the village. This building had three floors. Kuvik didn't know why.

This was the house where Kesha lived with Kannor and his wife. They didn't have any children. Kannor's wife had four domestic slaves. Only one of them wanted to join the escape attempt.

Kuvik entered the house through the back and stepped into an identical fireplace room. He didn't know the slaves' living arrangements, but he didn't have to go looking for Kesha.

The fire in the fireplace lit up her stark naked body lying on the stone floor in a pool of her own blood. Blood and filth saturated her hair. Blood also saturated a rope tied around her wrists, ankles, and neck.

The same rope secured her to the chimney pillar. She was the only person in the room.

Kuvik studied her for a minute thinking fast. He tiptoed past her, entered the house, and searched around until he found the stairs going upstairs. He knew enough about this village by now to know that no other Bounty Hunters lived here with Kannor and his wife.

Kuvik guessed that Kannor and his wife lived on the top floor and they proved him right. He found them asleep in a huge bed in the far northern corner of the house.

Kuvik killed both of them without a moment's hesitation, rummaged through the room, and found a pair of pants, a shirt, and a jacket of Kannor's.

He took them down to the fireplace room and rolled Kesha onto her back. He didn't know how bad her injuries were or what he would have to do to bring her back to consciousness.

She jolted wide awake the minute he rolled her over. She started to yell out before he covered her mouth. "Be quiet, Kesha!" he whispered. "It's me! It's Kuvik! I'm here to get you free, but you have to be quiet! I can't free you until you promise to be quiet."

She nodded fast and bit her lip to hold back emotion while he cut all her ropes. She sat up and pulled her knees against her chest to hide her body.

"I brought you some clothes," Kuvik whispered. "They're Kannor's, so they'll be too big, but you can't leave the village like that. Don't worry. He's dead. He won't come after us. I need you to get dressed and go through the village to free everyone else. Can you do that? Are you too injured? I can carry you out if I have to."

She shook her head.

He pushed one of Zori's knives into her hand. "Try to hurry. We don't have much time. Bring everyone to the weapons storehouse. I'll meet you there. Okay?"

She nodded again. He would have liked to take more time to help her, but he couldn't. Time was of the essence.

Chapter 24

K uvik snuck back outside of Kannor's house and set off for the weapons storehouse. He had to hide from another patrol and decided to eliminate that one, too. The more Bounty Hunters he eliminated, the fewer men they would be able to send after the fugitives.

He hid behind a different house, grabbed one of the men when he walked past, slit the guy's throat, and his comrade immediately came after Kuvik. The guy should have raised the alarm when he had the chance. Kuvik killed him, too, and hid them in a dark corner.

He got to the weapons storehouse just as Nelv showed up with Garvis and Phiri. "Akli is still out there freeing people," Phiri informed Kuvik.

Kuvik nodded and turned to the weapons storehouse. The Bounty Hunters had no way to secure it from the outside, so he had no trouble cutting the rope around the latch and letting himself in.

"None of you has any weapons training, do you?" he asked over his shoulder.

"No," Garvis replied. "Does that mean we don't get weapons?"

Kuvik pulled out a bunch of different blades and armed the three men. "I want you three to go through the village and hide in the dark undergrowth in the jungle over there behind that house. Do you see? Go over there and wait for me. Don't show yourselves no matter what."

"What if something goes wrong and you don't come?" Phiri asked.

"Then I want you to climb up into the trees as high as you can go and stay there. Stay hidden and stay silent no matter what. Now go. No more questions."

He sent them away just as a crowd of people showed up from Akli's cellar. All of these people had been tied up in the stalls near him.

Kuvik held his finger to his lips, armed everyone, and gave them the same whispered message. He sent them out into the jungle to join up with the three men.

Kesha showed up next. Her people kept quiet—as quiet as they could. She brought four mothers with young children. Three of them had to hold their hands over their babies' mouths to stifle the little ones' screams.

None of these mothers had their hands free and they didn't know how to fight anyway. Kuvik armed everyone else and even a few of the older children. He whispered to Kesha where to take everyone and sent them on their way.

Then Kuvik loaded himself with as many weapons as he could carry. His heart soared when he found his jawbone kukris and his shoulder bags in the pile. They happened to be near the top. The Bounty Hunters had captured him the most recently.

He hefted his kukris in his hands. The Bounty Hunters had even kept the four extra kukris that Dana had stolen from him during her betrayal. Now he had them back.

These were the weapons he would use to kill these bastards. These kukris thirsted for the taste of Bounty Hunter blood.

He stuck the tooth back into his pocket and pulled out one of his tooth knives—one of the teeth he'd already attached handles to. He could use this much more easily.

He went outside and listened for the approaching patrols. They entered the village from opposite ends. He probably should have run for it while he had the chance, but he just couldn't walk away from his enemies when he had them in his clutches.

He put all his weapons down in a corner, took his one tooth knife, and retreated to the far end of the village where patrols always entered from that side.

He ambushed the first patrol in the same way as the others, dragged the bodies into the undergrowth, and hid to wait for the next patrol. He eliminated all six of them and left the village sleeping peacefully.

Now would have been the perfect time to set fire to every house, but he decided against it. Some of these houses had children sleeping in them, not to mention slaves who didn't want to escape.

He left them alone, retrieved his stash of weapons, and met up with his group in the undergrowth. He didn't stop there to explain anything. He motioned for them to follow him and headed off deeper into the jungle.

His one thought was to get the mothers with babies as far away from the village as possible before one of them made any noise. He drove the whole group much faster than he normally would have. He kept them moving until dawn before he stopped.

He turned to face them and addressed them in a normal voice. They didn't have to whisper anymore.

"We're going to climb up into the trees and hide there. Any of you with your hands free, start climbing. You need to learn now and get used to doing it a lot. We're going to start traveling the Godless way. It's much safer than traveling on the ground. The Bounty Hunters won't come for us here."

Dorei's mother glanced over her shoulder toward the village. "What will we do if the Bounty Hunters come after us?"

"I'm certain they will come after us eventually. They won't be able to get to us if we're in the trees even if they find us. Now start climbing. Find a way to tie your weapons to your bodies or sling them over your shoulders like this. Keep both hands free."

"What about us?" one of the mothers asked.

Kuvik turned to them next. Two of the four babies had passed out during the night. One of the others sat on his mother's hip. She had to hold onto him. The other mother propped her infant daughter on her shoulder and bounced her up and down.

Kuvik thought fast, emptied his bags into each other, and gave two of the empty bags to the two mothers whose children were already asleep. They maneuvered their babies into the bags, hung them over their shoulders, and started climbing, too.

Kuvik dealt easily with the mother with the boy sitting on her hip. Kuvik got some vines from the jungle, tied them into a loose, sloppy net, wrapped it around the mother's body, and tied the boy on so the mother could use her arms.

Kuvik used one of his bags for the tiny little girl, too. She started fussing when her mother took her off her shoulder, but the little one stopped making any noise and stared around her in wonder when her mother started climbing. The motion soothed the baby.

Kuvik had to show everyone how to find comfortable spots for themselves in the canopy. He positioned each person in the secure fork of branches or anywhere else they could relax.

"Now what do we do?" Akli asked.

"Now we hide from the Bounty Hunters," Kuvik replied. "We can talk until we hear them coming. Then we need to keep silent until they leave. They won't find us and they'll eventually get tired of searching for us."

"So we're going to stay here the whole time?" Kesha asked.

"No, not the whole time. We're going to stay here until all of you are ready to travel through the branches."

"What does that mean?" Garvis asked. "How can we travel through the branches? We would have to go down to the ground to travel."

"We travel through the branches like this." Kuvik stood up and balanced along the branches. He moved from one side of their tree camp all the way to the other. He could have kept going, but he stopped there and came back. "The Godless do it all the time. It's faster and safer than traveling on the ground."

"I've never heard of that," Akli exclaimed.

"None of you has lived with the Godless, have you?" Kuvik cocked his head to listen to the jungle noises. "Some of us will have to keep watch for night creatures."

Kesha glanced around. "Are you sure about this? Won't the Bounty Hunters come after us if we stay here?"

"No more than if we travel on the ground," Kuvik replied. "They'll come after us more on the ground because we'll be more vulnerable. Anyway, any creature that attacks us we can use for food."

Garvis gasped. "How would we do that?"

"We would kill it to protect ourselves, wouldn't we? Why would we waste that perfectly good food if the animal is already dead?"

"But....how would we cook it up here?" Phiri asked.

Kuvik shrugged. "That's the tricky part. Some of us would have to go down to the ground, but we would have to do that to get food anyway."

One little boy about four years old started crying. "I'm scared!" he whimpered. "I want to go back to the village!"

"The sun will rise soon and then the jungle won't be so scary," Kuvik told him, but he saw all the rest of his people having the same problem. None of them had ever spent time in the jungle—not without the Bounty Hunters taking care of them.

He had escaped with thirty people. Four of them were the mothers with the four babies. Another five were mothers with children ranging in age from three all the way up to older teenagers.

Kuvik's mind went into a tailspin when he realized what he'd just done. This was what Hangman had been dealing with—for years. He'd traveled across country with babies and helpless pregnant women. He'd battled his enemies to protect them.

Kuvik turned his head away. He would have liked to cover his face when he finally realized the gargantuan task in front of him. This was going to be a thousand times harder than anything Hangman had ever faced. He had armed men to help him.

He had left home with his brother and two cousins. Even the three of them alone had been better than only one man. None of these people sitting in front of Kuvik right now knew how to use a weapon. That was the awful truth.

Then Red had joined Hangman's band and all the men had worked together—but before that happened, Hangman had recruited Hammer and his men. They had only been boys then.

Kuvik had to do something like that. He had to take it even further—and he had to do it now.

The babies woke back up. The mothers had to soothe their children and stop them from crying, but they could do it more easily, now that everyone was more comfortable. He had to unwind the net from around the little boy so his mother could hold him.

"As soon as we make our first kill, I'll make each of you a wrap so you can carry your children using only one arm," he told the mothers. "You'll have one arm free to climb and balance in the branches, so you'll need to learn to do that."

"Just tell us what to do," one of them told him. "We'll do whatever it takes so we don't have to go back."

A bunch of other people nodded.

Kuvik turned to all the men, teenage boys, and even some of the other younger boys. "All of you will need to learn to hunt and fight—and you need to learn fast. I can't protect all of you by myself. I need all of you to help me."

"We'll fight anyone you want us to fight, Kuvik," Akli replied. "We'll kill any Bounty Hunters who come after us."

"The problem with that is that none of you knows how to fight," Kuvik returned. "You told me yourself you would have gotten away a long time ago if you had only known how to fight. We'll travel farther away from the village and then you all need to start practicing. You'll practice fighting each other and you'll practice hunting—both to provide food for the band and to protect the band from creatures."

The others glanced at each other. "Are we a band now?" Garvis asked.

"We're as good as a band, so we might as well start calling ourselves one and operating as one. We aren't anything else."

"That makes you our Kral," a different boy replied. He must have been about twelve.

Kuvik's first instinct told him to deny it and say he wasn't the Kral to any band, but he changed his mind. "It would be an honor for me to be your Kral," he told them. "If we do this, you would have to follow my leadership as your Kral and I would have the final decision on what we do and how we do it. Do you all agree to that?"

More people nodded. Akli said, "Yes, of course, Kuvik. We all want that. We want you to tell us what to do."

Kuvik gave him a hard look and then scrutinized the other men and younger boys. "Do you all agree to that? Do you all agree to follow my leadership and answer to me as your Kral?"

"We want that," Phiri replied. "You're already in charge of us. You've already brought us further than anyone else ever could."

"Then my first decision would be to turn this into a Godless band," Kuvik went on. "I've never met any stronger, kinder, more powerful people anywhere. They're the best people I've ever met. I would turn all of us Godless. That means we would initiate into the Godless and run this band the Godless way."

"What does that mean?" Nelv asked.

"It means we would initiate boys into manhood at the age of fourteen. We would send your young people to the gatherings to marry at the age of gathering. We would travel until we meet up with another band of Godless....."

"Why would we meet up with another band of Godless?" Kesha asked. "Why can't we just run our band the way we are?"

Kuvik took a deep breath. "We can't do that because I'm not Godless. I haven't initiated into the Clan—which means I'm not qualified to initiate any of the rest of you. We would need a group of initiated Godless to initiate me and probably a bunch of you—which means you all have a long way to go to learn how to fight and hunt before you can initiate."

"What is required for us to initiate?" Akli asked. "Is it difficult?"

"You have to fight a creature—and it has to be a creature that's dangerous enough to test your courage and skill in front of the other men. You can't choose something easy that you're certain to beat. The other men will call you a coward. Your initiation is your chance to prove your worth and win the respect of other men."

"What about us?" Kesha asked. "Do the women have initiations?"

"No, nothing like that, but they all learn how to hunt and fight. I knew a woman who married into the Godless from the Follower Clan. She had never even held a weapon before she got married. She spent a long time struggling to learn how to defend herself just so she could walk to the stream for water without getting killed. It was hard, but she did it and she became one of the bravest women I've ever known. All of you could be like that. You could be strong, brave, fierce, independent people that anyone would tremble to confront you. Imagine that."

"That's what I want," Phiri murmured.

"Me, too," Garvis added. "I'm doing it."

"Then start preparing yourselves to fight," Kuvik replied. "The Bounty Hunters will come after us. It's only a matter of time. Your courage and ferocity will take you a long way, but you do need skills."

He barely got the words out before the party heard voices in the distance. Kuvik's group fell into a tense silence as Bounty Hunters swarmed out of the jungle coming from the village. They flooded the area searching everywhere.

No one in the treetops made a sound. The dark canopy hid everyone. None of the babies made a sound, either.

The Bounty Hunters kept going and eventually passed the spot. They traveled a long way into the jungle before they came back and returned to the village.

Kuvik followed them with his ears and became aware of everyone else doing the same thing. These people might not have learned to fight and hunt, but their mistreatment made them overly watchful and sensitive to any danger.

No one had to teach them how to listen for the sound of their enemies coming closer. Kuvik just needed to teach these people how to recognize the jungle sounds.

"Everyone settle down and try to get some rest before daylight," he told the group after the Bounty Hunters left. "We won't go anywhere before morning."

"I'm hungry," a little girl complained. Her mother immediately told her to be quiet and that going hungry for a little while was better than going back to the village.

The girl didn't answer, but those words told Kuvik all he needed to know. These people needed food. They needed water. They needed protection—and most of all they needed survival skills—the one most crucial thing they didn't have.

He had certainly bitten off more than he could chew with this one. He had a massive job in front of him and all the odds stacked against him.

Chapter 25

The sun rose on the high canopy and the jungle warmed up. The light and heat woke up the freed slaves of Kuvik's band. He really needed to find some other word to use for them. They weren't slaves—not anymore.

The morning sunshine shone a spotlight on all the glaring problems he had faced last night. Now he had no choice but to confront them.

"Everyone stand up," he announced. "If you have both hands free, you can start moving through the branches heading that way." He pointed south—away from the village. "You can slow down when you get out of sight of us. Then wait for everyone else to catch up and move on as a group. Don't stop traveling until sunset."

The freed captives moved off through the branches. They traveled slowly at first the way Kuvik expected them to. The children took to the branches much faster than anyone else.

The adults didn't climb too badly, either. They got used to it and sped up the longer they kept doing it. The four mothers stayed behind. So did Kesha. She seemed to have stationed herself as a guard over these mothers.

"You three put your children in your bags," Kuvik told the three mothers with bags. "You—wrap the net around yourself."

"I don't know how," the woman with the net replied.

"Then you better learn," Kuvik countered.

Kesha stepped forward. "I'll help you."

"No, you won't," Kuvik snapped and turned back to the mother.

She wasn't that old. She couldn't have been more than twenty-five. She was also extremely undernourished and badly beaten like everyone else in the group.

"What's your name?" Kuvik asked.

The woman gulped in front of him. Her voice trembled when she tried to speak. "Balea...." She choked. "Please don't leave me behind. I don't want my son to grow up with the Bounty Hunters."

"No one is going to leave you behind." Kuvik turned to the other mothers. "No one is going to leave any of you behind. I swear it. You just need to learn to do things for yourselves. What will you do if the men and I are out fighting the Bounty Hunters and some creature comes out and attacks you? You have to be able to defend your children." He turned back to Balea. "And you would need to bind up your son by yourself so you could use your hands to fight the creature off. You wouldn't want to leave him on the ground—and you couldn't put him down if you were in the branches. This is not that hard. All you have to do is wrap the net around yourself and him to tie him around your body. Just do exactly what I did yesterday. Go on. Do it."

"Leave her alone, Kuvik," Kesha interjected.

He turned on her. "Did you hear me before? I told everyone with two hands free to start moving through the branches. Now go on and do it. You accepted me as your Kral. Now go. This doesn't concern you."

She walked away and started moving through the branches with the other mothers. They moved slowly at first, but they eventually got farther and farther away. Kuvik stayed behind with Balea.

She swallowed hard, sat her son on her hip, and held onto him with one arm while she picked up the net. She had to find a way to wrap it around herself without holding onto the branches with her free hand.

She eventually sat all the way down, straddled the thick branch under her, and held on with her legs while she wrapped the net around her, pulled it tight, and tied it.

"You see? That wasn't so hard, was it?" Kuvik asked once she stood up. She had tied the net tightly enough so she could use both hands. Her son actually seemed to enjoy this. He smiled up at Kuvik.

Balea stared at the boy and then all around her. "I.....I don't know what's wrong with me...."

"What's wrong with you is that you just escaped from captivity where you never had to do anything. Learning these things is hard and it takes a long time. I lived with the Godless for five years. That's how I learned and you will, too. Now let's go. I'll stay with you so you don't fall behind."

She set off through the branches. She overtook the other mothers in no time, now that she could use both hands.

The others had adjusted their bags in different ways. One of the mothers with an older boy had sat her son upright so he could look around. Kuvik stopped them all to change the way they carried their children.

He tied up the bag with the infant girl in it so she rode right against her mother's chest. The woman wrapped one arm around the bundle and climbed with the other.

Kuvik changed the configuration with the sitting-up little boy so the bag hung on the mother's back. The boy sat upright and looked over his mother's shoulder. She could climb with both hands free.

The fourth mother had already arranged the bag in a similar position on the front of her chest. Kuvik tied it tighter and showed all three of them how to do it for themselves.

He stayed with all four mothers after that. He became aware of Kesha watching him like a hawk, but she never interjected or contradicted again. She traveled with him when he and the mothers set off south on their journey.

They overtook the rest of the band resting in the branches. "Should we travel together from now on?" Phiri asked.

"No," Kuvik replied. "I want all of you to travel as quickly as you can. You children should be able to travel very fast if you try. I want you to practice traveling as fast as you can. Godless warriors can run faster through the branches than they can on the ground. I want you all to get like that. If you get too far ahead, practice some more by coming back and finding us—and practice moving quietly. I could hear you all the way back there."

Some of his people laughed. They all set off again. Kuvik started to get extremely thirsty, so he called a halt in the canopy over a stream that evening.

He used some of his stolen weapons to hack branches from the surrounding foliage and started teaching everyone how to carve cups, bowls, and other utensils from the branches.

He spent hours explaining about leaf paste and Gooji sap. Some of the freed captives already knew about them, but none of these people knew how to find the leaves or the sap.

He used their utensils to bring up water from the stream. They all felt better after they drank some water.

Kuvik got to his feet and surveyed the jungle. "I think I better go hunting. We won't be able to keep traveling if we don't eat—especially not these children."

"What should we do if creatures come after us while you aren't here?" Garvis asked.

Kuvik opened his mouth to answer. He didn't have a good idea about what to say and what not to say. He hadn't thought that far in advance.

Going hunting by himself would mean leaving these people completely defenseless. They could wind up dead much quicker out here by themselves than they would have in the Bounty Hunter village.

A shriek cut him off before he could say anything. He looked up into the sky and saw a large male Ridgebeak diving straight for the party. One of the younger girls looked up toward the sound, too. She screamed when she saw the Ridgebeak.

Kuvik leapt off his branch. "All of you stay exactly where you are!" he ordered. "Don't move or you could all die! I want you all to watch this very carefully. Consider this your first lesson in how to hunt for your food."

Kesha started to stand up. "What are you going to do?"

He pointed at her and snapped a lot louder than he intended to. "Sit down and don't move!"

She shrank from him and sat back down. He didn't have a moment to lose.

He sprang across five branches to where Balea sat with her son. She'd taken the net off so she could sit him on her lap.

Kuvik snatched the net just in time, dove out of the way, and took shelter under a cluster of branches. He pulled one of his jawbone kukris, but he needed both hands free to catch the Ridgebeak.

He wasn't as strong as he had been with the Godless. He would have to be careful and execute this kill perfectly or he would be a dead man. He would become the Ridgebeak's meal instead of the other way around.

The Ridgebeak dove. The canopy thinned right there to give the giant bird just enough of a view of the people sitting in the branches. The Godless never would have made a mistake like that. Kuvik must be out of practice from staying away so long.

He didn't have the luxury of failure this time. He clamped the thin back ridge of his kukri between his teeth and took hold of the net with both hands. The bird's shadow blocked out the sun.

He tensed every muscle, waited for the bird to plunge through the branches, and the creature extended its talons to seize its prey.

It went after Akli. Akli raised a weapon, but he didn't react fast enough.

Kuvik dove off his branch, flung all his weight at the Ridgebeak, and spread both arms. He didn't try to tackle the bird's body, wings, or head. He aimed for its feet.

He widened the net to cover as much of the talons as possible and then closed his arms to wrap the net around them. The momentum of his jump pulled the talons together.

He almost collided with Akli, bounced off the branch next to where Akli sat, and Kuvik tumbled off into open space two hundred feet above the ground.

His weight plummeted and yanked the bird right out of thin air. Kuvik plunged downward through the canopy pulling the bird with him. The Ridgebeak was a lot bigger and slammed against dozens of branches.

The force of its fall and Kuvik's weight dragging it down shattered the bird's bones. The bird screeched its head off, but the surrounding branches stopped it from flexing its wings and taking fight again. It couldn't get away.

Each blow injured the bird more and made it less and less able to fight back. Kuvik held onto the net for dear life. These crashes broke his fall and saved him from smashing to his death.

The thicker branches ended fifty feet from the ground. He saw the ground coming closer, swung off, and let go in an arc. He landed on a nearby branch and let the injured Ridgebeak hurtle past him.

He jumped as soon as it passed his branch. The bird slammed into the ground and he landed on top of it.

He didn't hesitate for an instant, scrambled over its body to straddle the bird's neck, and bludgeoned it in the skull with his kukri. He struck five times in rapid succession until the bird flopped twitching on the ground.

Chapter 26

Kuvik toppled off the Ridgebeak's dead body, sprawled in the dirt, and crawled away to catch his breath. That fight cost him a lot more strength than he could afford to spend.

He didn't realize just how weak he was. He really needed to get his strength back—and that meant he needed food.

He slumped at the base of a tree gasping and wheezing. He lay there for what felt like a long time before he dragged himself to his feet. Now he had to butcher this creature.

He surveyed the jungle around him. The noise and smell of blood would attract other creatures. He would need help to defend his kill while he cooked it and cured the leftovers for travel—if this group left any leftovers.

He glanced up. Every member of his band stared at him from the branches above his head. Maybe now they would start to realize what it took to survive out here. They all better put their helplessness aside real quick.

He waved up at them and beckoned them down to the ground. They took a long time to climb down. Even those who had been traveling easily through the canopy found it much harder to climb down. They had to look at the ground.

He decided not to tell them about the Godless jumping from that height, grabbing and swinging from branches to slow their falls, and even bending saplings over from that height to swing down to the ground.

His people all assembled on the ground.

"That was incredible, Kuvik," the twelve-year-old boy exclaimed.

"Thank you, little brother," Kuvik replied. "You'll be doing it yourself before you know it."

"How did you learn to do that?" Akli asked.

"I learned exactly the way you just did. I learned by watching other people do it. The Godless men I know do things like that all the time. It's the only way to combat these creatures. Now you're all going to work together as a band, build a fire, butcher this Ridgebeak, and start cooking it for our food." Kuvik made a snap decision. "Akli, I want you, Phiri, Garvis, and Nelv to stand guard around the camp with your weapons ready. I want you all to keep watch and be ready to defend the band against any creatures that come. The rest of you get to work. We're all hungry and we don't want the blood to attract the creatures."

Everyone got to work. The mothers with older children gave their young ones to the girls to take care of.

The group talked much more excitedly that night. Kuvik didn't have the heart to tell them to be quiet. This was the first time they'd got a chance to enjoy their new freedom. They deserved it.

They acted much more like a band and a lot less like a bunch of beaten-down slaves. They actually didn't act like slaves at all.

He pretended not to notice Kesha slipping away from the group. She vanished down the stream and came back an hour later with her clothes and hair soaking wet. She had washed all the dried blood and muck off herself from before her escape.

She caught Kuvik watching her and she didn't look away. Neither did he. He didn't regret that he had been the one who found her Kannor's house. He wasn't the only one who understood what had happened to her there.

He spent the rest of the evening lounging by the fire and letting everyone else do the work for a change. He talked the whole evening and late into the night about Godless ways and how they did everything. His people drank in every word.

The children started to copy how he described Godless children behaving. Some of them started to practice swinging their weapons at trees, branches, and insects. Kuvik had to replace these weapons with sticks so the children wouldn't hurt themselves or each other.

Even some of the men and younger women tried to practice fighting each other. Kuvik gave them as many tips and lessons as he could.

Everyone ate a lot that night. They ate as much as they could possibly hold—and he turned out to be right. They left not a single scrap of meat on the Ridgebeak's bones. The band had nothing left over to take with them.

That didn't matter because everyone went to sleep much happier that night. He made them all climb into the branches first. He didn't let anyone sleep on the ground.

He took the Ridgebeak's hide, talons, and a bunch of different bones with him. He chopped out the Ridgebeak's skull, scooped out the brain, burned off all the skin and tissue in the flames, and used the skull as a bowl.

He selected different bones to make into tools and weapons later. The children bombarded him with questions about what he was doing and why. Then they bombarded him with questions about how he would turn the creature's bones into tools and weapons.

Everyone settled on the branches in the dark. Silver moonlight shone down from above and gave enough light for everyone to see each other and the surrounding jungle.

Dorei's mother wound up sitting next to Kuvik. He'd found out from listening to other people talk that her name was Linnoth.

"Thank you for tonight, Kuvik," she murmured. "I would gladly die after tonight. It was all I ever dreamed about the whole time I was a slave."

"Yeah," Akli breathed. "Tonight makes it all worth it."

"None of us is ever going back," Kuvik replied. "Not ever. You're all going to learn to fight and we'll take out any Bounty Hunters who come to recapture us."

"Why do you think they haven't come yet?" Kesha asked.

"I killed some of them before I left," Kuvik replied. "I didn't kill enough to make a difference, but....." He hesitated.

"Tell us everything," Akli insisted. "We deserve to know the truth."

"If you really want to know what I think, I think they're amassing an overwhelming force to hunt us down," Kuvik replied. "I think they want to make sure we don't get away with this. They want payback for the men I killed—and a few other people. They want to make sure they bring enough people—which means we have to be ready for that."

"How do we get ready to fight an overwhelming force?" Garvis asked.

"I've already told you. We use unconventional fighting methods—or methods that are unconventional to the Bounty Hunters. They don't fight in the trees. They don't do anything in the trees. The trees aren't part of their fighting landscape. That makes the trees our one advantage. The quicker you all get up to speed on how to use the trees, the better our chances of victory."

"Victory?" Nelv asked. "You really think we can win—us—against the Bounty Hunters?"

"Of course we can win," Kuvik countered. "What does winning mean? It means we got away. It means we live in freedom for the rest of our lives without ever going back to the Bounty Hunters, either now or later. We can do that easily. All we have to do is stop them from retaking us."

"Something tells me it won't be as easy as that," Phiri remarked.

Kuvik stiffened and looked around at those nearest him. "Will you listen to yourselves? You're talking like you're already defeated. You can't think like that. We have tools at our disposal that are much stronger than anything the Bounty Hunters have. We have allies and weapons and advantages that leave them in the dust."

"What allies, weapons, and advantages are those?" Kesha asked. "They know how to fight. We don't."

"We have the whole jungle," Kuvik fired back. "Will you listen to me? The jungle is our most powerful weapon. We don't need to fight the Bounty Hunters because the jungle will do it for us. We can use the jungle against them. Do you think the Bounty Hunters can fight Krakelows?"

"What's a Krakelow?" Balea asked.

Kuvik came dangerously close to losing his temper right then, but like magic, he actually heard a Krakelow coming toward the party through the branches.

The sound sent a prickle across his scalp—and then he heard Bounty Hunters coming closer. Kuvik got to his feet. "This is your next lesson. I want you all to watch me very, very carefully. Don't move and don't make a sound. Stay where you are. I'm going to use the jungle to kill those Bounty Hunters. Just watch."

He left everyone sitting in the branches, climbed away from them, and positioned himself up and to the side of the rest of his band.

The Bounty Hunters made a lot of noise coming through the jungle. They announced their arrival long before they got near the band.

The Bounty Hunters must have had a way to track the escaped fugitives—either that or some of their men had been searching the area and maybe heard the girl's scream earlier.

He didn't think the Bounty Hunters were versed enough in the jungle's ways to recognize a diving Ridgebeak. The Bounty Hunters wouldn't have put the puzzle pieces together that the Ridgebeak must have been going after prey in the treetops.

The Krakelow kept getting closer at the same time. It approached from a different direction heading for the people crouched in the branches. Any Godless would have moved out of the creature's way to avoid the inevitable confrontation.

Kuvik didn't tell anyone to move. The Krakelow and the Bounty Hunters converged on the band, but the Bounty Hunters got there first. They found the remains of the fire, the Ridgebeak carcass, and all the signs of the hours the band had spent on the ground.

The Bounty Hunters even found marks on the trees to indicate that the band had climbed up into the branches for the night.

The Bounty Hunters walked around on the ground talking about everything and speculating how to get the escaped fugitives out of the trees. Kuvik decided to bait the trap a little more by jumping up and down on his branch to rustle the leaves.

His actions sent the Bounty Hunters into a frenzy. They paced around faster, talked louder, and called their friends to come to the spot. They talked in rushed, animated bursts about how they had trapped the escaped slaves in these trees.

The Bounty Hunters thought the slaves couldn't get away without coming down to the ground. The Bounty Hunters thought they could camp out on the ground right there and ambush the band when they came down for food or water.

The Krakelow's scales scratched on bark. The sound kept getting closer. The creature picked up speed coming faster and faster to fling itself at the party. One Krakelow could wipe out the whole group in a matter of minutes.

Kuvik retreated to a different set of branches, pulled one of his kukris, and took a fresh grip on it while he counted down the seconds.

The Krakelow launched itself out of the branches, coiled its long body, and whistled through the air heading straight for the spot where the band crouched in hiding.

Kuvik jumped off his branch, sailed through the air, and dropped in a downward arc to intercept the creature. He hacked his kukri across the middle of the Krakelow's back. The Demonex teeth on the inner surface of the jawbone cleaved the Krakelow in half.

Cutting a Krakelow in half made it more dangerous—not less so. That one blow knocked the Krakelow out of the air and it fell straight downward right into the middle of the Bounty Hunters.

The Krakelow landed on top of five Bounty Hunters, enveloped them instantly, shattered into dozens of segments, and all the segments streaked outward to attack all the other Bounty Hunters in the area.

They screamed, bellowed, and tried to get away. The segments pulled down a dozen more men. Only a handful got away. They left more than seventeen bodies on the ground at the base of the tree.

Kuvik watched before he retreated back to the band's hiding place. "We'll need to leave here in the morning," he announced. "The bodies will attract creatures and more Bounty Hunters. They'll find out we camped here. We need to move before they find us again."

Chapter 27

Kuvik balanced in the branches and watched his people getting farther and farther ahead. They traveled faster by the day, but they still didn't travel as fast as Godless. These people had a long way to go.

Everyone with their hands free practiced fighting each other whenever possible. They also practiced fighting small creatures whenever one presented itself.

Kuvik had taught his people how to kill almost everything, but he hadn't gotten around to teaching them about Gorlocks and Crushers yet. He decided to save that one until next year at the earliest.

He cast a glance behind the party. They'd been traveling southward for a week and kept encountering continuous Bounty Hunter patrols coming after the fugitives.

The Bounty Hunters already knew by now that the escaped captives were heading south. Kuvik had been able to reduce these patrols and send them running home by ambushing them with creatures and other dangers.

He'd even lured an army of ants into the Bounty Hunters' path and left none of them alive. The Bounty Hunters always sent more patrols to follow. They never broke off the search entirely the way he hoped they would.

How long would they keep following? He couldn't lead the Bounty Hunters to any other Godless band—or any other band from any other Clan. That wouldn't be right.

He no longer worried about his people being able to take care of any creatures they met in the canopy. He'd taught his people to use their hearing to avoid creatures like Krakelows and to keep an eye on the skies for Ridgebeaks and Boultars.

An uneasy feeling made him hang back and let them move ahead of him. He didn't recognize what caused that feeling. He would have been able to handle any other Bounty Hunter patrols that came along.

His old idea about the Bounty Hunters sending a much larger force—that idea never really went away. Why else would they delay for so long before coming after the band?

The Bounty Hunters would have been hellbent on either killing or recapturing this band. The Bounty Hunters would consider it a matter of honor and reputation that they not let any captives get away.

The Bounty Hunters would have been even more zealous about retaking and making an example of such a large group of captives who attempted to escape—especially a group that had left so many dead Bounty Hunters.

Kuvik had stuck it to them by killing those men. He had known he was sticking it to them at the time and he did it anyway. Now the survivors would have to retaliate and try to make the whole band pay for it.

A different sound drifted out of the northern jungle. That's what gave him the uneasy feeling. He didn't recognize that sound.

He set off running through the branches. He hadn't traveled this fast while he had been traveling with his band. He only ran like this when he went off alone to scout the surrounding countryside.

He retraced the band's route for twenty miles before he stopped in the high branches. He saw something moving in the distance to the north. He recognized it the instant he saw it, but he stayed where he was to confirm it.

The Bounty Hunter force he'd predicted moved through the trees, emerged for a few minutes—just long enough for him to see how big it was—and then vanished into the dense jungle again. There could be no question. They were coming.

He turned around and took off running his fastest back to his band. He had to think. He had to come up with a strategy for dealing with the Bounty Hunters. He would have to rely on his men. That was the bottom line. It no longer mattered if they were ready or not.

He overtook the band in an hour. They didn't move fast enough to outpace him. He wasn't sure anymore if they moved fast enough to outpace the Bounty Hunters.

The Bounty Hunters had brought only fighting men. They could travel day and night. They could send one party ahead while the other slept and leapfrog over each other to catch up with the escaped captives.

Kuvik dropped out of the branches in front of the band and everyone stopped in front of him. He saw in their faces that they already knew something was wrong.

"They're coming," he blurted out. "The overwhelming Bounty Hunter force I told you about is coming. They're heading south right now coming straight for us."

He held up his hand to stop anyone from asking questions at a time like this.

"All the women and children—keep heading south exactly the way you have been—but try to pick up the pace. Try to travel faster to put more distance between yourselves and the Bounty Hunters. Don't risk yourselves by traveling faster than you can move safely. Just move with a little more urgency. You men—and you boys—you come with me. We have some work to do."

"What about the rest of us women?" Kesha asked. "We want to fight the Bounty Hunters, too."

"If you want to fight, you can defend the weaker women and children who can't defend themselves," Kuvik replied. "The women and children need guards around the clock. The men and I won't be able to do it. I'm relying on you to do it. That's more important—and you might need to hunt for them if we get separated." He turned to the others. "Let's go. You all know what to do."

The two parties separated. Kesha and the other women closed the mothers and children in a guarding posture and vanished heading south.

Kuvik stayed behind with ten men and four teenage boys. They had all discussed at length what booby traps and creatures they could use to ambush the Bounty Hunters.

Krakelows and ants were the most obvious choice, but luring the creatures into the Bounty Hunters' path was the hardest part—and the most dangerous to the men as much as to the enemy.

Kuvik didn't want to take the time to lure creatures here. It made more sense to use creatures that were already here. He and his men set off along the track to intercept the Bounty Hunters. They made it easy to find them.

Kuvik pointed out dozens of spots along the way where he and his men could ambush their enemies. He left certain men and certain boys at strategic intervals along the way to spring these traps one after the other when the Bounty Hunters came within range.

Kuvik made it to within a dozen miles of the forwardmost Bounty Hunters, gave a few last-minute instructions to his men, and dropped out of the branches.

He landed on the ground between the trees where he knew the Bounty Hunters would come right up to him. He stood there waiting. He didn't draw his weapons.

A faint rustle overhead told him when his men retreated out of the area on the same track. He puffed out his cheeks in a deep sigh. He was going to enjoy this. He would enjoy any activity that involved killing Bounty Hunters—especially in large numbers.

They walked right up to him. Some of the Bounty Hunters in the front of their army didn't realize at first that he was even there. Others did and got their friends' attention to point him out to them. The Bounty Hunters stopped and stared at him.

"Remember me?" he yelled out to them. "I'm the one who killed all your men. I killed Kannor and his wife. I killed everyone who died that night. I'm the one who stole your slaves and I'm the one who will lead them to freedom."

His words produced exactly the effect he wanted them to. The Bounty Hunters bellowed in rage and charged him. He turned and ran for it.

He could run a lot faster now than when he had been their prisoner. He'd been eating well, running a lot, and he didn't have any injuries this time.

The Bounty Hunters weren't used to running long distances. He didn't want them to tire out, so he dodged sideways into the trees, headed to the right, and started to slow down.

The Bounty Hunters saw themselves closing in on him. They doubled down and ran faster to try to catch him. He didn't speed up. He actually slowed down more, which caused them to put on a fresh burst of speed.

He did this time and again until he decided that they couldn't run any faster. At the last second, he burst through a cluster of bushes and launched himself into the branches.

The Bounty Hunters rushed through the undergrowth right behind him and blundered straight into a Cursed Sand pit.

Those running behind followed too fast to stop themselves. Dozens of them fell in and fell on top of each other until they filled the pit all the way to the top.

The creature at the bottom went crazy slashing, killing, pulling men down into its den, and grabbing those on top to do the same thing.

The Bounty Hunters panicked and stepped on top of each other trying to climb out. They wound up pushing each other down harder and prevented their comrades underneath from getting out.

The creature realized just how many victims had actually fallen into its hole. The creature kept escalating its efforts and yanking men down one after the other killing faster and faster.

The creature wound up killing almost forty men before those at the edge of the pit stopped rushing into the area. They dragged a handful of men out of the hole in time to save their lives. The rest went down and didn't come out.

Kuvik watched from the treetops and waited for the noise to die down. Then he cupped his hands around his mouth to amplify his voice and laughed extra loudly to get the Bounty Hunters' attention.

"Ha ha! You pathetic idiots!" he crowed. "Keep coming after me! You'll all die out here! I'm going to kill every last one of you! You will never lay a finger on me or my people ever again! Come on, you gutless cowards! Come and get me!"

He took off running his fastest through the branches. He didn't look back—not for a few minutes at least. He headed back to the original line of travel where he'd left his men.

He checked behind him after ten minutes and saw exactly what he expected to see. The Bounty Hunters gave chase—and they did it at a run this time.

They traced his movements through the branches, pointed upward to tell each other where he was, and dogged him all the way back to his friends.

He laughed when he passed Phiri. Phiri did a double take. "What are you doing?!"

Kuvik couldn't help but laugh. "They're coming! Get ready! Now's your chance to throw all that Follower education away for good. Now you get to kill some people."

He kept running for another hundred yards. The Bounty Hunters ran with their faces pointed up at the sky. They didn't look where they were going—not that it would have helped them if they did.

They ran right under the branches where Phiri sat waiting for them. He balanced on one branch and held himself in place by wrapping his leg around an upright limb to hold himself steady.

He spotted the Bounty Hunters coming, swung a large metal axe Kuvik had stolen from the Bounty Hunters' weapons storehouse, and hacked the huge blade into a different branch.

It shattered instantly. The outer bark surrounded no solid wood underneath. The branch cracked, plummeted toward the jungle floor, and a massive torrent of Abnormits and thousands of larvae spilled out onto the ground.

They rained all over the Bounty Hunters, smothered dozens of them, and the Abnormits immediately started eating their way through the whole force. Screams echoed out of the sea of Abnormits.

The creatures brought the Bounty Hunters to a standstill. Those in the back far enough away to escape the Abnormits turned and ran away to the north. They didn't stop until they regrouped ten miles away from the spot.

Kuvik climbed down the branches and stopped next to Phiri. The two friends stared down at the Bounty Hunters disappearing under the mass of white. A few dark adult Abnormits squirmed among the larvae all eating as fast as they could.

"Wow," Phiri murmured. "That was.....that was awful. I didn't think it would be this bad."

"How do you feel after making your first kill?" Kuvik asked.

Phiri remained silent for a long minute. Then he looked up and cracked a wicked grin. "I feel great. I want to do it again. I feel unstoppable."

Kuvik laughed. "Come on. Let's catch up with Akli. The Bounty Hunters won't wait around forever before they get moving again.

Chapter 28

Kuvik and Phiri found Akli in the branches. He stood on a branch and held onto another stout limb over his head to keep his balance. He stiffened when his two friends showed up.

"What's happening?" Akli asked. "I heard screaming."

"Phiri made his first kill," Kuvik replied. "Now it's your turn."

"Can I stick around and watch?" Phiri asked. "I need to live through my friends."

"Of course. You need to learn." Kuvik squatted down on Akli's branch.

"What are we waiting for?" Akli asked.

"We're waiting for the Bounty Hunters to catch up," Kuvik told him. "They have to wait for the Abnormits to go back into their nest."

"Where will they go?" Phiri asked. "They can't climb all that way back up to the same branch."

"I don't know where they'll go, but the Bounty Hunters will just go around the Abnormits. The Bounty Hunters saw me running this way. They'll catch up eventually."

Akli glanced over his shoulder toward the south. "Shouldn't we check to see if the women and children are all right?"

"Not unless you want to leave and go check on them. Phiri and I will carry out this ambush for you. You don't have to be here."

Akli scowled his most furious scowl and squatted down next to Kuvik. "Hell no. I'm not leaving."

Kuvik clapped him on the shoulder. "Now's your chance to get some payback."

"I sure hope this works."

"It will." Kuvik shifted onto his seat. "We really need to kill some larger creature—something that will give us enough meat to cure and take with us. I'm hungry. I don't like traveling without some dried food on hand."

"It would take more than one large creature to accomplish that," Phiri pointed out. "Thirty people would devour a whole Crusher before the meat went bad."

"He's right," Akli replied. "Have you seen the way some of those children eat—and I thought I was hungry."

"They're young and growing," Kuvik pointed out. "They have a lot of years of neglect to overcome. I guess we all do."

"How does it work in the larger, more established bands?" Akli asked. "How do they ever have enough food?"

"It's like I told you," Kuvik replied. "They kill any creature that attacks. All the men are always hunting and bringing in their kills. The women do the same thing. If one of them goes down to the stream for water and a Dushag attacks, the woman kills it and takes it home. People constantly bring in kills and the women butcher them up for everyone to share. The Godless never had any shortage of food when I was with them."

"How will it work for us to marry if we aren't initiated into the Clan?" Phiri asked. "Will we have to live alone—even when we're traveling with all these women? Why can't we marry each other? We have no way of knowing when we'll meet up with another band or if we ever will."

"I've considered that," Kuvik replied. "This is the way I see it—and since I'm Kral, it would be my decision anyway. You were a Follower before, weren't you?"

"You know I was," Phiri replied. "What does that have to do with anything?"

"The Followers go to the gatherings—and you're older than the age of gathering now. So am I and so is Akli, which means that none of us would be able to go to the gathering anyway."

"I'll never marry," Akli grumbled. "No woman will ever want me again."

"You might be surprised," Kuvik told him. "Besides, countless men go to the gathering every year and leave without wives. They live their whole lives alone, so you're no worse off than they are. Anyway, this is the way I see it. The women are all over the age of gathering, too, so it would be the Kral's decision if the men and women pair off and who they pair off with. That would be the law in any Clan—any Clan that follows the law of gathering—which we are. Those of you who know which Clan you belong to can follow the law of your original Clan since you haven't actually initiated into any other Clan. Those of you who don't know which Clan you belong to can follow the law laid out by your Kral. That's me. So you're all right. You can pair off with any woman you want as long as she's unmarried, willing, and over the age of gathering. Any underage girls can either go to the gathering if we're near enough to one or they won't go if we aren't near one. Then they'll pair off with whoever we have that they feel like pairing off with."

Phiri's head shot up. "You would actually do it that way?"

"I don't see that we can do it any other way," Kuvik replied. "We would do it that way if we all belonged to the same Clan and we hadn't just come from the Bounty Hunters after getting captured from dozens of different Clans. That would be the law no matter which Clan we came from. Am I right?"

Akli's head snapped around and he glared at Kuvik. "Why do you say I might be surprised? How can you say that? Why would you give me false hope when you know it's impossible?"

Kuvik didn't mention how he'd found out about Akli and Akli didn't ask—not that it mattered. Dorei was already dead. Akli couldn't exactly take it out on him for telling Kuvik his secret.

"Do you think every woman in the world wants a man for his body?" Kuvik countered. "Do you think there isn't a woman in the world who would want you for more than that?"

"Every woman in the world wants children, you bastard!" Akli raged. "Don't you sit there and tell me they don't! You know they do! Why else would they get married?!"

"What about the women who are beyond childbearing?" Kuvik fired back. "Use your head! What about the women who already have children and don't want any more? What about the women brutalized by Bounty Hunters since these women were little girls and they can't face lying with a man ever again? Don't you think they would want a strong, caring, protective man who wants to care for them? Don't you think you would make them feel safer simply because you can't hurt them that way again? Think, Akli! You're young. You have your whole life in front of you. There are women in the world who would thank God to get together with you. Don't give up on yourself. I can think of a lot of women who would want a man like you."

Akli looked away, clenched his mouth shut, and didn't answer. Kuvik gripped Akli's shoulder again and squeezed. Then Kuvik let the matter drop. He didn't want to hurt Akli any more than he already had been.

Kuvik didn't know if any of the women in his band would ever get together with Akli. They would be a lot more likely to get together with him than a woman from another Clan—and vice versa.

The women in Kuvik's band understood Akli. They all knew what had happened to him and why. They would be much more likely to get together with him than with a man from another band who didn't understand their shared past.

None of that mattered to Kuvik right now. He wouldn't mind any of his people pairing off. They deserved to find happiness. Why shouldn't they find it with each other?

The three men sat in silence for a while before Kuvik noticed movement in the distance again. He stood up. "They're coming. They're making their move."

Phiri and Akli both stood up, too. Phiri retreated further into the branches. Kuvik faced Akli. "Now's your chance, brother. Give it to them real good. Understand?"

Akli dipped his chin once. "Don't worry about me. I'll get them."

Kuvik squeezed both of Akli's shoulders. "I can't wait to see it. We'll be watching."

Kuvik climbed up and joined Phiri. The two men found a comfortable branch to sit on.

Akli descended to the ground and stood in front of the approaching Bounty Hunter column exactly the way Kuvik did. Vines and trailing fronds hung from the branches overhead.

The Bounty Hunters saw Akli, slowed, and eventually halted to confront him the same way they'd confronted Kuvik.

"What the hell are you doing out here?" one of the Bounty Hunters snapped.

"You all know who I am," Akli replied. "I'm Akli. You all participated in punishing me when I tried to escape before."

"Did you enjoy it that much?" another snapped. "You seem to be asking us to do it again."

Akli shrugged. "I escaped, didn't I? You haven't taken me back yet."

"We will," the first Bounty Hunter countered. "Don't you see how many more of us there are than you? We have hundreds of warriors out here. You're only one man."

"I don't see you trying very hard to capture me," Akli taunted. "Are you afraid? Are you worried I'll defeat you and kill dozens of your men the way my friends did? Is that what you're worried about? You aren't having very good success. How many have you lost already—a hundred? Two hundred? How many of the escaped slaves have you taken back so far? None. What does that tell you? We defeated you. You're losers. You lost to a bunch of slaves who have never held a weapon before in their lives—just like you'll lose to me right now."

The first warrior bellowed out, "You piece of filth!" and barged forward. His actions set off an answering wave in the warriors behind him. They all surged forward to pounce on Akli.

He never moved except to raise his hand, grab one of the nearby vines, and he yanked it hard.

It pulled a bunch of other vines free from the trees overhead. A dozen twisted limbs untangled from each other and thousands of snakes tumbled out of a tightly wound nest hidden among the leaves.

The snakes fell right into the thickest mass of Bounty Hunters. The snakes attacked in fury, lashed themselves around any body part they could get hold of, and their razor skin cut through flesh with no effort at all.

The Bounty Hunters went down by the dozen—or maybe even the hundreds. Akli stayed where he was and watched the whole grizzly scene without moving a muscle. The Coffincreep didn't come near him. They attacked those nearest them—the Bounty Hunters.

The Bounty Hunters screamed, turned inward on their own party, and tried in every possible way to tear the snakes off. The nest contained snakes of every size and age. Some were as big as a man's arm and twice as long as a Krakelow.

The youngest Coffincreep were barely bigger than a child's finger, but their razor-sharp skin cut just as well as the adults' if not better.

The creatures severed every hand that tried to pull the snakes away. The Coffincreep cut off the Bounty Hunters' heads, cut their bodies in half, and severed their legs at the hip joint.

Countless Bounty Hunters went down under the mass of seething bodies all whipping, snapping, and slicing with lightning speed.

The Coffincreep didn't stop once they killed someone. They bounced off the ground and off of fallen bodies, sprang onto anyone still standing within range, and started all over again.

The surviving Bounty Hunters ran for it. They retreated back to exactly the same place where they'd regrouped after their encounter with the Abnormits.

Akli stayed on the ground and watched until the bitter end. The Coffincreep really did know how to get back up to their nest. They were much more intelligent than Abnormits and had built their nest themselves.

Both young and old Coffincreep finished off the remaining Bounty Hunters, slithered into the trees, and reassembled in the same cluster of limbs where they'd built their nest to begin with.

The snakes started to wind their bodies around each other. They formed an enormous ball of twisting, writhing, slithering flesh. The ball widened and they pulled the surrounding tree limbs and leaves inward to hide the nest.

Akli stayed until silence and stillness descended over the jungle. He watched the Coffincreep until they vanished from sight. Then he turned his hard, ferocious eyes downward to the bodies of more than a hundred dead Bounty Hunters lying at his feet.

He glared and then spat on them before he climbed up into the branches and rejoined his friends.

"Do you feel better now?" Kuvik asked.

Akli nodded and looked away. "Yeah. I do."

"Great. Let's go meet up with Nelv. I don't think the Bounty Hunters will try again today. We can spend the night and wait for them to come tomorrow."

Chapter 29

Kuvik, Phiri, and Akli retreated into the jungle and found Nelv sitting in the crook of a tree. He didn't stand up when the three men joined him. "How did it go?" he asked. "I heard screaming.

"It was glorious," Akli murmured.

Phiri laughed out loud. "Yeah. It was perfect."

Nelv's features pinched. "I don't know if it will be like that for me. I might completely screw it up."

"No, you won't," Kuvik replied. "You're gonna be outstanding."

Nelv glanced down toward the ground. The sun was going down and starting to cast the jungle in shady colors.

Kuvik followed Nelv's gaze. The party had chosen this spot because three mother Crushers stood guard over their nests just below where the four men sat right now.

All three mothers must have laid their eggs at the same time. All three clutches had hatched at the same time. The young Crushers were all about the same size. They came up to their mothers' knees, so each Crusher was as tall as a large man.

Each clutch contained nine young. That made twenty-seven young Crushers, each with enough power in its jaws to snap a person in half.

Their mothers still considered them babies—which they were. They could barely hunt for themselves. They were at the age when their mothers took turns going out into the jungle, catching live prey, and bringing it back for the young ones to play with.

"They're really kind of cute," Phiri remarked. "When you look at them the right way."

"That's easy for you to say," Nelv countered. "You don't have to go down there and face them."

"Just remember what I said," Kuvik told him. "You're a fast runner, so you'll have to take advantage of your speed."

"Don't remind me," Nelv muttered. "We don't have to go over it again. You'll only fray my nerves worse than they already are."

"I'm really glad I went first," Phiri went on. "I'm glad I get to see all of you spring your traps. I'm learning so much."

"I'll tell you what I'm learning," Akli interjected. "I'm learning that it pays to be cold and ruthless. The jungle shows no mercy and neither should we."

"Just remember to be cold and ruthless to your enemies," Kuvik replied. "You can do whatever you want to your enemies as long as you take care of and protect your own. That's the whole point. The point isn't to be cold, ruthless, and hurtful to your own people. That's what's wrong with the Bounty Hunters. They bring it home and treat their own that way. That's no way to live."

"Don't the Godless do it that way?" Phiri asked. "I heard they're just as cruel."

"The Godless aren't cruel at all," Kuvik countered. "The Godless don't take captives—from anyone. If you're their enemy, they kill you. If you aren't, they leave you alone. They don't capture anyone, not even women. Do you want to hear a story? My friend Hangman told me his father Shadow's band was in battle against another band. Shadow was only sixteen at the time. He found the enemy Kral's daughter hiding in the jungle. He immediately started making plans to return her to her father. That's what the Godless do with captured enemy women. They send them back to their Clans. The Godless don't mistreat any women and children, especially not their own. I lived with them for years and never saw any one of the men raise his hand against anyone in the band—not even once. I never saw any of the men even raise his voice to anyone in the band. They're the most upright people anywhere. The Followers tell their children the Godless are bloodthirsty and cruel so their children will grow up peaceful and not wanting to be warlike hunters and warriors."

Phiri's eyes widened. "You know about that?"

"I told you I know a woman from the Followers who married into the Godless band. She told me everything about it. She said her family told her the Godless eat their own children."

Akli gasped. "Is that true?"

Phiri looked away. "Yes, it's true."

"The Godless are too interested in raising their children to adulthood just like every other Clan," Kuvik pointed out. "The Godless would never do anything to put their children in danger. That's ridiculous."

Silence fell between the men. The jungle got a lot darker.

"Are you sure the Bounty Hunters won't come at night?" Nelv whispered.

"They'll want to keep an eye open for any other dangers we bring out against them," Kuvik replied. "Anyway, it wouldn't be safe for you to run around in the jungle in the dark—and the Crushers won't do anything until morning, either. Just make yourselves comfortable. We won't do anything more tonight."

"How do you know so much about the jungle, Kuvik?" Phiri asked.

"I told you. I learned. No one is born knowing this stuff. Not even the Godless are born knowing it. That's what they taught me. They learn as children and they grow up learning to fight and hunt. They get used to it over decades. You can't expect yourselves to know everything right away. Think about it. You have to learn and that means making mistakes. You're all doing fine so far. You're doing much better than I thought you would."

"What did you think—that we would die within the first day?" Akli demanded.

"I thought some of you would. I thought some of you would get too scared and go back to the Bounty Hunters on your own. I thought it would take you a lot longer to be ready to fight and kill and hunt. I couldn't be happier with your conduct."

"Would you be happier if we were real Godless?" Nelv asked.

Kuvik heard the glaring resentment in those words and didn't try to hide that he heard it. He turned to face the young man. "Listen to me, little brother. The Godless warriors of my band told me for years that I was Godless even though I hadn't initiated. I could have initiated long ago, but I chose not to because I thought I wasn't worthy to be one of them. They told me I already was—that I had been Godless since the day I committed myself to them, their families, their Kral, and their ways. They said the initiation was just a formality. That's how it will be for you. You'll get stronger. You'll get braver. You'll learn to hunt and fight and defeat your enemies in open combat so you don't have to keep springing these traps on them. You'll do all of that—and you'll become Godless if you really want to be. You'll be as Godless as any man born into the Clan. Then your initiations will be just a formality. Everyone will already respect you and know your worth. They'll know you're an honorable man who would do anything to protect his family, his band, his Clan, and his brothers. When that happens, we'll be real Godless together and I won't be any happier or prouder then than I am right now."

His words ended their conversation for the night. He left the others with a lot on their minds—just as he had a lot on his mind.

Kuvik entertained not the slightest doubt that these men sitting with him right now would become Godless warriors. They would grow, learn, fight, and get stronger. They would initiate and earn the respect of their families and bands. Kuvik saw it all in front of his eyes.

He really couldn't have been prouder of them. They had exceeded his wildest expectations. The fact that they weren't those strong, capable Godless warriors yet meant nothing—because they would be. Their fate and their futures were written in the stars.

He fell asleep first that night—which was a first for him and them. They were all still awake when he fell asleep and they were all awake when he woke up. Did they sleep at all?

Nelv didn't appear to have gotten any sleep. He kept a close eye on the Crushers. They were still asleep when Kuvik woke up—or at least the mothers still sat on their nests when he woke up.

The mothers were just starting to stir and open their eyes as daylight crept over the jungle. The mothers looked around and made their first rumbling noises.

Akli and Phiri looked better rested than Nelv. He showed his nerves as a deeper level of fury—even deeper than what Kuvik was used to seeing from Akli.

Nelv kept gritting his teeth and glaring at everyone and everything. His eyes flashed more dangerously as the hours passed.

Kuvik stood up and climbed higher and to one side in the branches where he could see in the Bounty Hunters' direction. He didn't see any movement yet, so he stayed where he was and kept watch.

The three men below him didn't talk. Akli probably recognized when to leave someone alone when they got that worked up. Phiri didn't say a word to anyone. The tension between the three of them escalated to the breaking point.

The mother Crushers moved off their nests and the young ones started moving around for the day. They hopped out of the nest and ran around in their little clearing, but they never went too far away from the nest.

The mothers stood over their young to guard them. The mothers kept making deep, booming rumbles in their chests. The young Crushers made higher-pitched cheeping sounds that occasionally came out as squawks.

One of the mothers went out hunting while the other two stood guard. One of the remaining mothers sidestepped extra carefully and positioned herself over both clutches of young.

The other mother came back in a little while with a fully grown female Demonex. The Demonex was still alive and hardly injured at all.

The mother Crusher released the creature in the middle of the clearing and the young Crushers attacked. The Demonex fought back, but they overwhelmed their prey and dragged it down.

So many young Crushers shared the spoils that they didn't get more than a few mouthfuls each. That wouldn't satisfy their hunger at all.

Kuvik looked away to check the Bounty Hunters' position—and saw them. They were on the move, but they came much more slowly this time. They didn't rush. They kept a close watch on the surroundings for any danger.

He descended and informed Nelv that the Bounty Hunters were coming. He stood up, nodded once, and climbed down to the ground. He positioned himself at a distance from the Crusher nests.

The Bounty Hunters made a lot of noise coming closer. Kuvik, Akli, and Phiri had no trouble tracking the Bounty Hunters' position.

Nelv waited until the Bounty Hunters barely came within line of sight of him. Then he sprang behind a tree and hid there.

The Bounty Hunters knew better than to run after these escaped fugitives without keeping an eye on the terrain ahead and around them.

Running away from them wouldn't work anymore. Nelv planned to use a different strategy to lure the Bounty Hunters to the Crusher nests.

Only a few Bounty Hunters spotted him before he vanished out of sight. They stopped in their tracks and brought the rest of the column to a halt while those few men explained what they'd seen to everyone else.

Then the Bounty Hunters held a lengthy discussion about what to do. They went on for a long time about how they needed to be careful so these escaped captives didn't lead the Bounty Hunters into another ambush.

They were still trying to decide what to do when Nelv dove out from behind his tree and sprinted to another one a little farther away—a little closer to the nests.

The Bounty Hunters broke off their conversation mid-sentence. They stood in silence staring at the place where Nelv had disappeared behind his second tree. The Bounty Hunters took even longer before they started talking again.

"He's right there behind that tree," one of the men pointed out. "He can't be boo-by-trapping anything there. We can see where he is. We can just walk over there, surround the tree, and catch him. We wouldn't be risking anything. What are we waiting for?"

"You don't know what these slaves are capable of," another argued. "The last three we've seen have all sprung booby traps on us. What makes you think this one is any different? He must be planning something."

"What could he be planning?" another asked. "He's standing behind a tree. We could at least walk over there and get closer to him."

"What makes you think he isn't trying to lure us under another pile of creatures like the last two times?" a fourth man countered. "These slaves know a lot more about the jungle than we do. They've already killed more than two hundred men. We can't keep taking these risks."

"How can the slaves know anything about the jungle?" the second man demanded. "None of them has lived in the jungle. They don't know anything."

"Well, someone does," the fourth man pointed out. "Someone must be telling them where to hit us and how to do it. We should be careful."

"We are being careful," the first man fired back. "We won't go anywhere that we see anything dangerous."

"We didn't see anything dangerous before the last three ambushes," the second man reminded him. "We're the ones who don't know enough about the....."

He broke off again when Nelv darted to the next tree. It stood right outside a rim of foliage with the Crusher nests hidden right behind that curtain of leaves.

The young Crushers scuttled around all over the ground near their nests and under their mothers' protection. The undergrowth hid the Crushers from the Bounty Hunters. The undergrowth even hid the enormous mothers.

Kuvik didn't understand how the Bounty Hunters didn't hear the mothers rumbling to their young ones. He would have recognized that sound a mile away. The Bounty Hunters didn't know the sound for what it was.

The first man turned away. "I'm going over there. He's one man and I'm not going back to the village emptyhanded. We came all this way to capture these slaves. We have one standing here right in front of us. He doesn't even have a weapon on him. Anyone who wants to can come with me."

He crossed the rest of the distance between the Bounty Hunters and Nelv's tree. The other warriors hesitated and then followed him. Nelv must have been watching them much more closely than Kuvik realized.

Nelv waited until the last possible second before the Bounty Hunters got near enough to capture him. He saw them closing in, lunged out of his hiding place, and dove for the wall of greenery separating him from the Crushers.

The Bounty Hunters saw him and sprang forward to pounce. They could see everything between themselves and the undergrowth. They could see there was no danger here.

He snapped a bunch of branches and then "accidentally" lost his footing trying to clamber through the leaves. He fell in the middle of the tangle—just enough to pull the undergrowth aside and create an opening.

The Crushers startled to high alert at the noise. They all looked up and saw dozens of armed men standing beyond the gap. The Crushers also saw Nelv lying there jumbled in leaves and branches. He made the whole thing look like a colossal accident.

The Bounty Hunters froze in shock. They didn't move fast enough before one of the mother Crushers bellowed to shake the whole world.

She took two deep, thumping footsteps forward, stomped her massive foot down on the branches to widen the gap, and all three clutches of young Crushers rushed the opening to go after their prey.

Nelv executed his plan to the letter, sprang out of the leaves, and sprinted sideways around the edge of the clearing. His quick actions got him far enough away from the Crushers for him to vault into the branches and save his own life.

None of the Crushers paid the slightest attention to him—not with all this other prey standing right in front of them. The young Crushers flooded out of the clearing and went into a frenzy killing as many Bounty Hunters as the young ones could catch.

The Bounty Hunters surged away to flee, but their own numbers trapped them right where the young Crushers could get to them easily.

The Bounty Hunters tripped over each other, trampled each other to the ground, and made each other helpless for the young Crushers to slaughter.

They didn't waste time eating all this fresh, convenient meat. They sprang from man to man killing each one and moving on. The young Crushers spread up the line of Bounty Hunters and didn't stop until the survivors all ran away.

The mothers did the same thing. Their booming footsteps echoed through the jungle while the mothers snapped men off the ground, pulverized them in their jaws, and tossed them away before grabbing the next victim.

Nelv climbed up and sat on the branch next to Phiri. Phiri clapped him on the shoulder. "Congratulations. That was perfect."

Nelv laughed and wound up blushing. "It was fun, actually. I enjoyed that."

Kuvik got to his feet. "Let's meet back up with the rest of the band. We can keep an eye on the Bounty Hunters and spring a few more traps on them to slow them down if we need to. I think they got the message for now."

Chapter 30

Kuvik spotted the band before he got there. He found the women and children settled on the ground around three fires. Four women were in the process of butchering a Dushag to share with everyone.

Kesha and three other women stood guard. They drew their weapons and then relaxed when they saw the men approaching. "What's going on out there?" Kesha asked.

"We delayed the Bounty Hunters and got rid of a bunch of them." Kuvik sat down by the fire. "Is everything under control here?"

"Everything has been quiet." Balea handed Kuvik a bowl of the Dushag meat and then scrutinized the other men. "You all look different."

"These men killed Bounty Hunters today and yesterday," Kuvik announced. "These men made their first enemy kills. It was a beautiful sight. They wiped out close to three hundred Bounty Hunters."

The whole band exclaimed over the feat. Everyone wanted to know the story. Phiri, Akli, and Nelv told their stories. Everyone else laughed and congratulated the three men.

"When do *we* get to make our first enemy kills?" Garvis asked. "You pulled us back before we had a chance. That isn't fair."

Kuvik laughed at him. "Actually, if you really want to know, little brother, I was thinking about going back out and hitting them again."

"Great!" Phiri exclaimed. "I want to do it again."

"Not you," Kuvik countered. "That's what I'm saying. You, Akli, and Nelv would stay behind to guard the band. I would take out Garvis and the others so they could get in a few enemy kills, too. We would see where the Bounty Hunters are, find out where they're planning to go next, and arrange a few nasty surprises for them along the way."

"Would we do the same things?" Garvis asked. "Would we lay the same traps?"

"That depends on the landscape and what's available," Kuvik replied. "I wouldn't let you do anything that called for you to run anywhere or anything like that. We would have to think of something else for you."

"What about us?" one of the teenage boys asked.

"Can I go, too?" the twelve-year-old boy asked. "I want to make enemy kills."

Kuvik turned to face them. The older boys ranged in age from fifteen to seventeen.

Thedo was the youngest with a friendly, outgoing personality and a cheery willingness to try anything. He treated the band's escape from the Bounty Hunters like a giant adventure full of all kinds of exciting new experiences for him to try and enjoy.

His mother was Nanta, the mother of the baby girl too young to hold herself up. Nanta had one other son about six years old, Thedo's younger brother, Vars.

Thedo paid a lot of attention to Vars. Thedo's affection took the form of friendly teasing and occasional attempts to gently rough Vars up.

Vars, on the other hand, was as fuming, sullen, and ferocious as Akli. He didn't appreciate Thedo's affections or his sense of humor.

Vars took it as a personal offense that Thedo made light of the band's escape, the jungle's many dangers, and the severity of the escaped captives' past.

The middle two teenage boys were twins named Los and Lago. They were the kind of twins who seemed to have melded into one person—or they wanted the outside world to think they were.

They acted the same and sometimes finished each other's sentences. They didn't let on if either of them had personalities of their own. They kept that hidden from the rest of the world.

They didn't mention if they had families and no one asked. Both boys had been tied up in the same cellar stalls with Akli when he freed the captives there.

The oldest boy was Elem and he had also been in the cellar with the others. He had a quiet, thoughtful, almost dreamlike quality as if he rarely came back to this earth unless he absolutely had to.

His captivity might have exaggerated that tendency since he didn't have any reason to come back. He may have developed the habit of checking out of reality and staying out of it.

The twelve-year-old was named Tren. He was an orphan with no parents or other family. One of the other mothers had brought him along with her children when they'd left the Bounty Hunters' village.

Tren actually reminded Kuvik a lot of Hangman. Tren had an electric, almost lunatic personality. He took unbelievable risks, ran faster through the branches, dared bigger and more often than anyone else, and his recklessness almost always paid off.

He had a hard-driving way of always pushing to the maximum limit in anything he tried. He would go as far as Kuvik and the other adults let him go and even farther unless someone reined him in. He saw no reason to hold back on anything.

Kuvik didn't know Tren's story. Kuvik might have come to the conclusion from Tren's attitude and behavior that he had completely given up on life and no longer cared if he lived or died—but it wasn't that. He did care.

He held nothing in reserve. He threw everything he had into every challenge. He acted as if he didn't see the point in doing anything at all if he didn't do it all the way.

Kuvik couldn't help but respect the kid, especially when Kuvik saw the way Tren was growing up. Kuvik had seen this too many times in Godless children. He knew exactly what kind of man Tren would grow up to become. Kuvik couldn't wait to see that.

Kuvik addressed Tren first. "I wish I could take you, but you're under the age of initiation. Wait a few years and perfect your fighting skill first. Then you can come out with us. I'm sure you'll become a great warrior. You just need to grow some and hone your skills. You can do that by helping the men guard the band. These women and children need your blade more than we do. Concentrate on that. I know you'll do a good job."

Tren looked away to scowl in another direction. He didn't answer.

The band consisted of fourteen men including Kuvik, Akli, Phiri, Garvis, and Nelv. That left nine who still needed some kind of direct enemy engagement.

"There are too many of you for all of us to go," Kuvik decided. "You boys can stay behind. I'll take the grown men this time. You'll get your chance later."

None of the teenage boys argued. None of them cared as much as Tren.

Kuvik decided to tell these boys the story of Hammer's band, how they had escaped from Renegade captivity by taking up arms against their captors, and how they had grown into a Godless band in their own right. These boys needed to hear that.

The band enjoyed a nice peaceful night on the ground. They ate the entire Dushag and left nothing behind.

Kuvik let himself relax. He didn't have to worry about the Bounty Hunters sneaking up on the band—not tonight. He and his men had killed a lot of them, sent them running, and made the Bounty Hunters think twice about coming after the band again.

The band could take one night to just sit around and enjoy each other's company. These people had earned that. The men who had killed Bounty Hunters had bought their comrades these precious hours when none of them had to worry about their enemies.

The freed captives talked, joked, and laughed. They told funny stories from their time with the Bounty Hunters. No one talked about the bad times. Kuvik told a few stories of his own and made the others laugh.

They all retired into the branches with full stomachs. Kuvik woke up early the next morning and didn't hurry to get up and go do anything. He didn't have to.

He let the rest of the band sleep in—or he would have if the babies hadn't woken everyone up at the usual time. Everyone had to get busy tending the children and organizing the band's next moves.

Kuvik took his nine men, gave his final orders to Akli and the others about continuing their journey south and guarding the band from any danger, and Kuvik and the others headed north to intercept the Bounty Hunters.

Kuvik found them camping in the jungle even farther north than where they'd regrouped before. They'd brought quite a few slaves with them. The slaves were in the process of taking down a bunch of huts while the Bounty Hunters talked among themselves.

Kuvik and his men stayed hidden in the branches and listened to their conversation. Kuvik didn't recognize any of these men. All the warriors he knew and recognized were already dead.

Most of the warriors' conversation was just repeated comments he'd already heard the previous day.

"We can't risk the slaves carrying out another strike on us," one of the warriors murmured. "We've lost too many men already."

"How can a bunch of slaves carry out such devastating attacks?" another asked.

"We have to report this to Halmeron anyway," a third pointed out. "We have no choice but to go back north, tell him what's going on, and get his decision on whether we come back out or not."

"What will we do if he decides to come back?" another asked. "He might decide to send an even bigger force and we would lose even more men."

"I'll tell you what I'll do if that happens," the second remarked. "I'll stay near the back of the column. I'll let someone else walk into all these ambushes. I'll be the first to turn and run for it. I don't care if they call me a coward. I'm not going to throw my life away over a bunch of slaves. Let them go. That's what I say. We can get more slaves anywhere. These people are too much trouble. Just let them go before they bring down the whole Clan."

No one had an answer for this. No one argued with him or told him outright that he was a coward for saying it.

No one told this man that he should be more concerned with protecting the Bounty Hunter Clan's reputation by bringing in these slaves and making examples of them to strike terror into everyone else's hearts.

The party continued to pack up and get ready to go. The Bounty Hunters waited for their slaves to finish tying up their bundles.

Kuvik didn't wait around to see the column move out. He signaled his men forward and they set off through the trees. Some of the men of Kuvik's band could run through the branches. Others could move fast, but not quite as fast.

They put plenty of distance between themselves and the Bounty Hunters. Kuvik and his men scouted the countryside ahead, found a bunch of different features of the landscape they could use to ambush the Bounty Hunters, and Kuvik gave instructions to all his men.

He didn't position them there the way he did last time. He kept his group together. He wanted to be able to adjust to conditions as they changed. He also wanted his men to see each other's ambushes so they could learn from and appreciate each other's kills.

They made it a few miles in front of the Bounty Hunters before the column moved out. The Bounty Hunters announced their movements to the world by making plenty of noise.

Kuvik and his men found an open stretch of ground on a direct north-south line from the Bounty Hunters' camp. They would have to cross this open area before they reentered the shelter of the jungle.

Chapter 31

Kuvik and his men hid in the canopy on the opposite side of the open ground. Kuvik gave some specific instructions to his men and directed them to climb all the way up to the very topmost branches.

The men stuck their heads up into the open air above the jungle's highest branches. Kuvik crawled out, swam onto his stomach on top of the dense foliage, and floundered around where the leaves and branches supported his weight.

"Come on!" he called to his men. "All of you come out here and swim around!"

"What do we want to do that for?" a middle-aged man named Gurn asked. He only had one eye and he let his stringy grey hair grow down to his shoulders.

"You want to kill Bounty Hunters, don't you?" Kuvik asked. "This is how you do it."

"I don't see you killing any Bounty Hunters," a young man named Senau pointed out. He was the youngest and only a few years older than Elem.

"If you don't come now, I'll tell all the women that you were too cowardly to make any enemy kills," Kuvik teased.

Three other men followed Kuvik's instructions, started paddling around on top of the canopy, and then the rest did the same thing. They flopped around and grunted and groaned from the effort.

"This is stupid," Gurn snarled.

Kuvik laughed at him—and cut himself off when he heard a shriek in the air. Kuvik looked up and saw a flock of Boultars circling in the air.

Kuvik sat up enough to check the Bounty Hunters' position. Then he went back to floundering. He and the other men swam around each other and occasionally fell on top of each other when the branches sprang in unexpected ways.

Kuvik kept a close watch on both the Boultars and the Bounty Hunters. The Boultars descended a little lower and circled right over the exposed men. The Bounty Hunters kept getting closer. They didn't notice anything out of the ordinary.

They approached the other side of the open ground. The Boultars dove to a height directly above the men—close enough to strike.

"Now!!" Kuvik ordered. "Get down—now!"

He sat up, straightened his legs, and plunged back under the canopy. The other men must have been counting down the seconds. They did the same thing, dove under all the leaves, and took refuge out of sight where the Boultars couldn't see them as well.

The Boultars could still have attacked the party, but the Bounty Hunters emerged from the trees just then and walked right out into the open in full view of the whole flock of Boultars.

The Boultars took the more easily accessible prey, veered toward the open field, and fell on the Bounty Hunters en masse.

The Bounty Hunter column wound up having exactly the same problem as always. Their own numbers blocked them from retreating in time.

Those in the back didn't see the danger until it was too late. They walked out into the field and met their deaths from the Boultars.

The Boultars started by attacking the first Bounty Hunters to step out of the trees. Thirty Boultars descended on the Bounty Hunters tearing them apart, impaling them with their beaks, and clubbing them into tree trunks with brutal swats of the creatures' wings.

The Boultars saw more Bounty Hunters trying to flee, took to the air, and landed behind the fleeing Bounty Hunters to cut off their retreat. The Bounty Hunters got trapped on the field with the murderous Boultars going on a killing spree.

The Boultars slaughtered every Bounty Hunter they could catch. The others had to shrink deeper into the jungle on that side where the Boultars couldn't get to them.

The Bounty Hunters had to cower there and watch the Boultars dismember and devour every single dead Bounty Hunter on the field. The Boultars stayed on the ground for a long time to gorge on their kills.

"You're right," Senau murmured while Kuvik's party watched. "This is so worth it."

"What's next?" Gurn asked. "When can we lay another ambush?"

"Let's scout around and see what we can find." Kuvik stood up. "We have some time before the Bounty Hunters catch up."

Kuvik and his men returned to the band four days later after carrying out continuous ambushes on the Bounty Hunters.

"Are they gone?" Kesha asked.

"They're as gone as they're going to get," Senau replied. "We reduced their column down to twenty men. They won't come back—not for a while."

Kuvik threw himself down by the fire. Someone in the party had killed a full-grown Gurlg. This was a new achievement, but he didn't ask who had killed it. He would probably find out pretty soon anyway.

The men he had left behind and a bunch of different women worked together to butcher the creature, cook the meat for everyone to eat, and to dry the rest for travel. The Gurlg was the biggest creature any of them had killed so far.

Nelv brought Kuvik a bowl full of the freshly roasted meat. "Thank you, little brother," Kuvik exclaimed. "This is a great way to come home."

"Home?" Akli asked. "Where is home, anyway? Where are we going?"

"I don't know about the rest of you, but I'm going south to Godless country where I belong," Kuvik replied. "Any of you can return to your own Clans if you want to or you can come with me. It's up to you. You're free now. We escaped from the Bounty Hunters. What we do now is up to each of us."

The others exchanged glances. The men and women working on the Gurlg carcass continued with what they were doing while the others ate or did other camp tasks.

Kuvik only now just noticed the men and women working on the Gurlg. They acted closer than he remembered. They shared more eye contact, helped each other more, and smiled at each other more often. Were they pairing off with each other?

One of the younger women seemed to be taking an interest in Akli. Her name was Mapa. She would have been jaw-droppingly gorgeous if she'd only put on some weight and didn't have so many bruises all over her face and body.

She already looked a hundred times better than she did in the Bounty Hunters' village. Kuvik didn't know her history, but she was definitely of childbearing age.

He recognized the unmistakable signs of Akli acting protective, helpful, and attentive to her. They worked together on one side of the creature while everyone else worked elsewhere.

Kuvik forced himself to look away. Whatever went on between them was none of his business. He found it hard not to feel protective of Akli, though. Kuvik didn't want Akli to get hurt, but he was a grown man and would have to take care of himself.

Nelv brought Kuvik back to reality. "I have nowhere else to go," Nelv murmured. "This band is the most I've ever had."

"We all feel that way," Phiri pointed out. "You're the only person here who got cap-tured as an adult, Kuvik."

"Did you mean what you said when you said we could come with you?" Tren asked. "Could we really become Godless?"

"Of course," Kuvik insisted. "I would never turn any of you away. We escaped together. We'll stay together unless one of you wants to leave. I don't know if any of you have families back home who might be waiting for you. That's why I said it. Any of you are welcome to come with me. The more of us go, the safer we'll be. We can help protect each other in numbers. We can guard the vulnerable women and children—and you'll all get better at fighting. I can help you learn and you can help each other. That would be the best thing as far as I can see. I don't want any of you to go, but I would be happy for you if you wanted to go back to your families."

"Don't you have a family, Kuvik?" Senau asked.

"The Godless are my only family," Kuvik replied right away. "If I can't find my old band, I'll join another one. They're lawful people and they treat strangers well."

"Can I ask you a question, Kuvik?" Garvis asked.

"Of course, little brother. Anything."

"You talked before about how the Godless initiate their boys into manhood. You said you hadn't initiated yet—and you also said you could have but you didn't because you didn't think you were worthy to become Godless—at least not yet."

"Yes. I did say that."

"Then would we have to initiate—as adults? Is that how it works if an adult from another Clan wants to join the Godless?"

"Yes, exactly," Kuvik replied. "You go through the same process of fighting a creature of your own choosing. The Godless change your name. The men have different names from the ones their parents gave them at birth. The name is a mark of respect, honor, and manhood. It's a sign that you've earned the right to go out and hunt and fight with the men of your Clan."

"Then.....how would it work for me?" Garvis asked. "How would I fight a creature that big when I have an injured leg?"

"Oh, I see what you're asking. The process works the same. What you need to do is develop your fighting skills to accommodate your leg. Your leg hasn't slowed you down in traveling through the treetops, has it?"

Garvis frowned. "No, I guess not."

"Your leg won't make any difference in how you use your arms and hands. You have to develop your own style to work around your leg. Think about it like this. Imagine a grown man tried to fight a full-sized adult Crusher."

Phiri gasped. "No grown man could kill a full-sized adult Crusher! That's impossible!"

"My friend Hangman fought a full-grown Crusher for his initiation," Kuvik returned. "He was alone. He was small and weak. He was fourteen years old and he won."

A tense silence fell over the group. "That sounds incredible," Tren murmured. "I wish I could have seen that."

"You need to think creatively. You obviously can't use strength alone to fight a Crusher or a Gorlock or a Ridgebeak or a Demonex or any other large creature. You need to use other advantages like speed, maneuverability, and changing your position to get to the creature's vulnerable spots. You need to weaken the creature in crucial areas to slow it down, stop it from attacking you, and bring it down before it gets to you first. Fighting any creature isn't about showing off how big and brave and powerful you are. It's about winning and walking away with your life, your health, and your limbs intact. Who cares what it looks like? You can strike at the creature's eyes. You can get behind its back and slash its throat. You can roll underneath it and cut the tendons on the backs of its ankles so it can't stand. You have something none of these creatures have. You have your wits. None of these creatures can combat that." He turned back to Garvis. "That's what you need to think about. You need to think about how you can outmaneuver the creature and strike at it without your leg getting in the way and slowing you down. You all need to think that way to make up for your weakness and your lack of skill. I'm not saying it's your fault or there's anything wrong with you because of it. Everyone has to do it that way. Not even the biggest, strongest Godless warrior can use strength and power to fight a Crusher. Everyone has to use their wits. That's how they do it."

"Tell us more, Kuvik," Nelv insisted. "Tell us everything."

"It would take too long for me to tell you everything tonight. We can talk about all of that later—if you plan to come with me." He looked around. "Do any of you want to go?"

No one spoke until Gurn broke the silence. "We all want to stay. This band....it's everything any of us wanted when we were captives."

"Then we'll leave on our journey heading south tomorrow," Kuvik announced. "We'll divide the men and anyone else who feels capable of fighting. We'll post guards to protect the women and young children. We'll assign scouts to travel behind us to search for any

Bounty Hunters pursuing us. The scouts will also range around the country and keep an eye open for any other bands—either friendly or hostile. We'll start acting as our own band until we find somewhere we feel like stopping and staying for a while."

Chapter 32

Kuvik sat in the fork of a tree high above the canopy and squinted south. A slight sway in the distant foliage showed him where his band was moving through the treetops on their journey.

The party had been traveling for three weeks with no sign of the Bounty Hunters returning. Kuvik and his men still kept watch just in case. The band had to stay on constant watch so everyone would be ready to respond if the Bounty Hunters did come back.

Kuvik turned his gaze northward, but he didn't see anything. He could search all day and all night and never find anything. The Bounty Hunters didn't come back.

He probably would have searched all day and all night, but he usually forced himself to stop before it got that bad.

Preparing his people as much as possible, training them as much as possible, and taking every possible precaution to protect them—it had become an obsession for him.

The chances kept dwindling with every mile the band kept traveling south. The Bounty Hunters wouldn't come this far to retake the escaped captives. The Bounty Hunters had to give it up sometime.

The chances got stronger every day that they wouldn't come back at all. Kuvik knew that, but he still found it impossible not to dwell on it. Had he and his people crossed that threshold already?

He couldn't slacken his vigilance in case they hadn't. Getting surprised or ambushed by the Bounty Hunters now would have been disastrous.

It actually wouldn't have been disastrous. His people knew how to hunt and fight so much better now than when they first escaped. They had risen to the occasion and exceeded his wildest expectations.

The four teenage boys had essentially joined the men on all their maneuvers. Kuvik didn't stop them. Tren joined them, too. He didn't ask for permission after that one time when Kuvik refused him. Tren just came. He belonged there somehow.

The five boys had taken Hammer's story as their personal mantra. The five of them had committed to doing exactly the same thing that Hammer and his band did.

These boys planned to become the most outstanding warriors the world had ever seen. They planned to initiate into the Godless Clan just as soon as Kuvik's party found another Godless band to initiate them.

Kuvik had to explain at length more than once why he couldn't initiate anyone. He had explained again and again that he would have initiated all of them a long time ago if he could have—all except Tren, of course.

He could have initiated any time he wanted to. The kid could fight literally anything. He was a powerhouse.

The rest of Kuvik's band had taken his stories about the Godless to heart. Everyone used unconventional fighting styles that emphasized speed, cunning, maneuverability, and unpredictability over power, strength, and frontal assaults.

Tren was a master of these techniques. He could outsmart anything and he struck with ruthless ferocity whenever he found a critical opening.

Kuvik was still sitting there staring north and thinking things over when Akli, Phiri, and Nelv came up to him through the branches. They could all travel as fast as any naturally born Godless.

He had to tear his gaze away from the north to confront his people. Staring north had become his default way of drifting in his thoughts and reviewing his tactical situation. Sometimes he didn't even look for the Bounty Hunters. Looking north helped him think.

"The west side is all clear," Akli told him. "We went forty miles north and didn't find anything there, either."

"Did you meet back up with Senau's party yet?" Kuvik asked.

"They haven't come back from the east side," Nelv replied. "They might have gotten delayed, but it's still within the time. We don't need to worry about them yet."

Kuvik turned around. "I guess it's time for us to rejoin the band anyway. Let's go. It's almost sunset."

Akli held out his hand. "Do you mind staying for a minute? I need to talk to you."

"Sure. What's wrong?" Kuvik asked.

Akli shot Senau and Phiri one of the furious glares Akli had become famous for. His manner had softened as he got used to freedom, but he could still pull out the most dangerous facial expressions when he needed them.

Senau said, "See you back there," over his shoulder and he and Nelv took off through the branches. They left Kuvik and Akli alone. They had become much closer in the last several weeks. They considered each other friends.

"What's on your mind?" Kuvik asked. "I can see something's bothering you."

"You're Kral of this band," Akli began.

Kuvik grimaced. "Call it what you want. We're brothers. Tell me what's bothering you."

"That's what's bothering you. I don't need a brother. I need a Kral."

Kuvik stiffened. "What do you need a Kral for?"

"Nolon made a move on Mapa last night," Akli blurted out. "He came up on her in the dark and tried to handle her. She came running to me crying in the middle of the night. She doesn't feel safe with him walking around free."

The hair stood up on Kuvik's arm. Nolon was one of the older men in the group with his hair turning grey. He might be around forty.

He was taller and broader in the shoulders than any other man in the band. He didn't have a wife or any other family in the group, but Kuvik had noticed him expressing interest in at least three other women.

Kuvik cringed when he heard Akli's story. "Let me guess," Kuvik muttered. "This isn't the first time."

"He's done it two other times—or I should say those are the only times she's told me about. She's told him to leave her alone, but he doesn't listen. I confronted him once before. He laughed at me and tried to say that no woman her age would willingly go with me when she could have a man who would give her children and the future she deserves. He spouted off a bunch of insults about how I'm not a man and I should bow out of her life with my dignity intact before I get humiliated."

Akli clamped his mouth shut in a deadly scowl of pure fuming rage. This wouldn't be the first time that Kuvik recalled Dorei's warning. *Don't make Akli mad.* Nolon apparently hadn't gotten the message.

"You're Kral of this band and Mapa isn't my legal wife," Akli snarled. "I would kill the bastard right now if she was. I would strangle him with my bare hands, tear his arms off, and shove them down his throat. I can't do that. You're our Kral. You have to be the one to deal with him—and I'll tell you something else, Kuvik. Mapa isn't the only woman in the band who is afraid of him. You have to stop him. I don't care what you do—but I won't rest as long as he's still a member of this band. I'll always sleep with one eye open and I'll never leave her alone with him as long as he's still alive. I don't care what any man says. I'll never let him lay a finger on her. She's suffered too much already."

Kuvik only nodded. "Good. You do that. I'll take care of Nolon. You can tell Mapa that he'll never bother her again."

Akli stared at him for a second and then narrowed his eyes. "Are you sure? He's a lot older and bigger than you."

"Don't worry about it. I'll take care of it. I'm happy for you and Mapa. I can see that you make each other happy."

Akli nodded, mumbled, "Thanks," and turned away. The two men returned to the band in silence.

Kuvik had a lot to think about on the way there. He had been called on to arbitrate these disputes more and more as time went on. His role as Kral had become undisputed and accepted by everyone.

Everyone treated him as Kral of this band. Everyone expected him to handle every disturbance that came up and to take responsibility for everyone's safety.

He and Akli made it back to camp by sundown. The band camped on the ground tonight while some of the women helped butcher and process a Gorlock that Tren had killed.

He seemed to favor the bigger creatures. He liked to test himself against them, especially after hearing about Hangman's and Cross's initiations. He and the other boys couldn't get enough of all those initiation stories.

Kuvik sat down on the ground by the fire and immediately got mobbed by a bunch of the children. They crowded around him, sat on his lap, leaned against his back, put their arms around his neck, and hung all over him.

Even the babies waddled over to study and grin at him. They liked touching his bald head and showing him pebbles and pieces of sticks they had found on the ground.

The others sat around sharing the Gorlock meat. Senau and his scouts came back a little while later and told Kuvik that the east side of their route was clear, too. Then everyone relaxed.

Akli and Mapa sat down next to each other the way they always did. She served him his food and they talked in low tones between themselves.

Four other couples had paired off, but none of them had come to Kuvik to ask if they could officially marry. No one had asked yet.

Los and one of the teenage girls had been getting friendly with each other. Kuvik had been forced to step in and remind both of them that they couldn't do anything intimate with each other until they passed the age of gathering.

That was the last he had heard or saw of that.

Chapter 33

Kuvik studied Nolon across the camp circle. He sat next to Balea tonight three places down from Kuvik. She was one of the three other women Kuvik had seen Nolon trying to get close to.

She must have seen the same thing because she didn't respond to him except in short, one-word answers. She rarely made eye contact with him. He also tried to get close to her children, but she maneuvered them away from him.

Kuvik waited for the mood to relax a little more. Gurn and Garvis both sat between Kuvik on one side and Balea on the other. Gurn got up. Kuvik took that moment to scoot down the circle into Gurn's place and then Garvis did the same thing.

Kuvik moved again and wound up sitting next to Balea. She gave him a pleading look like she wanted him to rescue her from Nolon.

"Take your son and move to my other side," Kuvik murmured. "Don't say anything to Nolon. Just move—now."

She did it immediately, picked up her son, stood up, walked around Kuvik, and he scooted into her old place before she sat down on his other side.

Nolon was in the middle of talking to Elem on his other side. Nolon didn't notice Balea moving until he turned around and discovered Kuvik in her place.

Nolon's eyebrows flew up. "Hello!"

"Which Clan are you originally from, Nolon?" Kuvik asked.

Nolon frowned. "Why do you ask that?"

"I'm curious. Which Clan are you originally from?"

"I'm from the Whisperers Clan." Nolon hesitated. "I thought you knew that, but I guess you wouldn't since we've never talked about it."

"How old were you when the Bounty Hunters captured you?" Kuvik asked.

"I was twenty. I was with my family band and the Bounty Hunters surprised us. We knew they were in the country, but we didn't realize they were so near us or that they were coming our way. We thought they were going somewhere else."

"Did your band take you to the gathering when you were younger?"

Nolon smirked. "I went, but there were too few women. I was one of those that left without a wife."

Kuvik only nodded. So Nolon had never been with a woman. He probably thought he could get one now.

"I'm assuming your parents, relatives, and Kral taught you the laws of gathering," Kuvik went on. "A man who goes to the gathering and doesn't come home with a wife has to stay alone for life. Isn't that the law?"

Nolon's smile evaporated. "What are you saying?"

"I'm asking if your parents, relatives, and Kral taught you the laws of gathering. They must have. You grew up in the Clan until the age of gathering. You went to the gathering. You came home and you lived with your Clan for another two years before the Bounty Hunters captured you. That's a long time. You must have learned the laws. Didn't you?"

Nolon gulped. "Yes, I learned the laws."

"Then you know it would be illegal for you to touch any woman you weren't legally married to. It would be illegal for you to touch any woman even if she wasn't legally married to another man. You would only be legally entitled to marry if you got your Kral's consent. Until then, you have no right to lay your hands on any woman no matter who she is. Isn't that the law?"

Nolon's face went through a few different spasms before he said, "Yes, that's what my Clan teaches."

Kuvik didn't wait around to continue this conversation. He stood up and raised his voice for everyone to hear him. "Pay attention, everybody. I know that Nolon here has been making advances to some of you women. Some of these advances have been illegal in nature and he's transgressed the law by pushing himself on women who were unwilling. We all know that Nolon isn't legally married to any woman in this band, so any advances of this kind would be a gross violation of the law. It would be up to me as your Kral to decide how to punish these offenses, so I want any woman here to stand up and speak in front of all of us to tell us what he's been doing and how he's trespassed on any of you. Speak now so we can make sure he doesn't do it again to someone else—and to make sure he doesn't do the same thing again to you."

Kuvik expected another tense silence to fall over the group, but Balea stood up right away. "Nolon forced himself on me four different times. I pushed him away every time and told him to leave me alone, but he wouldn't listen. He said he could be a husband to me and a father to my children. When I told him I would never marry him, he threatened me and said he would do a hundred times worse to me than the Bounty Hunters ever did if I told anyone." She glanced at Kuvik. "I'm sorry I didn't tell you. I should have."

"Thank you," Kuvik told her. "Thank you for telling us now." He faced the circle. "Anyone else?"

Kesha stood up. "He only came onto me once. He didn't go as far as putting his hands on me. He tried to. He came at me, but I pulled my knife on him and told him to stay away from me. He laughed at me and said I would never be anything but Kannor's whore. He said I shouldn't even be alive right now and I would die soon to settle the score."

She sat down and turned her face away so she didn't have to look at anyone. A different woman named Giwa stood up. "He never did anything but talk to me," she stammered. "I guess you could say he flirted with me. I don't know if that counts."

"Were you receptive?" Kuvik asked. "Did you flirt back at him?"

"I started to and then I noticed him doing it to a few other people, so I stopped. He didn't stop and I guess you could say I didn't stop him. I just decided to let it run its course. I figured if he was interested in other people he would lose interest after a while if I just didn't respond. I had no idea he was out there doing all of this."

She sat down and silence really did fall over the group. The crackling fire sounded extra loud in the stillness.

Kuvik glanced over at Mapa. She and Akli exchanged glances and she stood up.

"Mapa?" Kuvik asked. "What do you want to tell us?"

"He......he......" she stammered and eventually faltered to the point where she couldn't go on.

Akli raised his hand and slipped it into hers while she stood next to him. The feeling of his hand holding hers pushed her over the edge and she burst into tears. She covered her face with her other hand. She didn't let go of Akli's with her other hand.

Kuvik waited. He would have waited all night for her to say what she had to say.

"He came at me three times!" she howled out in choked sobs. "He followed me when I left the camp for water. He pushed up against me and used his body to grind against me while he pawed at me with his hands. I told him to stop, but he wouldn't!" She burst out in wretched sobs. "He knew what happened to me and he did it anyway!"

"Are you saying.....?" Kuvik tripped over the words. "Are you saying he took you all the way?"

She nodded, but she was crying too hard to answer. No one else made a sound.

Akli eventually stood up, put his arms around her, and pulled her back down to sit on the ground next to him. He kept shooting Kuvik death glares while Akli held her.

Kuvik took a deep breath. He never expected to have to preside over something like this as Kral of any band. Now he had to make it count.

He waved to everyone sitting around the fire. "I want all of you to back away—at least ten feet from the fire. Clear a space—not you, Nolon. You come and stand over here in front of me."

Everyone hustled to back off, including Akli and Mapa. Nolon hesitated. He glared at Kuvik, too, but Nolon didn't quite cast the same intimidating impression as Akli.

"What are you going to do?" Nolon snapped. "You aren't really a Kral, you know. You're just another escaped captive-slave like the rest of us. You don't have any authority."

"I'm going to give you a choice, Nolon—because I'm a nice person. I might be willing to send you out into the jungle on your own and banish you from our band. I probably would do it that way if we had just escaped from the Bounty Hunters. The problem is that you're too good a hunter and warrior now, so you would probably survive and either come back to haunt our band or you would just go around and do the same thing to someone else."

Nolon scowled a little deeper. "What's the choice, then?"

"You agreed with the others when they made me Kral," Kuvik pointed out. "You didn't offer any objection then. I seem to remember you even nodding when the others said I would be Kral of this band. Do you remember that?"

"What does that have to do with anything?"

"As Kral of this band, I could tell my warriors to kill you in punishment for your crimes, but I'm not going to do that. I don't want them to do it. I feel a special responsibility to protect these women and to give them the justice they deserve with my own hand. We don't have time to wait until morning to feed you to the ants. So the choice I'm giving you is this. You can accept me as your Kral, which means that you would accept my sentence and submit to it without fighting back. I know the Whisperers Clan follows the law when it comes to these things, too. You obey your Kral without question and accept your Kral's decisions no matter what. Don't you?"

Nolon's features turned to granite. "What's the other choice?"

"The other choice is that you don't accept me as your Kral, you do try to fight, and I kill you anyway. The only question is if you want to die as a wretched, traitorous, Clanless criminal or if you want to die abiding by the law of your fathers before you. The only question is if you want to bring even more shame on your Clan than you already have. I'm sure your parents, relatives, and Kral would be disgusted if they could see you now."

Nolon's face twisted in a mass of knotted, hideous fury. "Don't you dare say anything against my Clan."

"I'm not saying anything against your Clan, you worthless waste of human flesh. I'm saying it about you. You don't deserve to walk the face of the Earth after what you've done." Kuvik finished his sentence by pulling one of his tooth blades from his waistband. "It sounds like you've made your decision."

Chapter 34

Nolon answered Kuvik by pulling a knife of his own. It was a short, straight, two-sided metal hunting knife taken from the Bounty Hunters' weapons storehouse.

Some of the others retreated farther away in the dark. The mothers pulled their children well clear. Nolon raised his weapon, flexed his knees, and circled Kuvik to the left.

Kuvik stayed where he was. He didn't even waste his time raising his weapon. Nolon had come from the Whisperers Clan, which meant he'd learned to fight when he was young.

Kuvik had seen Nolon fight before. Kuvik couldn't know what Nolon had been like before his capture, but his skills had either deteriorated or vanished completely. He didn't start off any better than Phiri who never learned to fight at all.

Nolon continued to circle until he got all the way over to Kuvik's left side. Kuvik barely turned his head to follow Nolon's progress.

Kuvik wanted to humiliate Nolon in front of all the women he had hurt, but Kuvik also wanted to teach Nolon a lesson. He actually thought he could flout the law by denying Kuvik as Kral just to suit Nolon's convenience in the moment.

Nolon had been one of the most enthusiastic about Kuvik becoming Kral. Nolon had never raised any objection before. He had no reason to do it now just because it suited him.

A decent man would have fallen on his knees and let his Kral do what he wanted to carry out the sentence—but then again, a decent man wouldn't have hurt these women in the first place.

The fact that Nolon knew what these women had been going through with the Bounty Hunters and still did it anyway made it so much worse. Mapa was right about that. That was the worst violation ever.

Kuvik couldn't leave someone like that alive. Nolon was a menace to everyone every-where. He didn't belong in the human race any longer.

Kuvik still didn't raise his blade to defend himself. He didn't have to. He faced front and waited for the attack he knew was coming.

Nolon circled all the way to Kuvik's left and drew level with Kuvik's shoulder. Nolon lunged in and raised his knife to strike.

Kuvik didn't even turn his head to see what he was doing. He tossed his blade to his left hand and swiped his arm out to the side. He slashed his blade upward and cut Nolon deep from his navel all the way up to his collarbone on the right side.

Nolon roared in pain and jolted back, but not fast enough. Kuvik spun around, threw his blade back to his right hand, and slashed Nolon again coming down the other way. He carved an identical gash down Nolon's chest to his hip.

Blood poured from both wounds. Nolon stared down at them in horror and then raised his eyes to lock on Kuvik's while Nolon staggered backward to get away. He bared his teeth in a half-furious, half-terrified grimace.

Kuvik was all done playing games with this treacherous bastard. Nolon had been alive on this planet too long already. Kuvik lunged forward and swiped his blade in one more swoop that slashed Nolon's throat.

Kuvik stopped where he was while Nolon dropped his knife and his hand flew to his throat.

He kept toppling backward until he tripped on something and sprawled backward on the ground. He landed on the bare dirt next to the fire and lay there gasping, convulsing, and gargling on his own blood.

His eyes raced around the dark canopy above his head while he tried in desperate panic to stop the flow of blood coming from his neck. No one moved or breathed until he stopped moving and lay still.

Kuvik stared down at the body. So that was the end of his first challenge to his leadership as Kral. He could beat any man here in a fight and they all knew it. He didn't even train with them because he was too far ahead of them.

He waited a little while until all the blood stopped flowing from Nolon's neck. That blood would cause the band problems. They needed to get away from it and the party still had a lot of work to do to finish butchering the Gorlock.

He bent over, grabbed Nolon by the wrist, and towed the body out into the jungle. Kuvik left the body next to an Abnormit mound. The Abnormits were all inside right now, but they would find the body soon enough and get rid of it.

He went back to the fire. None of the others had moved. He picked up Nolon's knife and used it to scrape all the bloodstained dirt off the ground. He scooped it up into a bowl, carried that to a safe distance from the fire, and bumped the dirt out.

He rinsed both blades and the bowl in the stream before he went back to the fire. No one had moved. Everyone stared at him in horror. He went back to his old place, put his tooth blade in his waistband, and set Nolon's weapon aside. Someone somewhere would use it.

He took a deep breath to steady himself and faced his people. Akli and Mapa stood across the circle from Kuvik. Akli held her in his arms while she hid her face on his shoulder. She kept her head turned the other way so she wouldn't see what happened to Nolon.

"Come out here, Akli," Kuvik ordered. "Bring Mapa with you."

Akli had to take his arms off Mapa to step out. He took her hand and led her into the circle glaring at everyone. She wasn't crying anymore. She wouldn't look at anyone.

They stopped in front of Kuvik. Akli glared at Kuvik in outright murderous challenge.

"Do you want to marry this woman, Akli?" Kuvik asked.

"Yes, of course I do," Akli replied.

"Mapa?" Kuvik asked. "Do you want to marry this man?"

"Yes, of course I do," she squeaked under her breath.

"Then consider yourselves legally married from now on. You can defend your wife any way you please from now on, Akli. You can take care of her and give her everything she needs. No one will ever stand between you again."

Akli stared at Kuvik in stunned disbelief. Mapa's head shot up and her eyes fell out of their sockets. She gasped out loud—and then she and Akli spun toward each other and hurled themselves into each other's arms.

They embraced much harder in front of everyone. He burst out laughing. She burst out in tears. He swept her feet off the ground and spun her sideways.

Everyone watched them celebrate together in their own private little bubble of their own. Akli eventually put her down and they pulled apart. Tears glistened in his eyes, but he had never looked so happy.

He dove in and kissed her once still laughing in tearful emotion. He grabbed her hand and led her out of the circle of firelight into the dark where no one could see them.

They left an even more meaningful silence in their wake. Akli and Mapa were the first domino to fall. They were this band's first legally married couple. They definitely wouldn't be the last.

Kuvik sat down in the place where he'd been sitting before his conversation with Nolon. The others slowly drifted back into their places, too. Giwa came over, handed Kuvik a bowl of cooked Gorlock meat, smiled at him, and walked away.

He read no subtext in that smile. He never read any subtext from any woman of this band. None of them expressed any interest in him.

He'd never told any of them about Yoa. That was his own private little secret. He didn't share it with anyone.

He dreamed about her every night. He dreamed about the way she acted with him the night they had escaped from the Bounty Hunters. He would always treasure that memory.

He would get back to her someday. He never doubted that for a second. She and the other Godless were the one thing keeping him going. They were the light at the end of a long, dark tunnel through this nightmare.

He ate his meat in silence. The others eventually started talking again. The band came back to life. Conversation flowed the way it should. He put Nolon's challenge behind him. Kuvik put everything about Nolon behind him.

Kuvik stared into the flames and let his fantasies run wild about how life would be when he made it back to the Godless.

He replayed his memories of his time with Hangman's band. He saw every face and experienced all the connection with each person one after another.

He sat there in his own world while the rest of his people climbed up into the trees for the night. He didn't watch to see if Akli and Mapa came back. Whatever happened between them was no one else's business but their own.

A twig snapped in the fire in front of him. It brought him back to reality. The fire was starting to die down. He should climb up into the treetops and go to sleep, too. He and his band had a long road to travel tomorrow.

He glanced around. He was the last person still on the ground. The others had already packed up what was left of the Gorlock meat and removed the carcass and bones.

He sighed. He had no reason to stay down here and dwell on all his old memories. The past slipped farther and farther away from him the longer he stayed out here. He didn't even know how long he'd been gone.

Hangman's band could be long gone by the time he made it back to Shadow's territory. Hangman, his men, his family, Yoa—they could all be dead. Kuvik could be holding onto these dreams for nothing.

Someone came out of the shadows behind him just then. He didn't realize anyone was still up. Akli and Mapa had gone off in a different direction.

Kuvik startled when Kesha sat down next to him. She smiled up at him and slipped her hand onto his knee. Her touch made him freeze. How did this happen within seconds of him thinking about Yoa?

"You should take a wife, Kuvik," Kesha murmured. "You're Kral. You should take a wife and have your own family."

"I will never take a wife." He pushed her hand off his knee and looked away. He would have gotten up and walked away, but that would probably have been too insulting.

He didn't want to insult her. She couldn't possibly know about Yoa.

She frowned. "Why won't you take a wife? You're strong and healthy. You would make a great father." She raised her hand and stroked it up and down his bare back. "Don't tell me you don't long for the company of a woman—your own woman."

The feeling of her hand touching him sent a lightning bolt through him. He jumped up and knocked her arm away before he realized what he was doing. "Don't touch me!" he snapped.

She got to her feet, but she didn't follow him, thank God. "I admire you for saving me from Kannor," she called after him. "I admire you for what you did for all of us and I admire you for what you did tonight. You're a great man and a great Kral. I only meant you should have a wife who admires you and cares for you as much as I do. I don't see you connecting with anyone else in the band. Why not me?"

He paced on the other side of the fire so he wouldn't go near her. He couldn't get rid of that feeling of her hand on his back. It gave him the shivers.

"I don't connect with anyone else in the band because I'm already engaged to a girl in the Godless Clan," he replied over his shoulder.

She snorted at him. "Engaged? You're either married to her or you aren't. If you didn't marry her, then she would be free to marry anyone else. She wouldn't wait for you. Her family wouldn't let her. They would marry her to someone else when you didn't come back."

"That doesn't matter because I'm going back to her. I'll never marry anyone else."

She crossed the camp to get closer to him. He had to stop himself from either shoving her away or running.

She halted in front of him. "This is all nonsense, Kuvik. You might never make it back to the Godless....."

"Yes, I will. I won't stop until I do."

"This girl could already be married to someone else by then. You've been gone too long already."

He only nodded. "Maybe, but I'm going back anyway. I owe my loyalty to my Kral and my Clan. Nothing will stop me from going back to my own band."

He didn't say another word. He sprang into the branches over his head and scrambled up into the canopy to join the rest of the band.

Kesha stayed down on the ground for a long time. She was still down there by the time Kuvik fell asleep. Now he had to make sure he stayed away from her. She wouldn't do anything when the rest of their party stood around watching.

Chapter 35

K uvik balanced along a branch, put some distance between him and the band, and scouted ahead. His scouts had already covered this part of the territory, but he went ahead and checked it anyway.

The men scouted the surrounding country much more closely the farther south they traveled. They also scouted more thoroughly to the north.

Freedom tasted pretty sweet these days. No one wanted to give it up. It kept getting more precious by the day. The band would defend it with all they had if anyone tried to take it from them.

The band traveled much faster these days. All the children ran quickly and easily through the branches. The mothers with babies traveled fast, too. They had all perfected the art of carrying their children in wraps and bundles of various kinds.

The older children and teenagers carried the younger ones who didn't know how to climb. The whole band had developed a much more efficient rhythm for helping each other and protecting each other as much as possible.

Kuvik never dreamed he would be this contented with any other band than Hangman's, but Kuvik found that with these people. Hardship and shared danger had brought them together in unimaginable ways.

Senau and Giwa were definitely pairing off. Gurn was in the process of pairing off with Dorei's mother, Linnoth. Neither couple had asked Kuvik if they could get married, but it was only a matter of time.

Kuvik followed the band's progress for the rest of the day. He didn't see any dangers they couldn't handle.

The four teenage boys almost always posted themselves as guards around the women and children when Kuvik didn't specifically assign one of them to a scouting party.

Tren was the only exception. He usually split off from the band to go hunt creatures he spotted in the jungle, even if he spotted one at a distance. He took the role of provider very seriously and no one tried to dissuade him.

He didn't split off today. He stayed with the band until they camped for the night. They camped in the trees and ate his leftover Gorlock meat.

"How far south do we need to go to meet up with your band?" Akli asked around the fire.

"I'm not sure," Kuvik replied. "I don't recognize this country. I just planned to keep going until I get back to country I do recognize."

"I don't think he knows where he's going at all," Kesha interjected in front of the whole group. "I think he's leading us on a fool's errand to nowhere."

"Kesha!" Balea gasped. "Watch your mouth!"

Kesha chopped her hand through the air in Kuvik's direction. "He isn't even a man! He doesn't want to get married. I think there's something wrong with him. Maybe he doesn't like women. Akli is more a man than Kuvik is."

Kuvik froze, but he didn't allow himself to respond. He didn't allow himself even to raise his eyes to look at her or any of the others to see how they reacted.

"What do we really know about him, anyway?" she went on in front of everyone. "We only know what he tells us. He could be making up all these stories. He might never have lived with the Godless. He might not know anyone there. He might not be going back there at all." She got to her feet, spun around, and pointed at him. Her voice started rising. "Do any of you know which Clan he's originally from? Huh? Go on. Ask him. He hasn't told anyone, has he? No one knows. I think he's making it all up."

"That's enough, Kesha," Phiri snapped. "Kuvik is the one who got us out of the Bounty Hunter village. He's the one reason we're alive out here with our freedom and a chance to live our lives in peace instead of being captive slaves. I don't need to know which Clan he's from. I already know everything I need to know about him."

"You're one of *his* slaves," she sneered. "You do anything he tells you to, don't you?"

"He's our Kral," Nelv interjected. "That's what a Kral is. We do what he says—and he's always right. Every decision he's made has been right."

She snorted at him. "You're more his slaves now than you ever were with the Bounty Hunters. When are you going to think for yourselves instead of always letting someone else tell you what to do? He has no authority over us. He isn't qualified to take us anywhere. Ask him if he's ever done anything like this before. Ask him if he even knows how to deal with being the leader of a band."

No one answered. The silence spoke volumes. A few people cast glances at Kuvik, but he didn't look up. He didn't say a word to defend himself.

He never asked for this. He would gladly have escaped from the Bounty Hunters by himself. He would gladly have let everyone in this band go in one direction while he went off alone in a completely different direction.

He never asked for anyone to make him Kral or for them to blindly obey him. He certainly never mistreated anyone.

He would lose absolutely nothing if they all walked away and left him alone. He might almost have preferred it if they did. Then he wouldn't have to deal with this crap.

This was his second challenge as Kral. He had to deal with Kesha. He had to silence her. The only alternative was for him to leave the band on his own. He could do it easily. He could survive in the jungle alone.

They couldn't—or not as well. They would all be better off with him than without him. Most of them understood this. He didn't even have to ask. They stood with him.

They didn't answer her because they all knew how ridiculous her statements were.

He kept thinking one thing. One thought blocked out all the others. He kept remembering what she looked like when he had found her unconscious, naked, bloody, and ravaged on the floor in Kannor's house.

That was her. That was the real Kesha.

This whole thing—her whole tirade in front of the group about how he wasn't a man—this was just her counterassault for him rejecting her. He had hurt her feelings and she retaliated by trying to hurt him back. That's all this was.

He didn't stick around to hear anything else. He got up, climbed down to the ground, and walked off into the darkness by himself. He got a safe distance from the camp where no one could see him, jumped back into the branches, and climbed.

He found a spot where he could observe the band and the surrounding terrain. He felt a profound sense of relief in his moment of solitude. Being Kral of all these competing personalities unnecessarily complicated his life.

He decided not to put up with anything like this again. He would deal with any misbehavior much more harshly. This band's cohesion was one of its greatest assets. He wouldn't let anyone undermine it for any reason.

He waited a while until Kesha went off on her own. She climbed down to the ground and headed off to the stream for some reason. He didn't see why and he didn't care.

He dropped out of the branches faster than anyone else in the band could travel. They still couldn't match his skill when it came to running and climbing in the treetops.

He dropped down behind Kesha and made enough noise to get her attention. She turned around. She started to open her mouth, probably to fire off at him again.

"Don't say a word," he snapped. "In fact, don't say a word ever again to anyone in this band. Is that clear? Don't open your mouth about me in front of anyone. Your other option is that you pack up and leave right now. You're either with this band or you're gone. You can leave by yourself or I can send you away."

She snorted at him. "You don't have the authority to send me away. You're nothing. You aren't a Kral. Nolon was right about that."

He didn't rise to the bait of her comparing him to Nolon. "I don't have to be your Kral. You don't have to be a part of this band. You can go somewhere else if you don't like it. You will leave if you say one more word against this band. Your actions are destroying the band's cohesion. That is unacceptable. Either get back on board with doing things our way or go off on your own. This will be your last warning. I won't tell you again."

He vaulted into the branches and left her standing there. Now he had to back up that decision with action. One more infraction and he would throw her out. That was the bottom line.

He wouldn't be a Kral at all if he didn't follow through. He couldn't make a threat like that without carrying it out.

He would do it just for his own peace of mind. He would do it just to get rid of the headache of having her around. He had too many problems and concerns already without one of his own people adding to it and making it worse.

He had a flashback of Aster betraying Hangman's band to the Renegade Clan. She was a traitor because she put her band in danger—on purpose.

That's what Kesha was doing. What would stop her from alerting the Bounty Hunters to the band's location if she thought Kuvik was so bad? Who did she think was qualified to lead the band in his place—herself?

He didn't need to ask that because he was Kral. Everyone else considered him their Kral. If they didn't, then they didn't belong in a band with him and he didn't belong in a band with them.

He didn't need to be in a band with them and he certainly didn't need to be Kral. He was doing these people a favor by being the Kral they needed him to be. He was doing them an even bigger favor by even staying in the same band with them.

He'd been doing them nonstop favors since they first escaped and even before that. He could stop doing that anytime they wanted him to. His life would only get easier if he did.

He climbed up and returned to his place with the others. Everyone was already going to sleep anyway, so he did the same thing.

Chapter 36

The band set off on their journey the next morning. Kesha acted as though last night's confrontation never happened, so Kuvik let it go. Maybe she would do the same thing and fall in line. Maybe she would go back to being one of his most reliable people.

She'd never given him any reason to doubt her before. She should have known better than to make a move on him like that when he'd never expressed any interest in her in return.

It might have been different if he'd singled her out or tried to talk to her more. Maybe then she could have made an overture like that.

Everything might have been fine between them if she'd only accepted it when he told her he wanted to go back to Yoa. Kesha could have just taken the news graciously and dropped the subject instead of turning against him like this.

He tried again and again to put the subject out of his mind, especially when she didn't do anything else hour after hour.

The mothers with young children and babies stopped for a rest at noon. The men returned from scouting forays to stand guard over the band while they ate some food and drank some water in the treetops.

Everyone engaged in the usual subdued small talk until the time came to move on.

"Why do we keep going south anyway?" Kesha blurted out in an extra loud, provocative tone. "I say we go in a different direction."

"Shut up, Kesha," Akli snapped. "No one is interested in what you think or say."

"The Bounty Hunters already know we're heading south," she went on. "That's the first place they'll look for us."

Kuvik stood up and walked off down the branch to the next tree. "You can go anywhere you want—all of you," he snapped over his shoulder. "I'm going south. I don't care what the rest of you do."

Everyone else in the band got to their feet and followed him without a word. The men outright glared at Kesha. No one said anything for a long time. They kept traveling at their former pace.

Kuvik stayed in front of everyone and flatly refused to turn around to check if they followed him or not. He honestly didn't give a crap if they came with him. He was traveling alone for all he cared. They didn't exist—any of them.

He kept going until sundown. The band would normally have stopped long before that to give everyone an hour or two of daylight to make camp, especially if anyone had hunted any new kills.

He didn't stop until the sky started to get dark. He descended to a stream still pretending he was all by himself out here.

He dropped to the ground, squatted by the stream, and the others gathered around him. He didn't look up to see if Kesha was with them. He took some of Tren's dried meat out of his shoulder bag and ate it.

Kuvik could easily hunt for himself. He didn't need someone else to do it for him. He didn't need to mess with these people at all. He definitely didn't need to put up with any of their stupid antics and spiteful backbiting behavior.

He heard the mothers and children around him. Some of the youngest children came up to him and tried to hang and sit all over him like they usually did. He stopped himself from pushing them away.

He didn't want to look at, talk to, or smile at them, either, but he made himself do it. None of this was their fault. They were innocent in all of this. They had no idea it was even happening. They probably didn't understand a word Kesha had said about him.

They loved him the same as always. He never had to doubt them. He would have seriously let them down if he left. He owed them his best effort even if the adults pissed him off at times.

He started to laugh at something Balea's little son was doing. He was crawling well now and trying to stand up. He almost always fell over when he tried.

An ear-splitting scream echoed out of the jungle right then and startled everyone to high alert. Kuvik listened for only a second. It was a woman's scream—and then he recognized Kesha's voice.

He already feared the worst by the time he took a running leap into the branches. He raced through the treetops toward the sound. It didn't stop. The sound led him straight to her.

He hurtled through the canopy and fought down a wave of cold sweat when he saw her staked to the ground at a distance with her arms and legs spread all the way out.

Akli, Phiri, Nelv, Gurn, Senau, Garvis, and the teenage boys crouched in the branches above her. They all watched Tren back into the clearing sprinkling pollen on the ground in front of a massive swarm of ants. He led them straight to Kesha.

She roared out in wordless screams as he tossed a handful of pollen on top of her and jumped into the branches out of the ants' reach. They followed the trail closer.

Kuvik rocketed through the canopy trying to get there in time, but he was too late and she was too far away. The ants climbed on top of her. He would lose his life if he went down there now.

He stopped and watched her vanish under the tide of black bodies. Her screams spiked into the stratosphere and then muffled when they covered her face. She disappeared and they ate her down to the bare dirt.

He stared at the spot until Tren dropped out of the branches and started scattering more pollen to lead the ants away from the band. He backed away deeper into the jungle and the ants went with him.

Kuvik couldn't tear his eyes away from the place where Kesha had been. He never planned to get rid of his problem like this—not in a million years.

Hadn't he just been thinking a little while ago that she was no better than Aster—that she put the band in danger for nothing—that she would betray the band to the Bounty Hunters just to retaliate against Kuvik?

The other men descended to the ground, too. They milled around the spot talking. He saw it all. They must have planned this behind his back.

He plummeted out of the trees and landed near them. He barely waited for them to turn around and face him.

"What the hell is wrong with you?!" he snapped. "How could you do this without even consulting me?!"

"We did it to support you," Gurn replied. "We did it out of loyalty to you and to protect you from her constant efforts to undermine you."

"I don't need you protecting me!" Kuvik fired back. "You all made me your Kral! Didn't you? Didn't you?! Am I your Kral or not?!"

"Of course you are, Kuvik," Nelv replied. "That's why we did it. She was a traitor for challenging you like that. She deserved to die. You're too forgiving if you let her live—even to leave the band."

"That's my decision to make—not yours!" Kuvik snapped. "I would be the one to decide if she went to the ants or if we banish her or not! You don't make those decisions without consulting me. That's what being Kral is! I decide—not you! Is that clear?! You're the ones who undermined my authority by going behind my back. Do you get that? All of you betrayed your oath to me. I should punish all of you!"

"You're right, Kuvik," Akli murmured. "We didn't think of that. We did cross you. We do deserve that. We'll accept your judgment."

Kuvik fought himself under control. "Do not EVER let me catch you doing anything like this again. Do you understand? We have too few women as it is. We can't afford to go executing one of them if we can avoid it. Is that clear? You don't ever make a decision like this without my approval. I'll be the one to decide how anyone gets punished for anything—including you! Is that clear?!"

He stood there glaring at everyone in front of him. Tren came back in time to hear the second half of Kuvik's tirade—including the part about punishing these men for going behind his back and making the decision on his behalf.

Tren slowed and watched from the other side of the clearing. None of the men answered until Akli murmured under his breath again, "It's clear, Kuvik. We won't do it again."

Kuvik spun around and got in the other men's faces. "Let me hear all of you say it—all of you!"

"Yes, it's clear," Phiri replied.

They all said it and some apologized to him. He gave them one last withering glare and stormed off back to the camp. He threw himself down by the stream again. The children didn't come near him.

It was a good thing they didn't. He was fuming too badly to deal with them. Did all the women in camp think that he was the one who threw Kesha to the ants for talking badly about him? Did they all think he was the one who made that decision?

He didn't say or do anything to change their minds. The men came back a little while later. No one talked about what happened. None of the women asked where Kesha was. Maybe they would think he sent her away after all. He could only hope.

He didn't understand his own reaction. What difference did it make to the band if she left on her own or if the men threw her to the ants? She was gone either way.

Why did it have to end like this? Why did she have to get so bent out of shape about him saying he didn't want to get together with her? Why did she have to get so irrational about it? She would be alive right now if she'd only kept her head.

He probably shouldn't have gone off on his men like that, either. They only wanted to protect the band—which meant themselves. Threatening the band meant threatening them. They had a right to protect themselves against any threat, even from her.

He stayed quiet for the rest of the evening and ate his own food by himself. He had enough. He didn't need anything else, but Mapa brought him some roasted meat a little while later. She must have kept it aside somewhere along the way.

He mumbled his thanks without looking up. Things had been going so well for the whole band. Why did this have to happen?

He couldn't expect everything to go well all the time. That would be asking too much. The band had enjoyed such good times lately. Life had never been better. It was bound to turn the other way eventually.

He couldn't expect to be Kral without someone challenging him. Nolon wouldn't be the only one and Kesha probably wouldn't be, either.

Kuvik didn't picture any of the others doing it, especially none of the men or boys. He held all of them in the palm of his hand. He already knew that.

The next challenge would come from somewhere. He just had to deal with it when it did come.

Chapter 37

The band climbed some steep mountains that took days to traverse. Kuvik had to send out constant scouting parties before they found a pass with a trail the band could follow.

The band had to travel along the ground here. They couldn't use the treetops. The jungle dwindled and disappeared. It no longer offered any protection from the air. The band had to hide from airborne creature attacks more here.

Kuvik tried to keep everyone entertained with stories about Hangman's band's adventures in the northern mountains. Kuvik told everyone about Wildling's initiation and his habit of carrying a rope with him everywhere.

The members of Kuvik's band and especially the children knew all the names of all the people involved in his stories. The children liked to hear about all the people they were getting to know through his wider and wider elaborations of everything he knew about them.

A few of the other members of his band also had interesting stories to tell about their lives before their captivity. Some of these people had already been old enough to remember their home Clans before they got captured.

These stories bonded everyone more closely together as they got to know each other better. Kuvik still didn't talk about his home Clan. He didn't talk much about his time in the Hungry Ghosts, either. He didn't want to elaborate on that.

Everyone avoided talking about their bad experiences, both with the Bounty Hunters and everywhere else. Everyone here had enough bad memories to last a lifetime. No one needed more of them.

Kuvik stood on a tall rock and watched his people file through the pass. He checked the skies, but he didn't see any creatures close enough to put the band in danger.

A few Boultars and Ridgebeaks soared high in the sky, but they wouldn't be able to get down here fast enough. His people would have plenty of warning and they would be able to hide in time.

The trail wound down the other side of the hill. The men kept constant watch on the countryside—and Kuvik turned his gaze northward, hopefully for the last time. He hadn't seen a single Bounty Hunter since the band's last assault.

The band might encounter more Bounty Hunters here. The Bounty Hunters might have invaded this country, too. They just wouldn't be from the same band that had held these people as captives.

He jumped off the rock and followed everyone down the hill. The group picked up their pace, now that they could walk downhill.

A line of jungle cut off their view of the valley. The trees would protect the band better in there. The four boys burst into a run and got there first to scout the area. Kuvik didn't call them back.

He decided to call the band to a halt early tonight so they could get some extra rest. Climbing these mountains taxed everyone more than usual. Traveling through the treetops was easy compared to this.

The band entered the jungle and continued to walk along the ground. Kuvik didn't correct that, either. The boys ranged outward on either side. Neither Kuvik nor any of the men or boys saw anything to threaten the band here.

The trail passed along the edge of a high hill that sloped down to a tumbling, rocky river down at the bottom of the valley. This looked like a fertile, prosperous country—so where were all the people?

The high hill eventually merged with a steep mountainside. The trail crossed the cliff. It still offered plenty of space for the band to walk comfortably. Nothing about it looked dangerous.

The trail wound around the mountain and headed across the cliff toward another high hill covered in jungle. This one looked similar if not identical to the one the band had just left.

They made it halfway across the distance when a deep rumble shook the mountain. Kuvik looked all around him, but he didn't see anything that might have caused that noise.

He picked up his pace. "Get into the trees!" he told everyone. "Get onto that hillside."

The band started forward, but at that moment, for no reason Kuvik could understand, the cliff face dissolved beneath his feet. The band burst into a run sprinting for the trees ahead. He lunged forward to join them, but not fast enough.

The cliff crumbled under him and he plummeted away along with tons and tons of solid rock falling all around him.

He crashed down in an overpowering torrent of rubble pounding all around him, but it moved and flowed like water. It tumbled him in all directions and slammed him from side to side.

The cascade went on for a long time. He might have hit his head and lost awareness of how long it took. He couldn't be sure.

He came to his senses lying under piles of rock. Blocks and slabs lay all over him—or it felt like it. He groaned when he felt the bruises covering his body, but at least the Bounty Hunters weren't the ones who did it to him this time.

He lay still for a second and concentrated on breathing. His body ached from countless bruises, some worse than others, but he didn't feel any broken bones, thank God.

He finally flexed his muscles and tried to push against all the debris and boulders on top of him. He might get trapped under here and never get out.

The layer of stuff on top of him turned out not to be as thick and heavy as he initially thought. Boulders, blocks, and slabs did lie on top of him, but the pile wasn't so heavy that he couldn't move it.

It took all his effort, but the weight started to shift as soon as he pushed against it with any serious strength. Gravel and random shards fell away the minute he started to unsettle the pile. That made it easier.

He heaved harder and used all four arms and legs to push against the debris on top of him. More boulders fell away and then one much larger slab toppled off. The rest broke apart easily and he pried himself out of the heap.

He toppled off and fell across a whole field of similar debris lying all over the river valley. The landslide formed a wide, rounded mound leading all the way down to the rocky streambed he'd just been admiring from the upper hillside.

He staggered to his feet, turned around in a full circle, and looked up at the mountain behind him. A section of cliff face had calved off in this landslide. It had gouged a deep groove in the mountain high above his head. The gouge looked tiny from here.

He could trace the cliff sideways to the patch of trees where his band had taken refuge. He just didn't see any way to get up there. Steep hillsides, cliffs, and more mountains blocked him in on both sides.

The river ran down the valley next to him. It went a long way without showing any opening where he might be able to get up there. He couldn't climb up there now—not in his condition. The trip might take days.

He glanced around at the valley floor. A family of Stalkions and a full-sized adult male Gurlg had gotten caught in the landslide. They lay dead among all that rubble.

He decided to camp here and process all this meat for travel before he made the journey to catch up with his band. He knew where they were and he knew where they had been going. He could catch up with them easily if he ran.

He got straight to work and didn't stop until sunset. He built a fire by the river, butchered the Stalkions first, and hung up the meat to dry. Then he started on the Gurlg.

He still had his jawbone kukris and his tooth blades, so at least he didn't have to start from scratch. He studied some of the Stalkion tusks, but he couldn't see a way to utilize them. They were too big to take with him when he didn't have any use for them.

He cooked enough food for himself to eat that night and maybe the following day. He dried the rest. He sat by the fire thinking about a lot of things that night. He'd just been thinking how easy and uncomplicated his life would be without his band weighing him down.

Now he missed them. He liked them and had even come to love them. He had bonded with his men and the boys. They became brothers. He had gotten very close to some of the mothers and children.

He genuinely wanted what was best for all of them—and they were what was best for him. They caused him problems at times, but his life was better with them than without them.

He felt the same thing for them that he used to feel for Hangman's band. Kuvik had been through a lot with them—with all of them. He had committed himself to them and become part of them. They had become part of him. He would always carry them with him.

He did miss Yoa. She was the one thing this new band couldn't give him. Kesha didn't even come close. Seeing her as a Bounty Hunter captive didn't touch him the way seeing Yoa as a captive did.

Maybe Kesha needed him more. Maybe she needed him a lot more, but his heart belonged to Yoa and always would. He didn't understand why until he remembered the way she took care of him after their escape.

He had been barely functional then. She had taken care of him. He trusted her with his life. He would never have felt that way about Kesha. He couldn't think of any other woman he trusted as much as he trusted Yoa. He trusted her with his heart and soul.

He stayed awake late into the night working on his traveling food and thinking about her. She shone in front of him as a guiding star to show him the way home. He wouldn't find his way home until he found his way back to her.

He knew all the old reasons why she might not be waiting for him. She might have married someone else. She might be dead or disfigured or she might have completely forgotten about him and moved on with her life.

He knew all of that, but he still held her as his lode star—his touchstone. He would find his way back to her one way or the other. He would find out whether she still wanted him or if she was even still available to him. Then he would decide.

He fell asleep in that certainty, woke up the next morning, and worked all the following day to finish processing all that food. He had to cure a section of the Stalkion hide to make another bundle to carry on his back. All the food wouldn't fit in his bags.

He set off on his journey on the third day, followed the stream, and eventually came to the second high hillside leading up to the trail where his people had escaped the landslide.

It took him another two days to climb up that hillside and get to the trail. He made camp immediately as soon as he got there. He was too exhausted to go on.

He continued south running as fast as he could go. He had no idea how far ahead the band might have gotten, but it couldn't be that far. The women with children had to walk. The rest of the band had to keep pace with them.

He should have overtaken them by the third day, but he didn't. The trail wound through the mountains always heading south. He didn't see any forks the band might have taken or anywhere else they might have gone.

He continued for two more days before he decided to climb another mountain to survey the landscape from above. He perched at the very top where he could see everything for hundreds of miles in all directions. He didn't see any people anywhere.

He stayed on the rock for a long time trying to decide what to do. His people weren't here. His gut told him to scream out and call to them to find out where they were. What could have happened to them?

Nothing had happened to them. Something had happened to him. He was the one who had gotten swept away in a landslide—so where were they?

Wouldn't they continue south? Wouldn't they think he planned to continue south and go that way to meet up with him?

Almost all the men in the band wanted to join the Godless the way he talked about. They would keep going south and hope to meet up with him. Wouldn't they?

He couldn't do anything about that now. He didn't know where they were, where they were going, who might have taken charge in his absence, or what they might have decided to do.

He could only keep going south on his journey back to Shadow's territory. Kuvik had nowhere else in the world to do. He only hoped and prayed his friends would find him there—or somewhere else along the way.

He climbed down from the rock and set off south again. He couldn't decide whether to run or walk and he still had plenty on his mind, so he decided to walk.

Traveling alone went a lot faster even at a walk. He didn't have to constantly stop to give the women and children rests. He didn't have to always organize his band's campsites, scouting parties, and constant watch for human and nonhuman enemies.

He didn't make camp anywhere. He traveled from the moment he woke up until the moment he went to sleep at night. He ate on the march, slept at the base of trees or in the jungle canopy, and kept going. He occasionally even ran.

He passed through another jungle valley and entered another mountain range. This one was much steeper, more treacherous, and the peaks were much higher. It cost him more effort to climb each hill, cliff, and pass, but he saw one advantage in all of this.

He scaled the highest peak he could find and at last, at long last, after all this time, he finally spotted the Jagged Points in the distance. They lay to the east with the mountains surrounding the Ashtaw Valley to the west and slightly south of them.

He crumpled on the ground in a heap of emotional relief when he finally saw familiar country. He could make it now. He knew where he had to go. He just had to go back to the Ashtaw Valley. He would be able to pick up Hangman's trail from there.

He spent hours on top of the mountain in the whipping wind. He didn't want to lose sight of those peaks in the distance. He stayed up there for so long that the sun started to go down. He wound up spending the night there, but he didn't care.

He slept better that night than he'd slept in a long, long time. He had finally made it. He could make it the rest of the way. He knew where he was. Nothing could go wrong now and he would still make it even if it did.

Chapter 38

K uvik spent three more days scaling down the mountains, coming out south of them, and finding the path his people would have followed if they did come this way.

He traveled for another week, passed through another stretch of jungle, and crossed another set of hills overlooking another valley. He hunted for himself along the way, but he never stayed in one place for very long. He never made camp unless he had to.

He stopped at the head of the valley when he saw the trail of smoke from a campfire. It curled into the air in the distance and showed him exactly where the other group was camped. Was that his band? The trail led into another patch of jungle.

He had to divert away from his journey to the Ashtaw Valley, but he did it gladly. He couldn't pass up a chance to meet up with his band. He could always head for the Ashtaw Valley afterward and take his band with him.

His friends would be ecstatic when they heard that he knew how to find the Godless. They would all be thrilled that they were entering another band's territory and could meet up with the people they'd been looking for all this time.

He traveled faster to meet up with whoever had built that fire. He ran all the way there, but he still had to stop and sleep twice on the way.

The smoke trail continued for the whole three days. It didn't stop even once. That was strange. His band should have continued to travel. They shouldn't have stayed in one place for this long.

He kept running until he got within a few hundred yards of the camp. He actually stopped dead in his tracks when he turned a corner and saw who it was. It wasn't his band. It was the farthest thing from his band that he could possibly imagine.

He gaped in horrified disbelief when he saw a bunch of Hungry Ghosts sitting around a fire. They chewed the remains of another Stalkion.

Kuvik found himself staring at these people as if for the first time. He found it nearly impossible to believe that he'd ever considered himself one of them and acted the way they did.

They didn't wear clothes. A few women sat around with the men. Their stark white body paint did nothing to hide their bodies. Both sexes completely ignored each other's nakedness.

How indecent the Hungry Ghosts looked compared to the Godless. The Godless never would have been caught dead exposing themselves like this.

The Hungry Ghosts didn't laugh, smile, relax, or enjoy each other's company. They barely talked at all and mumbled when they did. They avoided all eye contact as much as possible, hunched over the fire, and stared down into the coals while they ate.

Kuvik considered walking off in the other direction. He had no further business with the Hungry Ghosts, but ancient conditioning drew him back. He probably would have left, but he recognized two of the men.

He actually recognized almost the entire group. He knew these people only too well, but he stayed for these two particular men. They were his own brothers. The Hungry Ghosts had captured all three of them along with the rest of their family when Kuvik was just a boy.

He couldn't walk away from his brothers—not without at least talking to them.

He went through a moment of surreal vertigo. Was he even seeing these people in the flesh? Was he seeing some kind of premonition or echo from his past? Was this some vision of what his future would have been like if he had stayed with the Hungry Ghosts?

His future wouldn't have looked like this because he would be dead now. He would have killed himself when Hangman, Viking, Cross, and Alien tried to capture him.

Kuvik would have killed himself the moment Hangman released him. That's what Kuvik would have done if he had been a real Hungry Ghost.

He wasn't a real Hungry Ghost. He had turned his back on the whole Clan and became Godless instead. Did any of that really happen? Maybe he was the apparition—this version of himself standing on the outside looking in.

Maybe the real him was sitting around that fire with the others the same way he always had sat around the fire with them when he was one of them.

Maybe everything that had happened between him and the Godless was just a dream he made up in his head. Maybe he had been here with these people all along.

He didn't look like a Hungry Ghost now. He didn't look Godless, either. He didn't look like he belonged to any Clan. He didn't know who or what he was.

He did know for certain that he was a brother to those two men over there. He had been their brother since the beginning—since long before he became a Hungry Ghost, before he became Godless, before he became a Bounty Hunter captive.

He would always be a brother to those men no matter what else he might become. He would be a brother to them no matter where he went or who he bonded with or which Clan he said he belonged to.

They were his only real family—his blood. He couldn't walk away from them.

He hardened his resolve, took a few deep breaths, and walked the rest of the way into camp. He sat down next to his older brother. Actually they were both older. He sat down next to the older of the two.

His name was Noe. Kuvik's middle brother's name was Mocce.

The Hungry Ghosts didn't use anyone's names. They referred to themselves and each other as, 'Maggot'. It had taken Kuvik a long time before he had been able to tell Hangman what his name was. Kuvik hadn't heard it or used it in years before that day.

He hadn't heard or used his brothers' names in years, either. His brothers might not even remember what their real names were. Kuvik had to think all the time during his years with the Hungry Ghosts to remember his own relatives' names.

The Hungry Ghosts didn't believe in relatives. They didn't believe in families or marriage or raising children. Life meant nothing to them and neither did people. Nothing meant anything to them.

Kuvik sat down next to Noe. Kuvik adjusted the position of one of his bags and pulled out some Boultar meat he'd prepared for his journey. He'd finished the Stalkion and Gurlg meat a long time ago.

He stared into the flames and started chewing while he thought about how to initiate a conversation with his brothers. Talking to them would be hard. The Hungry Ghosts would hear and intervene to stop Kuvik from trying to talk any sense into them.

His movements caught Noe's eye. He looked up—and he froze when he saw Kuvik. The light of recognition came on in Noe's eyes immediately. He knew exactly who he was looking at.

He opened his mouth to speak—and gulped. Kuvik smiled at him. Kuvik would have liked to throw his arms around his brother then and there, but he didn't. The Hungry Ghosts wouldn't understand.

Kuvik would have given anything to wash all that paint off his brother, dress him in some real clothes like a real man, and take him out of here. Kuvik would have liked to do that with both of them.

Noe didn't look away. His eyes overflowed with so many questions, connections, and realizations. His gaze darted all over Kuvik's body.

Whip scars covered his chest, stomach, back, arms, and legs. Kuvik never had to think about his scars as long as he stayed with his band. Everyone there had something similar and maybe a lot worse. Everyone understood. He didn't have to explain anything to them.

Mocce noticed something wrong and glanced over. He didn't hold back. "Kuvik?" Mocce husked.

Kuvik's eyes welled up with tears. "Yeah. It's me. How are you? I didn't know you were here. I would have come a long time ago if I had known."

"What are *you* doing over there?!" another man barked across the circle.

Kuvik glanced up. The man was older than Noe by at least eight years. Kuvik didn't know the guy's name. Kuvik didn't know any of the Hungry Ghosts' names. They had never told him.

This man had always been something like a leader to the group, but he acted more like a disciplinarian. His main function was to stop anyone from acting normally and to enforce the rules of everyone acting like real Hungry Ghosts.

He took it as his personal responsibility to discipline anyone the Hungry Ghosts captured. He taught them the Hungry Ghosts ways—and he taught them the hard way. He could be as brutal as the Bounty Hunters.

The only difference was that this guy didn't punish anyone as long as they did act according to the Hungry Ghosts' rules. A person only had to follow the rules and act the way all the other Hungry Ghosts acted to avoid punishment.

The disciplinarian recognized Kuvik instantly, too. The guy glared at Kuvik across the fire. "What are you doing here, Maggot?" the guy snarled.

"I'm not a maggot," Kuvik countered. "I'm not a Hungry Ghost anymore. My name is Kuvik. I came here to see my brothers." Kuvik pointed to his brothers, and his final act of ultimate defiance, he called them by their names. "This is Noe and this is Mocce. They're my family."

"They're maggots," the guy snarled. "You put on your paint and act right or you'll pay."

"I told you I'm not a Hungry Ghost anymore."

"Where have you been?" a different man demanded. "You've been gone a long time."

"I've been living with the Godless. They captured me and....."

"They're swine," the disciplinarian barked. "They're filthy animals. All they care about is rutting and breeding and eating. They're no better than animals."

Kuvik opened his mouth to argue that the Godless led beautiful lives and he couldn't think of anything better to aspire to than to become one of them.

"You're staying, aren't you?" Noe asked from Kuvik's other side. "You have to stay. You can't go—not again. You have to stay."

Kuvik turned to his brothers. They both stared back at him with the same confused torrent of emotions waging in their expressions.

He could think of a lot of things to say to them, but he didn't want to say it in front of all these other people. The disciplinarian would only contradict, call it blasphemy, and probably attack Kuvik for saying it.

"At least you escaped from the Godless," the second man remarked. He was a bony guy about the same age as the disciplinarian.

Kuvik thought of this guy as essentially a mouthpiece for the disciplinarian. The second man's only function was to repeat or reinforce whatever the disciplinarian said.

Whether the disciplinarian said something was good or bad, this guy agreed. The mouthpiece elaborated on whatever the disciplinarian said as though the mouthpiece had thought of it himself.

"Were you with the Godless the whole time?" one of the women asked. "It's been so long."

"You should have escaped sooner," the disciplinarian snapped. "You should have painted yourself before you came back—and why are you wearing *those*?" He pointed at Kuvik's pants.

Kuvik didn't answer. Explaining anything to these people wouldn't make any difference.

In that moment when he decided not to answer, he felt his mind slip. Sitting around the fire with these people somehow tricked him into thinking he'd never left at all. He had been here all along. He was still a maggot. He thought exactly the same way they did.

He only had to think about it for a split second before their whole ideology came flooding back into his mind. It didn't even flood. It just switched. He switched instantaneously from the Godless way of thinking back to thinking like a Hungry Ghost.

He didn't care about anything. He didn't care about getting married or having children or his own comfort. He didn't even care if he lived or died. Years of suffering the worst possible treatment at the disciplinarian's hands made sure he didn't care if he lived or died.

He understood their mentality only too well. Seeing them sitting around him naked and painted—it brought it all back in a heartbeat. He was one of them. He always had been one of them. He could never be anything other than one of them.

That whole way of living, thinking, and being came perilously close to completely sucking him under.

It probably would have if he hadn't been able to look down at his own body and see himself sitting here unpainted and wearing his pants with his bags crossed over his torso.

His jawbone kukris and his tooth knives hung from his waistband. Those weapons offered the most glaring testimony of the last however many years of his life. He couldn't even remember how long he'd been away from the Hungry Ghosts.

He could never go back to them. He didn't want to go back to them. He didn't want to think this way or live like this. He wanted to go home to his band. He wanted to go home to Yoa and Hangman and Viking and all the others.

He glanced over at his brothers. "I didn't escape from the Godless. I lived with them willingly for five years. They were the happiest years of my life. I got separated from my band and captured by the Bounty Hunters. I've been traveling all this time to get back to my people." He looked back and forth between Noe and Mocce. "You should come with me."

"Be quiet!" the disciplinarian snapped louder. "Put your paint on. You're an abomination the way you are."

Kuvik glanced at his brothers again. He had to remind himself that both of them had been firmly embedded in the Hungry Ghosts' mindset all these years.

They didn't have Hangman to pull them out of it. They didn't have a whole band of people showering them with kindness, care, and help to guide them in how to regain their humanity.

His brothers didn't have their humanity at all. The Hungry Ghosts had robbed them of it the same way the Hungry Ghosts had robbed Kuvik of his humanity. It took the combined efforts of dozens of good, strong, solid people to pull him out of it.

His brothers deserved as much or more. They deserved his best effort. He couldn't walk away from them without at least trying to give them the same chance.

Kuvik didn't move to go put his paint on. He didn't know where the group got their paint these days. He had no idea this group of Hungry Ghosts was even in the area. He thought they would have been hundreds of miles away from here.

How did they even get into this part of the country? The group had been much farther north from the northern mountains before Kuvik and his comrades took up residence in the artillery battery.

Not that it really mattered how the Hungry Ghosts got here. He didn't put on his paint. He didn't take his pants off. He didn't make himself back into a Hungry Ghost. He wanted to offer his brothers an example of what they could become if they broke out of all of this.

Kuvik didn't say anything—not now. His brothers confirmed everything he was thinking by turning around, facing front, and going back to staring into the fire. His presence alone would offer the best evidence he could give them for how to get out of this.

He didn't move. He just sat and thought his own thoughts for the rest of the evening. He didn't feel the same overwhelming pull to sink back into all those terrible, hopeless thoughts. He sure hoped his brothers weren't thinking that way, but they probably were.

Chapter 39

Kuvik peeled himself off the rough ground and sat up. He'd fallen asleep around the fire with the Hungry Ghosts. They lay asleep all around him. They looked so bizarre with their bodies exposed and covered in white paint.

The black soot around their eyes and faces made them look like skeletons. They didn't look human. The white paint made their naked bodies look demonic and grotesque. They reminded him of giant Abnormit grubs.

Their thinking acted the same way on his mind and spirit. Their attitude had a way of eating its way into his guts, rotting him from the inside, and devouring him until he had nothing left.

He had to save his brothers from this. Someone had to. He was the only one free enough to get through to them. He could always leave if it didn't work. He could just continue his journey and let them stay if they really wanted to.

Noe woke up first, sat up, blinked at the smoldering embers of the dead fire, and then turned around to stare at Kuvik.

"Kuvik!" Noe whispered. His features trembled all over the place.

"I can get you out of here," Kuvik whispered back. "I can take you and Mocce far away. You can get your lives back. You don't have to live like this. We're better than this. You know we are. Please dear God tell me you don't believe everything they taught you about how your life means nothing and we're all better off dead. Please say you don't believe that."

Noe opened his mouth, but he couldn't make a sound. The turmoil crossing his face twisted Kuvik's stomach in knots. He wanted to grab both of his brothers and carry them out of here by brute force if necessary.

"Do you remember what it was like when they first captured us?" Kuvik whispered in a deadly undertone. "Do you remember how the disciplinarian punished Mother and made us all watch her screaming and crying in pain while they brutalized her?"

Noe clamped his eyes shut, looked away, and gulped. Kuvik pressed his advantage. Noe did remember.

"This is no way to live, Noe. You know me and I know you. You and Mocce and I are brothers. We're family. That means something. You both mean the world to me and I know I mean the same thing to you. The Hungry Ghosts can't change that. I came here to take you and Mocce away. You have to come with me. We can be human again. I've been living that way ever since I left. It's so much better that way, Noe. We don't have to live like this. We *can't* live like this. I *won't* live like this—not when I know how good it can be on the outside. Come on. Say you'll come with me and leave all of this behind. People are kind and helpful and loving and caring out there. People will give you everything to help you. Let me take you there. Let me take you where people can care about you as much as I do. Don't stay here. Don't throw your life away for nothing."

Mocce must have heard him. Mocce woke up just then and sat up to join the other two. He swiveled around to face Kuvik.

Mocce had a much harder, tougher, more dogged personality than Noe. Noe was more thoughtful, introverted, and sensitive. He had a quiet kind of strength—or he used to before the Hungry Ghosts captured their family.

"You would take us out of here, Kuvik?" Mocce asked. "You would take us away from the Hungry Ghosts?"

"I would take you in an instant if I thought you wanted to go," Kuvik replied. "I can take you right now. We can stand up and walk out of here right this minute. These people won't be able to stop us. I know where we can go. We can get there in a few days. People there will help us and take us in. We don't have to live like this. We're better than this. We're family. We matter—to each other and to the rest of the world. What we do matters. We can give the world something of value. We can find people who respect us and want us around—people who would grieve if we died."

They all had to stop talking when the other Hungry Ghosts woke up. Noe and Mocce cast frightened glances around at the others in the circle. None of the three brothers said any more about it.

Kuvik let the matter drop. He had planted the first seeds in his brothers' minds. It would go like this. It would take time to break them out of this.

Kuvik had to be patient and wait. He had to keep his memories of the Godless alive and keep trying to convince his brothers to escape. Kuvik had to do all of that without getting sucked back into the Hungry Ghosts himself.

The disciplinarian glared at him when the guy woke up and looked around at the world. The disciplinarian didn't say anything about Kuvik not wearing paint and not leaving the way the disciplinarian told him to.

No one else in Kuvik's experience had ever defied the disciplinarian like this. Kuvik couldn't remember any outside person intruding on the Hungry Ghosts like this. No one wanted to come anywhere near them.

The group didn't stay in the same camp for long. Everyone stood up from their places. They went into their wild, chaotic, frolicking dance. Kuvik never understood what the dance was supposed to mean. No one had ever explained it to him.

Noe and Mocce joined in. Kuvik stood off to one side and watched. These people really were deranged—or maybe they just went along with it because everyone else went along with it.

The dance ended pretty soon and the Hungry Ghosts moved off toward the east. No one mentioned why they went that way.

They passed the remains of the Stalkion they'd killed yesterday. The Hungry Ghosts must have killed it, but they didn't preserve the meat. They ate enough to satisfy themselves and left the rest.

Abnormits, Blitzwords, and a few other creatures were already starting to devour the rest of the carcass. This shouldn't have surprised Kuvik. He already knew the Hungry Ghosts' ways.

He couldn't tolerate that kind of waste now. The Godless never would have wasted so much perfectly good food. That food could have kept a family band alive for days.

The Hungry Ghosts just abandoned it. They would just kill another creature later today or tomorrow to feed themselves. They didn't care what they killed or if the food went to waste. Killing meant nothing to them.

He didn't say anything. He fell in line with his brothers and went with them. He wanted to be on hand if and when he ever got another chance to talk to them alone.

He would just keep trying until one or both of them told him they weren't interested in leaving. He would always keep trying as long as he thought either of them wanted to leave.

The Hungry Ghosts seemed to be heading for another mountain range farther east. Kuvik didn't know why. There was no reason why. There never was a reason why for anything when it came to the Hungry Ghosts.

The Hungry Ghosts didn't do anything for any particular reason. They just went wherever they went for no reason at all.

He glanced behind him toward the mountains leading to the Jagged Points. He could get back there if he needed to. He knew where to go to find Hangman's band, Shadow's band, and all the Godless.

The Hungry Ghosts traveled all day. They didn't stop to rest. They didn't even stop at the streams to drink water. Kuvik let his thoughts drift.

He'd always found it strange that the Hungry Ghosts hunted for food and drank water at all. Why did they waste the effort if they really thought their lives were worthless and not worth living? Why stay alive at all?

The disciplinarian and others had taught Kuvik and his family the Hungry Ghosts' ways. These people always taught that human beings would be better off dead and the world would be a better place without them in it. Death was the ultimate and only nobility.

The Hungry Ghosts would take any opportunity to kill themselves if even the slightest circumstance went against them. Some Hungry Ghosts killed themselves randomly for no reason. They just decided one day that life wasn't worth living anymore.

So why didn't they all do it that way? Why didn't they all do it immediately? The disciplinarian wasn't young. He must have been living for a long time—but why would he?

A person had to try pretty hard to stay alive in this world. The Hungry Ghosts had to work together to hunt and bring down creatures for food.

The Hungry Ghosts had to be careful during these hunts. They had to be just as careful as everyone else during hunts. They had to be careful that the creature in question didn't kill one or more of the Hungry Ghosts instead.

Why go to all that trouble just to stay alive? It would have been much easier if the Hungry Ghosts didn't hunt at all and just let themselves starve to death. That's what they really would have done if they really believed that life wasn't worth living.

Kuvik was in the middle of thinking all of that when someone rushed him from behind and smashed him across the back of the head with something very hard and solid.

His knees buckled, and before he even realized what was happening, the Hungry Ghosts surrounded him all kicking and beating him with sticks and clubs. He curled into a ball and waited for it to be over.

They yelled insults and obscenities at him while they did it.

"Maggot!" one of them yelled.

"Swine!" one snarled.

"Filth!" one of the women screeched.

Kuvik became aware of Noe and Mocce hitting him and kicking him, too, but they didn't say anything. Kuvik couldn't even resent them for participating in this. They'd been part of this world for decades. Kuvik couldn't expect them to come out of it overnight.

The beating went on for a long time until someone kicked him in the head and he drifted out of consciousness.

Chapter 40

K uvik woke up tied hand and foot in the jungle. The Hungry Ghosts sat nearby. The sun was starting to go down. Kuvik must have passed out.

The Hungry Ghosts weren't eating anything tonight, but they had built a fire. They always did. That was another thing. They shouldn't have needed light or whatever the fire did for them if their lives weren't worth anything.

He tried to shift his position to make himself more comfortable. The Hungry Ghosts had stripped him naked and smeared their white paint all over him to make him look like one of them.

He spotted his pants, shoes, bags, and even his weapons lying in a pile nearby. The Hungry Ghosts hadn't gotten rid of any of it. Maybe the Hungry Ghosts planned to just leave all his possessions behind when the group moved on tomorrow.

Then he realized something else. The Hungry Ghosts probably didn't recognize his weapons. He'd never seen anyone else fighting with weapons like his. He had improvised them from Demonex teeth and jawbones.

Maybe the Hungry Ghosts didn't realize these things even were weapons—or maybe it never crossed the Hungry Ghosts' minds that someone would want to use a weapon against them.

He had another flashback to the time when the Hungry Ghosts captured his family. He remembered the day vividly and he remembered everything the Hungry Ghosts did to his family afterward.

These were his enemies. The Hungry Ghosts were just as dangerous, just as vicious, and just as cruel as the Bounty Hunters. The Hungry Ghosts just did it in different ways.

He would definitely need weapons to fight this enemy. Today's beating was just the beginning. They would keep escalating until they broke him and forced him to accept their ways.

They wouldn't stop until he actually started to think like they did. He could do it easily. He could slip into that dark hole with no effort at all. He already felt himself leaning into it.

He had to fight every single minute to hold onto the memories of his life with the Godless. Memories of his life with the Godless had gotten him through his ordeal with the Bounty Hunters. The same memories would get him through this.

He only had to think about Yoa. He had to get back to her no matter what. She loved him. She took care of him. She wanted to marry him. She might not be able to wait for him, but she would always love him the same way he loved her.

That feeling flooded his heart and forced all the dark thoughts away. He could have a family with her. He could initiate into the Godless. The men would welcome him as a brother. He could give something back to the Clan and family band that had given him so much.

That would be a life worth living. He actually pitied the Hungry Ghosts for their way of life. They had no idea what they were missing.

All those things waited for him away from these people. He only had to get free from here—and hopefully take his brothers with him.

He couldn't get to his weapons. He would have to do something about that.

The Hungry Ghosts would have to untie him before they left here tomorrow. One night. He just had to put up with this for one night.

They had painted him and made him naked like themselves. Maybe the disciplinarian would untie Kuvik and let him move around to see if he behaved the way he was supposed to.

Kuvik's movements got the disciplinarian's attention. He looked up and glared at Kuvik. "You turned against our ways. You abandoned the cause."

"What cause?" Kuvik asked.

"You're worthless!" one of the women snapped. "You always were! You're a piece of filth if you even dirty the ground by being here. You should have killed yourself a long time ago. That's what you would have done if you had any honor at all."

Noe glanced over his shoulder in Kuvik's direction and looked away without saying anything. Kuvik caught a glimpse of his brother's expression in that moment. Noe's features revealed all the same turmoil of confused emotion as before.

Mocce didn't look at Kuvik, but Mocce didn't say anything, either. He would have joined in if he really believed what the Hungry Ghosts were saying. They were all supposed to join in to chastise someone who stepped out of line and didn't behave correctly.

Kuvik's brothers' silence spoke volumes. They didn't berate him for turning against the Hungry Ghosts' ways. They both responded to his invitation this morning. They both wanted to leave.

"You were never any good," the disciplinarian growled again. "You and your whole rotten family. I knew you were worthless the first time I laid eyes on you. I knew you would come to nothing—and look at you! Look what happened to all the others. The same thing will happen to you and the world will be wiped clean of your filthy, rotten presence."

"Why do you hunt?" Kuvik blurted out. He didn't try to stop himself. The disciplinarian's comments could only be referring to one person—Kuvik's mother.

The disciplinarian had been the one responsible for breaking her. He had torn her apart, body and soul, until she had nothing left. She eventually really did kill herself the way the Hungry Ghosts told her she should.

Kuvik and his brothers had to watch that. They had to watch the Hungry Ghosts do the same thing to Kuvik's father and two sisters, too.

The Hungry Ghosts captured a bunch of Kuvik's other relatives at the same time. The same thing happened to them. Only the three boys survived.

Kuvik's mother was the one he really took personally. She was the one he held out as the ultimate example of what the Hungry Ghosts were capable of. She was the one he still resented them the most for killing.

They killed her. She didn't kill herself. They forced her to do it. They twisted her mind and broke her spirit through repeated brutal treatment until she thought she had no choice but to do it. She wouldn't have done it at all if not for them.

The disciplinarian bared his teeth at Kuvik in a vicious snarl. "What did you say to me, Maggot?"

"Why do you hunt?" Kuvik asked again. "Why do you hunt at all if life isn't worth living? Why don't you let yourselves starve? Why do you hunt at all? Why don't you kill yourself now if the world would be better off without you? You say the world will be better off without people. You're a person, so the world will be better off without you, too. Do you plan for everyone else to die, but you'll still be alive by yourself? What are you waiting for?"

The disciplinarian's features shivered with rage. Kuvik couldn't remember ever seeing the guy so furious, but Kuvik didn't care. He wanted to hurt these people. He wanted to shove their ideology down their throats.

"You worthless piece of filth!" the disciplinarian hissed. "How dare you question me?!"

"You're the one who is supposed to teach us the Hungry Ghosts' ways," Kuvik went on. "How do you explain this? Huh? Explain it to me so I understand. Why are any of you even still alive? How old are you? You must have been alive for a long time. You've been alive for years ever since I first met you—but you haven't killed yourself. You keep living every day. You hunt for your food. You build fires every night. Why do you go to all that effort just to stay alive? Why don't you show us how noble you are? I think you're the one who has turned against the Hungry Ghosts' ways. I don't think you ever believed in the Hungry Ghosts' ways. I don't think you ever believed that your life was worthless and not worth living. You would have died a long time ago if you really believed that."

The disciplinarian shot off the ground, bellowed with rage, and seized a stick off the ground near him. Kuvik hadn't noticed before that all the Hungry Ghosts had kept the same stick he used to beat Kuvik earlier.

Kuvik probably shouldn't have antagonized the guy that much, but Kuvik couldn't bring himself to regret his words. He wanted to show what a fraud the guy was. Kuvik wanted to expose the disciplinarian in front of all these people he crushed under his heel.

He charged Kuvik and all the other Hungry Ghosts joined in. They attacked him and started beating him again until they knocked him out again.

Chapter 41

Kuvik woke up in darkness. The fire still burned nearby. The Hungry Ghosts lay asleep around it. He couldn't see his pile of clothes, bags, and weapons. The shadows concealed them, but at least he knew where he could get his hands on some weapons.

He had to get out of here before morning. That was all there was to it. He had to find a way to break or cut these ropes. He twisted over onto his side to try to see if he could get his mouth close to the knots around his wrists.

The Hungry Ghosts had tied him with his arms in front of him and his bound wrists tied to a tree. Another length of rope went from his wrists around the trunk to his bound ankles.

The rope held his body at a strange angle. That would make it harder to get free. It would be hard and he would have to be careful. He had to use the darkness to his advantage. He had to take this opportunity while the Hungry Ghosts slept.

He started to maneuver himself into position when Mocce stirred and sat up. Kuvik froze and stopped moving around. He didn't know where his brothers stood. One of them could turn against him and alert the other Hungry Ghosts that he was trying to escape.

Mocce stared into the flames for a minute and then glanced over at Kuvik. Kuvik felt all the bruises all over his body. The paint probably hid them, but it wouldn't hide the swelling.

He met his brother's gaze and looked away. Kuvik didn't want to deal with either of his brothers if they were going to try to tell him to cooperate and become a Hungry Ghost again.

He would abandon them if they did that. He had to save himself first. He wouldn't let them drag him back into this nightmare.

Mocce waited a minute and then scooted over to squat in front of Kuvik. Kuvik had to stop himself from staring at his brother's nakedness. None of these people realized how indecent they looked.

Kuvik shouldn't have been able to see his brother's naked body. Being able to see it violated some fundamental law of the universe. Kuvik would up twisting over onto his side to stop Mocce from seeing his body.

Mocce didn't notice. "I want to go with you, Kuvik," Mocce whispered. "I want to get out of here. What do we have to do?"

Kuvik's head shot up. "You do?"

Mocce nodded. "I hate this place and I hate these people. I even started to hate you and Noe because I thought you believed in the Hungry Ghost Clan. I hate everything about this. I never wanted to be here. I just didn't know how to leave. Come on. Let's go. We can go right now the way you said."

"Does Noe want to go, too?" Kuvik asked. "I don't want to leave him."

Mocce glanced over his shoulder. "I don't know if he wants to go or not. I don't know if we should ask him."

"Go over there and bring me my clothes and bags." Kuvik nodded toward where the Hungry Ghosts had left his belongings.

Mocce went and got the pile. Kuvik's heart turned a somersault when he saw his weapons.

"Take that tooth thing and cut these ropes," Kuvik instructed.

Mocce did everything perfectly. He grabbed one of Kuvik's tooth blades and cut the rope binding Kuvik's wrists. Then Mocce cut the rope on Kuvik's ankles.

Kuvik pounced on his weapons, grabbed another tooth blade for himself, and started pulling on his pants as fast as he could. He had to sit down to scoot them up his thighs and hips.

He must have made more noise than he realized. The mouthpiece guy sat up, saw Kuvik getting to his feet fully armed, and also saw Mocce sitting there holding a weapon.

"What are you doing?!" The mouthpiece guy started to get to his feet, too. Then he shook the disciplinarian awake. "These guys are trying something!"

Their voices roused everyone else. The other Hungry Ghosts hustled to their feet and started to move in. Kuvik sprang forward and raised his weapon to guard Mocce.

"We're leaving here!" Kuvik announced. "We're free men and we're leaving! Come on, Noe! You come with us! Any of you who want to leave, you come with us now! You can live your lives, have families, and find some meaning outside this nightmare. You don't have to follow these stupid rules anymore!" He swiped his blade at a few people trying to get closer on his left. "I'll kill any of you that tries to stop us or harm my brothers! Don't come any closer unless you plan to leave with us!"

One man stepped forward. "I'm going with you."

"Me, too!" one of the women agreed.

"Get behind me!" Kuvik snatched up one of his jawbone kukris and transferred his tooth blade to his other hand. "Come on, Noe! You're coming with us!"

Noe darted across the gap and got behind Mocce. Mocce stood up, positioned himself next to Kuvik, and raised his weapon to defend the group.

"This is your last chance to go with us!" Kuvik picked up his shoulder bags and hung them across his chest. He got white paint all over his pants and bags, but he would just have to clean that off later.

One other man came forward. "I want to leave, too."

The disciplinarian jumped out of position and grabbed the guy by the arm. "No, you don't!"

The first man spun away and yanked his arm out of the disciplinarian's grasp. The disciplinarian raised his stick again.

Kuvik refused to stand by and watch that. He jumped forward, slashed his tooth down the disciplinarian's arm, gashed the flesh wide open, grabbed the guy, and dragged him across the camp to the others.

Kuvik pushed all three of the deserters behind him and started to back away. He kept pivoting from one side to the other and brandishing his weapon to threaten everyone.

"Don't come near us again!" Kuvik snarled. "I swear I'll kill anyone who tries to stop us. That's what you want, isn't it—for me to kill you? We're free people! You have no claim on us! We're leaving!" He pushed everyone farther back behind him—out of the firelight.

The disciplinarian clutched his bleeding arm. "You won't get away with this!"

Kuvik didn't answer. He really didn't see how these people could stop him, but he didn't want to take any chances. He untied his extra kukris from his bag strap and passed them out to everyone else—Noe and the three deserters.

All four of them raised their weapons to defend themselves against the Hungry Ghosts. Kuvik's party backed farther away into the darkness. Just a few more yards and they would be free.

The Hungry Ghosts waited right up until that moment. In the end, the mouthpiece guy was the one who grabbed another stick, bellowed out in fury, and charged the party.

All the other Hungry Ghosts rushed forward at the same time, grabbed different objects, and attacked. Kuvik's allies responded perfectly, stood their ground, and defended themselves.

Four different men came after Kuvik. He slashed with his tooth blade and cleaved with his kukri, but they surrounded him and backed him farther into the shadowy jungle.

He spun from one direction to another and crushed in one of their skulls. Paying attention to one man gave the others an opening to move in. Their stick blows fell all over his back, shoulders, and head. They drove him down onto his knees.

He couldn't let them beat him down. He struck back, pivoted sideways on one knee, and smashed his kukri hard against one man's leg. The guy roared in agony and buckled onto the ground.

Kuvik ignored more blows pummeling his body, lunged to his feet, and slashed his blade upward at the first person he came to. He didn't realize until he eviscerated the person across the midsection that it was a woman.

Her vital organs tumbled all over the place and his blade snagged a major blood vessel somewhere. She staggered away.

He didn't have time to deal with her before the last man charged Kuvik and raised his stick to cave in Kuvik's skull. Kuvik reacted without thinking and swung his kukri at the man's head.

Kuvik hit the guy's neck by mistake, shattered it, and the guy folded in a heap on the ground.

The man with the broken leg writhed, grimaced, and roared on the ground. Kuvik crushed his skull, too. The other two were already dead.

Chapter 42

Kuvik stood still breathing hard and trying to listen for any noise coming from the jungle. He didn't hear anything.

He stumbled back to the fire. It still blazed in the middle of the night, but he was the only person here. He didn't see any of the Hungry Ghosts, his brothers, or the people who had agreed to leave with him.

He did find his jawbone kukris and his other tooth blade lying on the ground as if his brothers and the other deserters had just dropped the weapons here. That didn't make any sense when they'd been ready to fight just a few minutes ago.

Did the Hungry Ghosts take the weapons away and leave them here? Kuvik couldn't understand it. He searched as much of the area as he could. He didn't find anyone except the four people he'd just killed.

He even called out to his brothers and asked where they were. He would rather lure the Hungry Ghosts back here. Then he would at least know where his brothers were. They weren't here. He was alone.

He ranged wider around the camp and even climbed into the branches. He searched the whole area for a long way in all directions. He didn't find any trace of anyone.

He returned to the fire and sat down next to it. The silence throbbed in his ears. What had happened to them? He sat up for the rest of the night waiting, watching, and listening. He kept his weapons out and ready, but no one came. No one threatened him.

He didn't keep the fire going. The Hungry Ghosts had built it up big enough to make it last a long time. He let it burn out by morning.

He waited until the first streaks of grey dawn light spread through the sky. He could see enough of where he was going now. He climbed into the canopy and ran through the treetops for hours to scout the area again.

The Hungry Ghosts only traveled by walking. They never ran and they never walked fast. He should have been able to overtake them. He covered a lot more territory in a complete concentric circle around the camp. He still found nothing.

He returned to the dead fire circle in the afternoon. He wouldn't find his brothers by staying here. He might as well leave.

He waited for another five hours. He didn't know why except that he couldn't bring himself to just abandon his brothers. He had come all this way and suffered all this trouble for their sakes.

He had come within inches of rescuing them—and now this happened. He didn't want to just give up.

He didn't have the first clue even which direction to go to look for them. He might spend the rest of his life searching for them and still never find them. He didn't want to do that—not when he knew where the Godless were.

He finally got to his feet, heaved a broken sigh, and headed off toward the eastern mountains he knew would lead him to the Ashtaw Valley.

He still had some extra food in his bags, so he camped in the treetops and ate it that night while he thought things over. He would never find out what happened to his brothers.

He'd never really thought about them when he'd left the Hungry Ghosts to join Hangman's band. He'd always assumed his brothers had completely converted to the Hungry Ghosts. It never occurred to him that his brothers might secretly want to leave.

He didn't secretly want to leave. He'd given up all hope of ever getting away from the Hungry Ghosts. He'd let their thinking completely take over his mind. He'd let it embody him so he never thought about anything else.

He never would have considered leaving the Hungry Ghosts before he met Hangman. He'd always assumed his brothers felt the same way.

Maybe they did feel the same way. Maybe the disciplinarian and his people somehow convinced Noe and Mocce to drop their weapons and return to the Hungry Ghosts where they belonged. Kuvik would never know.

He couldn't throw his whole life away to save them. Was that wrong? Would going after them be the right thing to do? Where would he even go to go after them? Which direction should he travel to go after them?

That was the real problem. He would have gone after them if he'd known where they were. He would have gone after them in a split second and stopped at nothing until he freed them, now that he knew they wanted to break free.

The Hungry Ghosts might have killed them both—but the Hungry Ghosts would have left the bodies behind. The Hungry Ghosts would have left the deserters' bodies behind, too, if the Hungry Ghosts had defeated them in a fight.

He finally put his head down, fell into an uneasy sleep, and kept moving the next day. He traveled for three more days and eventually ran through all his remaining food stores.

He stopped on a high tree branch and went through all the stuff in his bags. He still had four Demonex teeth plus a bunch of the other bones. He planned to use them to make tools. He just hadn't gotten around to it while he'd been with the Bounty Hunters.

He didn't even know how long he'd been with them. The time had blurred into itself. He'd spent so much of the time in a brainless fog.

He needed to go hunting right now, so he better start looking around for another creature to kill. He continued on his journey, but he didn't travel as fast. He usually ignored creatures as long he still had enough food supplies to keep him going.

He didn't see anything promising until evening. He wanted to kill something big so he could process a lot of food and travel faster afterward. He would rather wait around for a few days for his food to dry instead of stopping to hunt all the time.

He spotted a Crusher in the distance, but that was too big. He decided to go for a Gorlock instead.

He came upon three of them. They were in the process of running down a flock of Gurlgs including several mothers and chicks.

Kuvik ran up behind the Gorlocks and waited for them to finish off their prey. The Gorlocks had to separate to catch them all. Each Gorlock wound up at a distance from the others. Kuvik snuck up on a large male Gorlock bent over his meal.

Kuvik positioned himself in the branches above the creature, poised there, and jumped off to land on the creature's neck.

Kuvik gripped his kukri in one hand and his blade in the other. He planned to land a crushing blow on the back of the Gorlock's skull. If that didn't kill the creature, he would slash its throat. He would be high enough up the Gorlock's neck to control its head.

He plunged toward the ground, but mere seconds before he landed on the creature, something collided with him from the side and sent him somersaulting away.

He realized too late that it was another person. The two of them rolled over and over each other, and before Kuvik could react, the person scrambled on top of him, straddled him down on the ground, and raised a blade to skewer him through the chest.

Kuvik tightened his grip on his kukri to defend himself—and then his eyes fell out of their sockets when he recognized the person on top of him. "Tren!" Kuvik gasped.

Tren froze. "Kuvik?!" he whispered.

The Gorlock got their attention by bellowing at both of them. The creature lunged before either of them could move. The Gorlock tried to snap at Tren and wound up butting him hard with its snout instead.

The impact hurled Tren away. He slammed into a tree trunk. The Gorlock would have spun around to attack Kuvik next, but he reacted quicker.

He rolled under the Gorlock's chin, slashed his tooth blade across the Gorlock's throat, and rolled clear to escape the gush of blood pouring from the creature's neck.

The Gorlock reared back bellowing in fury—and then it crashed down hard on its stomach. It thrashed in its death throes for a while and then wilted to twitching before it lay still.

Kuvik pried himself off the ground, stared at the Gorlock, and then went to check on Tren. He lay sprawled on his side with his long hair spilling all over his face.

Kuvik picked the boy up, carried him back to the clearing, and laid him on his back. Tren was out cold. Kuvik combed the hair out of Tren's face and found himself gazing at the boy with choking affection.

Tren would be able to lead Kuvik back to the band—his band. God, he needed those people! Thank Almighty God he had found them again. He needed them more than anything.

He examined Tren's body, but Kuvik didn't find any injuries other than a lump on the boy's head. Kuvik left him there, built a fire, and started butchering the Gorlock.

He brought a bowl of water from the stream to clean his blades and found Tren just waking up. Tren groaned, cradled his head, and dragged himself upright. "What happened?" Tren croaked.

"The Gorlock hit you. It knocked you into a tree. Don't try to get up or do anything yet," Kuvik told him. "Here. Drink some water and I'll make you something to eat."

Tren glanced at him. "We thought you were dead, Kuvik."

Kuvik smiled at him. "I thought I was dead, too, little brother, but I guess I'm not. Where are the others?"

Tren jerked his thumb over his shoulder. "They're over there—at least...we are."

Kuvik frowned at him. "What do you mean?"

"Akli, Mapa, and Nelv are over there. It's just us now."

Kuvik's stomach plummeted into his shoes. "What about....what about the others?"

"We don't know where they are," Tren mumbled. "We.....well, a lot of things happened and we got separated. We couldn't find them—so it's just us now. I'm sorry, Kuvik. Things fell apart after you left. We tried. We really tried." He gulped. "I wish I was old enough to be Kral."

Kuvik gripped his shoulder. "Don't worry about it, little brother. I'm sure whatever happened wasn't your fault. We'll make some food, cure the rest of this meat, and go back to the others. I'm sure they're worried about you."

Tren looked up and bit back a grin. "They're going to be thrilled that I found you."

Kuvik laughed. "I don't know if you found me or I found you, but someone found someone, didn't they? Stay here and drink some water while I put some meat on the spit."

Kuvik stood up and got back to work. He felt so much better, now that he knew where at least some of his people were. He cut a hunk of the meat off the carcass and set up a spit to cook it, but Tren didn't stay sitting down.

He got up and started working alongside Kuvik. "I thought I told you to stay sitting down. Is this the way you obey your Kral?"

Tren laughed. "I'm not that hurt. Besides, we aren't a band as long as it's just the two of us. We're just brothers traveling."

Kuvik turned away, but he couldn't help smiling. "Fine. If that's the way you want it."

"Where have you been, Kuvik?" Tren asked while they worked. "What happened to you after you fell off the mountain?"

"I got caught in a landslide that swept me down the mountain. I tried to find you, but you were already gone. I tried to follow your trail, but I lost you in the end. I didn't know where to find you, so I kept traveling south."

Kuvik stopped there. He didn't want to talk about the Hungry Ghosts. He couldn't remember nor did he even care if anyone from his band had found out that he'd once belonged to the Hungry Ghost Clan.

He didn't want to talk about this latest experience. It still felt too raw.

Tren and Kuvik cut up all the meat, put it on tripods to dry, and then sat down to eat together. Kuvik didn't ask about what happened to the band after he'd gotten lost in the landslide. Tren acted like he didn't want to talk about that, either.

"I found the territory where I got separated from my Godless band," Kuvik told him. "We can find our way to the band from there."

Tren's head shot up. "Really?! That's great. We don't know where to go."

"Have you just been wandering around all this time?"

"We kept going south. We figured we would meet up with someone eventually. We had nowhere else to go and no reason to go there."

"Are the others all right—the others who are with you?"

"As far as I know. Akli and Mapa are very close, of course. Nelv is.....he's quiet. He's gotten a lot quieter since we lost you. He withdrew....after everything that happened. He hardly talks at all now."

Kuvik stared into the flames. "I guess we could have expected that."

"He talked to you more than anyone. Maybe he'll come out of it once you come back to the band."

"Do you still call yourself a band? Is Akli your Kral now?"

"No, we don't call ourselves a band. It's just the four of us. We don't have a Kral. Akli is the only grown man of the group apart from Nelv and Nelv doesn't talk, so Akli makes most of the decisions. It seems to work that way. Mapa follows Akli and Nelv never argues. It wouldn't work for me to argue with Akli, so I guess you could say he's in charge if anyone is."

Kuvik clapped Tren on the shoulder again. "I'm so glad I found you. It's great to see you."

"You, too," Tren murmured. "Losing you was a hard blow—for all of us. A lot of people gave up after we lost you."

Kuvik stood up. "Let's finish dealing with this meat so we can go back to the rest of the group."

The two friends worked long into the night. Kuvik eventually had to tell Tren to lie down and get some sleep. Kuvik disjointed what was left of the Gorlock bones and dragged all the remains into the jungle for the creatures to chew on.

He found himself studying the Gorlock's fangs and teeth. He didn't need any other weapons, but using his kills' teeth and spines as weapons was becoming a new obsession for him. He had to stop himself from taking any of them with him.

Chapter 43

Tren and Kuvik divided the Gorlock meat between two big bundles, slung them across their backs, and set off with them through the treetops. Tren led the way back to another rocky, tumbling river running through the jungle.

He turned off to follow it south. The two friends traveled a long way and eventually caught up with the other three. They walked single file along the ground with Mapa between the two men and Akli in the front.

Tren dropped down into the trail in front of them and made Akli jump back. "Don't do that, Tren!" Akli bellowed. "I've told you not to startle me like that!"

Tren burst into a grin. "Wait until you see what I've brought you, Akli! You won't believe it!"

"What did you kill this time—another Crusher?" Akli fired back.

Tren only pointed behind the group. They turned around and saw Kuvik crouching in the branches. The three travelers gaped at him in disbelief while he climbed down to join them.

Mapa got over her surprise first. "Kuvik?!" she choked. "You're alive!"

He smiled at her and then at the two men. "I've been looking for you everywhere. It was pure good luck that I found Tren."

Akli made a choking noise in his throat and turned his face away to hide emotion. Nelv blinked at Kuvik in pure, wretched misery. Mapa gawked at him with her mouth open and her eyes falling out.

"Let's keep going," Kuvik suggested. "I know where we can find the Godless. We can get there in a few days. Come on. You go ahead, Akli. Tren and I will follow you."

Akli started walking again. Mapa fell in behind him and Nelv followed her. Tren and Kuvik brought up the rear. The party traveled for the rest of the day and made camp on the ground that night. Mapa built a fire and Tren and Kuvik shared out their Gorlock meat.

Akli finally broke the silence. "We never thought we'd see you again," he choked. "I don't.....I don't feel right leading this group when you're here. You should take over."

"I'm not here to take over anything, brother," Kuvik told him. "We're all friends here. We can travel as friends and brothers. We don't need a Kral."

Akli stared down into the flames. Kuvik had never seen his people so defeated since they first escaped from the Bounty Hunters. They looked even more defeated now.

"A lot of bad things happened...." Akli mumbled. "I'm ashamed to tell you."

"Then don't tell me. I don't need to know. I know you all did what you could to keep the band together. I don't blame anyone for what happened. I wish I could have been there to help you, but I probably couldn't have stopped it even if I had been there."

"No," Akli murmured under his breath. "No one could have stopped it."

"Then why would you be ashamed? It isn't your fault. It's no one's fault. These things happen out here. It's a miracle any of us is still alive after everything that's happened to us. We can be grateful for that—that we're still together and we can enjoy this evening."

"Where do we go to get to the Godless band?" Mapa asked.

Kuvik pointed toward the southwest. "There's a mountain range over there. I got separated from my band there and they were heading east—across the mountains to Hangman's father's territory. We'll retrace our steps to the west side of the mountains and pick up the trail from there. We'll be heading east into Godless territory, so we're bound to run into someone's band even if it isn't his."

"It doesn't seem real," Akli murmured. "We've traveled all this time without knowing where we're going. It's hard to believe we might actually get somewhere and not have to travel anymore."

"We can only hope. Let's get some sleep. We can keep going tomorrow. We'll come out of this jungle and we'll be able to see where we're going."

The group went to sleep, got up early, and set off again with little fanfare and not much fuss. The group traveled much more quickly and stayed in one place for much shorter periods of time, now that no one had to wait for mothers and little children.

Kuvik had to continually stop himself from asking any probing questions about what had happened to the rest of the band. He could see plain as day how much the recent past had hurt these people. Whatever it was must have been really bad.

They traveled faster, but they still traveled on the ground. Kuvik didn't know why and he didn't ask.

They came to the edge of the jungle and he spotted the Jagged Points to the southwest. He set their course to skirt the west side where he could get to the Ashtaw Valley.

The party had to cross another stretch of open country between the jungle and the mountains. Kuvik scanned the area, but he didn't see anything to threaten the party. The whole territory lay open in all directions.

His many experiences in the jungle and on this particular journey set his nerves on end. How many times had he just been thinking that he didn't see anything threatening right before something catastrophic happened?

He glanced over his shoulder toward the jungle behind the party. He didn't see anything there, either, but something back there put him on edge. He stopped walking, turned around, and stared.

Tren came up to him. "What's wrong?"

"I'm not sure." Kuvik hesitated. "I guess it's nothing."

"Do you see something?"

"No, there's nothing there." Kuvik turned away, but he wound up looking behind him a few seconds later.

Something was wrong. His nerves threatened to snap. He felt something creeping up behind him—something deadly. He didn't know what it was. He couldn't put his finger on it.

He faced front and tried to stop himself from looking behind him again. He kept walking, but he caved after only a few minutes and looked back.

He didn't expect to see anything, but he did. He actually stopped in his tracks again before he could fully believe what he was seeing.

A wall of flame and smoke erupted out of the jungle behind him. He didn't understand how it could flare so big so fast, but it did. It blasted out of the middle of the jungle, unfurled a cloud of smoke into the sky, and started clawing its way across the countryside.

He burst forward and shoved his friends in front of him. "Run!" he bellowed. "Run for it!"

The whole party broke into a run heading straight across the open ground. The mountains jutted into the sky over there. Kuvik didn't know where he could find shelter from the fire, but he sure as hell wouldn't find it here.

He scanned the terrain ahead and spotted another river to the northwest. It lay against the sheer, rocky mountains where he'd first seen the Jagged Points.

He turned his friends in that direction. "This way!" he yelled. "Get to the river! Hurry!"

They all ran their hardest. Mapa ran the slowest. The others slowed down to stay with her. Kuvik made the mistake of looking behind him. The fire ate its way through the jungle heading straight for the open country. The flames sure moved fast.

He didn't understand what was happening. He didn't need to. He grabbed Mapa by one arm and pulled her forward. "Come on!"

She ran another mile before her legs started to give out. He thought fast, but Akli got to her first. He grabbed her, threw her over his shoulder, and took off running with her. He didn't try to be gentle.

Nelv and Tren sprinted ahead. Kuvik tried one last time to slow down and stay with his friends. The fire swallowed the jungle in a sheet of blistering flame and crawled out into the open fields.

The fire could move so much faster out here. It consumed grasses, bushes, and low-growing trees in a carpet of flame coming closer by the second. Kuvik had to fight himself not to run for the river and leave his friends behind.

Mapa's weight slowed Akli down. Kuvik went back for both of them, but he didn't feel right about telling Akli to hand Mapa over. Kuvik couldn't be sure he would be able to run faster than Akli.

Nelv and Tren put more distance between themselves and the others, but the two friends were still nowhere close to the river. Kuvik looked back.

The fire spread across the open country impossibly fast. It was coming faster than anyone could run. Kuvik considered one last time if he ought to just stay and perish with his friends. He would rather do that than go on alone.

A blast of scorching heat singed his cheeks in that one instant when he turned back to check how close the fire was coming. That puff of searing air ignited his adrenaline. He turned around and ran for his life. He ran as he'd never run before.

A deep, animalistic, almost guttural woof of flames thumped and pounded behind him. One cruel gust after another scorched his back getting closer all the time. He would die if he slowed down even for an instant.

He barely noticed when he ran past Nelv and Tren. Kuvik just had to keep running no matter what. He had to get to the river at all costs.

The heat built to an inferno. Blisters erupted on his back just as he got to the riverbank. He hurled himself off the side and an almighty explosion went off behind him.

The concussion hurled him halfway across the river before he plummeted into the water. He submerged and the cool, blissful water closed over his head, but he could still see roiling flames billowing and coiling above the surface. He didn't dare to go up there.

He held his breath, turned around, and stroked underwater until he made it to the opposite bank. He dragged himself up, collapsed there, and flopped onto his back before he remembered.

He screamed when the rough grass pricked all his blistered skin. He had to roll onto his side so he could rest there. He sat up—and stared across the river at the other side consumed in flames.

The fire raged as high as ever, but it didn't last. This country didn't have enough vegetation to keep the fire going for very long. It burned out just as fast and left the whole area charred to a black wasteland.

Kuvik staggered to his feet and stumbled up and down the river staring across it. There was no one there.

"No!" he whimpered. "No!!"

They didn't come back. The fire left not a single trace of any of his friends.

"No!!" he yelled louder and the rising tide of anguish and revolt overwhelmed him. They were all gone—for real this time. He couldn't even pretend that they were still out there traveling somewhere.

He collapsed on his knees, screamed out once, "NO!!" and crumpled in tears. He buried his face in his hands and let all the heartbreak pour out.

He cried for all of them—his brothers, his band—all the people dead and lost along the way. He had only ever wanted to live a peaceful life with them and make something good in the world.

They never even got a chance. Why did Tren have to die? Why did such a staunch, brave, smart, thriving boy have to die? He could have been something great. He could have been Kral of his own band and he would have been incredible.

He could have protected his people, raised a family, and made the world safe for future generations. They all could have.

Why? Why did they all have to die? Why did Kuvik's family have to get captured by the Hungry Ghosts in the first place? Why did the Hungry Ghosts even have to exist? It wasn't fair. None of this was fair.

Kuvik collapsed back onto his seat, too wretched and devastated to go on. This was the worst insult yet. The Gorlock meat in his bags right now was an insult to Tren's memory.

Kuvik would have given anything to go back to that night he'd shared with Tren by the Gorlock carcass. Why couldn't all the nights be like that? Why did this world have to be so cruel and unforgiving?

Kuvik was still sitting there when night started to fall. He couldn't bear the sight of that charred landscape. He had to get away from it—from all of it.

He turned away and started heading west. He didn't care where he went or even if he walked straight back into the hands of an enemy Clan. He almost hoped he would.

He came the closest that night of falling back into the Hungry Ghosts' pit of black hopeless, meaningless defeat. He didn't want to be alive right now.

Chapter 44

Kuvik walked all night just trying to shut his mind down. He felt better in the morning once he reentered another stretch of jungle. The fire didn't make it this far. The landscape looked normal here.

He stopped at a stream, drank some water, ate some of his food, and put leaf paste on his back. The burns didn't break the skin. He didn't need Gooji juice. The blisters just hurt like crazy.

He didn't stop to sleep all that day, but he camped in the treetops and slept that night. He slept normally every night after that.

He kept traveling, passed the Jagged Points, and turned south until he saw the mountains surrounding the Ashtaw Valley. He still had to travel for another four days before he got there.

He found a well-beaten trail winding up the hills to the valley's northern rim. He stopped at the top and looked down at thousands of Ashtaws grazing on the valley floor. The whole scene couldn't look more peaceful.

He took a rest there just to fully appreciate his victory, no matter how small it might be. He had made it. He had found his way back here. He would find his way the rest of the journey to rejoin Hangman's band. Kuvik no longer doubted that.

He only stopped for a few minutes to enjoy the view before he continued along the rim trail heading southeast toward the route to Shadow's territory. A few Ashtaws paused their grazing to watch him.

He surveyed the countryside to the east. Everything looked the same as he remembered.

He made it halfway around the valley rim before he noticed strange movements among the Ashtaw herd. Some of them didn't just mill around grazing.

He climbed up on some rocks, looked down, and his stomach turned another somersault. A group of Ashtaws ran around in an open stretch of grass away from the rest of the herd.

These Ashtaws' movements didn't startle the others. The other Ashtaws just kept right on grazing as if they understood these creatures' strange movements.

Kuvik stiffened when he noticed people riding on the Ashtaw's necks. Each person sat in a sling harness high up the Ashtaws' necks near the head. Each person used another harness to steer each mount by the head.

The creatures turned, wheeled, pivoted, stopped, and went on running according to their riders' instructions. Human yells and spoken commands drifted on the wind to Kuvik's ears.

He couldn't move. Someone was down here domesticating these creatures and teaching them to obey commands. Was Hangman's band here? Did they settle in the valley after all?

Whoever was down there certainly controlled the Ashtaws well. The mounts didn't misbehave even once. They didn't rebel or fight back. They didn't act like carrying riders mattered to them at all. The Ashtaws were used to it.

Kuvik had to find out who was here. He had to find out if Hangman's band was here.

He turned around, jumped off his rock, and set off at a run toward the south. He knew a way he could get down onto the valley floor and at least talk to one of the people down there. Who were they? Did he know one of them?

He fought down excitement while he wound his way along the valley rim. His heart pounded—and then someone launched out of the cleft between two rocks above his head.

The attacker slammed Kuvik down on the ground, bowled him over and over, and then the attacker launched to his feet before Kuvik could recover.

The attacker slammed his foot down on Kuvik's chest to pin him, raised a spear, and thrust it down toward Kuvik's neck.

He froze when the sharp point buried itself in his neck. The attacker stopped just short of impaling Kuvik through the neck. The attacker held the spear there to hold Kuvik down.

Kuvik flattened himself on the ground. He couldn't move—but he didn't need to. He stared up at a Godless warrior glaring down at him. It was Cross, Hangman's younger brother.

Cross's features went through a rapid series of spasms. "Kuvik!!" Cross gasped. "You're alive!"

Kuvik opened his mouth, but he couldn't answer. Overpowering emotion overcame him. He was looking at one of his closest comrades—one of his brothers. They were here. He had found them. He was home.

He gulped down a lump in his throat. He couldn't speak even when Cross took the spear away, grabbed Kuvik's arm, and pulled him to his feet.

Cross squared his shoulders, hugged Kuvik, gripped him by the shoulders, and peered deep into Kuvik's eyes. "Are you okay?" Cross asked. "Did I hurt you? I'm sorry I attacked you. I didn't recognize you. We've had so many enemy incursions. We have to strike first if anyone invades."

Kuvik still couldn't answer even to nod or shake his head. He wasn't okay. He wasn't sure he would ever be okay again.

Cross read his mind. Cross always knew when someone needed help. He patted Kuvik on the shoulder. Kuvik tried not to notice Cross's eyes dipping to the scars all over Kuvik's body.

"Come with me," Cross murmured. "I'll take you to see Hammer. He'll take care of you."

Cross set off at a walk up the valley rim heading south. Kuvik followed. He didn't know what to think. Was Hangman here or not?

They returned to the spot where Hangman's band usually descended into the valley. This spot occupied the far southeastern corner of the valley. This was the spot where Kuvik had planned to turn east to follow Hangman's trail.

Kuvik spotted a cluster of Godless warriors standing around on the rocks near that spot. Cross picked up his pace, went over to them, and they crowded around to listen to him.

Kuvik hung back. He knew every man in the group—and he understood now. They were Hammer's men. Hangman and his men weren't here. Only Hammer's band was here.

Cross told them what was going on and they came over to Kuvik. Hammer stood at the front of the party. He didn't try to hide his gaze roving all over Kuvik's scarred body.

"You made it back," Hammer remarked. "You have no idea how good it is to see you, brother. Come stay with us tonight. We all missed you. Let us welcome you."

Kuvik glanced around. "You're here alone, aren't you? Hangman's band isn't here."

Hammer's features hardened. "It's a long story. Come to our camp. I'll explain everything. Then you can decide what you want to do."

He gave some gesture to his men and then beckoned Kuvik forward. Hammer sure acted like Kral of his band. His men stayed behind while Kuvik followed Hammer down the hills behind the valley. He didn't take the eastern trail.

He led the way farther south, down a bunch of steep paths, and into a maze of trackless gorges packed with jungle. "What's going on?" Kuvik asked. "Where are you taking me?"

"Our long camp is down here. This area is more defensible than anywhere around the valley. We patrol the valley and stop any incursions there so no one finds this place."

Hammer stepped out of the trees and stopped at the mouth of a box canyon buried in miles upon miles of jungle and more gorges.

Kuvik stared into the canyon. Women moved back and forth between shelters built in the Godless style. A few young children toddled and even ran back and forth between the houses. The children's shrieks, cries, and laughter echoed off the canyon walls.

"Shadow threw us out," Hammer went on. "Hangman led his band back to Shadow's territory after you disappeared. We rejoined his band, but he didn't want to accept me as joint Kral with Hangman. Shadow felt that he had to assert his authority over Hangman and especially over me since I'm so much younger. Shadow believed that the territory could only have one Kral and he was it. He tried to get me to submit. I probably would have done it, but then he tried to forbid me and my men from continuing to court our sweethearts. He decided to send all the girls to the gathering, which meant that my men and I would be out of luck. We couldn't tolerate that, so we left. We broke with Shadow's band and we came back here. We've been living here ever since."

"But......these children...." Kuvik faltered. "How long.....how long have I been gone?"

Hammer cocked his head and frowned at him. "You don't know? You vanished five years ago. None of us ever thought we would see you again." He waved Kuvik forward. "Come to my house. You look exhausted and I can see you've been on a long, hard journey."

Chapter 45

Hammer sat down in front of one of the shelters. Kuvik stumbled after him, but Kuvik stopped in his tracks when a woman crossed the camp to meet up with Hammer.

She smiled at him, kissed him, and handed him a water gourd. She said something to him and continued working nearby while he sat there relaxing.

Kuvik couldn't stop staring at the girl—except that she wasn't a girl anymore. It was Vina, Hammer's sweetheart. She was all grown up into a beautiful Godless woman and she was massively pregnant.

She happened to glance up and her jaw dropped when she recognized Kuvik. He couldn't stand the look in her eyes, so he looked away and hustled over to the shelter to sit down next to Hammer.

A little boy about three years old raced around the shelter right then, collided with Hammer, and made Hammer laugh. He kissed the boy, put him on his feet, and sent the boy running off somewhere else before Hammer turned his attention back to Kuvik.

Hammer handed Kuvik the water gourd and then picked up one of the jawbone kukris hanging from Kuvik's waistband. Hammer turned it over in his fingers and raised his eyebrows at the bloodstains around the jagged teeth.

"These are incredible," Hammer remarked. "I've never seen anything like them. They look outstanding. Which creature are they from? No, don't tell me. Let me see if I can guess. They're Demonex, aren't they?"

Kuvik nodded. "I didn't have a weapon when the Ashtaw carried me away."

"I won't insult you by asking what you've been doing and where you've been while you've been gone. I can see it was hard on you. You're welcome to stay here as long as you want to. All my men consider you a brother. We would love it if you stayed with us."

Kuvik looked away. "Where's Hangman? Is he still alive?"

"He's still with Shadow's band as far as I know—him and all the others. Mora and their children are all still alive the last time we checked."

"You checked?" Kuvik repeated. "How could you check? Where are they?"

"Shadow's territory is down the eastern gorges—here." Hammer sketched a crude map in the dirt at his feet. "Shadow threatened to kill any of us who ever set foot in his territory again, so naturally I have to treat him as an enemy now even though I don't consider him an enemy. We send scouts into his territory every now and then to check where his band is camping, how many warriors they have—all that kind of thing. They left the area for a while. I don't know where they went. Then they came back and reoccupied the gorge country. They've been there ever since."

Hammer cocked his head and scrutinized Kuvik on the side.

"I won't be offended if you leave to go with them," Hammer went on. "I know you have a special bond with Hangman—and I don't blame you. I miss him a lot. Losing him was the only really bad thing that happened from our departure."

"I'm sorry....." Kuvik mumbled. "I wish I could stay. You have a beautiful camp and a beautiful band...."

"You don't have to explain," Hammer replied. "You'll always be welcome here if you change your mind. Just take my warning. Shadow isn't Hangman. Shadow doesn't welcome strangers the way Hangman does. What happened between you and Hangman never could have happened if Shadow had been Kral. He would have killed you or let you kill yourself. He never would have given you a chance or welcomed you or let his people have anything to do with you. Hangman is the only Kral who would have done that—and he is definitely the only Kral who would have recognized me as Kral of my own band. No one else would have done that. Anyone else would have forced me and my men to knuckle under and submit exactly the way Shadow tried to do. Hangman is.....he's unique."

"That's all the more reason I have to find him," Kuvik murmured. "Besides.....Yoa is there."

Hammer only nodded. "I know. You don't have to tell me. We're here because we wouldn't give up the women we loved. You should go get her."

"Is she......is she married?" Kuvik hardly dared to ask.

"I don't know. I know Shadow is a stickler about sending girls to the gathering when they get old enough. That's all I know."

"So.....you haven't seen her there?" Kuvik swallowed hard. "You haven't seen her with their band?"

"She's there. She's definitely there. I just can't tell you if she's married or if she ever has been married. Shadow is still alive, so I don't see how he could be her Kral without sending her to the gathering when the time came. He would at least marry her off to one of the single men if he didn't send her to the gathering. That's just the way he is."

Kuvik looked away. He had a hard time controlling his emotions—now that he knew Yoa was so close. He had to stop himself from standing up and leaving this very minute.

"I know it isn't what you want to hear," Hammer went on. "I wish I could tell you something else. I understand that you have to leave. I would have crossed Hell itself to find Vina if anything separated me from her."

Kuvik couldn't answer. Vina came back in a little while and served both men some freshly cooked food. She smiled at Kuvik. "It's so wonderful to see you back, Kuvik," she exclaimed. "Welcome home."

He couldn't bring himself to answer, so he just stared down at his bowl until she left him alone with Hammer again.

None of these people would ever understand. He didn't want them to. He didn't want to poison their blissful lives with the horror of his past—any of it.

He would carry these scars for the rest of his life. Everyone would see them all over him. He had come back so much more heavily scarred than when he left.

These people would all understand that he must have gone through something terrible. They didn't need to know what it was. He wouldn't feed their nightmares with that. It was bad enough that he would live with the nightmares in their place.

He had to change the subject. "The Ashtaws....your people are riding them."

Hammer laughed. "It took a long time and a lot of trouble. It was messy at first—really messy. Don't judge us based on what you see now. It wasn't like this then. We had to fight other Clans to establish our territory. That made it more important that we use the Ashtaws against them. We wouldn't be here now without the Ashtaws."

"I'm amazed you actually accomplished it," Kuvik remarked. "Mora would be amazed."

Hammer made a face. "We wouldn't even have been brave enough to go near the valley without her advice. We just modified all of her ideas. She was the one who really made it happen."

"You were smart to bring your people back here." Kuvik glanced up at him. "You're a good Kral. I can see that."

Hammer turned red and looked away. "Being Kral isn't all it's cracked up to be. I just try to do the best thing for my people. That's the best I can do."

"I know," Kuvik replied and realized he may have said it a little too quickly.

Hammer definitely picked up on it, but he didn't say anything. Kuvik found himself studying the man next to him. Hammer had aged and matured in five years. He wasn't a boy anymore. He was more a man than Kuvik ever thought possible.

"It's so good to see you, brother," Hammer exclaimed. "It's always good to see a friendly, trusted face in the country. Heaven knows we have enough enemies around."

"Yeah," Kuvik murmured. "It's so good to see you and your men, too. You're all doing so well. I'm happy for you."

"I'm sure it will be like this for you as soon as you go home. You deserve it."

Kuvik looked away. "I didn't know. I'd been away for so long."

"No one deserves happiness more than you do. What you had in the Godless is the least that you deserve. If you can't get it from Shadow's band, you should come back here. We'll take care of you."

Kuvik could barely whisper, "Thanks." That word didn't even cover it. He had good people just waiting to take him in. He could take his pick. That was more than he ever hoped for.

He had family. He would be as at home here as he was with Hangman's band. Kuvik didn't have to question that. He knew every man in Hammer's band. Kuvik called them all brothers. They would always take care of him.

The thought staggered his mind as much now as when he first met Hangman. The concept of someone else taking care of Kuvik, being kind to him, and making sure he had everything he needed—it conflicted with everything else he'd ever known.

Everything outside this little world told him the opposite. Everything told him he was alone against a harsh, hostile, violent, malicious world that would hunt him down, break him, and leave him for dead.

He had to readjust his thinking all over again as if he'd never met the Godless.

Dreaming about his life with them, fantasizing about it, and keeping those pictures and feelings always in the center of his mind—they didn't prepare him to actually live it in person.

Hammer didn't push it. He knew Kuvik too well. Hammer saw too much when he looked at Kuvik, so Hammer kept his eyes turned most of the time. He pretended to busy himself with other work like sharpening his weapons while they talked.

Sitting here next to a man Kuvik knew and liked—a man he trusted—it felt so strange and out of place. It didn't feel real to sit next to someone Kuvik didn't have to question or guard himself against.

He had felt that way about Akli, Nelv, and Tren, but Kuvik had traveled with them for such a short time. They had vanished before he could fully appreciate them.

He never had to doubt Hammer, Cross, or any of their men. These men formed the bedrock of time—the foundation of Kuvik's existence. He could finally reorient himself to reality, now that he'd found them.

Chapter 46

Hammer and Kuvik sat trading remarks for a while. Neither of them talked about anything too serious until Hammer's men came back. They all crowded around talking about Kuvik's return.

His men had a lot to say about everything they'd been doing since Kuvik's disappearance. The men didn't hold back, but they didn't ask him to reciprocate by telling them about his adventures.

He caught most of them shooting questioning glances at him. Did he really look that different? Maybe not, but he did look beat up. He had seen some hard miles since he saw them last. No one had to tell him.

They ate a lot that night and so did he. He stayed sitting next to Hammer as an honored guest until everyone went to sleep.

The camp roused the next morning with the usual noise of children crying and mothers trying to soothe them. Kuvik sat up and watched everyone going about their business.

Hammer had slept in his house with his family. He came out sometime later and handed Kuvik a wrapped, tied bundle. "Here's some extra food for your journey. Come with me and I'll walk you up to the valley."

The two men left without a word to anyone. They didn't talk almost all the way up there. Hammer broke the silence when the valley came in sight. "You remember what I said. You come back here if anything goes wrong."

"I will," Kuvik replied. "This will be the first place I come."

Hammer stopped at the base of the hills, faced Kuvik, and hugged him. "I wish I could convince you to stay, but I see that you have to go. Know that you always have a place here. You'll always be a brother to us—to me. Travel safely. Be careful. You're too good to waste."

Kuvik clamped his lips shut and nodded. He didn't trust himself to speak enough even to say goodbye.

These people valued him. These people knew his worth. They would grieve his loss. The Hungry Ghosts would never convince Kuvik again that he was worthless. These people cared. They wanted him back. They had been waiting for him all this time.

He tore himself away and walked off into the jungle. He had to fight himself every step of the way not to turn back and fall into the blissful contentment of Hammer's band. What a wonderful life that would have been.

Kuvik would go back there if anything happened to stop him from returning to Hangman's band. Shadow might not accept Kuvik. Shadow might refuse to initiate Kuvik or Shadow might refuse to let Kuvik marry Yoa.

Then Kuvik would come back to Hammer's band. Life felt pretty good knowing that he could always come back to people who cared about him. He wasn't alone in the world.

He traced the route Hammer had drawn in the dirt. It wasn't the most detailed map in the world, but it showed Kuvik where to go. He found a few different landmarks and had to divert and delay to let an army of ants pass through.

Part of Hammer's route passed through a series of high cliffs leading down to another expanse of jungle. Hammer had given Kuvik more information about the route last night. Hammer said Shadow used to keep his long camp here, but that it was deserted now.

It may have been deserted before, but it wasn't now. Kuvik saw from high in the cliffs that someone was living there. Talking to Hammer convinced Kuvik that whoever was living there wouldn't be Shadow's band.

Kuvik approached the area slowly, carefully, and cautiously. He stayed in the treetops, tiptoed along the branches, and advanced a few paces at a time so no one would see him observing the band from out of sight.

Another Godless band occupied the area. They had built shelters in Shadow's old long camp, but this wasn't any Godless band that Kuvik recognized. For a start, almost everyone here was male.

These men didn't bring any uninitiated boys, but that would have been normal for any band other than Hangman's. He really was unique in so many ways.

The men of this band didn't seem to leave, either. Hangman's men would never have stayed in camp this long unless they'd just returned from a long journey. Sometimes they wouldn't stay in camp even then.

Kuvik didn't see any men standing watch around the perimeter or even checking the surrounding jungle. Their behavior confused him. Didn't they understand the danger?

The whole point of establishing a long camp was to protect the women and children. The whole point was for a group of warriors to guard the camp while others went out to scout, hunt, and fight invading enemy Clans. Didn't these people understand that much?

Kuvik didn't know who these people were, but he remembered enough of Hammer's map to know something was wrong. These people were Godless—so why were they camping so close to Shadow's territory? Hammer made it sound like this was Shadow's territory.

He would have waged war against anyone who intruded on his territory. He wouldn't have wanted to wage war against another Godless band, but he would do it.

The story of Hammer's band and their fight against the marauders masquerading as Godless came back to haunt Kuvik. Was this another splinter of the same group? Were these people pretending to be Godless so they could invade Shadow's territory and attack his band?

Kuvik would have liked to skirt around these people and go straight to the gorge camp where he would find Hangman, Yoa, and all the friends Kuvik wanted so badly to see.

He couldn't just walk away from this—not without finding out if there really was a threat here.

He retreated into the jungle, found one of the paths leading to the long camp, and walked along it like he didn't know where he was going. He made sure to leave his weapons where they were.

He strolled into the camp and stopped there to look around at everything. His arrival got the warriors' attention real quick. Twelve of them stormed up to him and blocked his path even though he wasn't trying to go anywhere.

All of these men outsized him by at least three times. They were bigger, taller, and more muscular than any Godless he'd ever seen—even bigger than Alien if that was possible.

That was another clue. Real Godless moved around a lot. Men this big wouldn't have been able to climb through the branches as fast as they needed to.

Alien had been the biggest Godless man Kuvik had ever seen and he was considered a freak. That's how he got his name. The others were smaller, leaner, faster, and more agile. They didn't need size and bulk. They had everything else to make up for it.

"What are you doing here?" one of the men boomed.

"I'm looking for Shadow's band," Kuvik replied. "I heard this was his camp. I came here to find him. Do you know where he is?"

"There is no Shadow here," the same man fired back. "We're the only band in the area. This is our territory."

Kuvik raised his eyebrows. He might have been willing to believe that if he hadn't just heard from Hammer that Shadow's band still lived here. Hammer seemed pretty certain that Shadow would have defended this territory if someone invaded.

Kuvik put his money on Hammer. For a start, Hammer kept tabs on Shadow for tactical reasons. Hammer had no choice but to consider Shadow an enemy in a neighboring territory. Hammer had to know where Shadow was and what he was doing all the time.

Hammer was too smart to let a potential enemy just vanish on him. Hammer would at least have found out if Shadow had left the territory.

The same man narrowed his eyes at Kuvik and scanned him up and down. "Who are you?"

"My name is Kuvik. I've been traveling a long time trying to find Shadow."

"What Clan do you belong to? You aren't Godless."

"I lived with the Godless for years before we got separated. I'm a stranger, but they welcomed me into their Clan. I want to find my way back to them."

"We're the only Godless here," the same man repeated.

Kuvik chose his next words with care. "How long have you been defending the territory?"

The man's eyes narrowed just a fraction of an inch. "Ten years," he replied.

"Do you have dealings with Hammer? He's the Kral in the next territory over adjacent to you."

"I never heard of him," the guy snapped. "We don't deal with other local bands."

"But you must have met them at the gatherings," Kuvik pointed out. "You would have taken your daughters south at the age of gathering. You would have met the other local bands there. Your daughters would marry into other bands and their daughters would marry your sons and come to live here. Right?"

Kuvik cast another meaningful glance around. He made it out like he didn't notice the obvious lack of women.

"What do you want?" the same guy demanded.

"I told you. I lived with the Godless for years and I want to get back to them." Kuvik made a snap decision. "If you're the only band in the area, maybe I could stay with you. I know how to fight. I won't let you down."

The guy stared at him in shock and then burst out in laughter. "You?! You think you can fight?!" He exploded in laughter again.

Some of his men joined in. Kuvik waited for them to stop. Now he knew these people weren't really Godless. Real Godless would never underestimate someone because of his size.

"I bet I can beat any man here," Kuvik offered. "Put me against your best warrior, and if I win, you promise you'll let me stay."

The guy laughed again. "You're soft in the head, but I'll give you a chance just to get rid of you quicker. You can fight Blink over there."

He jerked his thumb at one of his men. Kuvik didn't see which one.

The others started to disperse. "Wait a minute," Kuvik insisted. "You didn't tell me *your* name."

"My name is Magic." The guy pulled himself up straighter. "This is my band."

Kuvik nodded. "Then you'll be my Kral after I win."

Magic snorted and retreated with his men. Blink stayed in the center of the camp and squared off against Kuvik. Blink wasn't as big as the others. He was actually about Alien's size.

Blink wore his hair long like the others. He braided the two side locks and tied them back with the rest of his hair hanging loose and flowing. He probably thought it made him look glamorous and handsome, but it actually came across as vain.

Kuvik only had to take one look at the guy to understand everything about him. He thought his size and strength could defeat anyone and anything.

He didn't understand the basic principle Kuvik had worked so hard to teach his people about adapting and using their wits to overcome superior force.

Blink pulled two enormous battle axes off his back to fight Kuvik. Just one of those axes could chop Kuvik in half, but he didn't even bring one of his kukris. He wouldn't need it. He only brought one of his tooth blades.

The other warriors laughed at him. They weren't even warriors. He didn't know who these men were and he was rapidly losing any interest in finding out. They were too stupid to defeat one man, much less a Godless band.

Chapter 47

Kuvik retreated to one side, took off his bags, and laid them in a pile near one of the shelters. He didn't want the bags to encumber his movements while he was trying to fight. He returned to the center of camp and faced Blink.

Kuvik held his knife blade down by his side the way he did when he faced Nolon. Blink made a big show of flexing his knees in a deep squat and pacing back and forth while he swung his axes from side to side.

Then he faced Kuvik and went into a rapid spinning flourish of whirling his axes around and around his head extra fast. Kuvik watched him from a distance. Blink would never get near Kuvik with those weapons. That much was obvious.

The other warriors stood or sat off to one side laughing, pointing, and talking extra loudly about the confrontation. They seemed especially amused by the sight of Kuvik showing up with just one small curved blade.

He stayed where he was until Magic yelled out, "Engage!"

Kuvik and Blink both stepped forward, but Kuvik still didn't raise his weapon. He kept his body relaxed and loose. This shouldn't be too difficult.

Blink went on the offensive first and charged Kuvik swinging both of those mighty axes at Kuvik's head and chest. Kuvik lunged forward, dove below Blink's waist where the axes wouldn't hit him, and rolled past Blink's left ankle.

Kuvik slashed his blade down the side of Blink's leg, laid open the calf muscle, and severed a bunch of the ankle tendons at the same time.

Blink roared in pain and fury. Blood poured down his leg and he hopped clear. He couldn't put his weight on his leg anymore.

Kuvik rolled back to his feet behind Blink and sprang to a safe distance to give Blink time to recover. He spun around, but he could barely walk at all. He only put his weight on his left foot for a second each time while he hobbled back into the center.

Kuvik took his former position but on the opposite side of the camp this time. Blink raised his axes, but he didn't spin them around. He compressed his face in a mask of cruel intent and narrowed in on Kuvik.

Kuvik waited for Blink to make his move again. Blink couldn't charge the way he did before. He leapt forward to close the distance, raised his axes above his head, and brought them down to cleave Kuvik in half.

Kuvik dove at the same time, rolled past Blink on the right side this time, and slashed an even deeper, more damaging cut down the side and back of Blink's right thigh. Blink actually toppled into the dirt.

He bellowed in rage and got up immediately, but he wouldn't stop grimacing in agony. Blood covered him below the waist.

He grabbed both his axes and rushed Kuvik immediately without giving either of them a chance to recover. Kuvik barely got to his feet and turned around before Blink came charging back.

He let out a ground-shaking roar, swung both axes from out at the sides, and chopped them down to cross them in the center this time.

Kuvik had to dart backward to get out of the way. Then he sprang back in, slashed sideways, and cut open Blink's left arm. The tendons and muscle released and Blink's axe fell to the ground on that side.

He spun around to face Kuvik with only one usable arm. Blink's other arm hung useless at his side gushing blood. Dead silence hung over the camp. None of the warriors made a sound.

Blink paused there holding up his one remaining axe. His features convulsed between desperate agony and trembling terror for his life. Kuvik actually felt sorry for the guy. Blink didn't have a clue what hit him.

He shook all over. He wouldn't be able to stay on his feet much longer and he knew it. He probably thought Kuvik would kill him now.

Kuvik *could* kill him. Kuvik could easily just sidestep the next time Blink made a move. Kuvik could step around him and slash Blink's throat easily. Blink didn't have the speed to avoid Kuvik nor the fighting skill even to anticipate a move like that.

Kuvik decided to take pity on the guy and leave him alive. A real Godless warrior would have preferred death to the humiliation of defeat.

This wasn't a Godless warrior. Blink was too cowardly to prefer death to a humiliating defeat. Blink would rather keep his life.

Blink seemed to make up his mind, took one step forward, and swung his axe in the most lackluster swing imaginable. He swiped from right to left straight across the middle with no subtly or artistry at all. He barely tried to hit Kuvik.

Kuvik stepped around him and gave Blink one last deep slash across the ribs. Kuvik cut him down to the bone. That cut would hurt, but it didn't put Blink in any danger.

Blink roared again and clasped both arms over the wound. He had to lower his axe to do it. He turned around to face Kuvik, but Blink didn't try to defend himself. The fight was over.

Now Kuvik was the one who rushed Blink, got inside his weapons range, and Kuvik swept his blade upward to hold it at Blink's throat. "Beg for your life," Kuvik ordered.

Blink instantly dropped to his knees. His whole face trembled. "Please don't kill me!" he blurted out. "Please...you win.....please don't kill me.....please...."

"Say you're a coward and a terrible fighter. Say you never should have challenged me and you aren't really a man if you could lose this badly to someone like me."

"I'm a coward!" Blink choked on the words and started to lose control emotionally. "I'm a terrible fighter! I never should have challenged you! I'm not a man if I could lose this badly! Please..... don't kill me....I'm weak....I'm a coward....please....you win.....you're the better man....please....."

Kuvik held his blade to Blink's throat for a second and then lowered it. Blink completely broke down, slumped, and bit back stifled sobs. Kuvik didn't need to see that. He walked away and crossed the camp to pick up his bags.

He wiped his blade on his pants and draped his bags across his body, three on each side. Magic came up to him while Kuvik was still standing there. "You're a good fighter," Magic remarked. "I'm sorry I misjudged you. You're welcome to stay with us."

"I've changed my mind," Kuvik replied over his shoulder. "I don't want to stay. I'm going to move on and keep looking for Shadow's band. Thanks anyway. I'm sure you and your people will thrive in this territory."

Magic frowned. "Don't judge us all based on Blink. We aren't all like that."

Kuvik turned around. He assumed Magic meant that Blink was a coward for conceding the way he did. Kuvik didn't consider Blink a coward—not because of that. Kuvik didn't make his decision based on Blink.

Kuvik leveled Magic with a direct stare, but Kuvik didn't hold it for more than a second. "Thank you again, but I'm going to move on. I don't want to settle with any other band than Shadow's. I wish you well."

Kuvik walked away. None of the warriors followed him out of the camp.

He walked a quarter of a mile down the trail heading for the eastern gorges, but he stopped there and climbed into the branches instead. He doubled back through the canopy and hid in a different place where he could observe Magic and his men in their camp.

Kuvik hid in the foliage and waited until nightfall. He watched Blink stumble to one of the shelters and collapse on the ground there.

Some of the other men came over to him in a little while, put leaf paste on his wounds, helped him bind them up, and the men made him some Gooji juice.

They treated him gently—probably because they all knew the same thing would have happened to them if they'd fought Kuvik in his place.

He eventually returned to join the other men, but he didn't talk loudly. He barely talked at all. He limped everywhere and took extra care not to move fast. He hardly moved at all, either. He wouldn't be any good in combat for a while.

Everyone else pretended the fight never happened. Even Magic played it off and relaxed that night until all the men went to sleep. They all slept in their shelters. They didn't leave a single man outside to stand guard.

Kuvik climbed down from the trees, dropped silently to the ground, and made his way back to Magic's camp. No one stopped Kuvik from entering. No one even saw him.

He stood at the center of the camp and turned in a complete circle looking around. These people, whoever they were—they didn't belong on this planet. They didn't belong in the company of other human beings.

These men were up to no good. They were essentially Bounty Hunters masquerading as Godless. That was the best they could possibly be.

He felt no qualms about killing Bounty Hunters, not even Bounty Hunter women. He would have killed Dana if he only knew where to find her. He felt no qualms about killing these people, either. Killing them would be a good thing.

He pulled his tooth blade and one of his kukris, transferred both to his left hand, and used his right to pick up a burning stick from one of the fires. He went around the camp and set fire to every shelter one after the other.

The men came running from outside and yelling out the alarm to their friends. Kuvik transferred his kukri to his right hand, stormed through the camp, and killed every last single man in the whole group. He left not one of them alive.

He stuck around just long enough to drag every dead body into the flames and watched the fire reduce all of them to ashes. If it was good enough for Tren, Nelv, and Akli, it was good enough for these bastards.

Kuvik retreated to the canopy and watched the camp burn to the ground. Nothing remained but a bunch of piles of cinders. Good riddance. Then he continued his journey.

He traveled through the treetops for three days until he entered the gorges. He had to travel along the ground between high walls. He slept sitting up on the ground against the walls.

The gorges had a way of numbing his mind. Part of him forgot why he was here. He just seemed to be traveling endlessly through a dream world of nothing with no past, no future, and no sense of even who he was.

He didn't remember until he turned a corner and saw another Godless camp spread out in front of him. Everything came rushing back and adrenaline started pumping through his veins. Women and children moved, talked, and worked everywhere.

Kuvik's heart stopped when he saw a group of men squatting across the camp under a bunch of trees. They talked to each other in earnest tones. None of the women or children went over there.

His eyes raced everywhere at once, but his gaze always came back to that one group of men. Another tidal wave of emotion started to overpower him. Was this real or did he hallucinate it like everything else?

One of the men over there noticed him, said something to others, and they all turned around to stare at him. One of the men stood up.....and Kuvik found himself staring at Hangman, Viking, and Red.

Hangman's scarred face hardened into a wall of granite. Kuvik knew that look only too well. He started forward and Hangman left his place to meet him.

The two men collided in the middle of the camp in an unbreakable hug. Kuvik felt himself falling, falling, falling. It was all coming down on his head faster than he could handle.

He was home. He was where he needed to be. All the trouble, all the heartbreak, all the pain and suffering—it all came true in this moment.

Hangman pushed him back and crushed both of Kuvik's shoulders while Hangman stared deep into Kuvik's eyes. Kuvik couldn't control his features. He felt himself starting to break down. He barely held himself together. He would disintegrate any second now.

"You're back!" Hangman whispered. "I can't believe it! You're back!"

Kuvik compressed his lips. He didn't trust himself to speak. He would probably fall apart even if he did speak.

The other men gathered around touching him and calling his name. He heard women and children calling out to each other and passing the world that Kuvik was back.

Hangman wouldn't let go of him. Hangman never stopped staring into Kuvik's face even once. Kuvik couldn't look away.

Kuvik hardly believed what was happening. He didn't know how to break out of this. Would he ever be able to live his life again after this stabbing pain in his heart? Would he ever lead a normal life?

Hangman pushed some of the other men away, took hold of Kuvik by the shoulders, and turned him sideways. Kuvik didn't understand why until Hangman stopped and kept turning Kuvik to the side to face him away from the group.

Kuvik found himself staring across the camp at a certain shelter in the distance. A woman stood in front of it. She didn't look like a fresh-faced underage girl anymore. She glowed with the prime of health, but a depth of sadness made her eyes soft and caring.

She stared across the camp at Kuvik standing there. He couldn't take his eyes off her.

"She never stopped loving you," Hangman murmured in his ear. "Her husband died and she's unmarried now. Go to her. She's yours. We'll initiate you in the morning and you can come home to her as her husband. Go, Kuvik. Go home to your wife."

Hangman propelled him across the camp. Kuvik's legs barely supported him. He staggered forward. Everything else vanished around him. No one else existed.

Yoa's presence guided him to her as powerfully as she had been guiding him all these years. She really was real. She was here and she was his.

The soft, caring warmth in her eyes overflowed in tears. He didn't have to say a word to understand exactly what she thought about his return.

His legs gave out and he fell on his knees in front of her, wrapped his arms around her waist, and buried his whole soul into the feeling of holding her in his arms at last.

Chapter 48

K uvik stood at the edge of the camp with Viking on one side of him and Red on the other. All the rest of Red's men crowded on his side. Feather, Banjo, Devil, Breaker, Grizzly, Bantam, and the rest of Shadow's men stood on Viking's other side.

The women of the band worked around their shelters, tended their fires, and supervised their children as usual. None of the women and children came near the men. No one did.

Kuvik glanced toward Yoa's shelter. She stayed inside and didn't come out. Kuvik had spent a lot of time with her last night, but he didn't spend the night with her. He slept by himself out in the jungle to prepare for his initiation.

She didn't come out now. She didn't want to see him leave.

Kuvik's eyes darted to the other side of the gorge camp where Hangman and his father stood talking away from everyone else.

Kuvik hadn't spoken to Shadow yet except in the briefest possible greeting. Hangman insisted on talking to his father first to explain who Kuvik was and why Hangman and the men planned to initiate him immediately the very morning after he returned.

Hangman didn't say anything else about his father. Neither did the other men and Kuvik didn't ask. Kuvik was prepared to take Yoa away from Shadow's band if Shadow offered any objection to Kuvik and Yoa getting married.

Hammer would initiate Kuvik if Shadow didn't do it. Hangman didn't say so outright, but he heavily implied that he would initiate Kuvik himself if Shadow offered any objection at all.

Kuvik didn't have to worry about Viking or any of Red's men, either. They had been pushing Kuvik to initiate for years before he disappeared.

Hangman had been over there talking to his father for a long time. Kuvik didn't understand the complex relationship between them. He didn't want to. It couldn't be anything good if it was complex.

They finally broke off their conversation and crossed the camp to meet up with the other men. Hangman said, "Let's go," and the whole party left the camp without a word. Shadow led the way. The other men followed.

They filed out of the camp, out of the gorges, and all the way back to the steep cliffs leading to the Shadow's old long camp. All the men stopped there and gathered around Kuvik.

"You lead us from here," Hangman told him. "Take us where you need to go and we'll watch."

Kuvik pointed behind them. "Follow that cliff to the edge. You can wait in the trees. I'll meet you there. Here. Take these." He took off all his bags and weapons and handed them over.

"Aren't you keeping anything?" Red asked. "Take a blade, at least."

"I don't need it," Kuvik replied. "I'll get everything back from you after I finish."

"Have it your way." Hangman hung all Kuvik's worldly possessions over his shoulder and held out his hand. "Good luck."

Kuvik nodded. "I'll see you on the other side."

He waited while all the men filed away from him. A few of Red's men shook hands with Kuvik and even clapped him on the shoulders as they passed him. They all wished him well and assured him that he would be fine.

He nodded, thanked them, and tried his hardest not to let nerves get the better of him. He felt better after they all vanished into the trees and left him alone.

He settled into a deeper part of himself. He understood himself better when he was alone. He knew exactly what to do. This wasn't a performance. It was just another hunt on his journey. He'd fought and killed bigger, tougher, more dangerous creatures.

He headed off into the jungle and passed along the clifftops on the opposite side of the gorge.

Shadow, Hangman, Viking, and the others would pass along the opposite cliff and watch him from over there. He wouldn't see them. They would keep hidden and let him fight his own fight.

He followed the cliff edge to its very end and stopped on a high, flat rock sticking out of the very far end. It hung out in space miles above the valley floor. He could see for hundreds of miles in every direction. He couldn't see a single person.

The men might not be there. He might go through all of this for nothing. They might not see his initiation fight and then he would have to do it all over again.

He just had to trust his friends—his brothers. These men wouldn't leave him alone—not now. They took initiations too seriously—especially his.

They all wanted to call him Godless like themselves. They wanted to call him their brother and see him marry Yoa. They all wanted to forget that he'd ever been gone.

He looked up into the sky and shut his eyes in the sunshine. It felt good to be free and home. His journey was over. He had found his way. He didn't have to go anywhere or do anything. He could finally start building the life he promised his brothers.

He would have liked to share it with them and with all the members of his own band, but living it himself would have to be good enough. It was good enough. It was everything.

A screech got his attention and made him open his eyes. He looked up and saw a Ridgebeak diving for him. This one was a male and it was much bigger than any he'd fought before.

Even a mother Ridgebeak would have been big enough and deadly enough to make a perfectly acceptable initiation opponent. This male was easily twice the females' size.

Kuvik tensed all over. All the relaxed happiness of a moment before evaporated out of his mind, but he didn't flex his knees or raise his hands or give any other sign that he was readying himself for the fight of his life.

He kept his eyes on the bird. It plunged out of clouds, pointed its nose to the cliff, and tucked its wings against its body to pick up speed.

Kuvik froze for the moment of confrontation. This was it. He had to kill this creature or die trying. He wouldn't go back to Yoa at all as anything but her husband. That meant killing this creature no matter how big and strong it was.

The Ridgebeak hurtled toward the ground at impossible speed. He didn't move.

Time slowed to a standstill, but he felt nothing but ironclad certainty that he would win. He couldn't fail. This Ridgebeak couldn't do anything to him that his enemies hadn't already done.

The Ridgebeak shrieked again and, at the last possible second, it swung its feet forward and spread its talons to nail him to the rock.

Kuvik sprang back just in time and the bird hit the rock with bone-crushing force. Its own momentum slammed it down hard and Kuvik struck. He dove back in, grabbed the bird by its chest feathers, and brought its head down with all his strength on the stone.

The blow stunned the bird, but not enough. It reared away from him and flexed its wings to launch so it could fight him head on.

He jumped away just in time to miss a swipe of its beak and the bird took that moment to lift off the rock to rise into the air.

He dove in again and made sure to do it beneath the creature's beak this time. The bird pumped its wings, lifted off, and its talons cleared the rock right in front of Kuvik.

He pivoted around on his knees and turned his back on the creature right where its talons would be able to grab, slash, or impale him. The Ridgebeak started to swing its talons forward to make its final strike.

The bird arched its wings forward to gain a little more height. Kuvik leaned back, stretched his spine, and grabbed the Ridgebeak by the feathers of its lower stomach right above its legs.

He threw all his weight forward and curled over on himself. He vented all his power on the creature, hurled it forward, and slammed it down onto the rock with every ounce of his strength.

The creature fell flat on its face with its wings outstretched, but Kuvik wasn't finished. He lunged out from between the bird's legs. The creature's giant body lay in front of him where it wouldn't hold him down.

He sprang on top of it, landed both his knees at either shoulder joint to pin its wings down, and dove for the head. The bird reared back trying to get up. It raised its head just as he got there.

He flung all his weight down on his elbow against the back of the creature's skull, nailed the Ridgebeak face down on the rock again, and scrambled forward to straddle the back of the bird's neck.

He grabbed the bird by the head and slammed its face down into the rock again and again with all his might. He drove it down right on top of the beak with every shred of power he could muster.

He unleashed every scrap of rage, pain, and brutal thirst for bloody revenge on the creature. He didn't stop even after he heard the beak shatter and felt the skull crack in his hands.

The creature's head lost its shape, but he still kept driving it down again and again until there was nothing left for him to hold onto.

He stumbled back gasping and dripping with sweat. He wavered there on unsteady legs. Blood saturated his arms past his elbows and dripped from his fingers.

He collapsed onto his knees and slumped sideways onto his elbow. He couldn't hold himself up. It was over.

He stared at the Ridgebeak hardly daring to believe it was really dead. He kept expecting it to get up and attack him again. He didn't realize until this moment just how big the creature was. He hadn't seen a Ridgebeak this big before.

He didn't realize when he first spotted this creature that he would be fighting something this big. He probably would have changed his mind if he had realized.

He sat up a little straighter and studied the creature. He should take a trophy from this creature—but what to take? He already had enough weapons and the talons didn't make for good weapons anyway—not as good as the Demonex tooth.

He was still sitting there when the men came along the cliff to meet up with him. He got to his feet. Shadow hung back while Hangman came forward. Hangman smiled in his crooked, compressed way.

"It's an honor to call you brother," Hangman murmured. "You're a true man of the Godless Clan and your name is Phoenix. You're a privilege and a blessing on our Clan. We're honored to have you with us and to welcome you among us. Now let's cut this thing up and eat it. We're all hungry."

The other men surrounded Kuvik all hugging him, congratulating him, laughing at his exploits, and talking over the fight in detail. They'd seen it all.

They all exclaimed over the size of the creature. Bantam picked up one of the Ridgebeak's feet to show how big its claws were. "Can you believe this?" he gasped. "You wouldn't catch me out there on that rock facing a creature this size."

"Wait a minute, little brother," Kuvik told him.

Kuvik retrieved his weapons from Hangman and cut off one of the claws. Then he plucked one of the Ridgebeak's longest wing feathers and put both into his bags.

The other men built a fire in the jungle and started cutting up the Ridgebeak to eat and cure to take back to the band. The men lounged around the fire telling stories and sharing jokes for hours.

Kuvik sat on one side of the fire with Hangman on one side of him and Viking on the other. Shadow kept apart. Hangman, Viking, and all of Kuvik's friends were the ones who initiated him into the Clan. They didn't need Shadow for that.

Kuvik heard the other men talking about him. They all kept referring to him as Kuvik. None of them used his new name. He didn't understand why, but it somehow seemed fitting and not insulting as Godless law stated.

He couldn't imagine anyone calling him anything other than Kuvik. It was his name. He didn't think it indicated disrespect or referred to him as an uninitiated boy the way it would if someone used a Godless man's childhood name.

The name *Kuvik* sounded like a mark of respect. It sounded like the man they all admired and wanted to welcome into their Clan. It sounded like the man Kuvik wanted to be.

He didn't correct them and they didn't correct each other. It didn't really matter in the end because he was one of them now.

He charred the flesh off the talon, wrapped a length of hide around the socket joint, and hung the talon around his neck. That was trophy enough. He would have to think about what to do with the feather.

"I suppose you'll have to start growing your hair out," Viking pointed out. "I can't picture you with long hair. I really can't."

Kuvik laughed. "Maybe I won't. Maybe I'll leave it short."

Viking shrugged. "You can do what you want with your own hair. No one can tell you not to." Viking grinned at him. "Yoa seems to like you this way, so why not, right?"

Kuvik blushed and grinned back at his friend. The men finished eating, picked up the giant joints of meat, and started the long hike back to the camp to deliver all this food to the rest of the band.

Kuvik went with them, but he didn't carry anything. Everyone in the band would eat his kill tonight—and he would go home to Yoa's shelter and stay there. He would never leave it again.

End of Book 6.

Keep Reading

Rise of the Giants Series: Book 7: The Angler War

The conflict between Hangman and his father erupts off the charts after Hangman and Mora return from their time trapped in the Angler Valley. The safety and security of the band Hangman worked so hard to rejoin turns into his worst nightmare when his father begins to suspect that Hangman is trying to take over and overthrow his father as Kral of the band.

With tensions at the breaking point and the other warriors speaking openly against Shadow's decisions, a new, more ruthless and powerful enemy Clan threatening the band is exactly what the Godless don't need right now. The band will need all of Hangman's strength, speed, cunning, and strategy to keep everyone alive—but what happens when his own father turns against him and stops him from fighting to protect those he loves?

The result will lead to a much bigger disaster the likes of which no one in the band has ever seen before. Hangman and his father can no longer peacefully coexist. One of them must challenge the other—which means one of them will rise to become Kral. The other will die.

You can find it at your favorite book retailer.

Sign Up Once--Get all Theo Mann's free books including brand new releases

S ign Up Once--Get all Theo Mann's free books including brand new releases

In a world where everything is out to kill you, humans must fight for survival every day against huge dangerous creatures and enemy Clans. The Godless Clan has enough to worry about already. They don't need to fight their own.

Sixteen-year-old Shadow knows exactly what to do when he discovers a girl from an enemy band hiding in the jungle. He takes her captive as a prisoner of war, but the Godless have a strict code of honor when dealing with women—even enemy women.

He and Katha will have to fight for their very survival and overcome generations of mistrust before they make it back to their people—who just might be the most dangerous enemies either of them has ever faced.

Sign up at www.theomann.com to read it for free

About Theo Mann

I write 70 books per year—and yes, before you ask, all these books are my original creative work. Nothing written under my name is AI-generated or ghostwritten because I write better than AI and any ghostwriter out there.

People don't read fiction for entertainment or to escape from reality. People read fiction to see their humanity reflected in another person's character and story.

This is my promise to you. When you read my books, you'll see your own humanity reflected in the characters and stories. I take this commitment to my readers very seriously. My books are an intimate form of communication between us. I would never disrespect my readers by turning that over to a machine or another writer. This is my bond between me and you as my reader.

I write 20,000 words per day as my daily work output. If anyone with a public platform would like to challenge me to prove this in a controlled environment, feel free to contact me on this website's contact page.

I worked as a professional ghostwriter for fifteen years. Now I'm on a mission to set a Guinness World Record by writing 700 books over the next ten years and 1400 books over the next twenty years, all originally written by me. See my website for the full book list.

I'm also the author of *Proof for the Existence of God* and the *Crimes Against Fiction* blog. You can find all my nonfiction work at www.crimes-against-fiction.com.

If you have a story idea, or if you would like me to explore a series in more depth, or if you'd like me to explore a character by writing a spinoff series about that character or world, leave me a message on my website's contact page. I answer all reader emails, so ask me anything, tell me what you liked and didn't like, and let me know where you'd like your favorite series to go. I would love to hear your ideas and find out what you'd like to read next.

Find out more at www.theomann.com.

www.ingramcontent.com/pod-product-compliance
Lightning Source LLC
Chambersburg PA
CBHW071901020726
47502CB00003B/842